Samuel Reynolds Hole

The Memories of Dean Hole

Fourth Edition

Samuel Reynolds Hole

The Memories of Dean Hole
Fourth Edition

ISBN/EAN: 9783337092764

Printed in Europe, USA, Canada, Australia, Japan

Cover: Foto ©Raphael Reischuk / pixelio.de

More available books at **www.hansebooks.com**

THE MEMORIES

OF

DEAN HOLE.

"From grave to gay, from lively to severe."

FOURTH EDITION.

LONDON:
EDWARD ARNOLD,
37, BEDFORD STREET, STRAND, W.C.
Publisher to the India Office.
1892.

LONDON:
PRINTED BY WILLIAM CLOWES AND SONS, LIMITED,
STAMFORD STREET AND CHARING CROSS.

TO

SIR HENRY FOX BRISTOWE, Q.C.,

VICE-CHANCELLOR OF

THE COUNTY PALATINE OF LANCASTER,

THE PLAYMATE OF MY BOYHOOD,

AND THE FAITHFUL FRIEND OF MY MANHOOD AND OLD AGE,

THIS BOOK IS AFFECTIONATELY DEDICATED

BY

THE AUTHOR.

The Deanery,
Rochester,
1892.

INTRODUCTION.

THESE Memories are the holiday task of an old boy, who desires, and hopes that he deserves, to rest, but is too fond of work to be quite idle. He would float awhile, " with languid pulses of the oar," upon the Cherwell, that, like the *Dido* of the unripe scholar, *vento profecta secundo*, he may come again with second wind to the eight-oar on the Isis. And, though he cannot aspire to combine with his own relaxation any signal service to his fellow-men, even as Bishop Christopher Wordsworth, when he was weary, amused himself by translating Theocritus, he ventures to hope that, from the varied experience of a long and happy life, among all sorts and conditions of men, he may communicate information which will be interesting, and suggestions which may be useful.

CONTENTS.

ARCHERS.

CHAPTER I.

ARTISTS.

CHAPTER II.

CHAPTER III.

CHAPTER IV.

CHAPTER V.

AUTHORS.

CHAPTER VI.

CHAPTER VII.

CHAPTER VIIL

CHAPTER IX.

CRICKETERS.

CHAPTER X.

ECCLESIASTICS.

CHAPTER XI.

CHAPTER XII.

CHAPTER XIII.

CHAPTER XIV.

CHAPTER XV.

CHAPTER XVI.

CHAPTER XVII.

GAMBLERS.

CHAPTER XVIII.

GARDENERS.

CHAPTER XIX.

CHAPTER XX.

CHAPTER XXI.

HUNTERS.

CHAPTER XXII.

CHAPTER XXIII.

SHOOTERS.

CHAPTER XXIV.

CHAPTER XXV.

OXONIANS.

CHAPTER XXVI.

CHAPTER XXVII.

CHAPTER XXVIII.

PREACHERS.

CHAPTER XXIX.

WORKING MEN.

CHAPTER XXX.

LIST OF ILLUSTRATIONS.

THE MEMORIES OF DEAN HOLE.

CHAPTER I.

ARCHERS.

Early associations in childhood and boyhood — The Royal
Sherwood Archers at Southwell—The Woodmen of Arden
—Horace Ford—Remarkable scores.

I BEGIN my recollections, as I began my education,
in alphabetical order. Again my first object-lesson,
"A was an Archer, who shot at a frog," presents
itself to the mental eye. He was an object, indeed,
but no longer of my admiration. He was impossible
as an archer, and immoral as a man. In defiance of
the first law of the craft, that the bowman stand
erect and firmly on his feet, he leaned forward on
one leg. The brim of his absurd hat would have
hopelessly prevented any approximation of the arrow
to his eye, but he appeared to be perfectly satisfied
in drawing it near unto his hip. He was encircled
with coils of tuneful brass, *æs triplex circa pectus erat ;*
and I was reminded of him, many years after I
made his acquaintance, when on a moonlit night,

B

having dined with the regiment of yeomen of which I was chaplain, and going down the inn yard for my dog-cart, I saw a brazen monster, gleaming, as it swayed to and fro, and accosting me, as it came alongside, with, " 'Ow de yer do, Mr. 'Ole?" Then I recognized one of our bandsmen bearing his ophicleide, whom I also knew as a clever house-painter; and when I proceeded to rebuke his intemperance, he gravely made reply, " Why, it were only t'other day as you was a-praising on me for graining your study door, and I do reckon to follow up natur' pratty close in oak, but I defy you at walnut!" I declined the challenge, and bade him go to bed.

I repeat that this educational archer was, both in posture and purpose, vile. What contemptible, cruel cowardice to array himself in such a costume to shoot at the harmless frog! I don't like frogs. I have been greatly disturbed by their nocturnes in Southern climes. I was taught in my early childhood that their conduct was not always filial; that they left their homes, and made proposals of marriage without the permission of their maternal parents, as it has been beautifully told in the Latin language—

> " Ranula furtivos statuebat quærere amores,
> ' Me miserum,' tristi Rolius ore gemit,
> Ranula furtivos statuebat quærere amores,
> Mater sive daret, sive negaret, iter."

But there is no suggestion that this bowman was a moral champion in quest of l'Enfant Prodigue, or even that he was a French epicure yearning for food ; and we should be harrowed by all the emotions which troubled the poetic soul of Mrs. Leo Hunter when she wrote her lamentations on " The Expiring Frog," were we not quite sure that our archer was incapable of hitting his mark.

Another vivid memory of my childhood is closely connected with archery. Many a time has the cistern of my little heart overflowed, when nurse read to us the tragic history of the irritable and nervous tailor, who could not endure the surveillance of the carrion crow from the aged oak hard by, and, shooting his arrow in the haste of his wrath—

> "Full many a shaft, at random sent,
> Finds mark the archer never meant "—

pierced the heart of the aged sow. I remember how we all fell a-sighing and sobbing, when we came to the supreme crisis of the tragedy—

> " The old sow's body was laid in the clay,
> Ding-a-ding, a-ding, a-ding O !
> All the little pigs came weeping away,
> And it's heigh-ho, the carrion crow,
> Ding-a-ding, a-ding, a-ding O."

Then came compensation. Diana smiled on me as I went, a happy boy, into the woods with the keeper, and he cut the stout, round, supple, shining hazel with my new knife (I still bear signs manual of its trenchant power), and I bought whipcord for the string at the village shop, carefully putting by a portion, having just read Miss Edgeworth's story of " Waste not, want not," and we went adown the brook for the stiff, straight reed, which we shortened into arrow form, and the blacksmith converted long nails into pointed piles, and the shoemaker fixed these firmly with waxed thread, and I sallied forth, as it seemed to me, a combination of Apollo, and Robin Hood, and William Tell, and of some stalwart ancestor, who following the banner, " Olde Nottingham, an archer cladde in green," and sending his arrows hurtling through the air, helped to win the great victory, on Crispin's Day, at Agincourt. How delightful it was when first I shot an arrow into the air, and it fell to earth I knew not where ; when I shot mine arrow over the house, and might have hit my brother, had I not been an only son ; when pigeons and rooks were eagles and vultures, and cats and dogs were tigers and bears ! I shot profusely, but, happily for her Majesty's lieges, I lost and broke so many arrows that my bow was soon laid aside. There still remained in use two instruments of terror (boys are a charming nuisance), namely, a cross-bow, made by the village carpenter, which ejected small portions of tobacco pipe, and a sling of stick, which propelled from a cleft at its upper extremity the smooth stones, which suggested on several occasions the exercise of the glazier's art. Civilization and science had not then achieved that infernal machine, the catapult.

In due course, I put away these malignant missiles, with other childish things, and, promoted to a full-sized bow and arrows, was permitted to practise with my father at the targets, elected a member of " The Royal Sherwood Archers," learned to—

> " Prove by shooting in a compass narrow,
> That I was born at Bow, and taught at Harrow ; "

and my " sacra auri fames," my longing to hit " the gold," was gratified by the annexation of my first prize.

Our meetings were held on a fair ground, overlooking the valley of the Trent and Southwell, half garden and half town, with its grand old church. The latter was largely indebted to Archdeacon Wilkins, who occupied " The Residence," for the restoration and maintenance of the fabric. Murray, his son, was rector, a man of much humour, and of practical energy in his work, for he was the first to introduce into the Midland Counties the harvest and choral festivals which are now universal; and I remember, as a specimen of his wit, the remark which he made upon our archers, " that, though the gentlemen shot well with yew bows, the ladies shot better with *beaux yeux*." And, apropos to his musical instincts, as we were walking down the main street of Southwell, he stopped opposite a bank, which was then kept by Messrs. Wild and Sons, and sang *sotto voce*, " I know a bank, wherein the Wilds' time goes."

One day the Roman Bishop of Nottingham, Roskell, came to inspect the minster. He was of portly and imposing aspect, and, when he was gone, the rector inquired from the chief mason what he thought of the visitor. " Well, sir," was the reply, " I saw nothing very particular about him. He seemed to me *the kind of a man as 'ud be pretty reg'lar 'ome at meal-times.*"

At Southwell Lord Byron lived when he wrote his " Hours of Idleness," and the book was published by Ridge, in the neighbour-town of Newark. " Ridge, Ridge," a friend said to me, as he read the word over his shop; " what a curious name!" " Much more remarkable," I could not forbear saying, " in the lifetime of his old partner, Furrow." But my companion seemed suspicious.

The readers of Byron's " Letters " will remember the name of the Rev. J. T. Becher, whose descendants still reside at Southwell. Not long ago, at a great ecclesiastical function—I think it was the enthronement of the present bishop—my friend, the present head of the family, who was rector's warden, was constrained to intimate to one of the vergers, an excellent servant, but enfeebled by age, that he must be superseded for the occasion by a younger man. The poor old fellow could not understand it, and at last exclaimed, in an astonishment of indignant grief, " *What me, as brought in 'Arcourt!*" Which meant that, at some distant period, he had walked before the Archbishop of York. We were long in persuading him that there was no diminution of respect.

The oldest societies in England are the Brough-

ton Archers, in Lancashire, of whom I have no information; the Toxophilite, whom I only know by the
high reputation which they most successfully retain
in London; and the Woodmen of Arden, of whose
pleasant meetings at Meriden, in Warwickshire—
where they have their hall and ball-room, their
dressing-rooms, kitchens, and cellars, their spacious
grounds, with targets and butts and clouts, their
servants clad in Lincoln green (reminding us of the
dear old "Heythrop," of which anon), where guests
are entertained with the most genial courtesy, and
fed on venison, archers' favourite food—I have joyous
memories. There, in the older days, when Coker
Adams and Coker Beck were the heroes, and in
later time, when my dear old friend Riland Bedford and others won bugles and arrows, it was my
exaltation more than once to win "the stranger's
bow." These meetings were more like private
parties than public assemblies, the members being
so well known to each other, and there was a merry
exchange of what the French call *badinage* and the
English *chaff*. For example, when the member
whom I have last named was standing on a chair,
reaching some of his archer's gear from his
" Ascham," another friend, a layman, who officiated
as judge and referee at this and at " the National"
gathering, addressed him with, " Now, rector, give
us a sermon." " If you wish," was the prompt
reply. " Shall I preach about *the unjust judge?* "

Archers are nomad and gregarious, and I became

acquainted with the best bowmen of their day, Higginson, who was one of the chief founders of " the National," Hippesley, Peckett, Luard, Maitland, Muir, Bramhall, Moore, the Garnetts, a triumvirate of brothers (of whom Charles, the eldest, shot the swiftest, strongest arrow I ever saw fly from bow), *cum multis aliis,* good men and true, whose names I do not recall. " But one I would select from that proud throng " as the prince and champion of all archers, Horace Ford. In the year 1845, at York, Mr. Peter Muir, of the Queen's Body-guard of Archers at Edinburgh, beat all competitors in the Double York Round, with a score of 537. Twelve years afterwards, at Cheltenham, Mr. Horace Ford took precedence, after shooting the same number of arrows, with a score of 1251, which has never been surpassed in public.

> " Micat inter omnes
> Julium sidus, velut inter ignes
> Luna minores."

But I have before me a letter, signed, " Yours to the pile, Horace Ford," in which he gives the details of a still more wonderful performance, made while shooting with the Rev. John Bramhall, who also achieved an admirable score—

FORD.

100 yards	144 arrows	127 hits	617 score
80 „	96 „	88 „	486 „
60 „	48 „	47 „	311 „
	Total ..	262 hits!	1414 score

BRAMHALL.

100 yards	144 arrows	114 hits	504 score
80 „	96 „	89 „	465 „
60 „	48 „	47 „	275 „
	Total ...	250 hits.	1244 score.

Ford also sent me some clever verses, written by his friend, Mr. Hughes, and entitled—

"LINES TO MISS VILLIERS.

"Of all the damsels whom the Muse
    Hath e'er summed up, as target-drillers,
I ne'er saw one whom I should choose
    To hold a candle to Miss Villiers.

"All the fair ladies on the ground
    Shot well, Peels, Hardings, Bakers, Millers,
Et cætera; but none were found
    Within two hundred of Miss Villiers.

"Our champion draws a yew as well
    As the old Agincourt blood-spillers,
But query if he can excel,
    At the same distance, this Miss Villiers?

"Peters, and ye, my staunch R. T.,
    When next we meet, let's all be fillers
Of a full pledge, with three times three,
    To the good health of fair Miss Villiers.

"Old Worcestershire may swell at heart
    With pride to call such grace and skill hers,
As we have witnessed on the part
    Of this redoubtable Miss Villiers!"

The poet does not descend to statistics, but I do not suppose that Miss Villiers ever attained the splendid score which Mrs. Legh made at Leamington in 1885, namely, 142 hits from 144 arrows, value 864!

Ford was ever ready to instruct ignorance, and he was pleased with a pictorial description which I sent him of "my archery before, and my archery after, six lessons from Professor Ford." In the first tableau one arrow was in the leg of a farm labourer, who was dancing with pain; another was in a hay-stack; and a third in the fleece of a sheep. In the second tableau the first was in the centre of the target, the point of the second in the "nock" of the first, and the point of the third in the "nock" of the second. On receiving this proof of my progress, he expressed his intention of retiring into private life.

Mr. Edwards, of Birmingham, a successful archer, communicated to me an incident which blended tragedy and comedy in a remarkable degree. He had received a dozen new arrows from Buchanan, and went forth to try them in a paddock adjoining his house. He had made eleven successive hits at sixty yards, and was delighted with his purchase, when a cow, which he had not observed, slowly approached the target, and pushed it down with its horns. "You will guess what I did," he continued. "It was no longer in my power to make a *bull's-eye*, but I touched up the other end of the *cow*." And the old nursery rhyme came into my thoughts, how

"Tidy hinched, and Tidy flinched, and Tidy cocked her tail;"

and the old schoolboy round-hand copy, "Retribution follows crime."

Two remembrances of graver import are associated in my mind with archery. Staying with a friend for a "bow meeting" in his neighbourhood, my razor, which I was stropping with the careless rapidity of youth, suddenly slipped from my grasp, and made a gash in the lower part of my left thumb, from which the blood streamed continuously. The wound required a surgeon, and was long in healing. *Pollice truncus*, but no poltroon, I resumed my archery as soon as I was able, but never again had the same firm grip of my bow.

In the same house, after the first day's practice of the year, my host and I decided to try a prescription for hardening the fingers of the right hand, which were sore from the bowstring, by striking them quickly on a heated poker, just touching the metal. The operation took place in the smoke-room, and the lady of the house, who came in during the process, volunteered to hold the poker, which was nearly red-hot. Suddenly, as she lowered it for an instant, her dress—which I think was made of tarlatan—caught fire, and to our horror she was at once surrounded with flames. Her husband lost his presence of mind, and tried to extinguish the fire with his hands. As he rushed to ring the bell for help, I bade her lie down, and, spreading out the large thick dressing-gown, in which it was then the fashion to smoke the evening cigar, I enfolded her completely, and effectually smothered the flames. The husband was in bed for nearly a fortnight, the wife a day or two, her right arm being badly burnt; the guest escaped unhurt, with a gratitude, which will never leave his heart, that he had been used to prolong the life of one of the most charming and beautiful women of her day.

Taking leave of this subject, so interesting from its associations with the past, and so powerfully presented to us by a modern poet, Mr. Conan Doyle—

> " What of the bow?
>   The bow was made in England,
>   Of true wood, of yew wood,
> The wood of English bows :—
>   So men, who are free,
>   Love the old yew tree,
> And the land where the yew tree grows.
>
> " What of the shaft?
>   The shaft was cut in England,
>   A long shaft, a strong shaft,
> Barbed, and trim, and true :—
>   So we'll all drink together
>   To the gray goose feather,
> And the land where the gray goose flew "—

I would commend archery as a most healthful and social exercise, forewarning all who have not made the experiment, that success can only be attained by acquiring a good style, and by constant practice (" Many prate of Robin Hood, who never shot with his bow "), and that with excellence there comes a powerful temptation to devote too much time to an amusement which, however fascinating, should be regarded only as a relaxation, subordinate and auxiliary to work and duty. Horace Ford expressed, in his later days, a sorrowful regret that he had spent so large a portion of his time' in archery.

CHAPTER II.

ARTISTS.

John Leech—His enjoyment of the country—Sherwood Forest
—Mr. Speaker Denison—On the hunting field—His sketch
of " A Contented Mind "—*Nascitur, non fit*—His drawings
on the wood—His hospitality—His friends.

I MIGHT have been an artist, but I met discourage-
ment. In my early childhood I had pictorial
instincts and a sixpenny box of paints, but my
mother not only reproved me for painting the
baby during the absence of its nurse, but objected
to the decoration of my own person and vestments.
Under a more auspicious patronage I might have
acquired the dexterity of Quintin Matsys, who,
having expended on his own pleasures the money
given to him for the purchase of a new suit, to be
worn at some grand ceremonial of the Court, to
which he was attached, painted on canvas a most
gorgeous costume, and wore it, to the admiration
of all.

Again, in boyhood, when, having received
lessons in drawing, I took home my show-piece, a

weeping willow by a ruined wall, entitled, "The Deserted Home"—no willow had ever such cause to weep, like Marius or Mariana, over a more desolate scene—my father first kindled, and then extinguished, my hopes by his commentary, "that it was just the sort of thing which he liked—for gun-wads."

Wherefore I retired from the School of Art, and satisfied myself, as most boys do, with marginal illustrations of my books, of the noble horse, as

"Læta per arva ruit,"

with portraits of those who taught me how to translate them, with mural delineations in chalk, and, in after-time, with such occasional cartoons in pen and ink as that to which I have referred, and which evoked the eulogies of Horace Ford.

How, then, it may be asked, dare you presume to write about artists? And I offer my apology in the language of the flower in the Persian fable, "I am not the rose, but cherish me, for we have dwelt together." My dearest friend for many years was John Leech. It was a memorable day on which we first met. I went literally "from grave to gay." In the morning there had been a consecration of ground added to our churchyard, by Bishop Jackson, of Lincoln; and a most incongruous incident had occurred in the distribution, by one of my parishioners, who had brought the wrong parcel from my study, of the "Schedule of the Caunton

Cottage Gardening and Horticultural Society," instead of the Form of Service; and in the evening I went to dine with a neighbour, and to meet Leech. I had always longed to grasp the hand which diffused so much pure enjoyment, and taught men how to be both merry and wise, and it was an epoch in my life, a green spot on the path of time, to look on his kindly, intellectual, handsome face. He had come into the Midlands, with his old friend Adams, to have a day with the Belvoir Hounds, and was greatly amused, with a *soupçon* of annoyance, at the ill-concealed attention which had been freely bestowed upon him. Some expected him to witch the world with noble horsemanship, whereas, fond as he was of hunting, he was a timid rider, and loved a placid steed. "Give me an animal," I have heard him say, "on which you can carry an umbrella in a hailstorm." Some hoped for a recitation in the familiar intonation of *Punch;* and all expected to see themselves next week in the pages of the *London Charivari.*

As to his appearance, it might be said of him, as Sterne said of Uncle Toby, that "Nature had written Gentleman, with so fair a hand, on every line of his countenance," and that, as Lord Peterborough said of Fénelon, he was "cast in a particular mould, never used for anybody else." After his death, his father sent me the *Illustrated London News,* having written in pencil over his portrait therein, "an exact likeness; the best extant." He was tall, but slight in figure, with a high broad forehead, large blue-grey Irish eyes (his family came originally from Ireland), and a face full of expression. When he saw anything which he disliked, when he was bored or vexed, there was "a lurking trouble of the nether lip," but the sunniest of smiles, ἀνηρὶθμον γελάσμα, when he was enjoying the ridiculous, or giving pleasure to his friends. He was modest in his demeanour, and silent as a rule, as one who, though he was not working, was constrained to think about his work. "*Les petits esprits*," Rochefaucault writes, "*ont le don de beaucoup parler mais de rien dire;*" but when Leech spoke, he spoke well, and when he was with those whom he loved, no one was merrier than he.

He dressed tastefully but quietly, like a gentleman, and was one of those who believe that cleanliness is next to godliness. Some years ago, I was writing letters in the morning-room of a great house, and one of two fine ladies, who evidently wished me to be edified by their conversation, inquired from the other, "Do you care, dear, for artists, and authors, and that sort of people?" And the answer was, "No, dear, I can't say I do. *They're so dirty!*" I ventured to suggest the names of individuals, distinguished in literature and art, who were manifestly as fond of ablutions as the *haute noblesse*, but they evidently did not believe me; and I must confess that I have met disciples of the palette and the press whose back hair has suggested both scissors and shampoo, and whose lighter raiment would be best described in Latin—

"Qui color albus erat nunc est contrarius albo."

The first time John Leech paid me a visit, it did me good to watch his enjoyment of country air and quiet. He sat under a tree, stretched himself, folded his arms, closed his eyes, and opened his mouth, inhaling, like one

> " Who feels, as in a pensive dream,
>   When all his active powers are still,
>   A distant clearness in the hill,
>   A sacred sweetness in the stream."

Like the Arctic voyager, when the sun shone once more, he "seemed to be bathing in perfumed waters." No child among the cowslips, no schoolboy home- ward bound, could be happier. I drove him to "the Dukeries," so called because at one time there was a conjunction of four ducal homes. Thoresby was the residence of the Duke of Kingston, succeeded by Earl Manvers, Clumber of the Duke of New- castle, Welbeck of the Duke of Portland, Worksop Manor of the Duke of Norfolk. Passing through Wellow, he seemed to be as delighted with the maypole on the village green, as was Washington Irving, when, in writing of his visit to England, he says, " I shall never forget my joy at first seeing a maypole." But when, having left our carriage, we wandered among the grand old oaks and the golden bracken, he closed his sketch-book, almost as soon as he had opened it, and murmuring, "This is too delicious," sat down in the sunshine.

We discoursed on Robin Hood (Robin o' the 'ood), who, by an ubiquity, only surpassed by that of our royal Charles, who seems to have slept in several beds on the same night, is supposed to have spent much time in this Forest of Sherwood (" the Shire Wood "), chasing the wild deer and harassing the tourist. Leech was pleased by an account, which I gave him, of a recent Archæological meeting at Newark, in which a learned antiquarian, after an elaborate history of Robin and his doings, was succeeded by a brother savant, who undertook to prove, by unanswerable evidence, that no such person ever existed. And I told him, apropos of outlaws, how, not many miles from the place where we sat, a Nottinghamshire gentleman was met as he was returning, on horseback, by night from Mansfield, where he had been to receive his rents, and having a large sum of money with him, by Dick Turpin, who stopped him with the inquiry, "Mr. Milward, I think?" "Noa, sir," it was answered in a vulgar provincial twang, "I bean't Mister Milward. I be his mon. The master's got a party at th' inn, and he won't be home till midnight." On he went unmolested, but it was long, after discovering the deception, before "Richard" was "himself again."

I invited all my neighbours to meet Leech at a garden party, my annual Fête des Roses, of which I had then three or four thousand trees; and, in memory of the fair ladies, who admired him, and the flowers, and the cooling cups, he afterwards made a charming picture of Mr. Punch, crowned with a wreath of roses and surrounded by smiling Hebes, offering sherry-cobblers, fanning him, and shading from the sun.

He was somewhat perplexed by one exuberant worshipper, who insisted on drinking his health at intervals, and assuring him that he was "the delight of the nation," and evidently felt, as Mrs. Nickleby, when one of her lovers would cut her initials on the pew-door during Divine service, that "it was gratifying but embarrassing."

He liked the sympathy of those who could appreciate the intention and execution of his work, but his countenance, his mixed expression of indignation and amusement, was a memorable sight to see. "A moment o'er his face a tablet of unutterable thought was traced," when a vulgar fellow, who travelled with us on the rail, asked him "how much he got for his funny cuts," and assured him that "some on 'em was tiptop, though he thought old Briggs was bosh." *

Everybody gave him heartiest welcome whenever he came and wherever he went. The Speaker,

---

* I had the pleasure of suppressing an intrusive fellow-traveller of this type, who brought into the carriage a strong odour of whisky, and, having bored me for some time with his imbecile remarks, roughly inquired, "What comes next to *Itchin?*" And when I answered, "*Scratching,*" the conversation flagged.

Mr. Denison, afterwards Lord Ossington, at whose house one met the potentates of the age, the American President, the English Premier, the popular prelate (I have in my recollection Daniel Webster, Lord Palmerston, and Bishop Wilberforce), mounted him, dined him, and told him, as few could tell, amusing incidents. Apropos of art, he narrated how, when making alterations in his house, he had sent away from a long gallery two waggon-loads of worthless pictures, copies from the great masters, to a dealer at Retford, who bought them for three or four pounds apiece. A worthy chemist from Southwell, very fond of pictures, went to inspect the purchase, and was so delighted with "A Monk at Prayer, by Murillo," that, as he told a friend on his return, he hardly dared to inquire the price, lest he should reveal his anxiety to purchase. Finally, on payment of ten pounds, he secured, and brought home, the treasure. There must have been some merit in it, for not many days after, Mr. Wright, of Upton, an accomplished scholar, the translator of Dante and Tasso, a clever artist, and the owner of many valuable pictures, saw it, bought it for eighty guineas, and gave it the best place in his collection. He died. The pictures were to be sold, and Messrs. Christie and Manson sent down an expert to prepare a catalogue. A proof was forwarded to the chief executor, who wrote back at once to express his astonishment that no mention was made of the gem of the collection, the Murillo. The explanation was depressing—a courteous intimation that the owner of the picture had made an injudicious purchase, and they could not advise that it should be sent to London.

On the hunting-field Leech was a most delectable companion, when he had a gentle, tranquil steed, and hounds were not running. No incident or object of interest escaped his keen observation. He directed attention to circumstances which were exceptional, characteristics which were quaint, things beautiful or ugly, where ordinary eyes saw nothing worthy of notice. I remember, in proof, that, as we were going from covert to covert, it was necessary to negotiate an ordinary fence. "Now," he said to me, "there is no hurry, nothing to fire your inflammatory spirit; wait awhile here and watch. You shall see that no two men, women, or boys, no two horses or ponies, will go through this performance, which seems so simple, in the same temper and style." His prophecy was exactly fulfilled. Some men gathered themselves and their bridles together, gripped their steeds, put their feet further through their stirrups, pressed their hats more tightly, and charged the obstacle, as though they rode to battle. Some held a loose and some a tightened rein. Some used the whip, and some the spur. Some were silent, and some addressed their animals with brief words of encouragement. Some kept their seat, and some rose so high as to open out an extensive view of the distant landscape between themselves and their saddles. The horse and his rider, who knew their business, went, the pace imperceptibly quickened, with serene confidence to the leap. The quadrupeds, like the bipeds, showed signal diversities of form. Some jumped a foot higher than the hedge, and covered four times the necessary space. Some cleared it, and that was all. Some broke it with their hind-legs, to the intense gratification of the timid, who were rendered yet more happy when an excited four-year-old or a blundering underbred brute went through it with a crash. Some suddenly refused, and then, if the rider was without experience, it was a case of "stand and deliver." Lastly, the mixed multitude, including that section which a friend of mine was pleased to designate as "The Pop and Porter Brigade," passed bravely through the gaps, and the gay cavalcade moved on.

When the chase began, Leech was not in the foreground. He was not physically strong; he had not hunted in his youth; his arm had been broken by a fall from his pony, and the recurrence of such an accident would have been disastrous to him and to us all. We, whose limbs were compara-tively of no importance, could afford to risk an occasional fall; and, apropos of such contingencies, he sent me, in reply to a letter, in which I informed him that I had been riding a most promising young chestnut in a long and difficult run, and that we had only had three mishaps, a sketch, which after-wards was published in *Punch*, as illustrating—

A Contented Mind.

"Well, Master Reynolds, so you've been riding the young un.   How does he go?"

"Splendid! never carried better in my life!   It was his first run, and we only came down five times!"

With the original, he wrote—

"Dear Master Reynolds,

        "I should immensely like a mount on this charming animal.—Yours ever,

"J. L."

The city and country mouse exchanged frequent visits, but with no unpleasant interruptions, as in the fable.   He came and went as he pleased, and could work or rest at his will.   He gathered welcome material in fields fresh and pastures new.   Sometimes he would say, "I must make a memorandum," and would trace a few mysterious lines in his sketch-book to be developed hereafter; and sometimes he would ask, with the meekest diffidence, if he were told an anecdote worthy of illustration, "May I use that?" as though you were conferring a priceless obligation, instead of receiving a privilege, in playing jackal to such a lion.   Sometimes he would have a horse brought out, and draw him.   Sometimes my wife sat to him in her habit.   Both may be seen in combination in one of his "Sketches in Oil," wherein a young horsewoman leaves the road, to

the horror and expostulation of the fat groom behind, and takes a fence into the adjoining field, to spare the poor animal's legs. The horse is the only true presentation—the lady in the picture is short instead of tall, and if I had proposed to any servant of mine to assume that coat of many colours, I should have received an immediate month's warning. Leech never published likenesses, except of public men in his cartoons, on principle, and I am not sure that he had the power, if he had desired it. He spent the best part of a day in endeavouring to produce a pencil sketch of the lady aforesaid, and then destroyed it as a failure.

It was like bringing water to some fair plant which was drooping in drought, food to the hungry, fuel to the frozen, to tell Leech a good story which the public had never heard, and which none could repeat to them so charmingly as he. I see that dear face light up once more as I relate how the farmer at the rent dinner (it took place, I think, on the Belvoir property) smacked his lips over the rich liqueur, and, turning to the footman behind him, said, " Young man, if you've no objection, I'll tak' some o' that in a moog;" how the coachman, unaccustomed to act as waiter, watched with agony of mind the jelly which he bore swaying to and fro, and set it down on the table with a gentle remonstrance of " Who-o, who-o, who-o," as though it were some restive horse; with other histories, many in number, which he made famous.

He was ever on the look-out,* listening, musing, realizing. "I am obliged," he said, "to keep my pencil in exercise, lest it should get above its work." But the real constraint was in the continuous demand, "*nulla dies sine lineâ.*" "There is always," he sighed, "a boy from the *Punch* office, diffusing an odour of damp corduroy through the house, and waiting for fresh supplies." Sometimes he could work with marvellous rapidity. I have known him finish three drawings on the wood before luncheon. Sometimes he said that his pencil was on strike, that it was a dangerous anarchist, and that he proposed to call out the military.

I have met with those who seemed to think that it gave him no trouble to produce his sketches (we are all of us inclined to regard other people's work as much more easy than our own), and that, like Gluck the composer, when he took his piano with a bottle of champagne into his garden and played joyous airs, his life was all music and sunshine; but at times he was sorely pressed. No artist had ever more enjoyment from his art. It was innate, as with all extraordinary genius—*poeta nascitur, non fit.* It was so in a marvellous degree with Handel, but the difference was that Leech had every en-

---

* So we read of Hogarth in his rambles through London streets, always on the watch for striking features or incidents, and accustomed, when any face struck him as particularly grotesque or expressive, to make a preliminary sketch on his thumb.

couragement (Flaxman, the sculptor, foretold his excellence), whereas Handel's father opposed his son's inclinations, and kept all instruments out of his reach, ignoring the wise advice of Lord Bacon, that "if the affection and aptness of children be extraordinary, then it is good not to cross it." He contrived to get possession of a clavichord, which he secreted in his garret, and played while others slept. It is recorded that he played the organ in the cathedral at Halle before he was seven years old, and that he began at the age of nine to study composition. I have seen some very clever drawings which Leech did about the same period of life, notably a coach with four horses, and two knights tilting in the ring, and no doubt his pleasure increased with his skill; but he was overworked, and sacrificed himself for the advantage of others.

No one knows what John Leech could do, no one has seen the supreme perfection of his art, who has not been privileged to admire his drawings when they were finished on the wood for the engraver. There was an exquisite delicacy of touch, which, even by such accomplished artificers as Mr. Swain, could never be reproduced in their integrity. The slightest divergence in an eyelash, or the curl of a lip, changed the expression and misrepresented his work; and I have heard him groan when *Punch* arrived at his breakfast-table on Tuesday morning, and he saw that some small aberration had detracted from his design and achievement. Happily there always remained an amount of excellence to satisfy and gratify all who saw them.

The mention of a Breakfast Table of which he was Autocrat (he had high admiration of Wendell Holmes) suggests his hospitality, and he was the most considerate and thoughtful of hosts. He gave to all his best. He had no *chasse-cousin*, no cheap wine, halfway on its road to vinegar, and so called because the French give it to poor relations when they wish to shorten their stay; and though he never pampered himself in private, nothing was too good for his friends, for whom he always produced, as Douglas Jerrold bade the waiter, "the older, not the *elder*, port." I asked him one day, after he had given us a merry little dinner at his lodgings, No. 1, The Crescent, Scarborough, how he made such good champagne cup. "The ingredients," he replied, "of which this refreshing beverage is composed, and which is highly recommended by the faculty for officers going abroad, and all other persons stopping at home, are champagne, ice, and aerated water, but, in consequence of advancing years, I always forget the seltzer."

I remember a dish of British Queen strawberries, of a size and colour to make a gardener take off his hat, crowned with a majestic monster, which would have made a dumpling; and he gravely requested a servant to remove the apex from the pyramid, and to have it carved on the sideboard.

But better than choice fruit, or food, or vintage,

though remarkably nice in combination, was the feast of reason and repartee provided by the clever guests whom he delighted to gather round him: Thackeray and Millais;* Adams, his oldest, and one of his dearest friends, who lived at Baldock in Hertfordshire, where Leech went a-hunting, and where our eighth Henry went a-hawking, and was nearly suffocated in a muddy ditch, his jumping-pole snapping in twain as he was vaulting over; Lemon, Shirley Brooks, and Tom Taylor—three successive editors of *Punch;* Douglas Jerrold and Percival Leigh; Tenniel, Holman Hunt, Du Maurier, Silver, Mowbray Morris (the manager of the *Times*), Dasent, Lucas, Knox (on the staff), and others, whose names I forget. Dickens was absent, because, when I first knew Leech, there had been an interruption of their friendship, but it was afterwards happily resumed. Their intimacy had been long and affectionate, and Dickens had nursed him in a serious crisis. Leech was his guest at Bonchurch, and while bathing was suddenly struck by a gigantic wave with a force which brought on symptoms of a congested brain, and for a time imperilled his life. Dickens wrote, " He was put to bed with twenty of his namesakes upon his forehead,

* A gentleman came into his studio, and, seeing his famous picture of " The Black Brunswicker," asked, " What uniform is that?" Millais, who had been at great trouble and expense to procure the exact costume, replied, " The Black Brunswicker." " Oh, indeed," said the visitor; " I knew it was one of the volunteers, but I wasn't sure which regiment."

became seriously worse, and was again very heavily bled. The night before last, he was in such an alarming state of restlessness, which nothing could relieve, that I proposed to Mrs. Leech to try magnetism. Accordingly, in the middle of the night, I fell to, and, after a very fatiguing bout of it, put him to sleep for an hour and thirty-five minutes. A change came on in his sleep, and he is decidedly better. I talked to the astounded Mrs. Leech across him, as if he had been a truss of hay."

He took me to dine at the weekly congress, the hebdomadal board, of *Punch*, which was held on Wednesday, in Bouverie Street, when the subject of the next large cartoon was fixed by the authors and artists. Afterwards he told me, " You are an honorary member of our mess," a compliment which I most gratefully appreciated, and which, I was informed, had only been offered to one other favoured guest, Sir Joseph Paxton. I need not say how elated and exhilarated I was, to be where " the sparks of wit flew in such profusion as to form complete fireworks."

Thomas Hood—I write the name with reverence, because no English poet, except Shakspere, has united in one brain and heart such pathetic and humorous power, who was among authors as Garrick among actors, alike excellent in tragedy and comedy—Hood was one of his select friends, and he went to see him, he told me, shortly before his death. He was weak, and emaciated in body, but the old bright spirit was strong within him. "Ah, Leech," he sighed, pointing to some pungent plasters, which his doctor had put on his chest, "*so much mustard, and so very little beef!*"

Samuel Rogers said to him, "Mr. Leech, I admire you much." He was just beginning his success as an artist, and was gratified by this commendation, as he supposed, of his art. "Yes," repeated Rogers, "I admire you much. I saw you brushing your own hat, and the man who, in these days, does anything for himself, is deserving of admiration."

CHAPTER III.

ARTISTS— *Continued.*

A little tour in Ireland—Leech on the ocean wave—His visit
to Blair Athole—A fiend in human shape—His wife and
children—Sketch from Biarritz—Bull-fight at Bayonne—
The last new Rose.

LEECH proposed that we should take a fortnight's
holiday in Ireland, and I accepted his invitation
with an eager gladness, which was somewhat
subdued when he suggested, " You shall write, and
I will illustrate, an account of our little tour." *
Nevertheless, my hesitation was brief; for I knew
that the sauce would compensate for the want of
flavour in the fish, and that the dulness of the
drama would be redeemed by the splendour of the
scenes. He sent me a sketch of his delight on
the ocean wave, being, in fact, an early and helpless
victim to *mal de mer*, and having stated in a letter
to Charles Dickens, whom he visited at a chateau in
France, that on his arrival at Calais he was received
by the congregated spectators with a distinct round
of applause, as being by far the most intensely and
unutterably miserable object that had yet appeared.

* " A Little Tour in Ireland."   Illustrated by John Leech.
London : Edward Arnold.

D

From the hour of embarkation to that in which we parted, our journey was all "sweetness and light." To have had as a companion "an abridgment of all that is pleasant in man;" to have realized Sallust's maxim, "*eadem velle, eadem nolle, ea demum est*

amicitia;" to have shared his quick perception and keen appreciation of all that was grand and lovely in nature, and of all that was eccentric and laughable in man—

"His eye begets occasion for his wit;
For every object that the one doth catch,
The other turns to a mirth-moving jest "—

as we looked over the Bay of Dublin from the hill of Killiney, wandered among the solemn mountains and lakes of Connemara, all but danced with joy over the first salmon which he caught at Kylemore, shot the weir between the upper and lower lake at Killarney, rowed by moonlight to Innisfallen, talking to the boatmen about the O'Donoghue, and listening to the bugles as they set the echoes flying, travelling mile after mile of tranquil enjoyment in the cosy Irish car;—these are memories to make an old man young. He was perfectly successful in all his attempts at delineation but one—the portrait of a most offensive odour in Cork Harbour, which, he said, taking out his book and pencil, " was quite strong enough to sketch." He had previously achieved a representation of a sneeze, which is still in my possession.

Soon after our return from Ireland, he wrote me an account of his visit to Blair Athole. He was delighted with the scenery and the gracious hospitality, but (as the lady said, when she was congratulated on her daughter's engagement, " Jenny hates the man, but there's always a something ") his spirit was perturbed by the lateness of the dinner-hour, which depended upon the ducal siesta, and was sometimes delayed until 9 p.m., and also by the presence on the dinner-table of a small but obese dog, who, as the footmen took up large hot-water dishes and handed them to the company, watched his opportunity, and crawled from one vacant space to another, that he might enjoy the warmer locality.

Asking the reader's permission to record my memories as they present themselves, I would narrate another canine incident, also connected with the dinner-table and warm water, which I heard from an eye-witness. In a London home it was the custom to place a foot-warmer, before the repast began, in front of the chair of the hostess, who was chilly and infirm from old age. On this occasion the guests were early, or the footman was late, and the latter was still under the table when the former took their seats. The lady of the house became conscious of some motive power below, and thinking that it came from a favourite retriever, who was allowed to roam where he pleased, fondly addressed it as " Rollo, good Rollo!" and, failing to hear the protest, " It's not Rollo, grandmamma—it's Alfred," affectionately patted the head as it emerged from the table, with a halo of powder, and an expression of perplexity which Leech himself could not have copied.

I have before me nearly one hundred and fifty of his letters—one, " written with a pen which had no mouth, and bolted," *all* in haste. A large proportion consists of invitations or replies thereto. When I pleaded my reluctance to leave my garden, he sent me a sarcastic view of a " *rational being admiring a chrysanthemum !* " bade me seek " the more refined and intellectual qualifications to be found in a pantomime," and called upon me to remember how we had enjoyed together the consummate acting of Robson in *The Porter's Knot*, so pathetic that a young man in the stalls near to us, who, before the performance, had been " turning to mirth all things of earth," when the drama was over, murmured to his friend, with tears in his eyes, " Awfully jolly, awfully jolly ! "

Leech was himself a clever actor, and played in private theatricals at Sir Lytton Bulwer's house at Knebworth, with Dickens, John Forster, Frank Stone, Mark Lemon, Cruikshank, Egg, and others : also, for charitable purposes, as " Slender " in *The Merry Wives of Windsor*, at the Haymarket, the St. James's, and Miss Kelly's theatres. Shirley Brooks describes him as being by far the most effective figure, in a combination of ancient and modern costumes, classic tunic over dress black trousers and patent-leather boots, new silk hat with wreath of laurel, spectacles, umbrella, etc., at a fancy ball, which was given by their mutual friend, John Parry. His first public appearance was when, with two or three other medical students, he sang, " for the fun of the thing," at night in the streets, the concerts being profitable as well as amusing. He told me that on one occasion a listener, to whom he presented his hat, produced from behind his back a small violin to intimate that he was one of the profession.

When I invited him to have a day with the
Rufford, and promised him a horse which had won
his confidence, he denounced me as a fiend in human

shape (I never quite understood why he put a
college cap on my head); and afterwards, in reply
to a similar proposal, he wrote to say that his

work, chiefly for " the almanac," would not even permit him to ride his pony, which was " swelling wisibly before his wery eyes " in the stable. Moreover, he was devotedly attached to his home, for

he was a " Douglas, tender and true," and the best of husbands and fathers, as well as the best of friends.

> " The gladdener of ten thousand hearths,
>   The idol of his own."

" Love at first sight, firstborn, and heir to all," constrained him to seek an introduction to Miss Eaton, to woo and win ; and though, when I first knew her, the bloom of *la première jeunesse* was gone, there remained abundant evidences of the charms which dazzled the eye, bewildered the brain, annexed the heart, of John Leech, bachelor, and reappeared continually in the pretty girls of *Punch*.

He has given us numerous manifestations of his delight in children, and one of the most delicious drawings he ever made is that scene in the nursery, where a child of seven appears, in a hat, neckerchief, and coat (tails touching the floor), evidently the property of the elder brother, as the family doctor, solemnly prescribing for the sick doll, while a wee lassie of four summers respectfully holds his (rocking) horse.

Mrs. Lemon, the wife of the editor of *Punch*, and designated sometimes by irreverent minds as Judy, told me that Leech was sadly disappointed in the first part of his married life that he had no children ; then a child was born and died, and then there were two more, a son and a daughter, whom I knew from their early days.

The son, George Warrington, had many "notes of fatherhood." A mere child, he must wear a little velvet coat like his papa's, and he expressed a wish to have the hair removed from the top of his head, that it might resemble the parental pate, which had what the Americans term "a snow line," where vegetation ceases. I see the dear little fellow now, standing before his miniature easel, and, with a most solemn gravity, richly colouring, in a style of polychromatic splendour hitherto unknown, the engravings of the *Illustrated London News*.

He was remarkably quick and shrewd. On the arrival of a new nurse, he informed her at once that his papa had said that he was a sort of boy who required peculiar and kind treatment (a quotation, I have no doubt, from the mouth of his indulgent father, which he was not intended to hear), and that he would trouble her to bring him an orange and a cake. On another occasion, when he was staying in my house, and my wife's maid remonstrated with him, and threatened to tell his mamma, he immediately made answer, "Oh yes, go, if you like; and I shall go too, and say how you idle away your time with nurse."

Leech had an original and effective method of reprimanding his children. If their faces were distorted by anger, by a rebellious temper, or a sullen mood, he took out his sketch-book, transferred their lineaments, with a slight exaggeration—

> "pictoribus atque poetis
> Quidlibet audendi semper fuit æqua potestas"—

to paper, and showed them, to their shameful confusion, how ugly naughtiness was!

The boy went to Charterhouse, and was the first to win the "Leech Prize for Drawing," given annually in honour of his father, who had been there as a scholar with Thackeray. Thence he went into Lincolnshire, a tall, handsome youth, to learn on a large farm the science and practice of agriculture; and then, not being strong, he set forth with a friend, the captain of a ship, to Australia, and as they were returning one night from the shore at South Adelaide, the boat was upset by a sudden storm, and young Leech was drowned.

His sister, of whom Leech might have said with Byron, "*Ada,* sole daughter of my home and hearth," a gentle, delicate, affectionate girl, had her home in ours soon after the death of her mother, who was separated but a brief while from him whom she so dearly loved, and remained with us until her marriage with Mr. William Gillett. Alas! she too died soon after the birth of her child, Dorothy, now the only living descendant of John Leech.

Ada possessed a most charming miniature by Millais in water-colours of herself as a baby, with the hand of her father appearing round her waist. I never saw it without thinking of the lines—

> "O for the touch of a vanished hand,
> And the sound of a voice that is still!"

And I remember another sketch by the same great painter, which Leech showed me with mirthful admiration, for it was equally adroit, though in an entirely different style, of "Old Mr. Leech and old Mr. Millais on their hunters." How thankful we ought to be that—

> "Heaven from all creatures hides the book of fate,
> All but the page prescribed, their present state"!

Leech took as much lively interest in my engagement and marriage as though he had been my brother; insisted on accompanying me, when I went on the somewhat anxious mission of discussing settlements with the young lady's guardian, to the door of his house; sent me a charming present of a gold horse, exquisitely modelled, on a large seal, and, having requested and received long notice of the wedding-day, " because," he said, " his coat, waistcoat, trousers, and especially his scarf, must be gradually and carefully developed," he appeared in due course, a combination of good looks, good temper, and good clothes, as my best man.

In the following year (1862) he went to Biarritz, and I received in one of his letters " the last sweet thing in hats (with a walking-stick, if you please)."

In his next he writes :—

" 32, Brunswick Square, W.C., September 18, 1862.
" MY DEAR HOLE,

" I have only just returned from *a bull-fight at Bayonne!* and find your kind note. Don't think me a brute, therefore, for not replying sooner, whatever you may think of me for assisting at such a disgusting display. I had heard of such things, but had always supposed that they were mere circus or Astley affairs, and never thought that any civilized people could delight in so much animal suffering. When I tell you that, besides *six* bulls, *seven* horses were sacrificed for the afternoon's entertainment,

The last new Rose — designed
for the Gardener's annual. —

you will imagine what an exhibition it was—to say nothing of such a trifle as one man being nearly gored to death. . . .

> "Yours always faithfully,
>> "JOHN LEECH.

"P.S.—I bathed 'in the Bay of Biscay O!' What do you say to that with your *Scarborough?*"

Then he sent me, with his congratulations, the accompanying sketch of my paternal joy.

CHAPTER IV.

ARTISTS—*Continued.*

Leech as a pugilist—In melancholy mood—New process of
enlarging his drawings—"Sketches in Oils"—Exhibition in
London—The beginning of the end—Thackeray's entreaty
—Thackeray's death—Leech's presentiment—His sudden
departure—His work.

LEECH was a man of peace, but when a fascinating
lady presented him with a piping bullfinch, he

announced that, with this bird as the crest upon his knightly helmet, he was prepared to maintain against all comers the supremacy of the donor, as Queen of Beauty. "In the lists," he added, " or any other ring."

There were times when from overwork, which troubles few, or from indigestion, which oppresses many, Leech took gloomy views of his surroundings. He affirmed and he believed, for he had not a *soupçon* of affectation in him, that he was wasting time on unworthy subjects and an inferior method, and he maintained the opinion, which prevailed in the time of Pliny, " *Nulla gloria artificum est, nisi eorum qui tabulas pinxere* " (" None but the painter of a great picture can be a great artist "); and that there would be no grand masterpiece, by which he would be remembered when he was gone, as the picture of the Transfiguration was placed by the dead body of Raffaelle. It was necessary on these occasions to deal with him very firmly—to ride the contumacious horse with the curb, and to give him a touch of the spur; to apply the asperities of sarcasm and the sound arguments of common sense; to attack his position with the light cavalry of ridicule and with the heavy brigade of grave admonition; to recommend medical interposition, depletion, and total abstinence; to suggest a keeper, and the difficulty he would experience in the exercise of his vocation under the embarrassments of a strait-waistcoat. Seriously, we, his friends, were unanimous, and he who was then the most famous painter of his day, Mr. Millais, joined us, in our indignant expostulation, and in assuring him that his work gave more pleasure to his fellow-men than all the pictures which were hung up in galleries and in rich men's homes, and therefore were comparatively unseen. We told him that he might as reasonably regret that he had not followed his original vocation, and become an eminent doctor, seeing that, *un médecin malgré lui,* he had done more by his chirurgery or handiwork to cheer invalids, raise the spirits of the doleful, and promote convalescence, than all the Royal College of Surgeons.

I believe that he was convinced, but, nevertheless, he made a compromise. Soon after the publication of our " Little Tour," a process was discovered by which his drawings could be enlarged, and he sent me some of the first results of the experiment, taken from his illustrations of our book, and afterwards coloured. The *modus operandi* is thus described : The principal agent is india-rubber. A block of this material, considerably larger than the engraving to be copied, is compressed to fit it exactly. In this state it is impressed, so as to become a counterpart of the engraving. On being removed, it at once expands to its full size, and the result is a reversed copy of the original on an enlarged scale. If the process is repeated, a much larger copy is obtained, and so on, until the necessary dimensions are realized. Then a prepared stone is applied to the enlarged indiarubber block, and the drawing transferred to it is again printed upon a piece of canvas, and is ready for the colours of the painter.*

By the aid of this discovery, Leech painted the "Sketches in Oils," which were exhibited in the Egyptian Hall, and were much admired by the public, although generally regarded, by artists especially, as being inferior in merit and interest to the original work.

And now, though I am writing beneath an Italian sky,

> "So cloudless, clear, and purely beautiful,
> That God alone is to be seen in heaven,"

a shadow falls upon my heart, and a chill, such as comes at sunset in these southern climes. It is the shadow of the valley of death. Thackeray was the first to alarm me as to the failing health of our friend, entreating me with all his earnestness to "get John Leech out of London. He was in a state of nervous debility, which would be fatal if he did not rest. Not only the street music, which he had always abhorred, but now any sudden or unusual sound, even the movement of a scythe over the lawn under his window, startled and distressed him." I could only answer that, though I was continually pressing him, even to importunity, I would make a more strenuous appeal. I

* See the *Athenæum*, June 27, 1862.

could not persuade him, nor would he leave his work, until he was ordered by his doctor to Whitby.

Thackeray little thought that he should be the first to go. They knelt together in the chapel at Charterhouse on the 12th of December, and dined in the old hall afterwards to celebrate Founder's Day ; and, little more than one week later, Thackeray was found dead in his bed. Mr. Leech told Millais of his presentiment, that he too should die suddenly. Hogarth had the same foreboding. He called his last picture " Finis," and broke his palette when it was completed. It was published in March ; and in October he died, just a century before Leech, suddenly, on his return from Chiswick, as Leech on his return from Whitby, in London, both having sought relaxation when it was too late.

A short time before he left town, the Speaker (Denison) told me that he had met him, and in answer to his expression of hope that he, who gave so much pleasure to others, enjoyed some portion of the repast which he prepared, he answered, with a sorrowful sigh, that he felt like a man who had undertaken to walk a thousand miles in a thousand hours, and who was oppressed by the fear of failure.

> " He saw a hand we could not see,
> Which beckoned him away ;
> He heard a voice we could not hear,
> Which said he must not stay."

The end here of the beginning of the hereafter came very suddenly. On the day before his death he had promised, and had commenced, a drawing for *Punch.* On the morning of that day he said to his wife, who in her widowhood repeated his words to me, " Please God, Annie, I will make a fortune yet." Messrs. Agnew had offered him £1000 for four original pictures. He proposed to give up his work for *Punch,* which overtaxed his strength, and to take a house in the country. But " God's finger touched him, and he slept." A sudden spasm, *angina pectoris,* and that noble heart was still. That right hand, cold and white as marble, could give and bless no more. His last words were, " I am going."

> "'I go,' he said; but, as he spoke, they found
> The hands grow cold, and fluttering was the sound.
> They gazed affrighted, but they caught at last
> A dying look of love, and all was past."

I did not hear of his death until the morning of All Saints' Day, when I saw the announcement, with a grief which I shall never lose, in the *Times;* and half an hour afterwards, in our village church, I was reading, to my unspeakable solace, in the First Lesson for the Festival, that " the souls of the righteous are in the hand of God, and there shall no torment touch them. In the sight of the unwise they seemed to die, and their departure is taken for misery, and their going from us to be utter destruction : but they are at peace."

I said the Burial Office as best I could at the grave, which was close to Thackeray's, and which was surrounded by his friends. The pall-bearers were the four consecutive editors of *Punch* (Mark

Lemon, Shirley Brooks, Tom Taylor, and Francis Burnand), Millais, Tenniel, Lucas, Mayhew, Silver, and Evans.   Dickens, and many other distinguished men, were mourners.   Looking up during the service, I was for a second startled to see what seemed to me at first an apparition, an exact likeness of what John Leech would have been had he lived to old age.   It was his father, whom I had not met before.   I pray, and hope, and believe that I shall meet his son, not by the gate of death, but of life, when

> " With the morn those angel-faces smile,
>   Which I have loved long since, and lost awhile."

The world was bereft of a benefactor, who had made it more happy and more wise.   He was a preacher of righteousness, manliness, sincerity, kindness, truth, and purity to thousands who would not obey the injunction that they should hear sermons. He suggested the grandeur of virtue by exposing the ugliness of vice, and the keen shaft of his ridicule pierced an epidermis which was proof against all other weapons.   He made a wide distinction between those who did evil wilfully, from a chronic malevolence, and those who were but seldom overtaken by a fault; and while he would hack about him, like Don Quixote among the puppets, when he fell among thieves, when he was intent upon unmasking hypocrites, or was engaged (to quote the words with which Sydney Smith once commenced an article in the *Edinburgh Review*) " in routing out a nest of consecrated cobblers," he dealt gently with the ignorant and weak. He sent all reprobates to the pillory, and bade the neighbours pelt; but he let folly go with a box on the ear, or with a rebuke, which hurt more than a blow.

His power was infinite, but he never abused it. The multitude of men who are uneducated, or have no time to read or think, and the multitude who are too idle to do either, are impressed by the clever caricature which they see in the windows of the shops, at the railway bookstall, or on the tables of their clubs, and may be influenced thereby for better or for worse. Leech never pandered to mean or sensual inclinations, and thoroughly despised the Spanish notion, "*Nada es mala que gana la plata*" ("Nothing is bad which gets money"). Cicero says, "*Duplex est omnino jocandi genus: unum illiberale, petulans, flagitiosum, obscœnum: alterum elegans, urbanum, ingeniosum, facetum*" (the refined, harmless wit of the gentleman, and the coarse, malignant, obscene jokes of the snob). We were together many days at a time. I have seen him under great provocations, but I never heard him utter a word that was malicious, lascivious, or profane, or saw him do an unkind act. He knew that—

> "'Tis excellent
> To have a giant's strength; but it is tyrannous
> To use it like a giant."

What sermons he preached against greed of gain, against that love of money for its own sake, which is verily the root of all evil, in that drawing of the old man building on the seashore with a

child's toy spade a little heap of sand, on which
are the letters "£ s. d."! The great waves are
coming to sweep all away. He heapeth up riches
and cannot tell who shall gather them, when the
word shall be spoken, "This night shall thy soul be
required of thee," and all the gold in the Bank of
England cannot buy him another moment of life.
And, again, in the bloated Jew, smoking his cigar
and watching a row of skeletons busily at work on
the tailor's board—

"Stitch, stitch, stitch, in poverty, hunger, and dirt,
  Sewing at once with a double thread a shroud as well as a
      shirt."

Or, once more, in the awaking after a night's de-
bauch of the betting-house frequenter, what a
warning is given to be content with that which we
have, and not to covet or desire other men's goods!

What a sermon against the dotage of lust in that
tottering old beau, who is offering a huge bouquet
to a *coryphée* behind the scenes! What a record of
the miseries of vice in the meeting of those two
unfortunates, seeking shelter from the pouring rain
on a miserable winter's night under the arched
entrance of a London house, and in the question of
terrible, though unintended, irony, "*How long have
you been gay?*"

He had intense enjoyment in the exercise of
his art, and he knew that the manifestations of
his humour would be everywhere welcomed with
delight, but he had no self-conceit. He ever re-

minded me of Ruskin's words, "I believe the first test of a truly great man is his humility. I do not mean by humility doubt of his own power, or hesitation in speaking his opinions, but a right understanding of the relation between what he can do and say, and the test of the world's sayings and doings. All great men not only know their business, but usually know that they know it; and are not only right in their mere opinions, but they usually know that they are right in them, only that they do not think much of themselves on that account. Arnoldo knows he can build a good dome at Florence; Albert Durer writes calmly to one who had found fault with his work, 'It cannot be better done;' Sir Isaac Newton knows that he has worked out a problem or two that would have puzzled anybody else: only they do not expect their fellow-men, therefore, to fall down and worship them; they have a curious under-sense of powerlessness, feeling that the greatness is not *in* them, but *through* them; that they could do or be anything else that God made them. And they see something divine and God-made in every other man they meet, and are endlessly, foolishly, incredibly merciful." Merciful to the sinner, not to the sin, for it is cruel to ignore or condone evil; and when Leech exposed the snob and the hypocrite to ridicule and contempt, he did a work of mercy in rebuking folly and vice, attacking it where it is most vulnerable, in its irritable self-conceit.

After his death Mr. Ruskin wrote to one of his

sisters, " John Leech was an absolute master of the elements of character; of all rapid and condensed realization ever accomplished by the pencil, his is the most dainty and the least fallible in the subjects of which he was cognizant; not merely right in the traits which he seizes, but refined in the sacrifice of what he refused."

One more word of praise. How little exaggeration or caricature there is in his drawings!—so accurate, so natural, so true, that they remind us of the compliment which Aristophanes paid to Menander, " O Life and Menander! which of you has imitated the other ? " How superior in the good taste which designed, as well as in their form of execution, to the coarse, personal, malignant caricatures of Gillray and Rowlandson, who put sharp stones in their snowballs, and shot with poisoned darts!

All mourned for him—they most who knew him best. Tenniel and Du Maurier, who have so successfully maintained the reputation which was imperilled by his death, still speak of him with a fond admiration. Shirley Brooks wrote, " That during twenty years of their weekly meetings, at which men of very different opinions spoke without restraint, Leech was never provoked into angry discussion, and no word spoken by him ever rankled in the mind of a colleague." *In pace requiescit.*

> " His life was whirling, burning,
>   In mazes of heat and sound;
>   And for peace his soul was yearning,
>   And now Peace wraps him round."

CHAPTER V.

ARTISTS—*Continued.*

Mr. John Tenniel—A clever reprisal—Mr. Frederick Tayler—
Mind your own business—Edward Lear—Herbert Marshall
—Frank Miles at Buckingham Palace—Herbert Ollivier
—Charles Furse—Mr. Kempe—Unintentional praise—
Musicians—Power of music—Sir George Grove and the
Royal College of Music—Sir John Stainer—Anecdote of
Gounod—Famous singers.

IT has been my privilege, in these latter days, to
revisit the home of John Leech in Kensington,
where I spent such happy days, at the invitation
of our mutual friend, Mr. Silver; to meet Mr.
Tenniel, and to see how affectionately time had
dealt with him. I could not induce him to immor-
talize an incident which had recently occurred to
me, because he said that he knew, and that I knew,
only one man who could have done it justice. In a
narrow London street, the hansom in which I was
seated was stopped by a line of carriages on one
side, and by a stationary cart filled with flowering
plants on the other. My driver civilly requested
the florist to move on and let him pass, but only
obtained in answer a defiant grunt and sneer. He
perceived in a moment, to my intense delight, that

he was master of the situation. He brought his horse's head into close proximity to the cart, and then slackened his reins; and when the animal saw his opportunity, and began to browse among the mignonette and geraniums, he called to the proprietor, "*He's a smelling on 'em!*" and that morose individual turned round to see a long stalk of pelargonium, with a large flower at the end of it, extruding from our quadruped's mouth, like a toothpick, and required no further inducement to clear the way.

I often met Mr. Frederick Tayler, the animal painter, in the house of Mrs. Bridgman-Simpson, who was, I have been told, the most accomplished of our English amateur artistes. She had visited the most picturesque places of the earth, and her home, especially her drawing-room, was a treasury of gems. Mr. Tayler was a most amusing companion. Give him an old shawl and bonnet, and he would sing in character such songs as "The Lost Child" with irresistible humour. He related to me an occurrence which illustrates the determination of some men to make money, *recte si possis, si non, quocumque modo.* He was walking in one of the streets of the City, when he saw in a shop window an engraving from his picture, which is known as "The Weighing of the Deer." Underneath a notice was written that "this beautiful engraving, from the original by Sir Edwin Landseer, could be purchased" at such a price. Mr. Tayler entered the repository of art, and meekly informed the proprietor that there was a mistake made about the engraving, as it was taken from a picture which was not painted by Sir Edwin Landseer, but by an artist of the name of Tayler. The information was received with a most bland equanimity, and evoked the following reply : " If you, sir, will be so good as to mind your own business, we shall be glad to follow your example." There is something almost sublime in the impudence and trickery of this knave of arts—one of those consummate scoundrels who " will lie with such volubility that you would think truth was a fool." I am indebted to Mr. E. Tayler, the miniature painter, for excellent likenesses of my wife and son; and to Mr. E. R. Tayler for a very striking picture which he painted, and entitled " Abide with Me," when master of the School of Art at Lincoln, before he went to Birmingham, and which was exhibited in the Royal Academy.

I knew Edward Lear, who was alike happy, as an artist in his pictures, and as a poet in his " Nonsense Verses." I met him first when he was painting in Charnwood Forest, and afterwards in his charming home at San Remo.

I claim the friendship of Mr. Herbert Marshall, though I knew him best as a cricketer and a vocalist, before he was famous in art.

Frank Miles I knew from his childhood, and was sorely grieved by his early death. Of him might

be quoted our Nottinghamshire poet's verses of
another Nottinghamshire man—

> "Unhappy White! while life was in its spring,
>   And thy young Muse just waved her joyous wing,
>   The spoiler came, and all thy promise fair
>   Has sought the grave, to sleep for ever there."

Frank was not only loved by his friends, but
was patronized by princes, and had to undergo
some cheerful chaff from his brethren. Returning
one night from a dinner, he invited a dramatic
friend, who does not restrict his love of comedy to
the stage, to take a seat in his hansom, as he should
pass his door. Unhappily for Frank, he was exhausted by a long day's work, and went sound
asleep in the cab. He did not awake until, aroused
by the driver, he rubbed his eyes and looked around
him, and anxiously inquired, "Where am I?"
"Buckingham Palace, sir! Buckingham Palace!"
"And why on earth have you brought me here?
I live in Tite Street, Chelsea." "Beg your pardon,
sir, but the gent as come along with you said I was
to drive you to Buckingham Palace."

Of my younger friends who are artists, Herbert
Ollivier is rapidly achieving greatness; and I confidently anticipate that Charles Furse will be in due
time among the magnates.

Of painters on glass, I rejoice in the friendship
of one who, as it seems to me and to many, in the
reverent spirit of his design, in his drawing and

colouring, far excels all others—I mean Mr. Kempe. I was told by a Cheshire rector that, going one day into his church, he saw in a side aisle, some distance before him, two Roman priests. He followed them, and, as they turned into a transept, he heard one of them exclaim, "Ah, that's something like glass! That's none of your post-Reformation rubbish!" "Gentlemen," he said, "you are admiring the window. It is very beautiful, and it was placed there by Mr. Kempe, *last week*."

Passing from the art which charms the eye, to that which delights the ear, I am ashamed to confess that the offerings which I have brought to the feet of the Muses—Euterpe, who presides over instrumental, and Polyhymnia, who presides over vocal, music—have been both shabby and few : the penny trumpet, the comb and paper, the broken drum, the keyless flute, the accordion touched in the wind; but I love music, though I may not call myself a musician, as being one of our most gracious blessings, from the lullaby which soothes the infant to sleep, to the solemn requiem for the dead. To children at school and to men stricken in years, to soldiers on the march and to sailors on the sea, in the factory and on the farm, down in dark mines and out in harvest-fields, the spirit is refreshed by "concord of sweet sounds." Always, everywhere, and by all, by the hewer of wood and the lord of the forest alike, "the song of one who hath a pleasant voice, and can play well on an instrument," is heard with a thankful joy by the prince and by the village smith—

> " Who goes on Sunday to the church,
>   And sits among his boys;
> He hears the parson pray and preach;
>   He hears his daughter's voice
> Singing in the village choir,
>   And it makes his heart rejoice.

> " It minds him of her mother's voice
>   Singing in Paradise;
> He needs must think of her once more,
>   As in her grave she lies
> And with his hard rough hand he wipes
>   A tear from out his eyes."

And when I speak of princes, I am reminded of the great revival of art in England by the late Prince Consort, and of the development and culture of musical talent by his son, the Prince of Wales, as founder of the Royal College of Music.

He is a true patriot who increases and improves the music of his country. Not many weeks ago it was my privilege to meet a gentleman who said to me in the course of conversation, " I have met with prosperity, and I have thought anxiously how I might lay out a portion of my wealth for the good of my fellow-men. I believe in the refining influence of music, and therefore I am building a college in which persons, having vocal or instrumental talent, will be qualified, as accomplished performers and teachers, to gratify and to educate that love of harmony which prevails throughout the land." He did not tell me, not being his own trumpeter (albeit, for the gratification of his neighbours in Yorkshire, he is the proprietor of a brass band), that this building would cost £40,000, and would be the New Royal College of Music. And I claim to number among my friends the president of that admirable institute, Sir George Grove, although I do not find in his "Dictionary of Music" (otherwise excellent) any account of the only concert in which I took part, and which I do not hesitate to say was, in the quality of the performance and in the enthusiasm of the audience, absolutely unique. It was given by under-graduates of Brasenose, who had tuneful proclivities, but had not received a musical education. I contributed "In my Cottage near a Wood," and was encouraged by applause, for which there were frequent opportunities, as my "Music, heavenly maid, was young," and hesitated not seldom between the notes. Another gentleman, who was learning the cornet, gave us "The Light of Other Days," with appropriate illustrations, having unhappily lost an eye! He appeared in the programme as "Herr Koenig." "Mario" was there, and "Grisi," though her boots were more masculine than feminine, and it must have been, I think, the only occasion on which she sang "The Tantivy Trot." Nor have I ever known an audience to be so excited and carried away by the music. They not only joined in the chorus, but, in accordance with "a way they have in the University" in their hilarious moods, they made free use of cries and exclamations which, as a rule, are restricted to the chase.

From gay to grave: I rejoice to include in my society of friends one who has done more than any other in our day to improve the character of our sacred music, and thereby the dignity of our worship—Sir John Stainer, D.M. Gounod said that "the midday celebration at St. Paul's was the finest service in Europe;" and of that great composer I would repeat, with the permission of Lady Stainer, an incident which she related to me. Calling one day in Amen Court, and shown into her drawing-room, his eye rested on an engraving of Beethoven, which he at once approached and addressed in impassioned words of reverence, delight, and love. Finally, he turned to Lady Stainer with tears on his face, and humbly asked her pardon, but he "could not refrain from offering his homage to the great master."

I have heard the great singers and instrumental performers of my time—Miss Love, Miss Sheriff, Malibran, Jenny Lind, Grisi, Rubini, and "his brother Tom Rubini," as the sailor named Tamburini, Lablache, Mario, Braham, Sims Reeves, and the *élite* of our English basses, baritones, tenors, and altos; and if I were asked to place those in order of merit who have won the largest approbation, my arrangement would be—Jenny Lind, Sims Reeves (for the English, profess what they may, still love their own music best), Malibran, Grisi, and Mario. The Swedish nightingale outsang them all.

Within my remembrance, great progress has been made in the quantity and quality of the music which we have in our homes; and this is largely due to the royal encouragement and institution to which I have referred. The pianists and pianos, the vocalists and the songs (the words retain their chronic debility—pressing invitations to private interviews, principally by moonlight; personal allusions to hair, eyes, lips, and limbs; frequent repetitions of *"we two," "you and I," "ever,"* and *"never"*), these are more numerous, and more capable; and the addition of violin music by the daughters of the house (I can remember when there was only one lady fiddler in our neighbourhood, and she was ever regarded, however pathetic were her tones, as a comic eccentricity) is indeed a sweet and welcome refreshment after the burden and heat of the day. A similar development has been made in painting and drawing. Where, when travelling, thirty years ago, you saw a single sketch-book, you see now a score. It emanates from the same sources, from schools of art, first established at Kensington, and now throughout the land.

I made a reference to a member of the Corps Dramatique, and my memory suggests a few words on the histrionic art. It was the custom, in the days of my boyhood, for the stars of the theatrical firmament to pursue at intervals their planetary courses through the country, and in the little playhouse at Newark on the Trent I have seen Edmund, the elder

Kean, Matthews, the father of Charles, accompanied by his friend, Mr. Yates, Liston, Macready, and others. There was a great disappointment one night at the non-appearance of Miss Foote, who had preferred an engagement with Lord Harington, whom she had married that day. The theatre was managed by Mr. and Mrs. Robertson, whose descendants have done such good service to the drama, by successful authorship as well as by successful acting, and they were highly esteemed. A country bumpkin, one market night, threw a turnip on the stage in front of Mrs. Robertson, who was performing admirably as " Jane Shore," and I distinctly recall her expression of disgust as she contemplated the offensive vegetable, and turned away with, " I'll play no more." ·

Clever actors and actresses, professional and amateur, were never so abundant as now, and in many pathetic pieces, and in comedy, they are excellent; but though we have had, and still have, actresses who can present the heroines of Shakspere to us as I believe he wished them to be presented (the " Ophelia " of Ellen Tree, afterwards Mrs. Charles Kean, was the most impressive piece of acting I ever saw), I have never seen the actor who did justice to the most sublime conceptions of the poet-king, the approximations being, to my mind, the " Hamlet " of Mr. Beerbohm Tree, and the " Shylock " of Mr. Henry Irving. My father always affirmed that we had no actor equal to Charles

Kemble; and, had he lived until now, he would not
have changed his opinion. When the landlord of
the inn at Newark told him that, just before leaving
for the theatre, Kean senior had supplemented his
after-dinner wine with a bottle of mulled madeira,
he exclaimed indignantly, "If the man had drunk a
hogshead he never could have played ' Richard.' "

Some of my brethren, ecclesiastical and lay, un-
reservedly denounce the drama, and because there
are some plays which suggest evil and condone guilt,
"as though," in Jeremy Taylor's words, "the ruin
of a soul was a thing to be laughed at, and deadly
sin was a jest," because some actors are immoral and
some actresses immodest, instead of doing their best
to expose and rebuke, to find an antidote for the
poison, to entice men and women from that which
is bad by placing beside it something that is better,
they condemn the whole system as corrupt. I
wonder that it never occurs to them to consider the
proportion of plays which present to the public the
victories of virtue, as compared with those in which
vice succeeds and is triumphant; the plays in which
truth, and honesty, and chastity meet their sure reward, and those in which they are made the objects of
scorn and ridicule, and in which the liar, the knave,
and the lascivious are promoted to honour. And
when they speak such bitter words of those who have
been led away and overcome of evil, and turn upon
them their virtuous backs, I should like to ask them
what they have to say, and whether they have said

it, to those who have availed themselves of their
social position, or their good looks, or their money,
to tempt, and lure, and degrade.

> "One had deceived her, and left her
> Alone in her sin and her shame;
> And so she was wicked with others;—
> On whom will you lay the blame?"

There is a class of men, sadly too numerous, who
cannot believe in use where there is abuse; who, if
they see a withered branch on a tree, call for an axe
instead of a saw, and cut it down instead of pruning
it; who regard decapitation as the only cure for
headache; and who, if they were rigidly consistent
with their creed, would go about naked, because
some people spend too much upon dress; would
abolish horses, because some jockeys won't let theirs
win; and would burn the vines, the barley, the oats,
and the hops, because some fools put an enemy into
their mouths to steal away their brains. "They
make a desert, and they call it Peace."

I have no more to say about actors, except to
express my high admiration of one, who, without
appropriate costume, without scenery, without a
prompter, and without an orchestra, possesses a marvellous power of personating, not only one character,
but all the characters of a long Shaksperian play;
who in the most minute particular, such as the three
distinct voices of the witches in *Macbeth*, never
forgets to vary his intonation. I mean my old, dear
friend, Sam Brandram.

CHAPTER VI.

AUTHORS.

HAD I not been an exception to the rule that early ambitions, if they be cherished and educated, are as the tide, which, taken at the turn, leads on to fortune, I must have been a great author. I never heard my nurse say that "I lisped in numbers," but I began to compose as soon as I began to think. I brought out my first tragedy when I was about eight years of age, and, with a remarkable anticipation and prescience of the sensational incidents which would be most acceptable to the popular taste, I did not weary my audience with preliminary explanations and dull details, but I conducted them at once to scenes of wild excitement, and to situations of terrible distress. My drama began, " Act I., Scene I., *Enter a man swimming for his life* ;" and if any of my readers will place themselves on a carpet, as in the act of natation, and endeavour to propel themselves along the floor, they will give me credit for a courage which was ready, like Cassius, to "leap into the angry flood, and swim to yonder point"—the point being an armchair placed halfway across the day nursery (the swimmer emerged from the night ditto), and representing the welcome shore. How I clutched, and crawled, and reached the land, and, looking back, saw buttons floating on the ocean wave, is beyond my comprehension now. There were other original conceptions. An archer, wandering through the forest, sees bright plumage in the thicket, and joyfully exclaiming, "Ah, a beautiful bird!" shoots, and then cries out in horror, "Alas, my father!" the beautiful bird being unfortunately the feathers in the parental cap, and the arrow having penetrated the parental skull. Then I took to history, and a thrilling effect was produced by the escape of Mary Queen of Scots from Lochleven Castle, the castle being represented by a four-post bed, and her Majesty by my younger sister, aged seven, appearing from between the drawn curtains, and gracefully descending into the boat, our nursery tea-table inverted. Here again was a difficulty as to propulsion; but the brave boatman (and author) jumped into the sea, and by some process, known only to himself, made the bark glide smoothly over the lake. Our audience, consisting of parents, sisters, and nurses, looked on admiringly; if they had laughed, we should have cried.

The chief merit of my plays was brevity. They occupied about seven minutes, and I have seen nothing so concise in dramatic performances except in a booth of strolling players at a fair in Newark, when, owing to the numerous attendance, a tragedy and comedy, with an interlude of singing and dancing, were executed in a quarter of an hour. I have forgotten the name of the tragedy, but the details were these—

Woodland scene. Small chapel in the distance, with bell-turret.

Enter GREGORY.

Gregory. 'Ark! I 'ear the chapel bell. (*Bell tolls at intervals.*) It is the signal that tells me my Hemmeline is no more! 'Ere comes Constantius to tell the 'orrid news.

Enter CONSTANTIUS, *on the wrong side, and salutes.*

Gregory (*turning with a scowl of disgust*). Constantius, thy looks betray the 'orrid news—my Hemmeline is no more!

Constantius (*with a broad grin*). Cheer up, bold Gregory! thine Hemmeline liveth; and Hedmund, thine henemy, lies dead at the chapel door!

Gregory. Then must I to the forest of Hawleens, and when victory has crowned my harms with triumph, I shall return, and claim her for my bride.

Bell. Curtain.

But when I quoted this example of compressed genius to Mr. Standen, the actor, whom I met on board the *Orient* on his way to Australia, he repeated to me the tragedy, yet more brief, of

"THE EMIGRANT'S RETURN."

In one Act.

Scene—a cottage in Ireland.   Enter Emigrant, who surveys the dwelling with emotion, and knocks at door.   Door opens.   Enter Inmate.

Emigrant.   Is my father alive ?
Inmate.   He is not.
Emigrant.   Is my mother living ?
Inmate.   She is not.
Emigrant.   Is there any whisky in this house ?
Inmate.   There is not.
Emigrant (sighs heavily).   This is indeed a woeful day !   [*Dies.*

Slow music.   Curtain.

I improvised scenes off the stage. When the sister aforesaid was contumacious, I pretended to be her lover, just returned from India (I don't know why, but I was fond of returning from India, also from the field of battle), and, surveying her with an expression of intense disappointment, sorrowfully sighed, " Alas, I left her a blooming girl ; I find her a withered maniac ! " My elder sisters, I am afraid, encouraged me in this and similar duettos, and there was something irresistibly comic in the serious resentment with which the "withered maniac," with her golden hair, blue eyes, and roseate cheeks, invariably heard the allegation.

I must have been nearly ten years old before I became a poet. I could not hear distinctly the words of the aged vicar, under whom I sat in my early school-days, and that which I heard I could not understand, therefore I feel no shame in confessing that my first and great epic, on "The Battle of Waterloo," was composed during his sermon. I only remember the first verse, but it will suffice, like some fragment of exquisite sculpture, to suggest the beauty of the whole—

> "We heard the rumbling of Great Gallia's drum,
> Onward we saw the hostile army come;
> Nearer and nearer to the plain we sped,
> Where many a veteran, many a stripling, bled."

I consider "the rumbling of Great Gallia's drum" to be one of the most striking lines in the language, and I have often wished, when in Paris, and other cities of France, that she had only one drum to rumble!

Then my Muse, *parva metu primum mox sese attollit ad auras ingrediturque*, The Nottingham Journal, in a poem entitled "Lines on the Death of William the Fourth," framed with mourning edges, and exciting the author with feelings of elation, which were anything but funereal.

Then I became an editor. *The Newark Bee* was

issued monthly, at one penny, by the same firm which had published for Byron, and was precious in the estimation of its contributors as the *Hours of Idleness.* No man, whatever may be his position and responsibilities, can be so impressed by a sense of his own importance as an editor, aged sixteen.

Afterwards, I wrote *de omnibus rebus;* and of making many books there was no end, from " Hints to Freshmen," * to " Hints to Preachers," leaflets, pamphlets, sermons, speeches, travels, treatises; but only one book, which it is not for me to name, has realized my hopes, reaching a twelfth edition, translated into German, and widely circulated in the United States by publishers, who have made no charge for their kind patronage.

The most difficult piece of writing I ever achieved was an account of the Carnival at Nice, written in a mask on the grand stand, under an unceasing and heavy shower of *confetti,* and afterwards published in the London *Guardian.* I proudly compared myself to Protogenes, who, when Rome was besieged by Demetrius, would not leave his studio, but proceeded daily in his work amid the noise of battering-rams and catapults, and the shouts of contending foes.

I do not presume to claim membership with the

---

* Fifty years after the publication of " Hints to Freshmen " I read the advertisement in an Oxford paper of a book under the same title, and wishing to see how the modern author had dealt with the subject, I wrote for a copy, and received my own composition.

Worshipful Company of Authors, but I have been honoured by their friendship. I paid a visit, going with his son from Oxford, to the Rev. Henry Lyte, who was Vicar of Brixham, and lived at Berryhead, by Tor Bay. It was good for a young man to be in the society and under the influence of such a true gentleman, scholar, poet, and saint, to be impressed by the beauty of holiness, and to be so happily assured that the voice of joy and health is in the dwellings of the righteous. He was revered by all who knew him, specially by those whose sympathies he prized the most—the poor. The fishermen came up from Brixham for supper, and sang their satisfaction in the old Devonshire chorus—

> " We'll stay and have our breakfast here,
> We'll stay and have a 'levener here,
> We'll stay and have our dinner here,
> We'll stay and have our supper here ; "

each line being thrice sung, and each triplet followed by the emphatic declaration (*fortissimo*)—

> " *And we won't go then !* "

" A 'levener " (some may desire the information) referred to a snack, or luncheon, which it was usual to enjoy one hour before the meridian.

Edmund Field, so long associated with Lancing College as chaplain, and so long beloved by the boys, was then Mr. Lyte's curate. Always zealous in the Master's service, he asked his vicar's permission to preach now and then on the sands, that he might compel absentees to come in. While Mr. Lyte hesitated as to the wisdom of such an innovation, though he was a foremost leader in the great Catholic revival, known as " the Oxford movement," a Dissenter adopted Field's intention, and, standing upon a small inverted tub, gathered round him for some Sundays a small congregation, who went by the name of " Bucket Christians."

Mr. Lyte wrote, as most men know, many pathetic verses—chiefly psalms, and hymns, and spiritual songs. In one of the latter he prays earnestly that he may be permitted to write, before he goes hence and is no more seen, some words which might be helpful to the souls of men, and by which he might be remembered for good.

> " Might my poor lyre but give
> Some simple strain, some spirit-moving lay,
> Some sparklet of the soul, that still might live
> When I was passed to clay !
>
> " Might verse of mine inspire
> One virtuous aim, one high resolve impart,
> Light in one drooping soul a hallow'd fire,
> Or bind one broken heart !
>
> " Death would be sweeter then,
> More calm my slumber 'neath the silent sod,
> Might I thus live to bless my fellow-men,
> Or glorify my God."

And what a gracious answer came ! Christians all over the world are singing, and will sing for ages, the hymn which he afterwards wrote, and which begins " Abide with me."

He was long time in delicate health; and staying at Nice, he became suddenly conscious, in the middle of the night, that the time of his departure was at hand. He summoned a servant, and asked that a priest of the English Church, if there was one in the hotel, should be found and brought to him without delay. After some little time a clergyman appeared, and gave him the last consolations of the Church. His name was Henry Edward Manning, then Archdeacon of Chichester, and afterwards Cardinal of Rome.

CHAPTER VII.

AUTHORS—*Continued.*

First meeting with Thackeray—Stories of giants—The Garrick
    Club—His delight in his daughter's success as an authoress
    —His allusion to " Vanity Fair "—Pen or pencil ?—" *Nemo
    me impune lacessit* "—The *Cornhill Magazine*—A letter in
    verse—" The Carver's Lesson."

I FIRST met Thackeray at dinner, when I was staying with Leech. When one of his daughters asked
him, " which of his friends he loved best ? " he
replied, after brief consideration, " John Leech."
And so he arrived in high good humour, and with
a bright smile on his face. I was introduced by
our host, and for his sake he gave me a cordial
greeting. " We must be about the same height,"
he said; " we'll measure." And when, as we stood
dos-a-dos, and the bystanders gave their verdict, " a
dead heat " (the length was six feet three inches),
and I had meekly suggested " that though there
might be no difference in the size of the cases, his
contained a Stradivarius, and mine a dancing-
master's kit," we proceeded to talk of giants. He
told me of a visit which he paid with Mr. Higgins,

" Jacob Omnium," who was four or five inches the taller of the two, to see a Brobdignagian on show, and how the man at the door had inquired " whether they were in the business, because, if so, no charge would be made."   And I told him how Sir William Don, when quartered with his regiment at Nottingham, was walking in the market-place, and was met by two mechanics, one of whom thus addressed him : " Sir William, me and my mate 'as got a bet of a quart of ale about yer, and we wants to know your 'ight."   And Sir William made answer, " My height is six feet seven, and yours is *the height of impudence!*"   Then I repeated to him the fine pentameter line, which happily he had not heard, written by the Eton boy in his description of Windsor Fair—

" Gigantes que duo, super honore meo."

As we were conversing, Leech's boy entered the room, and was immediately welcomed by Thackeray with " Come here, my young friend. You're my godson.   Come here, and be tipped."

We had many a pleasant reunion.   Whenever we met, he invited me to his house, and always, before the guests went home, he whispered in my ear, " Stay for the fragrant weed."   He proposed me for the Garrick Club, and there we often dined together.   I have few memories of his conversation. He said so many good things, being the best talker I have ever listened to, when it pleased him to talk, that they trod down and suffocated each other; but I have a distinct recollection of one most interesting discussion which he had with a learned professor from Cambridge. The subject of debate, suggested by the publication of Buckle's "History of Civilization," was upon the power of the human mind, and the progress of scientific discovery, to eliminate the sorrow and enlarge the happiness of mankind. The professor seemed to think that there would be hardly any limit to these attainments. Thackeray spoke, as Newton spoke about gathering pebbles on the shore, and affirmed that one of the best results of knowledge was to convince a man of his ignorance. He seemed to preach from the text, though he did not quote it, that the wisdom of this world is foolishness with God. It was a combat between pride and humility, and pride had its usual fall.

On one subject he was proud, but it was a pride which testified to his own freedom from self-conceit. He was proud of his daughter's books. " I assure you," he said (but we tacitly declined to be sure), " that Annie can write ten times more cleverly than I." She had, indeed, received a rich inheritance of her father's brains—exceptional, as it was large, because genius is not so regularly entailed as that old lady supposed, who inquired from the son of Canova " whether he intended to carry on his father's business ? "

I only once heard Thackeray allude to his works, and that in a serio-comic spirit, which amused both him and us. "I was travelling on the Rhine," he said (in company, no doubt, with "the Kickleburys"), "and entering one of the hotels on the banks, exhausted and weary, I went into the salon, and threw myself on a sofa. There was a book on a little table close by, and I opened it, to find that it was 'Vanity Fair.' I had not seen it since I corrected the proofs, and I read a chapter. Do you know, it seemed to me very amusing!"

He was more solicitous about his illustrations than his text, and derived more enjoyment, I believe, from his pencil than from his pen. Artists would sometimes venture upon critical comments. There was one sketch of a battle-field, which they said would have been purchased by the nation if the combatants had not been concealed beneath a canopy of smoke. But it was perilous to measure swords with one who was such a master of fence, and whose motto was, "*Nemo me impune lacessit.*' Sometimes there was a combination to chaff him, as swallows congregate to pursue a hawk; but "he did bestride this narrow world like a Colossus, and those petty men walked under his huge legs to peep about, and find themselves dishonourable graves." There was one member of the Garrick whose presence and speech seemed to irritate him, and who found pleasure in exercising his power as a gadfly on a thoroughbred horse. One night, in the smoke-room, Thackeray was in the middle of a most interesting story, when his enemy suddenly entered. To every one's surprise, Thackeray hesitated and stopped, on which his persecutor, assuming an air of the most gracious patronage, blandly encouraged him, with " *Proceed, sweet warbler; thy story interests me.*"

He asked me to write for the *Cornhill Magazine*, of which he was editor, and I sent some verses, which he commended so highly and rewarded so munificently, that I venture to introduce them. They were favourably noticed by the reviewers, and when I quoted them in a sermon, the late Dean said, as we came out of St. Paul's, to my grateful joy, " Were not those lines from Hood ? "

MABEL.

I.

In the sunlight!
Little Mab, the woodman's daughter, singing by the brooklet's
 side,
With her playmates singing carols of the holy Easter-tide ;
And the primrose and the violet make sweet incense for the
 choir,
In the springlight, when the roses hide the thorns upon the
 briar.

II.

In the lamplight!
With a proud defiant beauty, Mab, the fallen, flaunts along,
Speaking sin's words, wildly laughing, she who sang that
 paschal song ;
And a mother lies a-dying in the cottage far away,
And a father cries to Heaven, "Thou hast said, 'I will repay.'"

III.

In the moonlight!
By the graveside, in the churchyard, Mabel, where her mother
    sleeps,
Sick at heart, and wan with weeping, Easter vigil sadly keeps;
There the lost sheep, torn and bleeding, trailing thorns, with
    piteous bleat,
And the Shepherd, Who has found her, as her mother prayed,
    shall meet.

Here follows a letter, which he sent me, in reply to a request, made on behalf of a friend, for his autograph, and in acknowledgment of some game :—

"January 26th, 36, Onslow Square.

"My dear Hole,

"Did I ever write and comply with your desire To have a page of autograph? You're welcome to a quire. Tell your friend the lady, I have no pleasure higher than in writing pretty poetry and striking of the lyre, in compliment to a gentleman whom benevolence did inspire, to send me pheasants and partridges killed with shot or wire (but whatever the way of killing them, I equally admire), and who of such kind practices, I trust, will never tire. May you bring your birds down, every time you fire, this, my noble sportsman, is the fond desire Of

"W. M. Thackeray,

"Editor and Esquire."

And an invitation to Miss Adelaide Procter, who had recently contributed some impressive lines to the *Cornhill Magazine*, which were designated " The Carver's Lesson," to meet her mamma.

The Editor of the Cornhill Magazine presents his compliments to the Author of the Carver's Lesson and requests the honor of her company at dinner on Thursday 22. March. at 7.30. to meet her mamma.

My last interview with Thackeray took place not long before his death. I went with Leech, and the servant told us that he was engaged. As we were going disappointed away, Miss Thackeray opened the door and called to us. " Of course, papa will see you." We went up to his study, and found him sitting, *more suo*, with his face turned to the back of his chair, on which a small board was fastened for his writing materials. He sighed, and said he was wearied by his long monotonous work (it was nigh the end, for the last pages of " Denis Duval " were before him); and Leech said, " Why don't you have a holiday, and take the girls to the seaside?" He made no verbal answer, but, rising slowly, plunged his hands to the very bottom of his pockets, brought them out, shook, replaced them, and then resumed his seat. I have often thought of that unfinished manuscript, and recalled the words which the writer spoke, when looking at the fragment of a story by the late Charlotte Brontë: " Hundreds who, like myself, recognized and admired in ' Jane Eyre ' the master-work of a great genius, will look with a mournful interest, regard, and curiosity, upon this unfinished sketch from the same noble hand."

There has been a diversity of opinions about Thackeray, his temper, and principles; and they who did not understand him, have made some cruel mistakes. Whoever desires to know what sort of man he was, his love of goodness, and his contempt of evil, let him read " The Newcomes."

CHAPTER VIII.

AUTHORS—*Continued.*

Correspondence and interview with Charles Dickens—His affectionate admiration of John Leech—Rochester associations—His home at Gad's Hill—The study and garden—" Charles Dickens going out of fashion ! "

SOON after the death of John Leech, I communicated to Charles Dickens a wish which had been expressed by some mutual friends, that I should write a biography of the artist, and I received the following reply :—

> " Gad's Hill, Higham-by-Rochester, Kent,
> " Tuesday, twentieth December, 1864.

" MY DEAR SIR,

" I am very much interested in your letter, for the love of our departed friend, for the promise it holds out of a good record of his life and work, and for the remembrance of a very pathetic voice, which I heard at his grave.

" There is not in my possession one single note of his writing. A year or two ago, shocked by the misuse of the private letters of public men, which I constantly observed, I destroyed a very large and very rare mass of correspondence. It was not done without pain, you may believe, but, the first reluctance conquered, I have steadily abided by my determination to keep no letters by me, and to consign all such papers to the fire. I therefore fear that I can render you no help at all. All that I could tell you of Leech you know (probably) to the circumstance, that for several years we always went to the seaside together in the autumn, and lived, through the autumn months, in constant daily association.

" Your reference to my books is truly gratifying to me, and I hope this sad occasion may be the means of bringing us into personal relations, which may not lessen your pleasure in them.

" Believe me, dear sir, very faithfully yours,
" CHARLES DICKENS."

His kind wish was followed by more definite invitations to his house in London and to Gad's Hill, and I lost no time in availing myself of the privilege which he proposed. On my way to our first interview, I met a gentleman who was then on the staff of the *Times*, and he showed me a printed extract from a special edition, announcing the assassination of the President (Lincoln) of the United States. Dickens was shocked by the news, and " hoped they had caught the assassin." I told him that the murderer had not been apprehended when the telegram was sent, the pursuers having taken the wrong turn in following him from the theatre, in which the foul deed was done. Then came a twinkle to his eye and a smile to his face, and the sun of his humour shone forth from the cloud of his pathos, as he said, " Ah, yes, when the man pursued turns to the right, and the men in pursuit to the left, the difficulties of capture are materially enhanced."*

John Leech was, of course, the chief subject of our conversation. Dickens loved the man as much as he admired the artist. He was one of many who maintained that Leech should have been a Royal Academician, seeing that his works would outlive a very large proportion of those which were exhibited at Burlington House. He said very much the same which Mr. Forster reports in

* Dickens, on his return from America in 1868, repeated a very remarkable incident, which preceded the assassination, and which was related to him by Mr. Secretary Stanton, who, on the afternoon of the day on which the President was shot, attended a Cabinet Council, at which he presided. All who were present noticed a great change, an unusual gravity and dignity in his demeanour. " Gentlemen," he said, "something very extraordinary is going to happen, and that very soon." His hearers were much impressed by his serious manner, and the Attorney-General inquired whether he had received any special information. " No," he replied; " but for the third time I have dreamed the same dream. Once on the night preceding the Battle of Bull Run; again before another battle in which we suffered defeat. I dream that I am on a great, broad, rolling river, and I am in a boat—and I drift—and I drift—— But this is not business; let us proceed to business." *That night he was shot.*

his life; * that Leech was the first artist who had combined beauty with humorous art; that he had done more than any other man by this conjunction to refine and exalt the power of caricatures; and that he would leave behind him not a little of his time and its follies sketched with inimitable grace. He compared the coarse, bloated exaggerations of ugliness, which were inseparable from the pictures of Rowlandson and Gillray, with the natural lifelike delineations of Leech; and he added, "In all his designs, whatever Mr. Leech desires to do, he does. His drawing is charming, and the expression which he desires to produce is recognized at once. His wit is good-natured, and always the wit of a gentleman. He has a becoming sense of responsibility and of restraint; he delights in agreeable things; he imparts some pleasant air of his own to things not pleasant in themselves; he is suggestive, and full of matter; and he is always improving. Into the tone, as well as into the execution, of what he does, he has brought a certain elegance which is altogether new, without involving any compromise of what is true. Popular Art in England has not had so rich an acquisition."

Charles Dickens admitted my claim to be one of his earliest and most enthusiastic admirers, when I told him that, as a boy at school, with an infinite appreciation of cheesecakes, I had nevertheless saved half my income, sixpence a week, to buy the monthly

* See Forster's "Life of Charles Dickens," vol. ii. p. 384.

numbers of " Pickwick ; " and he expressed his hope
that I should be interested in some of the scenes of
his stories when I came to his home at Gad's Hill.
I little thought that circumstances, which I need
not detail, would prevent me from entering that
house until the illustrious owner had been many
years in his grave; or that I should pass the latter
portion of my life on earth among the scenes to
which he referred ; little more than a mile from the
home and school of his childhood at Chatham; not
two from the house which he desired in his boyhood, and bought when, after years of painful
poverty, he became rich, wherein he lived long and
happily until his sudden death ; not a hundred yards
from the High Street, in which the coach which
bore the Pickwick Club stopped at the Bull Hotel,
in which Mr. Winkle's horse conducted himself in a
most mysterious manner, with his head towards one
side of the way and his tail to the other, and in
which the house of " The Seven Poor Travellers "
has the inscription in stone over its portals—

" RICHARD WATTS, Esq.
by his Will, dated 22 Aug. 1579,
founded this Charity
for Six poor Travellers,
who not being ROGUES, or PROCTORS,
May receive gratis for one Night,
Lodging, Entertainment,
and Fourpence each "—

and is open nightly to those who may ask admission.
The " Proctors " excluded were (not the members

of the Lower House of Convocation, nor the peripatetic gentlemen in velvet sleeves who supervise our undergraduates, but) a swarm of hypocrites, professing to collect money for the Lepers' houses, and spending what they could obtain on themselves. I admire, as Mr. Pickwick admired, from Rochester Bridge, "the grand old keep of the ancient castle, its towers roofless, and its massive walls crumbling away, but telling us proudly of its old might and strength," and I gaze on the river, which flows by, as Mr. Micawber gazed, "with a view to setting up in the Medway Coal Trade." I walk on the seven miles of road between Rochester and Maidstone, which Dickens affirmed to be one of the most beautiful walks in England; and from the marshes, in which the child met the escaped convict, my son brings home the wildfowl which he has shot at flight-time, concealed, half-frozen, in his punt. I too enjoy, as Dickens enjoyed, the woods and glades of beautiful Cobham, having free access from the generous owner; and in its garden-grounds have sat in the Swiss Chalet, which the great actor (Fechter) gave to the great author, and in which, placed in a shrubbery, and bright with mirrors, reflecting the trees and fields around, he wrote, with flowers always on his table, and the birds singing around him, in the summer months. It was removed, after his death, to Cobham, and is safe from pocket-knives and petty larcenies in the careful custody of Lord Darnley. In this chalet he passed the greater part of his last day on earth, June 8, 1870, writing the unfinished story of " Edwin Drood;" and I never pass " the little graveyard, belonging to the cathedral, at the foot of the castle wall," in which he wished his body to be laid, I seldom go by the brass tablet which bears his name in our cathedral, without the joyful hope, which is inspired by those words, almost the last which came from his pen, concerning " the Resurrection and the Life." No thoughtful reader of his books can fail to trace those pure, deep, living waters of charity, which flow through the flowery, fertile banks of his wit and humour, to their spring, to his faith as a Christian, to that " unswerving faith in Christianity," to which his most intimate friend and biographer bears such earnest testimony, and which he himself so solemnly declares, and commends to his children, in his last will and testament.

Coming yet nearer home, I little thought, when, in that same history of " Edwin Drood," I read of " the ancient English cathedral, having for suffi-cient reasons the fictitious name of Cloisterham," but being Rochester, of Minor Canon Corner, and of " the dean, who, with a pleasant air of patronage, as nearly cocks his quaint hat as a dean in good spirits may " (Dickens forgot that the hat decanal is cocked always), " and directs his comely gaiters homewards,"—I little thought, one hundred and fifty miles away, that on this stage, and in that character and costume, I was to conclude the little drama of my life.

*   *   *   *   *

I have just returned from a pilgrimage (many a pilgrim has gone to a shrine with a far less reverent joy) to Gad's Hill Place. The present owner, Mr. Latham, has greatly improved, without altering the general appearance of the home of Dickens. He has introduced more light and air both into the house and grounds, developing the capabilities of the place, after the example of those who preceded him; but there is no material change. The dear old study remains as it was, with the dummy books on the door and on part of the walls, bearing the quaint titles which Dickens invented for them—

Kant's Eminent Humbugs, 10 vols.
The Gunpowder Magazine.
Drowsey's Recollections of Nothing.
Lady Godiva, on her Horse.
Evidences of Christianity. By King Henry the Eighth.
Hansard's Guide to Refreshing Sleep.
Strutt's Walk.
Malthus' Nursery Songs.
Cat's Lives, in 9 volumes.
History of the Middling Ages.
Five Minutes in China.
Swallows, on Emigration.
History of a Short Chancery Suit, in 19 volumes.
A. Carpenter's Bench of Bishops.
Butcher's Suetonius.
Crib's edition of Miller.

In the garden is the tiny grave, tombstone, and epitaph of "Dick," a beloved canary—

" This is the Grave of
DICK,
the best of birds,
born at Broadstairs,
Midsummer, 1851,
died at Gad's Hill Place,
14 October, 1866."

A critical autocrat recently informed me that " Charles Dickens was going out of fashion ; " whereupon I inquired, as one profoundly impressed, and gasping for more information, " whether he thought that Shakspere would be *à la mode* this season, and what he considered the newest and sweetest thing in the *beau monde* of intellect ? " " Pickwick," " Nicholas Nickleby," " Oliver Twist," " The Old Curiosity Shop," " David Copperfield," " A Tale of Two Cities," " A Christmas Carol," out of fashion ! Not while the English language remains as now, and they, who speak it, have brains to appreciate humour, and hearts to sympathize with woe.

CHAPTER IX.

OF the authors whom it has been my great privilege to number among my friends, there is not one whom I remember with a more affectionate regard than Dr. John Brown, who wrote "Rab and his Friends." "In memory's fondest place I shrine" the words which I heard from his lips, and read in his books—his admirations of all things pure, and brave, and true; his condemnations of meanness, falsehood, cruelty; his tenderness and compassion for the desolate and oppressed. That beautiful head, "with Brains, Sir;" that face, so bright with intellectual power, and with the purer sunshine of a divine charity, hangs "on the line" of the long gallery of portraits, on which imagination delights to gaze. No man was ever more beloved by his friends; few writers have been so intensely appreciated by their readers, though many more largely read.

I knew him first in Edinburgh, among those who loved him most dearly, because they knew him best. To know him at all was to love him much. He was one of those men whom, from the moment in which you hold their hand and look into their face, you believe, and find to be, sincere. Made to be a doctor, not only for his skill as a physician, his sympathies with suffering, his kindness to the poor, but because his very presence refreshed and cheered, there was warmth in his smile, and music in his voice, to revive the hopes of the sad. It is the doctor's duty, he said, to be kind. Kindness, as well as a merry heart, doeth good like a medicine. Cheeriness is a great thing in a doctor; his very foot should have " music in't, as he comes up the stair." The doctor should never lose his power of pitying pain, and letting his patient see this and feel it. His eye should so command, comfort, and cheer his patient, that he should never·let him think disobedience or despair possible. It is not true that doctors are hardened by seeing so much suffering. Pity as a motive, as well as a feeling ending in itself, is stronger in an old doctor than in a young, so he be made of the right stuff. He comes to know himself what pain and sorrow mean, what their weight is, and how grateful he was or is for relief and sympathy.

He paid me a visit in Nottinghamshire. On the

morning after his arrival, he went with me to our daily service in the church hard by. He talked after prayers to some of the old folks outside, and was specially pleased with one of them, an octogenarian, who, using two sticks, had remarked in our hearing to a companion, who required but one, "Why, Sammy, you're a poor crittur! why don't you *drive a pair*, like a gentleman?" And no man ever drove a pair, or two pairs, who was more "like a gentleman" than he who spoke those words. Not long before Dr. Brown's visit, he came to me, as we were going into church, and said, "Do you think, sir, you could bring in that prayer about giving thanks this morning? I'm eighty years old to-day, and I should like to thank God for all the mercies He has been pleased to send." He had one small room in a poor cottage, his income was three shillings a week, he had no relations and few friends, he was often ailing, and always infirm, and yet, he had not only learned, in whatsoever state he was, therewith to be content, but he was always happy. He was a Christian in spirit and in truth, and the last words he spoke to me just before his death were these: "I am not dying in darkness; I am dying in the light of life."

Dr. Brown went with me to the school, and heard the children sing their morning hymn, and, as we were returning to breakfast, he said to me, "I am a Presbyterian, and the son of a minister, but I must say that in this daily worship and communion with your people, old and young, you have an advantage which we do not possess, and which might beneficially occupy some part of the time which is so largely devoted to sermons—to sermons of which, not seldom, the chief result is somnolence!"

Not that he faltered in his faith, because he knew that the best of Christians may be overcome by an exposition of sleep, when lulled by a monotonous drawl, numbed by a frigid dulness, dazed by insoluble problems, or exhausted by vain repetitions. On the contrary, I find in one of his letters this delightful affirmation of his loyalty: "I have sent a funny little game Scotch terrier to the Bishop of Peterborough *—half Skye (original, short and hard hair), otter terrier; t'other ½ Scotch fox terrier, small and wiry. When young, this breed have their tail cocked up and their ears down, but when they come to years (ears) of discretion, the tail drops gracefully and slowly down, and the ears prick themselves, and their courage, up; and I have told the bishop that as the tail (gradually) falls, so falls the Church of England, and as the ears rise, so rises the U. P. Church."

In another letter he writes, "You know, I dare say" (but I did not know), "the lines addressed to a hunting dean, who sang a song in praise of the hounds, he being a grey-headed man—

> ' Cane Decane, canis; sed ne cane, cane Decane,
> De cane—de canis, cane Decane, cane.'"

---

* Dr. Magee, afterwards Archbishop of York.

John Brown, like Charles Dickens, is associated with Chatham. He was here (I am within five minutes' walk of Chatham) when the cholera first came in 1832, and he records his experience how serious a thing it is to be a doctor, and how terribly in earnest people are when they want him. This fearful malady generally came on in the night—" the pestilence that walketh in darkness "—and many a morning he was roused at two o'clock to go and see its victims, for then was its hour and power. One morning a sailor came to say he must go three miles down the river to a village, where the disease had broken out with great fury. They rowed in silence down the dark stream, passing the huge hulks, which were then on the Medway, and hearing the restless convicts turning in their beds and their chains. The men rowed with all their might in silence; they had too many dying or dead at home to have any heart for conversation. As they neared the place, the young surgeon saw a crowd of men and women on the landing. They were all shouting for him—the shrill cries of the women and the deep voices of the men coming to him over the water. As the boat drew near the shore, an elderly but powerful man forced his way through the crowd, plunged into the sea, seized John Brown, and carried him ashore. Then grasping him with his left hand, and thrusting aside with his right fist all that opposed his progress, he hurried him with an irresistible force to a cottage near. It was "Big Joe," in his fierce determination that the doctor's first patient should be his grandson, "Little Joe," convulsed with cholera. The boy got better, but "Big Joe" died that night. The disease was on him when he carried the doctor from the boat, and when his wonderful love for the child, supreme over all else, had fulfilled its purpose, he collapsed and died.

Dr. John Brown died on the 11th of May, 1882. Mr. David Douglas, his devoted friend, to whom we owe the publication of "The Journals of Sir Walter Scott," being my friend also, wrote to tell me of our loss, in words which he knew would comfort—that his mind was clear until the final separation; that he had taken an affectionate farewell of those most dear to him. When the dark shadow showed him that death was near, he asked that a favourite old nurse might be sent for, and greeted her, when she entered his room, with, "Come away, Mrs. Scott; you know you trysted to be with me at my death."

"Then," Mr. Douglas wrote, "one of the loveliest of human characters left this earth. It has been a great privilege to know such a man. I never met another who so attracted love from all classes and conditions of men and women." And he added, to my deep joy and gratitude, "I tell you all this, knowing the regard you had for him, and to thank you, on the part of his Edinburgh friends, for being the means of rousing him from his apathy by writing to him so cordially in October last. I look upon your writing to him as the turning-point from great depression to a state of mental vigour, such as he had not shown for twenty years. After receiving your encouragement, he entered heartily into the correction of his papers, and quite enjoyed the praises of a new generation of critics. He has been very happy in various ways since Christmas last."

One morning he came to me, his face beaming with pleasure, with an open letter in his hand, and said, "I am a happier and prouder man to-day than I have been since Thackeray first wrote to me." The letter was from Wendell Holmes, praising his last volume, and specially the history of "Pet Marjorie," which "he had read, re-read, and then insisted on reading for the third time aloud to his wife." Mr. Gladstone, Mr. Ruskin, Mr. Motley, and other distinguished men, were also his admiring friends.

*   *   *   *   *

I have known the four editors of *Punch.* The first, who started the periodical in 1841, Mark Lemon, and his successor, Shirley Brooks, intimately; the third, Tom Taylor, seldom but admiringly; the fourth, Mr. Burnand, slightly but gratefully, for the refreshment of my spirit's weariness, and specially for his modern version of "Sandford and Merton," which, like "Phyllis," never fails to please. Mark Lemon was portly, fatherly,

genial, a wise administrator, and shrewd man of
business, keeping his team well in hand, in good
condition on a liberal diet. He wrote a great
number of farces, melodramas, etc., which had a
brief success; but he had not the quick, brilliant
humour of Shirley Brooks. Tom Taylor was of a
more reflective, graver mood; and I remember,
at one of the *Punch* dinners, when he had just
brought upon the stage two of his pathetic pieces,
that Thackeray remarked of him, as he sat in
silence opposite, "All play and no work makes
Tom a dull boy." Nevertheless, he had any amount
of comedy as well as of tragedy in his mental
repertoire, and generally suggested the best subject
for the next week's cartoon.

I went, on Shirley's invitation, to the christen-
ing of his children, and Mark Lemon was there as
one of the sponsors. Some of our friends professed
to regard this arrangement with horror and indignation. They solemnly assured the father of the
babe that they saw through his diabolical intentions;
that all London, including the suburbs, was crying
shame upon him; and that, after anxious deliberation, they thought it their duty to lay an information before the magistrates, and to demand the
interference of the police. It was evident, they
said, that in engaging Mr. Punch as a godfather—
Punch, who habitually and daily assaulted babies,
beat them about the head with a stick, and dashed
them down upon the stones of the street—he, Shirley

Brooks, was bent upon infanticide; and that they were unable in consequence to sleep in their beds, terrified as they were by previsions of one, whom they had so dearly loved, appearing as Brooks, murderer, in Madame Tussaud's Chamber of Horrors!

All things, nevertheless, were done with due reverence; so much so, that Mr. Charles Knight, the historian, remarked, sitting next to me at the *déjeûner* which followed the ceremony, on the improvement which had taken place within his recollection. He remembered that when he was a very small boy, one of his godfathers came to him and said, "You see this half-crown; you shall put it in your pocket if you'll say 'D'" (he gave the monosyllable *in extenso*), "'d— Billy Pitt!'" There has indeed been an "improvement" since those "times of the Regent," in which it might be said of the nobleman or gentleman (so called) of the day that "his delight was in cursing," when their conversation was so blended with blasphemous oaths that this profanity was regarded by foreigners as a characteristic of our nation. Whenever an Englishman was represented in a French drama, he rarely uttered a sentence without an imprecation; and an old friend tells me that when he and his brother went to a French school, it was said of them in the streets, "*Voilà, les deux petits Godam!*"

I was present when Shirley Brooks first propounded a riddle, which I venture to repeat, as being one of the cleverest of its class, though it afterwards appeared in *Punch*. Lord Palmerston was Premier, and John Delane, the editor of the *Times*, was a constant guest at Lady Palmerston's receptions; therefore we were asked, " Why is Swan and Edgar's like the residence of Lady Palmerston ? " and were told, when we could not answer, " It is the best house in London for *mousseline de laine*." The sub-editor and three of the leading writers or writers of leaders in the *Times* were of our company, and the expression of doubt upon their countenances as to whether it was loyal and safe to scoff at Jupiter Tonans added greatly to the delight of those who felt no apprehensions. It was a very brief hesitation. They knew, as we all knew, that Delane was " above suspicion," and that no one would enjoy the enigma more than he.

*   *   *   *   *

Walking one day in front of my house, I was astonished to see a number of workmen preparing to set up the usual telegraphic apparatus on the roadside not far distant, and I wrote at once to the postal authorities, declining to have the presentation of a drying-ground for clothes perpetually in sight of my windows. The postal authorities sent down Mr. Edmund Yates, and Mr. Edmund Yates very promptly sent down the poles, which were contrary to the provisions of the Act protecting ornamental grounds. I much enjoyed his cheery society, and some of his recent experiences in connection with this new line of electric communication which had brought us together. There had been much opposition, and at a recent meeting a small, insignificant old gentleman had suddenly bounced out of his chair, and approaching Yates, who could have blown him away with a puff, in a state of incandescent excitement, shook his fist and yelled, " You minion of the Government! don't think you're going to cram your poles and wires down *our* throats. I defy you."

Afterwards he sent me his trenchant epigram, suggested by the gay clothing of the worshippers at a church, known as " All Saints' "—

> " In a church which is garnished with mullion and gables,
>   With altar and reredos, with gurgoyle and groin,
> The penitents' dresses are sealskin and sables,
>   The odour of sanctity eau de Cologne.
> But surely if Lucifer, flying from Hades,
>   Were to gaze on the crowd with its paniers and paints,
> He would say, as he look'd on the lords and the ladies,
>   ' Oh, where is All Sinners, if this is All Saints?' "

*　　*　　*　　*　　*

I have many happy recollections of authors; of an interview, in his beautiful home, with one of the most profound thinkers and writers of our age on spiritual, political, and social subjects—the author of " The Reign of Law ; " of letters from the Laureate, in one of which he crowns me as " the Rose-King," placing me on a " throne of purple sublimity," from which I have ever since surveyed with royal condescension the whole horticultural world; of pleasant, profitable hours spent with Professor Sir Richard

Owen in the Museum of Natural History at Kensington, and in his home in the park at Richmond, in which I learned more of the wonderful beasts and birds now extinct, of their habits and surroundings, than I could have acquired from years among books; of mirthsome months in the Riviera with Lawrence Lockhart; of a delightful visit from the writer of that famous book, "John Inglesant;" of an interview, too brief, with the author of "The Light of the World;" of conversations with Mr. Augustus Hare, who deserves to be called "the traveller's joy," seeing that without his "Walks in London and Rome, Venice, and Florence," the tourist would be, like Goldsmith's "Traveller," "remote, unfriended, melancholy, slow," and of learning from him how the lady, who had been reading one of his books, and had left it in her bedroom, suddenly exclaimed, as she was departing from her hotel, surrounded by the landlord and his servants and an admiring crowd, in a loud voice to her maid, "Oh, Eliza, Eliza, I've left my Hare on the dressing-table!"

*　　*　　*　　*　　*

"Kissing hands" is in some countries a graceful expression of a sincere respect and attachment; with us it is little more than a ceremonial sign of homage on appointment to some office of importance, and a form of osculation not much in vogue. But we rejoice to grasp the hand of those whom we love, honour, and admire; of good, true, generous men; of those "that handle the pen of the writer," to instruct, to gladden, and to warn ; and of those who delight our ears with exquisite music, and our eyes with the life-like portrait, the lovely landscape, the historical scene. In speaking of those great authors and artists whom it has been my privilege to know, I have seemed once more to hold the hand and see the smile of their friendship, and I venture to hope, as I withdraw from their presence, that my recollections may leave upon my readers, as they always have upon me, a more thankful admiration and regard.

CHAPTER X.

CRICKETERS.

The love of cricket—An Oxford song—The good influence of
cricket—Tom Barker—Fuller Pilch—Lillywhite—Mynn—
W. Clark—Guy—Box—R. Daft—George and Sam Parr—
Country stories—My match at single wicket—Umpires—
"The Free Foresters"—Remarkable incident at Leicester
—Extraordinary scores—Should clergymen play at cricket?

THE love of cricket, as of all manly games and
sports, is innate in the hearts of Englishmen,
especially in the northern and midland counties,*
and in Somersetshire, Gloucestershire, Middlesex,
Surrey, and Kent. It first develops itself, according
to my experience, in dab and billet, trap and ball,
rounders (who that has "run his side in" ever forgets the delicious sensation?); expands into fives,
rackets, tennis, and finally attains its full power and
joy in cricket! Wherefore I sang at Oxford, and the
voices of the athletes made the welkin ring; that is

* Nottinghamshire produces more first-rate cricketers than
any other county, and, the supply being in excess of the home
demand, they are to be found in various parts of the land.
For example, in the recent victory which the Notts eleven
achieved over Surrey at the Oval, their most formidable
opponent was Lockwood, a Nottinghamshire man.

to say—for I am not quite clear about the welkin, what it means, or how and when it rings—the undergraduates joined in the chorus :—

YE CRICKETERS OF ENGLAND.

AIR—"*Ye Mariners of England.*"

"Ye cricketers of England,
  Who guard the timbers three,
Whose game has braved a thousand years
  All other games that be,
Your pliant willows grasp again,
  To meet another foe,
As ye stand, bat in hand,
  Where the ripping swift uns go,
Or some crafty Clark,* with artful twist,
  Sends in the teasers slow."
        Chorus—"Where the ripping," etc.

"The spirits of your fathers
  Look on from glen and glade,
Their ghosts in ancient flannels clad
  Watch every ball that's played.
Where Pilch and mighty Alfred move,
  Those spectres long to show,
How to stand, bat in hand,"
        Chorus—"Where the ripping," etc.

"That England hath no rival,
  Well know the trembling pack,
Whom Charley Brown, by Calais town,
  Bowled out behind his back.†

---

* William Clark, the famous Notts slow bowler.

† Charley Brown was an eccentric supernumerary on the Nottingham ground, and had a marvellous knack of bowling from behind his back. He challenged and defeated three Frenchmen in the neighbourhood of Calais.

> The cricket-ball of England
>   Can brook no foreign blow,
> As they stand, awkward band,"
>   Chorus—" Where the ripping," etc.

> " Long, long, in park of noble,
>   And in the cottage field,
> This game of games to English hearts
>   Its manly joys shall yield;
> And oft at eve, when stumps are drawn,
>   The fragrant weed shall glow,
> As ye tell how they fell,"
>   Chorus—" Where the ripping," etc.

And ever since I sang that song, I have rejoiced to see children, on village greens and the waste places of our towns and cities, boys in the playing-fields of our schools, young men in our universities, and everywhere, all sorts and conditions of grown men, enjoying this grand old game; and I never had a reception which gratified me more, than when, fifty years after, I accepted an invitation from the Notts Incorporated Football Club to a welcome at their rooms, which I shall never forget, and to receive from a very large attendance—with such men as William Gunn in the foreground, and with men of authority and influence, magistrates and others, on the platform—" a vote of thanks for the support which I had always given to all that is manly and honourable in British sports and recreations." This club has four hundred and fifty members, and is rapidly increasing. They meet for friendly inter-course, pleasant conversation, reading the news-papers, chess and other indoor games, and smoke the

soothing weed, when the day's work is done. No
intoxicants are sold on the premises, and no
gambling is allowed.

I regard cricket with admiration, not only for
the enjoyment which it brings to those who play it,
and to those who see it played, but, as a philosopher,
physician, and priest, I not only believe that "all
work and no play makes Jack a dull boy," but that
no good work can be done continuously, without
that variety of occupation which brings comparative
rest, and refreshes both body and mind. So long as
we can run, as he who "fields;" and smite, as he
who bats; and aim, as he who bowls; so long as we
retain the keen eye, the strong arm, the lithe limbs
of the cricketer, we shall run after, and not before,
our enemies, break through his defences, and demolish
his batteries.* He is no statesman, no philanthropist,
much less a Christian, who does not prize, as of
prime importance, the health—the physical as well
as mental health—of a nation, the *mens sana in
corpore sano;* and a country has no benefactors who
more deserve its respect and gratitude than those
who give grounds for games.

Tom Barker was the first distinguished cricketer
with whom I was acquainted, and on an eventful day,
when I had accompanied my father to a meeting of
our County Club at Southwell, which Barker attended

---

* Our reviewing officers will tell you, in proof, that in
Nottinghamshire our Yeomanry, the South Notts and the
Sherwood Rangers, our Militia, and Volunteers, are excellent,
and second to none.

as a paid bowler, and when my seniors were leaving the ground and going for lunch to the pavilion, he said to me, " Now, my little man, I'll give you a ball." I took up a bat, and went with my heart in my mouth to the wicket; for Tom was a tall, dark man, and bowled at a terrible pace ; but he favoured me with a ball which was exquisitely slow, and which, in the most awkward manner imaginable, I spooned up into the air, and he called out, " *Bravo, bravo !*" and I was bound to believe him ; and we parted to our mutual satisfaction.

Then, on the Trent-bridge Ground at Nottingham, I saw all the great heroes play. Fuller Pilch, with his long reach, grand defence, and powerful hitting. Short, stout Lillywhite, who was the only round bowler, until Redgate (in white breeches and stockings) followed his example, with twice his amount of speed ; and round bowling became the rule. I saw Alfred Mynn, with his tall figure and handsome face, hit a ball which he could not resist, in practice before the match (the biggest hit I ever saw, or shall see !), over the booths, over the Bingham road, and some distance into a field of potatoes on the opposite side thereof; and we stood gazing as it rose, as rustics gaze at a rocket, and then relieved our oppression of astonishment with that universal note of admiration, " Oh ! "

And here I must relate an incident, which created such an intense excitement as I have rarely seen, and which was followed by a discussion, never to be solved, whether it was the result of intention or of accident. There was to be a great match between Nottingham and Kent. Mynn had recently made a big score, over one hundred runs, off Redgate's bowling at Leicester (in which operation, playing without pads, he was sorely bruised, and for some days was unable to leave his bed), and William Clark was absorbed by one anxious ambition, to bowl him, or get him caught. He walked about the ground before the play begun, and murmured at intervals to a friend of mine, who reported the interview, " If I can only get *him*—if I can only get *him!*" The ground was cleared; Mynn and his colleague went to the wickets, and the umpire called " Play." Then Clark bowled, and Mynn seemed to prepare to hit, but changed his mind, and quietly blocked the ball halfway between wicket and crease. Clark bowled again with a similar result, but the ball was stopped much nearer the wicket. A third ball came, but the batsman went back so far that as the ball fell from his bat, *a bail fell also!* For two seconds there was a profound silence; there might have been nobody, where many thousands were. We Notts men were mute with amazement, dumb with a joy which hardly dare believe itself. The " Lambs " could not utter a bleat. Then they roared like lions! They left their seats, and, not satisfied with shouting, they danced and capered on the sward!

I saw Box, who in those days had no rival in his

department, keeping wicket in his tall white hat.
Richard Daft, who was in his best day the most
graceful of bats (as Clark said of Guy, " Joe Guy,
sir, Joe Guy, all elegance, fit to play in a drawing-
room before her Majesty ") and the quickest of
fielders, told me an amusing story of Box. The
Eleven of England, like all other elevens, had
much harmless fun, and many a practical joke, in
their peregrinations, being ever in exuberant health
and spirits ; and on one occasion it was Box's turn
to be victimized.   He was scrupulously particular
about his hair, and one evening at supper, during
a match, he inquired whether any of his companions
could tell him of a good haircutter.   Sam Parr
replied that he had found a satisfactory artist in the
town, and gave Box his address.   Then a mischievous
design occurred to him, and early next morning he
went to the haircutter, and told him that he should
shortly introduce a friend, who was unfortunately
suffering from disease of the brain ; that the doctors
considered it a matter of great importance that · he
should wear as little hair as possible, and had, at
last, and after much opposition, persuaded him to
have it removed.   Box returned from the interview,
white and wild with indignation.   He might have
quoted the words of his namesake in the play, " I
have a great mind to register an oath that I will
never have my hair cut again.   I told the man only
to take off the ends.   He must have thought I meant
the other ends.   I look as if I had been cropped

for the Militia;" but he preferred, I regret to say, much more violent language. He all but assaulted Sam, and told him that his friend was a born fool, and that when he had asked him whether he was not taking too much off, the lunatic had said, "Oh no, sir; just a little shorter, sir; you'll feel so much better, sir—you will indeed." "I told the brute," said Box, "I didn't want to feel better; but it was no use, and I'm not fit to be seen!" He wore his hat at meals, and Sam said he slept in it.

My friend Daft owed me a story. Giving a lecture in the village in which he resides, I was pleased to see him in the audience, and made a detour from my main subject, that I might surprise him with a bit of cricket. And I did surprise him, when I affirmed boldly that cricketers nowadays did not know how to score as we of the olden time. I then narrated how, many years ago, I had played a match at single wicket against a friend and his retriever. The dog was really an excellent field, and brought the ball with great rapidity to his master. Unhappily for my opponent, the spectators were so clamorous in their expressions of interest, that the poor retriever lost his presence of mind, and started off with the ball in his mouth, as though making for Southwell, about a mile away. His master followed in pursuit, and I took advantage of his absence to make twenty-seven runs, before he returned with the ball!

George Parr's hitting, especially to leg, was, I think, the most cheerful performance I ever saw with the bat. He went to play for his village at a country match, and there was a sort of panic among the little fishes in the presence of this Leviathan. George ventured on an impossible run, and was manifestly out. But when the question " How's that ? " was put to the umpire, his courage failed. He hesitated, and, turning to the batsman, said, " Now, Mestur Parr, you know a great deal more about these things than I do ; what should you say ? " " *I* should say, ' Not out,' " was the reply. " And so say I, Mestur Parr," said the umpire. " Lads, get on with your gam'."

There are other quaint records of country umpires. My son was captain for a time of an eleven in a mining district, and refreshed me at intervals with his reminiscences. One worthy old fellow remarked, in returning thanks at a supper for the toast of the umpires, " My opinion of an umpire is, that he should be fair, and I don't hold with no foul dealings. What I always says is, Fairation with " (after a short pause) " just a slight leaning towards your own side." And I do not suppose that you would find an umpire without this little bias more quickly than Diogenes with his lantern could find a perfectly honest man.

In the same district it was solemnly decreed, at a general meeting of the club, that, though a certain umpire (I have his name, but must not reveal it) "in ordinary fixtures gave general satisfaction, yet, *taking into consideration the peculiarities of other umpires, he must be regarded as a little too fair for such important competitions as the Derbyshire and Wake Cups.*"

And when one of these " other umpires " exemplified his peculiarities by giving a man "in," who certainly was so when the verdict was uttered, but not when the wicket went down, a voice came from a distant part of the field, " Mestur umpire, I don't want to have no unpleasantness with you, but if you come that little gam again, I shall just step in, and pull out your mustassios by the rewts."

Within my own experience and neighbourhood, another umpire, in speaking after a match to the united elevens, made his confession thus : " Gentlemen, I think that the time has arrived in which I should offer you my hearty apologies for any prejudice which I may have shown in favour of local talent, and I confidently rely on your forgiveness, because I am sure that you must have noticed in the second innings I treated my own side with undue severity, in order to make an average." He might have added, that when it was evident that his friends must win, he regulated his verdicts, so that they should not win too easily.

One more delectable incident. I must alter the names of the *dramatis personæ*, but that will be the only fiction. Mr. Stumps, an umpire, has had a quarrel with Mr. Batts, and on the morning of a match, he addresses Mr. Bowles, *sotto voce* : " Mr. Bowles, that there Batts is going to play again you to-day, and if ever you says to me consarning that ruffian, ' How's that ? ' I shall lose no time in telling you, ' *You can chuck her up, Mr. Bowles.*' "

But the " out-and-I've-won-five-bob " umpire is now almost extinct, and the office of adjudication is entrusted to honest men, who love cricket too well to insult and spoil it.

Their long white coats are somewhat unsightly to us elderly gentlemen, who resent innovations; but their resemblance to the apparel of the kennel huntsman may reconcile them to hunting men.

I remain a member of several clubs, because it seems to me a duty to encourage, especially among boys and working men, this manly recreation. Next to my own county club (Nottinghamshire), the society which has given to me the greatest amount of personal pleasure is known as " The Free Foresters," and was founded by the Rev. W. K. Riland Bedford, to whom I have previously referred as an archer, Rector of Sutton Coldfield, and well known in the literary world as the author of " The Blazon of Episcopacy " (I asked him to supplement the arms of the bishops with the legs of the deans, but he has not complied), and other interesting books, in conjunction with his neighbours, the Garnetts, of Moor Hall and Bone Hill. The latter were accomplished cricketers, and an eleven of their house and name played and defeated a first-class team. This brotherhood of Foresters has included, and includes, the *élite* of the amateurs; such bats as Mitchell and the Lytteltons, and such bowlers as Goodrich (the best slow bowler of his day) and David Buchanan, *cum multis aliis.* When I knew them best, and sometimes had the pleasure of offering them hospitality, they were the most delightful of guests. They gave you an admirable display of cricket by day, and at night, as merry as crickets on the hearth, the most charming music, glees and madrigals, and dear old English songs, such as I had not heard since the Orpheus Club sang, in the gardens of New College, during the commemoration week,

> "O quam bonum est !
> O quam jucundum est!
> Poculis fraternis gaudere!"

and the *pocula fraterna* were splendidly represented by the college silver goblets and cups.

An accomplished cricketer related to me a very singular incident, which occurred during a match between the counties of Nottingham and Leicester. Before the game began, the captain of the latter eleven came to him, as being leader of the opposition, and inquired whether there would be any objection to their playing a young fellow, who was devotedly fond of cricket, but who unfortunately was suffering from mental derangement, and was an inmate of the asylum hard by. He was perfectly harmless and inoffensive, and often came to play with them, not only with his doctor's permission, but at his special request. Assent was readily given, and about an hour before luncheon the invalid came on the ground. My friend was making an excellent score, and remained at the wicket until the bell rang. As he was walking back to his place, he was accosted by the new-comer, who was put on to bowl, "Allow me, sir, to say that I have been watching you with much interest, and I deeply regret, I can assure you" (he spoke with a sad and solemn earnestness), "*that I must bowl you out.*" My friend, of course, cheerily replied that he should postpone such a consummation so long as it was in his power. The umpire gave the signal, the bowler uttered a sound, something between a who-op and a wail, and away flew the middle stump! The batsman laughed aloud, but the bowler surveyed with a rueful countenance the ruin which he had wrought; and with an audible lamentation, "So sorry!" went back to his post. At eventide a bell rang from his melancholy home, and quietly and sadly he left the ground.

The happiest, neatest, prettiest *bon mot* which I ever heard about cricket was said by Lord Winchilsea, at a dinner given to Lord Harris before his departure as Governor of Bombay: "It may be that, when the noble lord returns, the House of which he is a member, and which is now denounced by its enemies, may have ceased to exist; but, be this as it may, I have full confidence that he will be permitted to *play at Lord's.*" Meanwhile, there is every reason

to hope that he will show in ruling a Presidency
that power of keen observation, that insight as to
the capacity of subordinates, which puts the right
man into the right place, and won for him the high
renown of being " the best captain of an eleven in
England."

The annals of cricket are so full of remarkable
incidents, that memory is confused by their number,
and only two or three seem to raise themselves above
the multitude and demand notice. In the midland
counties we have always believed in the famous
one-innings match between Kegworth and the neighbouring village of Diseworth, which resulted as
follows : Kegworth, 1 ; Diseworth, 0. But as others
may regard this contest as legendary, I will restrict
myself to details of which there can be no doubt.
In July, 1884, Newman, a professional, in a match
between Wimborne and Poole, *made all the runs*
from the bat—the innings amounting to 27, of
which 4 were " extras " !

About the same date, in a match between two
London schools, St. Paul's and Highbury Park, St.
Paul's scored 8, including 4 extras ; and T. H.
Fawcett had the honour of carrying his bat through
the innings for a score of 1 !

In 1885, July 13 and 14, at Chichester, Mr. T. S.
Carrick, in a match between the West of Scotland
and the Chichester Priory Park Cricket Clubs, scored
for the former 419 runs, not out. He was batting
for two days, and his side made 745 for four wickets.

Just one more abnormal performance, because I know the performer. Colonel Fellowes, of the Royal Engineers, scored 22 runs from an over, 4 balls, bowled by W. G. Grace! The total would have been 24, but the last ball hit the wall of the pavilion, and came back into the field, making the result 6, 6, 6, 4!

Should clergymen play at cricket? Why not? If I were a bishop, and a young priest asked me the question, I should at once give an affirmative answer, with these restrictions : Your cricket must never interrupt or abridge your duty. You should not leave your parish, unless you have a curate, for a match of two or three days' duration, because fatal sickness may come suddenly, to the babe unbaptized, and to those who most desire or most need your help. You must be satisfied with the ordinary costume of clean white flannel (none so becoming), and not array yourself in gorgeous or fantastic raiment. You must despise the habit of " going in for a B and S," and let your moderation be known unto men in tobacco, as in all things else. When you have made a good innings, you will deserve your pipe.

It is rarely given to a clergyman to effect a complete transformation of character upon the cricket-field, as it was to one, who is now very highly esteemed in love for his works' sake, as a suffragan bishop, but he may exercise a very healthful influence. In the case to which I refer, the parson, who frequently played cricket with his parishioners and neighbours, was surprised and grieved to notice that one of those who joined in the game had a manifest dislike of his presence. The cause, whether some anti-clerical feeling, evoked by those agitators who tell working men that they are robbed and priest-ridden, or from some other prejudice, he never knew, but the aversion was obvious, and on one occasion was conspicuously displayed by the proprietor, who placed himself at the beginning of an over by the side, and within a few feet, of the ecclesiastic who was going to bat, and contemptuously replied to a remonstrance and warning of danger, " I'm not afraid of nothing as the likes of you can do to me."

There came a loose half-volley to leg, and the batsman hit it with all his strength. His malignant adversary, anticipating results, fell just in time to the ground, or he would in all probability have been stretched there in woeful plight. He was a miner, and, shortly after this escape, he was very badly hurt by an accident in the mine. Then the clergyman, to his surprise, received an invitation to go and see him, and, after several visits, he had the curiosity to inquire the motives which had dispelled his antipathy. " Oh," said the miner, " *that hit o' yourn to square leg for six converted me.*"

This incident was a phenomenon; nevertheless, the ordinary parson may win sympathies, and suggest reflections, quietly and unostentatiously, which may be profitable alike to him who gives and him who takes. A good man, wherever he goes with a good purpose, will communicate goodness; for virtue, thank Heaven, is a thousand times more impressive for good than vice is infectious for evil. Clergymen must not be hermits, but rather in the world though not of it; all things to all men, that they may save some. Great harm is done by their absence from those places and pastimes in which laymen see nothing immoral or religious, and the latter resent it, as suggesting the evil which they do not find. Moreover, it confirms the hurtful notion that the clergy are wanting in manliness, and is used as an argument by those who rejoice to disparage, and to denounce us as "a lot of old women."

We may not go where men are drunken, and curse, and swear, and are profane and obscene, and love to speak all words that may do hurt; where they lie and cheat, and defraud one another, and knaves are applauded for their cunning, and young men are robbed of their inheritance, and women who have lost "the shame, which is a glory and grace," are flattered and admired; we must turn away with the sad regret that a sport, which might have given entertainment to all classes, should be thus degraded and defiled. But we may go, and ought to go, where men may renovate true manliness; to the playgrounds where rich and poor, masters and servants, may forget the difference which divides them elsewhere, and unite in their common admiration of excellence, which is independent of money and rank, and offers itself to the ambition of all earnest men. And there never was a time when kindly communion of the upper, middle, and lower classes (as they are termed) was of more serious importance than now.

I may not leave this subject without offering humbly my tribute of praise to the great cricketers of our day; without expressing the hope that the champion, who has " beaten the record " of all time, may continue to demonstrate how long and how well the man who takes care of himself may play cricket (" he who striveth for the mastery is temperate in all things "), and that all the famous chieftains who bowl and bat may maintain their ancient glory, and may teach Young England how to play the most manly, the most healthful, and the most interesting of all our games.

Above all, I would tender, as a Nottinghamshire man, to Mr. Dixon and his decemviri my grateful admiration.

And good luck to our Australian brothers! They have done us good. They have taught the old folks at home a few things which they did not know. They have made John Bull sit up, when he was becoming drowsy and obese, in the belief that he was omnipotent; and they have proved, as Lord Shaftesbury said a wife would prove to the Pope, that he is not infallible. Moreover, such intercourse is good for nations, as well as for classes; and at a dinner which we gave to their eleven at Nottingham, it was pleasant to hear their expressions of affectionate regard for the dear old fatherland. "We always," my neighbour said to me, "we always call it *home*."

Concerning other games, I know little of football, except that it is a brave and gallant diversion, and that I rejoice to see thousands of our young men and boys enjoying it on a Saturday afternoon, instead of loafing about the streets, and boozing in the public-house.

Of golf I know less, and am too old to learn.

Lawn-tennis is a most precious invention (or rather restoration, for I was told by an archæologist, who went with me to Pompeii, that something very like it was played there, two thousand years ago), social, invigorating, graceful; and it has taken the place of a game—croquet—which was in every way inferior, and a sore trial to the equanimity of those, who suddenly found themselves expelled from honourable positions in society to the loneliness of some distant grove!

Court-tennis always seemed to me the most fascinating and scientific exercise; but it is far too expensive and far too difficult to be accessible to the public. I saw Barr, the Frenchman, beat the marker in our Oxford court with a bootjack, and make some marvellous returns with a ginger-beer bottle. He was a fat man, with little rapidity of action, but he seemed to know where every ball would finish its course, and was there to meet it on arrival.

CHAPTER XI.

ECCLESIASTICS.

Past and present—Fifty years ago—Zebah and Zalmunna—
The dawn of day—The Oxford movement—The foreigner's
visit—The American bishop.

I REMEMBER a remark made by the late Bishop of
London (Dr. Jackson), that when he recalled the
sad condition of apathy, indolence, and disobedience
into which the Church of England had fallen, it
seemed marvellous to him that it continued to exist,
that it should survive such manifest indications of
debility and decay. I did not share in his surprise,
believing that, as a branch of the true Vine, it may
droop, but it cannot wither, and though it may
bleed when it is pruned, whether by the merciful
Hand which purgeth it that it may bring forth
more fruit, or by the sword of the oppressor, it
can never die. Moreover, there was the remnant,
the seed, the seven thousand who had not bowed
the knee to the Baal of worldliness; and He who
said, " I will not destroy the city for ten's sake," in
His wrath thinketh upon mercy. The Evangelicals,
the Wesleyans, not then severed from the Church,

and devout Christians in all grades of society, kept the lamp from going out in the temple of the Lord. The pulse of spiritual life was feeble, slow, intermittent, but it encouraged hope. And so, while I record the memories of my boyhood and youth, were it only to suggest or to strengthen the gratitude which we owe for the revival of the faith, which worketh by love—my recollections of neglect and degradation—I remember also with a reverent regard those holy and humble men of heart who, few in number—"the fewer men the greater share of honour"—followed in quietness and confidence the steps of the Divine Master, and went about doing good, in schools and cottages, sick-rooms and mourners' homes, from that charity "which vaunteth not itself."

In some cases a comparison between the past and the present is greatly in favour of the past. I speak that which I know, and testify that which I have seen, having associated all my life with rich and poor alike, when I affirm that there was far more unity and far less discontent—a better feeling between masters and servants, employers and employed. Servants were not tempted by bribes, nor by facilities of locomotion, to wander from place to place; they remained in happy homes for long periods of mutual attachment, and there were no demagogues to suggest and organize distrust. I do not say that the disaffection and disunion which ensued were not provoked nor justified. I regard them, on the contrary, as the protest of right against wrong, as the fulfilment of the Divine warning, " Be sure your sin will find you out;" a truth which was echoed by the philosopher when he said—

> " The gods are just, and of our pleasant vices
>   Make whips to scourge."

I know that we were living in the lull which precedes the storm, and the big drops, which have been described as the tears of the tempest, weeping for the havoc it will make, began at long intervals to fall. I believe that the thunder-clouds then gathering on the horizon had never darkened day, if the Church had done her duty; if her rich laity, her nobles, squires, and merchants, had been more thoughtful and more generous as to the spiritual and temporal condition of the people; if the welfare of the mechanic and the labourer had been studied and promoted by Christian sympathy, instead of by politicians, fighting for place, and outbidding one another with promises to the electors of a beneficence which, if ever it be realized, will cost them personally nothing. If the subjects of education, dwellings, allotments, trades unions, labour and capital, had been dealt with in a religious, philanthropic spirit, instead of being pressed upon Parliament, and if that Parliament had never been, as Charles Dickens, who watched its proceedings for three and a half years, described it, a place in which " Britannia was brought out night after night to be roasted, like a trussed fowl, skewered with office pens, and tied up with red tape; a place in which he listened to promises which were not intended for fulfilment, and to explanations which only tended to mystify, which constrained him to declare with regard to patriotism, 'I am an infidel and shall never be converted;'" why, then there might have been confidence instead of suspicion, men of all ranks might have met each other in the streets with the smile of sympathy instead of with the scowl of aversion, and owners might have gone into factory and field, as Boaz went among his harvesters, with a "Lord be with you," and been answered with "The Lord bless thee."

In addition to this larger concord, there were other advantages and immunities, fifty years ago. Though the Wesleyans were fast breaking away from the Church, losing their affection for a mother who made no effort to retain it, we had no deserters to Rome; nor were we informed by professors and pedants that the Bible abounded in myths and mistakes; that we must take their word for it, instead of listening to Him Who bids us " hear the Church," and must receive their hypercriticisms, their theories, and doubtful disputations, as though they were the edicts of an Œcumenical Council, and in place of our ancient Creeds. Some have affirmed—and all inherit from our first parents an evil instinct to transfer blame : Adam accused Eve, and Eve the serpent—that the clergy were the cause of this sad declension. They were, undoubtedly (with few exceptions, chiefly, as I have intimated, of the Evangelical school), indifferent to their duties, and unworthy of their high vocation. They did as little as decency compelled, and that but once in the week. They ate of the fat, and clothed themselves with the wool, but they did not feed the flock. Nevertheless it must not be ignored by their accusers that the people loved to have it so. *Populus vult decipi et decipiatur.* It was as at Tyre, as with the people so with the priest, as with the servant so with his master, as with the maid so with her mistress. The parson could not prevent Lord Zebah and Squire Zalmunna from taking the houses of God in possession, from slumbering in their lofty quadrilateral forts. Had he lifted up his voice like a trumpet, and constrained them to hear a sermon, preached by Saint James, about rich men in gay clothing and poor men in vile, he would have been denounced at once as a Papist or a Methodist, and would have tasted the old port no more.

Within twelve miles of my home, Zalmunna came regularly to church, followed by a footman, carrying a Prayer-book, which he reverently suspended by a silver chain round the neck of his master on his arrival in the family pew!

My first memory ecclesiastical is of a time in which we never saw or heard of our vicar—days of pluralities and non-residence, suggestive of Lord

Brougham's splendid enigma, " What makes treason reason and Ireland wretched ?" answer, " Absent T." It was then that a certain Vicar of Strood was induced by a laudable, abnormal magnanimity to leave the benefice, which he preferred in some distant county, and to visit the fold, which he had entrusted to one of his hirelings; but he was so offended and repelled on his arrival by a nauseous odour, which came between the wind and his nobility from a basket of shrimps, held up as he passed through the street for his approval as a purchaser, and in process of swift decomposition, that he abandoned his benevolent intention, and sought the refuge of his sweeter home.

Our curate, who lived five miles away, rode over for one dreary service on the Sunday, dined, and we saw him no more during the week. He was much occupied in the pursuit of the fox, which, it is charitable to suppose, he mistook for a wolf, and like a good shepherd was anxious to destroy. The service was literally a duet between the parson and the clerk, except when old John Manners, the bricklayer, gave the keynote for the hymn from his bassoon, a sound which might have been uttered by an elephant in distress, and we sang—

" O turn my pi—O turn my pi—O turn my pious soul to Thee;"

or when the curate suddenly emerged from his surplice, which he placed on the side of his reading-pew, and appearing in his academical gown, went up the "three-decker" to preach. The altar was represented by a small rickety deal table, with a scanty covering of faded and patched green baize, on which were placed the overcoat, hat, and riding-whip of the officiating minister, who made a vestry within the sacrarium, and, sitting there in a huge surplice, had a conversation with the sexton before the service began, and looked as though he were about to have his hair cut. The font was filled with coffin-ropes, tinder-box, and brimstone matches, candle-ends, etc. It was never used for baptism. Zebah and Zalmunna would not have countenanced such an unseemly interruption of the service. Sparrows twittered, and bats floated, beneath the rotten timbers of the roof, while beetles and moths, and all manner of flies, found happy homes below. The damp walls represented in fresco "a green and yellow melancholy," which had a depressing influence upon the spirit, and the darkest and most dismal building of the parish was that called the House of God.

We had, I remember, a supplemental service at home on the Sunday, which I am sure was good for us, although we derived no benefit from the introduction of Blair's sermons, of which we children understood not a single sentence, and in which it is difficult to find any reference to the Christian faith. They only impressed me as being beautifully bound, in calf with gilt edges, and as being printed in large clear type. Perhaps, as the first day of the week was then regarded as the gloomiest of all, and no notice was taken of the Church's directions as to "days of fasting and abstinence," these sermons . were inflicted as penance. If so, they fulfilled their purpose; but I should say that, as a Lenten exercise, a course of Blair would be too severe for ordinary patients.

At last, the morning star, which announced the advent of a brighter day, shone through the darkness; and it is interesting to recall how gradually that gracious light broke upon the dreary scene.

As when some beautiful picture, which has been concealed and forgotten, removed in time of battle, lest it should be destroyed by the enemy, is found after many years, and is carefully cleansed and skilfully restored, and the eye is delighted with the successive development of colour and of form, and the lifelike countenance, the historical scene, the sunny landscape, or the moonlit sea come out once more upon the canvas; so in that great revival of religion, which began in England more than half a century ago, the glorious truths of the gospel, the ancient verities of the Catholic faith, were restored to a disobedient and gainsaying people, who had forgotten or slighted them so long. They were with us in our Bibles, in our Prayer-books, in our Sacraments, and means of grace, but they were hidden from our eyes, like the colours of the picture, by the dust of a long neglect.

Or as when, after some sad, restless night of pain, of feverish vision, and of fearful dream, joy cometh in the morning, and the sun shines upon a world

> " By suffering worn and weary,
> Yet beautiful as some fair angel still ; "

so with the awaking of our religious life from that sleep, which seemed like death.

The first agents employed in this work of restoration, the first promoters of " The Oxford Movement," invited and secured, through the press and from the pulpit, the consideration of their readers and hearers, as they appealed to the Holy Scriptures, to the Prayer-book, to the ancient Fathers, and to primitive practice, in their expositions of our privileges and of our duties as members of the English Church. They reminded us, and proved to us, that this Church was no modern establishment, devised by human prudence and depending upon secular support, but that it was founded in Apostolic times, or shortly after the decease of the Apostles, by those whom they had ordained ; that it was here when Augustine came to exalt and extend it ; and that in later days, having, like the Church of Ephesus, lost its first love, and remembering from whence it was fallen, it had been reclaimed and reformed ; that our bishops, though statesmen had the power to commend, and kings to command, their appointment, derived their dignity and power from consecration and the imposition of hands ; and that our clergy, however unworthy, were royal ambassadors, entrusted with messages of pardon, and with the benedictions of peace.

They taught us, at the same time, that these privileges were worthless, unless we *proved* our appreciation ; that it was vain, and worse than vain, to have the most excellent form of godliness on our lips, if in our lives we denied the power of it; and that they only, who receive the seed into an honest and good heart, can bring forth fruit with patience.

These soldiers were the pioneers, the advanced guard, of a victorious army, marching to the relief of a beleaguered citadel and of famished men, and they wrought a great deliverance. Ere they came, a foreigner visited this country and wrote a record of the impressions which it made upon him. After praising its scenery, valleys and hills and streams, its woods and cornfields, gardens and orchards, its wealth and industry, its great discoveries in science, its achievements in art and in arms, he goes on to say, " But most impressive, at first sight, to me was the sight, not only in cities and in towns, but in every village, of the church tower or spire, rising over the roofs and the trees, and hard by the pastor's peaceful home. Surely, I thought, we have here, not only a prosperous, intellectual, energetic, brave, and accomplished people, but they are devout and religious also. Imagine then my disappointment when, as I drew near, I found the graveyards were uncared for, the tombstones broken, defaced, defiled, the church doors barred and locked, and when I obtained admission, for which I was manifestly expected to pay, I looked on desolation and decay, comfortable apartments for the rich, with cushions and carpets, bare benches for the poor; and was told that the church was only used once in the week, and that the chief shepherd resided a hundred miles from his sheep!"

How great would be his surprise of joy could he return to us now! His utterance of sad reproach would be exchanged for some such words as those which were spoken, when the first influence of this reaction was felt throughout the land, by an American bishop, George Doane of New Jersey. Preaching in the parish church at Leeds, he said, " Brethren, right reverend, reverend, and beloved, it is written in the records of the Older Testament, that when the Ark of God was on its way to Zion, it rested for three months in the house of Obed-Edom, 'and it was told King David, saying, The Lord hath blessed the house of Obed-Edom, and all that pertaineth unto him, because of the Ark of God;' and as I have gone from scene to scene of varied beauty in this the most favoured land of all the world, as I have contemplated your prosperous industry, and enjoyed the hospitality of your happy, peaceful homes, and have remembered that over every sea floats the Red Cross of Saint George, and that on the limits of your Empire the sun never sets, I have asked myself, Whence to this little island, whence to Britain, once unknown to the civilized world, this glory and this power ? And the answer which has come to me instinctively is this : ' The Lord hath blessed the house of Obed-Edom, and all that pertaineth unto him, because of the House of God.' Yes, brethren, the power and glory of England comes from her pure and ancient Christianity. And the armament which guards her shores is the fleet which bears to distant lands her missionary zeal."

CHAPTER XII.

ECCLESIASTICS—*Continued.*

Personal recollections—Dignitaries—Archbishop Vernon Harcourt—Bishops Kaye and Jackson—Anecdotes of the Duke of Wellington.

MY own parochial experience of this great transformation and renewal reminds me of its progress from small beginnings. A new curate came to reside within three miles of our church; the next, within two; his successor actually in the parish, though at the extreme boundary; and then the appointment was given to me residing in my old home, not two minutes' walk from the church. Since that time a new school and vicarage have been built, " the House of God set in its state," the daily service and weekly Communion restored. And this may be said generally of the parishes throughout the land. As a rule, there is a resident and earnest clergyman, and a restored church; the children are taught, the sick are visited, the poor have the Gospel preached to them, and the worship is frequent and sincere.

My first recollection of dignitaries is of Archbishop Harcourt Vernon, who confirmed me at

Newark—a tall, aristocratic man in a wig, which became him well. There was in those days a scant administration and a large abuse of this Apostolic ordinance. Seldom offered, and only in cities and towns, the ceremony was attended by crowds from the surrounding districts, who came with little or no preparation, behaved with much irreverence and levity within the church, and outside as though at a fair. From a parish adjoining my own the candidates went in a waggon, and gave a fiddler half a crown to play them merry tunes on their journey!

Then came Bishop Kaye, who ordained me deacon and priest, ever to be remembered by those who had the privilege of knowing him, with admiration of his learning and veneration of his character. Spiritual and intellectual beauty made sunshine on his countenance, and

> "On his lips perpetually did reign
> The summer calm of golden charity."

He had, as I afterwards discovered from converse with others, an invariable system of dealing with those whom he examined personally for Holy Orders. He took an exact measurement of each before he let him go. He led us by the hand into shallow waters, and onward until we were out of our depth; and then, giving us one plunge overhead, he brought us gently and lovingly ashore. The process commenced, on my first interview, with easy passages from the Greek Gospels, and I was congratulating myself on the serenity and security around, when I found the waters rising rapidly, as I made mistakes in my translation of the shipwreck in the Acts, and finally lost my foothold and my Greek in the Epistles, as huge billows, lingual and doctrinal, 'surged and roared overhead. Then I grasped the outstretched hand of his sympathy, and heard, as I reached the land, that he was fully satisfied.

Nevertheless, there was not then the anxious forethought, the preliminary training, which are now bestowed upon those who are candidates for the diaconate and the priesthood. Too many young men were attracted by the leisure which seemed to accompany the life of a clergyman, and to a profession which brought ready admission into what is called good society. Some were to have rich livings by purchase, and some through family ties. There were none of those admirable training colleges to which the young graduate can now go for special instruction relating to the ministerial office, nor do I remember an instance of that reception in the house of the bishop, or in other congenial homes, which is now as general as it is wise and helpful. In my day we went to the hotels.

A singular incident occurred during a confirmation held by Bishop Kaye at Newark. A boy named Hage, from the neighbouring village of Balderton, looked so much younger than his years, as to have quite a childish appearance, and the bishop, as he approached for the imposition of hands,

paused and inquired, " My boy, what age are you ? "
He was immediately answered, " Please, sir, Hage
o' Balderton." Then his pastor came forward and
explained.

Bishop Kaye was succeeded by Bishop Jackson,
a loving servant of his Divine Master, an earnest
preacher of practical religion, fervent in spirit,
energetic in the duties of his office, so much esteemed for his sermons when Rector of St. James',
Piccadilly, that both the leaders in Parliament were
members of his congregation, and were alike desirous to offer him a bishopric.

He told me that one morning, when he was
preaching in the Chapel Royal of St. James', he
was much perplexed by the conduct of a verger,
who, at the close of the sermon, opened the door of
the pulpit, and just as the preacher was about to
step through, suddenly closed it with all his force,
and with a noise which rang through the building.
" I looked at him for an explanation," the bishop
continued, " and he informed me in a whisper that
his Grace the Duke of Wellington was asleep, and
that, not liking to touch him, they adopted this
method of rousing him from his slumbers." There
was no necessity to repeat the bombardment, as
" that good grey head, which all men knew," was
no longer nodding.

We all like to be reminded of our Great Duke—

> " The hero of a hundred fights,
> Who never lost an English gun,"

and I may therefore record some characteristic words
of his, repeated to me by one who heard them, Dr.
Blakesley, Dean of Lincoln. "I've just come from
Buxton," he said. "I haven't been there since I
was quite a youngster—ever so many years ago—
but the man at the inn knew me again!" He had
the modesty which forgets its own greatness, and I
quite believe in his meeting the lady who was going
up the steps to see the model of Waterloo as he
came down them, and in his saying, "Ah, you're
going to see Waterloo. It's very good, very good
indeed—I was there, you know."

He left behind him three memorable sentences,
which we ecclesiastics should quote continually to
those who revere his memory and confide in his
common sense. He said "that education without
religion would surround us with clever devils;"
and our prison records will testify to the truth of
his prophecy. He said to one who pushed aside a
poor man who was going up before him to the altar,
and bade him "make way for his Grace the Duke
of Wellington," "Not so—we are all equal here."
And when a young clergyman was speaking in
disparagement of foreign missions, he rebuked him
with, "Sir, you forget your marching orders, 'Go
ye into all the world, and preach the gospel to every
creature.'"

Bishop Jackson suffered much from depressing
headaches, but when in health he was always genial,
sometimes humorous. He said that the preben-

daries of his cathedral, being deprived of their *prebenda*, had "stalls without a manger;" and this remark suggests the clever epithet applied to them of "Rifled Canons," and an amusing story told of one of their brotherhood.

Under the old *régime*, when cannons were sometimes removed from their places on board a man-of-war for the sake of accommodation, they were replaced by short wooden dummies, which looked externally just like the real thing, but occupied much less room. A naval officer, who had taken offence at something which had been said at a dinner-party by a clergyman who had just been made an honorary canon, and who was somewhat autocratic, resolved to be avenged. He invited the whole party to inspect his ship next day, and when inquiry was made as to the use of one of these sham substitutes, which he had placed in a conspicuous position to attract notice, he replied, in a tone which all could hear, "*Oh, that wooden thing? It's only a dummy—a sort of honorary cannon!*"

One more explosion, but only from a minor canon. His temper was not always in harmony with his music, and he was afflicted by sullen moods, which made him *impiger, iracundus, inexorabilis, acer,* sudden and quick in quarrel, resentful of any interference. A sick man had been prayed for twice daily in his cathedral during several weeks, and when the constant repetition of his name became somewhat monotonous, the canon in residence, from whom I received the story, politely suggested that the words " for a sick person " should be substituted for the name of the invalid.   The request received a brief ungracious assent ; and at the next service, and just before the Prayer for All Conditions of Men, the minor canon announced in a tone of surly indignation, " The prayers of the Church are desired for a person *whom I'm not at liberty to mention.*"

Bishop Jackson much enjoyed " a doubtful compliment," which was paid to him by the young curate of the parish in which he lived, who was much attached to him, and said to him one day in conversation, " I can assure you, my lord, that my rector is such an exceptionally good man, and his wife is such an exceedingly good woman, and they are in every respect so infinitely my superiors, that, if it weren't for your lordship and Mrs. Jackson, I should feel quite uncomfortable."

CHAPTER XIII.

ECCLESIASTICS—*Continued.*

Bishop Christopher Wordsworth—His appointment to Lincoln —His spiritual, intellectual, and bodily excellence—His eirenicon to the Wesleyans, and his anxiety to promote reunion—The " Old Catholics "—The Greek archbishop— Strange incidents in connection with almsgiving—" Theophilus Anglicanus "—The last message.

BISHOP JACKSON was succeeded by Dr. Christopher Wordsworth, Archdeacon of Westminster. The late Bishop of Peterborough, Dr. Magee, afterwards Archbishop of York, said to me, " I was never in Bishop Wordsworth's society without feeling better from the interview." And it was impossible to know a man so saintly, so learned, and so kind, without a reverent and loving affection. There was a remarkable coincidence in the circumstances of his appointment. Having to preach in the Abbey at Westminster, I was staying with my old Oxford friend, Canon Prothero, in the house which had been occupied by Archdeacon Wordsworth, and having occasion to write to him I referred to the fact. He told me in his reply that in the room from which I wrote, close to the place of St. Hugh's consecration, he had received, on St.

Hugh's Day, the offer of the bishopric once held by "St. Hugh of Lincoln." His "praise is hymned by loftier harps than mine," but none could honour him more. Right worthy of the beautiful name of Christopher, he evoked and exalted Christian sympathies wherever he was, and men "took notice of him, as of the Apostle, that he had been with his Divine Master." He spoke eloquently and instructively on all subjects, even as King Solomon spake of trees, "from the cedar tree that is in Lebanon unto the hyssop that springeth out of the wall," and would descend from the heights of theology, or the classical slopes of Parnassus, to the humble abodes of the valley or the playgrounds of the school. "I have learned more," he said, "in sick-rooms, and from poor and simple folks, than from all the books which I have read." He left his library once, I remember, when the lake was frozen at Riseholme, and, putting on his skates, astonished and delighted the spectators. He never forgot the days when he played in the eleven of his school, or the match in which "Manning, caught Wordsworth, 0," seemed to intimate that the first of the two did not always play with a straight bat. He sympathized with all sports, games, and recreations which were manly and free from vice, and which could be enjoyed without dereliction of duty or unwise expense. When he was told that the wife of one of his canons had been driving tandem in a sleigh over the snow, his commentary was not at all in accordance with the anticipation and hope of the individual who laid the information : " I should greatly have enjoyed the drive ! "

He had the courage of his opinions, and swerved neither to the right hand nor to the left, when he believed that he was on the way of righteousness, however rough and steep. He disputed the presentation to a living which seemed to him to be illegal, and the lawsuit which ensued, and ended in a verdict against him, cost him nine hundred pounds. The clergy of his diocese subscribed and sent a cheque for the amount, for which he expressed his gratitude, and his hope that he might be allowed to expend the money on the restoration of the Old Palace at Lincoln.

Some criticized his " Eirenicon to the Wesleyans," as an imprudent interference, which would only widen the gulf between that community and the Church; but the result was that " he received," to quote his own words, " more applications from Wesleyan ministers for admission into Holy Orders than he could possibly entertain." " This morning," he writes to me in one of his letters, " I have three communications on the subject."

He had a great yearning for the reunion of Christendom, that all who profess and call themselves Christians might hold the Faith, as the Founder prayed, in unity of spirit.* The Archbishop

* He took a deep interest and a prominent part in the " Old Catholic" movement, and in the year 1872 attended the Con-

of Syra and Tenos was his guest at Riseholme, and on the occasion of a great Church function, in St. Mary's at Nottingham, I was honoured with an introduction. He spoke to me very kindly, but no chorus in the " Agamemnon " of Æschylus had ever perplexed me more than his Grace's modern Greek, and when I rejoined my friends, and was eagerly questioned as to the subject of conversation, I could only say, with the minor canon, that I was not at liberty to mention it. At the luncheon, which followed, the bishop proposed the archbishop's health, and the latter responded in modern Greek, and the physiognomy of the listeners was a study—some trying, some, I fear, affecting, to understand, and some assuming an expression of honest ignorance and hopeless stupidity, which was not encouraging to the speaker.

Many curious incidents are narrated having reference to the giving of alms. How Lady Cork was so impressed by a sermon, soliciting pecuniary help, that she borrowed a sovereign from Sydney Smith, who sat next to her, but could not make up her mind to put it into the plate, or to repay Sydney. How a certain quaint canon in a northern diocese was playing billiards in a country house, and having "lost a life" at pool, produced payment in the form of two threepenny bits, and when an exuberant youth exclaimed, " Oh, canon, you've

gress at Cologne, and addressed the members in a powerful Latin oration.

got to the offertory," effectually silenced his critic with the rejoinder, " *You recognize your miserable contributions, do you?* " And there is the authentic history of the lady, or rather of the female disguised as a lady, who came into the vestry after a collection, and asked that a sovereign, which she had put in the alms-bag, mistaking it for a shilling, might be returned to her ; and all doubt as to the course to be pursued was dispelled from the minds of the churchwardens by the absence of the coin, which the claimant hoped would be there. But all these (even were we to include the gentleman, not gene-rous, feeling the rim of his offering, lest he should give a fourpenny instead of a threepenny piece, and singing the while—

> " Were the whole realm of Nature mine,
> That were an offering far too small ")—

all these pale their ineffectual fire in the splendour of an incident, which occurred during the episcopate of Bishop Wordsworth, and at the consecration of a church in his diocese. There was a very large congregation, and the rector, seeing that there was only one alms-dish, made signs to a rustic from the chancel entrance to come to him, and bade him go into the rectory garden, through a glass door into the dining-room, where there had been a slight refection before the service, bring a dish from the table, take it down one side of the north aisle, and up the other, and then bring it to the clergyman at the place from which he started. The rustic disappeared, reappeared with the dish, took it, as he was ordered, and presented it to the people on either side of the aisle, and then, approaching the rector, whispered in his ear, " I've done as yer told me, sir. I've taken it down yon side the aisle, and up t'other —they'll none on 'em 'ave any." No order had been given to empty the dish, and *it was full of biscuits!*

No incident in *our* Comic Ecclesiastical History excites my admiration more than that which I have told; but America in this, as in all things else, challenges our precedence, and I must meekly acknowledge that the occurrence, certified to me by Dean Hart of Denver as an actual fact, substantiates her claim. "We have a certain parson," he writes, giving the name, " whom we keep on the frontier. He is a rough diamond, and has a knack with the miners. Not long ago, he went to a camp called Rico, borrowed the dance hall over the saloon for his service, 'rounded up his boys,' and the hall was filled. After the sermon came the collection, a very important feature. The preacher ran his eye over his audience, and selecting a certain 'tin-horn' gambler, known as 'Billy the Kid,' 'Billy,' he said, 'take up the collection.' Very much honoured, Billy took his big sombrero hat, and with an important and dignified air, as was fitting for the occasion, he made his way to the front, and held his hat for a young man on the foremost chair to 'donate.' The young miner dropped in a quarter (1s.). Billy looked at it, then, putting his hand under his coat-tails, drew his revolver, 'clicked' it at the donor, and said, with the utmost gravity, 'Young man, take that back; this here's a dollar show.' Then, with his hat and revolver, moving round the hall, he got as many dollars as there were people." One more curious incident from the States. An American bishop, whose praise is in the Churches, told me that a collector in a church in San Francisco, on receiving a shake of the head instead of a dollar from the hand of one whom he knew intimately, stopped to remonstrate, and said, "William, you must give something. You've heard what the rector has said—it's your duty." "My money belongs to my creditors," said William. "And who is your greatest creditor? To whom do you owe the most?" asked the collector. "Well, that's very true," replied William; "but just now He's not crowding me quite so much as the others."

The Church of England never had a braver champion nor a more loyal son than Christopher, Bishop of Lincoln. No book had so great an influence in its day upon young men, at our public schools and universities, and upon candidates for Holy Orders, to convince them of the Divine institution of their Church, and of their privileges and duties as Churchmen, as the manual entitled "Theophilus Anglicanus." With good will and kind words for all, he never accommodated his creed to his company, or sacrificed truth to peace. While with the charity which hopeth all things, he dare

not limit the Holy One of Israel, yet, knowing the
terrors of his Lord, he would persuade men to flee
from the wrath to come. When he prayed to be
delivered from false doctrine, heresy, and schism,
he believed in their existence, for he saw them
around him, and knew that they were perilous to
souls. He asked from others the obedience which
he always rendered to the rules of the Church.
He thought that the "Ornaments Rubric" meant
what it said, and that it was lawful, though it might
not be expedient, to wear the special vestments in
use throughout Christendom at our highest act of
worship. But he was equally opposed to additions
as to subtractions. He generously encouraged the
building and beautifying of churches, he was the
advocate of frequent and reverent services, but he
disdained the curtsyings, and osculations, and
tinkling cymbals introduced from Rome, as much
as he disliked the chill indifference of those who sat
to pray, and only cared for the preaching of tenets
which emanated from Geneva. He was neither
papist nor puritan, but one who believed in his
heart that "before all things it was necessary to
hold the Catholic faith."

Not long before he died, he sent me this message:
"Tell him, who is so fond of flowers, that no bed
in the Garden of the Soul is so beautiful as the
bed of sickness and of death, on which the penitent
seems to be in the presence of the Gardener and
to have a prevision of the flowers, and a foretaste

of the fruits, of Paradise. Tell him that these thoughts may give him a subject for a sermon." I never forgot his words, and waited for the opportunity to preach, as he proposed. It came in an invitation from his successor in the archdeaconry of Westminster to speak from the pulpit, which he so often occupied, in aid of a society, which he had instituted some fifty years ago, for the spiritual welfare of the district in which he lived. Then I endeavoured to develop the analogy which he had suggested—to contrast the soul, which is a watered garden, with that which is as a barren and dry land where no water is, the flowers and fruits of holiness with the cruel thorns and poisonous weeds of sin; and I essayed to show how every man may " make the desert smile," not only in his own heart and home, but in the abodes of ignorance and poverty and sin.

Abiit, obiit—I would fain say, as I pray, *præivit.* Dr. Hammond's epitaph might be inscribed over his grave—

> " Nihil eo excelsius erat, aut humilius,
>   Sibi uni non placuit,
>   Qui, tam calamo quam vitâ,
>   Humano generi complacuerat."

CHAPTER XIV.

ECCLESIASTICS—*Continued.*

Bishop King—The power of charity—Archbishop Tait—
American and Scotch bishops—Pusey, Newman, and Keble
—The Oxford revival—Indiscretion.

HE was succeeded by another *episcopus episcopo-rum*, Bishop King. And here I would say of our bishops generally, from the long and large experience of one who has been permitted to do some work for his Master in almost every diocese, not only in England, but in Scotland and in Wales, that all Churchmen should render hearty thanks to that great Shepherd of the sheep who has sent such loving, learned, and laborious men to take the oversight of His flock; and though I may not say much that I should like to say, personally, I may console myself by relating incidents with which they were connected, which have gone into circulation, and have become, as it were, public property.

I begin with an interview between the prelate whom I just now named and a deputation of aggrieved parishioners, who went from a neighbouring village to Lincoln, to lay their grievance before him. Being questioned on their return as to the result of their appeal, they seemed much perplexed and confused, and there was some hesitation before Mercurius, the chief speaker, delivered his report of the meeting : " We went to see the bishop, and he came out to meet us in his purple dressing-gown, and seemed so pleased to see us ; and said he was just going to have his lunch, and hoped that we would join him ; and we sat down, and he smiled and talked, and told us to come again, and behaved himself so gracious, that we would not find in our hearts to bring in anything unpleasant."

This triumph of charity, so honourable to all who won it, brings to my memory another meeting between Archbishop Tait and a shrewd layman, very characteristic of both. A passenger entered the railway carriage, in which I was travelling, with a bit of blue ribbon on the breast of his coat, and said benignly, after surveying my person, " A Catholic priest, I presume ? " " Yes," I replied, " I am a Catholic priest, of the English, not the Roman Church." He then inquired whether I objected to conversation, and being assured that I liked it, he told me that he was a Nonconformist teetotaler, and went about giving lectures. Being myself much engaged in the latter business, we made it our chief topic, and we were unanimous in our protest against an annoyance of which we both had experience, and which is caused by chairmen and others, who have been reading up the subject, " rising to say a few words of introduction " of the lecturer and anticipating some of his best points, statistics, and illustrations. I told him the story of the loquacious squire and the garrulous rector, who, by their preliminary speeches, occupied nearly all the time which had been allotted to a lecture in the village where they lived. The lecturer spoke for some twenty minutes, and then, looking at his watch, he said, " Ladies and gentlemen, I must now leave that I may catch my train, but I will ask your permission before I depart to suggest for your consideration an occurrence which took place on board a small American vessel. The captain, the mate, and a passenger dined together, and upon the occasion of a roly-poly pudding being placed on the table, the captain inquired from his guest, ' Stranger, do you like *ends?* ' and receiving a negative answer, went on to say, ' Oh, don't yer? Me and the mate does ; ' and he cut the pudding in two, giving one end to the mate and appropriating the other."

My companion said it was a good story, but he could tell me a better, in which he himself was the sufferer and the avenger. " I was invited," he said, " to speak about total abstinence at a mixed meeting, and, being nobody in particular, I was placed last on the list. Worse than this, the chairman introduced a lot of other speakers, and the whole audience were sick and tired, when he informed them that Mr. Bailey would now give his address. And I rose and said, ' My address is

45, Loughborough Park, Brixton Road, and I wish you all good night.'"

Then in the course of our conversation he told me of the interview to which I referred. He was working as a turner in Lambeth parish, when a servant came from the Palace with a note, inviting him to see the archbishop, who was anxious to obtain some information from him. "I was engaged in some important work," he continued, "which had just come in, and I sent my respects to his Grace, informing him that I could not spare the time to come. The same day, he came down to my work-shop, and stood for a couple of hours beside my lathe, until he had heard all I could tell him concerning the good works in which he was engaged. Then he thanked me, and asked, 'Is there anything I can do for you?' 'Well, your Grace,' I replied, 'we are giving a tea to our Ragged School next week, and our funds are very low.' 'What shall I give?' he said. I asked for a sovereign, and he said, 'Take two,' putting them on the bench close by. Then I remarked, 'Mrs. Tait, perhaps, would like to subscribe;' and he answered, 'I am sure she would,' and he laid down another sovereign. Then I thought, 'I may not have another visit from an archbishop; I must make the most of the occasion,' and I said, 'There's dear Miss Tait; we must not leave her out in the cold!' and he took out his purse and added half a sovereign more."

There is another story of an American captain

(which was told to me by the Bishop of Minnesota, and may therefore be included in my episcopal anecdotage), who reproved one of his passengers for beginning his breakfast on Friday, a day which the captain rightly observed as a day of abstinence, with a huge beefsteak. The beef-eater was silent, but he was on the watch for his time of retaliation, and all things come to him that waits. That same morning something went wrong on deck; the captain lost his temper, and, like the Scotchman, who went into the middle of the street and swore, at last he used words vile and profane. Then the passenger drew near and addressed him, " I guess, captain, that if you'd eat a little more and cuss a little less, you'd be much nigher the kingdom."

The bishop has delicious records of Indian sagacity—how the shrewd old chief, with the quickest insight into character and intention, will listen with an expression of the most solemn gravity and intense interest to some proposal which is designed to deceive and cheat him, and will suddenly, and in some quaint, unexpected manner, make it known to all that the fish sees the hook in the gaudy fly, and flaps his tail at the angler on the bank; that the days are gone, departed never to return, when lands, and ivories, and skins were to be had in exchange for glass beads, padlocks, and " Turkey reds."

A pious fraud, desiring to revive these ancient negotiations, was endeavouring to make a favourable impression upon a tribe of Indians by assuring them that he had lived such an unblemished life that he should not know how to cheat. " The winds of sixty winters," he said, " have passed over my head and left this snow upon it, but never from my childhood have I done a dishonest deed." Then, after a pause, the chief arose and said, " The winds of sixty winters have likewise turned the little hair I have to grey, *but they have not blown out my brains.*"

And when another visitor, also in search of advantageous contracts, came to them in a military uniform, and informed them that the Great Father (the President), knowing their valour in battle, had selected him from his warriors, as being most worthy to hold intercourse with them, another chief drew near, with a look of delighted, reverent admiration on his face, and said, " All my life I have longed, and hoped, and prayed that I might be permitted to see the white man in his war-paint, and now " (walking slowly round the object of his worship, a short, fat man in clothes which did not fit)—" now " (sitting down with a sigh of blissful satiety, after one last fond look)—" *now, I am ready to die.*"

Before I leave the States, my memory suggests that I should pass from lively to severe, and should chronicle an impressive incident—impressive as a proof that the seed which is sown in faith, and received in an honest and good heart, never fails to germinate, and that, where intentions are pure and earnest, the reward is sure—related to me by the Bishop of Albany.   His father, the eloquent and beloved Bishop of New Jersey, whose words I have quoted,* was staying with Dr. Hook at Leeds, and preached one Sunday, in the grand old parish church, a sermon upon Baptism, in which he pleaded with those who had not been baptized to prepare themselves at once, and to receive the Sacrament, as being necessary to salvation, wherever it might be had.   Dr. Hook thanked the bishop after the service for his excellent sermon, but deemed it only due to his congregation to add that, so far as he knew, they were all baptized. The bishop expressed his great regret that, under the impression that in Leeds, as in the place from which he came, large numbers were unbaptized, he had chosen this theme for his discourse.   Some months after he had crossed the Atlantic, a young man came to Dr. Hook, and told him that, walking through the streets, he had seen an announcement of a sermon from the Bishop of New Jersey.   He had at that time no religious convictions, and had never been taught the Christian faith; but he " thought he would see what a Yankee bishop was like," and went accordingly to hear him preach. He was so impressed by the sermon, that it became his dominant and most anxious thought; and he sought counsel and instruction, not only from

* Page 138.

human wisdom, but from Him who is always merciful to give light to them that sit in darkness and in the valley of the shadow of death, and to guide their feet into the way of peace. He was baptized, confirmed, and came now, as a communicant, to ask Dr. Hook what assistance he could render in any branch of his work.

Of the Scotch bishops who have left us, two, Alexander, Bishop of Brechin, and George, Bishop of Argyll and the Isles, were my dear friends. Forbes was with me at Brasenose, and was a delightful companion. No man could have more solemn convictions, or a more reverent spirit, but the sunlit, silvery waves of his humour danced and gleamed above the depths.

George Mackarness, like his brother, " Honest John," Bishop of Oxford, was beloved by all who knew him. Upright in mind as in mien, the kindness of his heart shone in his handsome face. Mine was, I think, the last house he visited, before he went to Brighton, where he died from cancer of the tongue—a fearful disease, but as his day so was his strength; a few lines written in pencil, shortly before he died, assured me of his perfect resignation, and of his bright and certain hope.

Why was St. Andrew selected to be the patron saint of Scotland? This question has exercised the clerical and lay curiosity, but has not been satisfactorily answered, unless the explanation, offered by the Archdeacon of Calcutta at a dinner which he attended on St. Andrew's Day, be confirmed as final, a consummation which we can hardly anticipate, though the archidiaconal conjecture was received with unanimous, nay more, hilarious, applause. "Gentlemen," he said, "I have given this difficult subject my thoughtful consideration, and I have come to the conclusion that St. Andrew was chosen to be the patron saint of Scotland because he discovered *the lad who had the loaves and fishes!*"

Passing from the prelates to a lower grade of the priesthood, I was greatly impressed as an undergraduate by Dr. Pusey's preaching, as afterwards by his published writings, by his saintly life, and his loyal love, faithful unto death, for the Church, in which he received from those in authority so much opposition and distrust. His manner was in itself a sermon, and he went up to preach with a manifest humility, which no hypocrite could assume, and no actor could copy.

Newman was a far more attractive preacher. There was such a pathetic tone in his utterance, of that which the French describe as "tears in the voice," such a tender appeal of plaintive sweetness, that I remember to this day the first words of the first sermon I heard from his lips— "Sheep are defenceless creatures, wolves are strong and fierce." But I fail to comprehend, regarding the matter in the light of consistency and common sense, why it was proposed that a statue of Cardinal

Newman should occupy the best site in Oxford; why the representation of a deserter should be set up in a barrack-yard of the Church Militant, as a model for the young recruits!

I can understand the gratitude and respect which built a college in honour of Keble, and a "house" in remembrance of Pusey; I can understand the Roman Catholics delighting to honour their illustrious proselyte; but the exaltation by English Churchmen of a man who forsook and denounced them, while they ignore the claims of her own champions, saints, and scholars, who have fought her battles and died in her ranks, is to me a mystery.

The revival of faith, and therefore of life, in the Church of England may be regarded in three phases, divided into three epochs. (1) It was, first of all, as I have endeavoured to show, a restoration of doctrine, as taught by the Church in her Prayer-book, with an appeal to history as to her right to teach. (2) It was then manifested in the restoration of churches, and of a more dignified and frequent worship; and (3) it has now reached the supreme height of its ascension, and is exercised by the noblest of all ambitions, to seek that which was lost, to bring back that which was driven away, to bind up that which was broken, and to strengthen that which was sick—to obey the Divine injunction, "Go out into the streets and lanes of the city, and bring in hither the poor, and the maimed, and the halt, and the blind. Go out into the highways and hedges, and compel them to come in." The shepherds have filled up the gaps in their fences and rebuilt the breaches of their walls in vain, if they do not seek and find the sheep which have wandered from the fold. They will not come until they hear the shepherd's voice—how can they hear without a preacher? Paul preached in the market-place and on Mars' Hill, as well as in the synagogue. If we would have " the common people," ὁ πολὺς ὄχλος, hear us, as they heard the Master, gladly, we must try to preach in the same spirit, and must go about doing good to the bodies and souls of men. We want the working men, and when they know why we want them, there is abundant proof that they will come. On this subject I shall have more to say.

The revival met with a fierce opposition, partly from earnest men, who were really afraid of Romanism or formalism; partly from the timid, who were averse to alter, or from the indolent, to enlarge, their work; but chiefly, as in most instances, from the worldly and irreligious, always prone and prompt to resent and ridicule any signs of an aspiration higher than their own, any examples of that better life which they rightly regard as a rebuke to their self-indulgence.

The bishops, with two or three exceptions, discouraged the movement, and sought rather to suppress than to guide this new-born zeal. Newman complained sadly of episcopal antagonism, and said he "could not fight against it." A friend of mine told me that when he went with others, who had been instrumental in building a new church, to the bishop (afterwards an archbishop) of the diocese, to submit to him their proposals as to the services, he expressed his surprise and dissent as to their intention of singing the Psalms, and asked them whether they were aware that this was only permitted to cathedrals and collegiate churches. They showed him the rubric, " Then shall be said or sung the Psalms in order as they are appointed," and he frankly confessed it had escaped his notice. When they expressed their desire that their church should be free and open to all, he expostulated, and inquired in a state of much perturbation, " Gentlemen, have you considered the number of police which will be necessary to keep order? "

They who preferred the surplice as ordered by the Church, in preference to the academical gown, were snubbed, hooted, hustled, and pelted in the streets. " Puseyites " were burnt in effigy, and then the defection of Newman caused a panic of consternation, raised a hurricane, which would have swept away the edifice, had it not been built upon the Rock. When Manning absconded, there was comparatively but a small regret. He was admired, but not loved, as Newman. Others followed, whose absence was more bitterly lamented, but by degrees the fish which were taken in the meshes of the

Roman net became few and small, some so diminutive, or in such flabby condition, that, even though they were gold and silver fish, a true sportsman would have thrown them in again.

Of course, there were in this, as in all great revivals, notably the Wesleyan, men who have a zeal, but not according to knowledge, and who insist on transgressing the boundaries marked out by their leader. · There are men who rejoice in walking on the rims of rocks, standing on the tip ends of precipices, skating on thin ice, going where they are forbidden to go.

There were, moreover, extravagances of ritual which not only enraged opponents and bewildered simple folks, but estranged the sympathies of many who desired a reverent and beautiful service, but were pained and offended by " the last new dodge from Rome."

I went to a high celebration in a London church, and, arriving after the service had commenced, was never able to distinguish one word of it, and only knew by close observation what part of the office we had reached. On another occasion, I went to celebrate at the altar of an absent priest, and was actually unable to find the service in a book which was there, full of hieroglyphics and illustrations to me unintelligible. I was wondering whether I could repeat from memory the more important portions, when I saw in the hand of the little server behind me a small twopenny Prayer-book, and this supplied all my need. In my own church, a stranger, officiating in my absence, remained so long bending over the altar, that my worthy churchwarden feared that he had some paralytic or apoplectic seizure, and went to his relief. And in a village church, some four miles away, a lady, dressed in the height of fashion, paused as she came up the aisle, and made such a low obeisance, that the vicar rushed from his prayer-desk to render assistance, under the impression that she had fallen or fainted.

When the country squire, preferring eyesight to hearsay, went up to town to judge for himself in the matter of high ritual, and inquiring from the first clergyman whom he met in the church to which he was directed, " whether it was Sacrament Sunday ? " was answered, " Five Masses have been already said," it seems to me that the reply, a combination of bad taste and braggadocio, was eminently qualified to make foes instead of friends.

Does not the Church of England supply us, in her ancient offices and prayers, with a most solemn and beautiful worship ? And when their adaptation is required, as for missions and other special services, have we not the full sanction and sympathy of those who have the rule over us ? If we lack anything, it will be given to us, if we work and wait, but not if every man doeth that which is right in his own eyes. "To obey is better than sacrifice." Moreover, it should ever be had in remembrance, that "there are diversities of gifts, but the same Spirit"—"differences

of administrations, but the same Lord "—" diversities
of operations, but the same God; " and that there
always have been, are, and will be, two great divisions
of Christians, alike sincere—those who welcome an
ornate ritual, with all that is attractive to the eye
and sweet to the ear, because it helps them to worship
in spirit and in truth; and those who love simplicity,
and avoid the accessories to which I have referred,
lest they should divert rather than direct their
thoughts. Why should there not be a mutual for-
bearance and respect? Why should Ephraim envy
Judah, and Judah vex Ephraim? Might we not
think more of those grand truths which we all
believe, and less of those minor matters on which
we differ, uniting in prayer for union, and seeking
to prevail, not by debate and controversy, but by
the most convincing of all arguments, example—the
practice of a religion which is pure and undefiled,
which visits the fatherless and widows in their
afflictions, and keeps itself unspotted from the world.
When we recall the past and meditate upon the
influences which we prize the most, we shall find
that they have come to us, not so much from good
books (with the one exception) as from good men
and women. The Christ-like life, unconscious of its
power, draws all men to the Cross.

CHAPTER XV.

The village church—The daily service—The choir—Loss and gain—"Finn may fiddle"—The school—"The child is father to the man"—Special services for children.

I REFERRED just now to our village church, and I would linger awhile among the memories which rise within it and without, like ghosts, or rather angels, for they are welcome messengers, and those which remind us of sorrow point upward to the Bow upon the cloud. Home—what sweet, pathetic music in the word! You have been at some great concert and have heard the most accomplished artists, vocal and instrumental, of their day, but no brilliant manipulation, no marvellous vocal range, has reached and troubled the fountains of your heart like that simple ballad of " Home, sweet home." You admired, or tried to admire, or pretended to admire, the more scientific music, but this melody took possession of the spirit within you. " A flood of thoughts came rushing, and filled mine eyes with tears."

Who does not love to recall, and yet more to

revisit, Home? The field in which we learned to bat; the pond on which, with fear and trembling, and legs much too far apart, we made our first uncertain slide; the hedge in which we found our first bird's nest; the brookside or the river bank from which we saw with an ecstasy, thrilling, intense, the bright new float, as it dipped and rose, and finally disappeared in the depths; and then we pulled our line with such a powerful effort that the prize at the end of it, a youthful eel or "snig," about four sizes larger than the worm which it had seized, rose high above our heads and fell some distance in the meadow-grass behind.

The dear old faces smile on us once more; we hear the merry voices of our playmates, so many of them silent; we see the curly heads, which are now grown white as snow. Some have failed, and some have won riches and honour. Some have wasted their time and worse—

> " The eye no more looks onward, but the gaze
> Rests where remorse a wasted life surveys;
> By the dark form of what he is, serene,
> Stands the bright ghost of what he might have been.
> There the great loss, and there the worthless gain,
> Vice scorned, yet sought, and virtue wooed in vain "—

and some have done bravely and well the work which was given them to do, and have dedicated their manhood to the Divine purpose for which it was created and redeemed.

And now I pass as an ecclesiastic—for this

chapter was to be ecclesiastical—as I passed daily for more than thirty years, from the church to the school. And here I venture to express my surprise that so few of the clergy obey the plain injunction which they have promised to observe, namely, that the curate, being at home, shall cause a bell to be tolled, inviting his people to pray with him in their parish church, and that the Order of Morning and Evening Prayer be said daily, not weekly, throughout the year. I would not recommend him to take his servants to church, because "*laborare est orare*" (true work is true worship), but to have a short service with his household, and, after breakfast, Matins. Two or three, at least, will be gathered together; and is not the church, as St. Chrysostom said, " the Court of the Angels," and when we go there, to quote a greater than St. Chrysostom, are we not going " unto Mount Sion, and the City of the living God, the heavenly Jerusalem, and to an innumerable company of angels, to the general assembly and Church of the firstborn "? It is good for the many who cannot come to be reminded that prayer is being offered for them, and to be assured that their pastor is at work, as they are; and I would advise that the time of this service be so arranged that, when it is over, he may go with his boys to the school. What boys? For many years I educated six boys and maintained a daily choir, at a cost of half a crown a week! The expenditure was—school pence for six pupils at threepence a week; twopence to each boy weekly, as a reward of regular attendance and good conduct; total, half a crown. We sang the *Venite* and a hymn in our shortened service, which lasted about twenty minutes, the daughter of my churchwarden or my wife playing the organ, and then I went with the boys to the school.

What a transformation I witnessed in our village choir—*quantum mutatus ab illo !*—which was crowded in a small gallery, set up in front of the beautiful western arch, and backed by a lath-and-plaster insertion, having a plain square window in the middle, and which, accompanied, preceded, and followed by flute, clarionet, fiddles, and bassoon, and all kinds of music, sang, I must say, lustily and with a good courage, though not unanimous as to time or key. The gallery is gone, the sun sets once more upon our evensong. We have an organ, better singing, far more reverence, though I have at times thought that the odour of peppermint was more distinct than the odour of sanctity, and though I often wish that there had been a reform rather than an expulsion. The performance of sacred music must always have some influence for good, and this might have been largely extended, as the surroundings became more suggestive of devotion, and the performers realized more and more the privilege and importance of their music. As it was, the practice of their instruments afforded them a pleasant and innocent occupation of their leisure hours.

Organs by all means, where they may be had, but why organs only? Drums and trumpets make grand music in our cathedrals, and why not the voice of harpers harping with their harps, and the instruments of softer tone, in our smaller churches? I am aware of the difficulty which exists in harmonizing the organ with other music; but it can be, and has been, dealt with, if we may not say overcome.

The loss, however, which has been inseparable from the progress of our Church service must not cast a moment's shadow upon the sunshine of our thankful joy, as we compare the present with the past. A friend of mine remembers the time when it was made known to the congregation assembled in the church of St. Peter at Marlborough that they were going to have an anthem, because the singers left the church during the service to fortify themselves for the enterprise with a refreshing beverage at the Six Bells over the way. There were irregular scenes elsewhere. In a Nottinghamshire village the rector employed the village tailor to make the livery of his groom. The artist in question, by name Kemp, was also a musician, and led the choir on his violin. From some cause unknown to me—perhaps there came a more fastidious groom—Kemp's raiment failed to please, and the rector sent his servant to Nottingham to be measured by Mr. Finn, who had a great reputation in his trade. He achieved an admirable outfit, but on the first Sunday of its appearance at church, there occurred an unforeseen disaster. When the clergyman gave out the hymn, there was no recognition, no preliminary note, from the gallery at the other end of the church. He repeated the announcement in a louder tone, but when he ceased grim Silence held her solitary reign. Once more he proclaimed the number, and read the first verse in vain. Then "Melancholy marked him for her own," and he stood gazing in mute despair at the orchestra. There was a brief consultation, and then an ambassador came up the aisle, and, standing in front of his perplexed pastor, delivered his message in a tone which all could hear, "*If you please, sir, Kemp says as Finn may fiddle.*"

I have had personal and quaint experience. At one period of our improvements, my precentor, who had retired from her Majesty's service, and was engaged in commerce—that is to say, had been a policeman, and was then a grocer—had a fine bass voice, and played our harmonium, but he had not received a classical education, and was somewhat rude of speech. We had recently held a local Choral Festival at Southwell, and had heard for the first time that exquisite hymn from the "Ancient and Modern" collection, which begins, "The strain upraise of joy and praise," and in which the word "Alleluia" occurs repeatedly. Shortly afterwards, on my expressing a wish to the leader of our choir that this hymn might be sung in our church, I received this answer : " Well, sir, we have had a go at it, and if I could only get Butcher Hodgson to cut his Alleluias a bit shorter "—as though he were chopping meat—" we could sing it almost any Sunday ; but William, when he gets hold o' them Alleluias, he seems as if he never knew when to let go of 'em."

On another occasion, when my old friend and neighbour, Mr. Cook, was entertaining several guests, I asked the precentor on Sunday morning what hymns he proposed for the following service. " Oh, sir," he said, " we must have ' Jerusalem the golden ' "—just then a favourite hymn—" this afternoon ; *Mr. Cook's very full o' company.*"

From the choir to the school. It is a pleasant help to the school master or mistress to have the sympathy of the clergyman in their monotonous life, and to have his counsel and mediation in the many difficult cases which arise in dealing with parents and others. It is right that the shepherd should know and should love the lambs as well as the sheep, and he has one of the brightest encouragements which are given to his work when he gains their affection, and is welcomed, when he meets them, with a smile. Moreover, the child is father to the man, and it is wise to watch the first indication of good and evil instincts, to strengthen and to suppress. When growth is small, and the ground is soft, you may eradicate weeds, but when the plant is established in the hard-set soil, " with men it is impossible." Not only should these tendencies, virtuous or vicious, be cherished or condemned, but special talents and capacities should have, when it is possible, a technical education. Serious mistakes are often made, a life rendered comparatively useless, and a loss inflicted upon the community, by thwarting these early inclinations. Minds are like soils; all, with culture, will produce in due season their various contributions to our store; but some parents insist upon planting roses, instead of rhododendrons, in peat, place their ferns in sunshine, and their Alpine flowers in the shade.

Not long ago, a clever boy put his fingers into one of his pockets, and produced a tooth. " This, mother," he said, "is a rat's tooth, and it is so formed because," etc., etc., etc. (here he gave a concise and clear explanation); "and this"—bringing out another —"is a hedgehog's tooth, and you perceive" (explanation); " and this "—extracting No. 3—" is a badger's tooth, differing from the others" (explanation); " and this "—fourth and final illustration—" is Sandy Macpherson's tooth. He sits next to me at school, and a very good sort of fellow he is." What cruel madness it would be to send this lad to sea, or to an office, instead of training him, as he will be trained, to be a professor of Natural History, and to make the world richer when he leaves it—as his grandfather, an archbishop, enriched it—with the results of his studies.

The children of our time have a great advantage in those special services, which are becoming general.

No surer process of estranging children from religion could be devised than that which made Sunday a desolation and a weariness, which sent them to long services, and sermons which they could not understand, with the inevitable result of fidgets, fightings, and misbehaviour in all its branches, severely rebuked and punished by those who, *me judice*, should have themselves been put in the corner as the authors of irresistible temptation.

I found large coloured prints, which I procured from the Society for Promoting Christian Knowledge, and from the National Society, and which I placed on an easel on the chancel steps in front of my little flock, to be a most powerful auxiliary force—

"Segnius irritant animos, demissa per aures,
Quam quæ sunt oculis subjecta fidelibus;"

and when their eyes were somewhat heavy, it was a pleasant sight to see them open wide, and sparkle with interest, as some new scene was set before them.

We had, of course, our share of strange and silly replies. My sister was teaching in our Sunday school, and asked, "What was meant by the Law and the Prophets?" A bright little girl immediately answered, "If you please, ma'am, when you sell anybody up." The law presented itself to her mind in the person of the bailiff distraining for debt, and of the auctioneer selling the effects; the profits being the results of the sale.

There was the eager boy, who will speak before

he thinks, and who informed me, without a moment's delay, when I inquired what proof we had of St. Peter's repentance, " *Please, sir, he crowed three times.*" *

* We country folk have no monopoly of these eccentric errors. A clergyman in Holborn asked a little girl, who sometimes appeared in pantomimes and other fairy scenes, how many Creeds there were. And the reply was, "Two, sir— 'Postles and Lyceum " (Nicene). And a boy, also in the vicinity of the Law Courts, included "the Epistle to Phillimore " (Philemon) among the writings of St. Paul.

CHAPTER XVI.

ECCLESIASTICS— *Continued.*

The country parson and his people—The Ranters—The village
demagogue—The village artist—The club—Decrease of
drunkenness—The " Rang-tang."

PASSING from the school to the parish, I must
confess that I am sometimes perturbed in spirit,
when I hear the country parson (very unlike George
Herbert's) complaining that he has nothing to do,
nobody with whom he can associate, or when I hear
his friends bemoaning him, as one who is " buried
alive, utterly thrown away," etc. ; and no one can
be in doubt why, where such men are, there is
disaffection and dissent.   Men who go where their
charity and their duty should lead them, will make
dear friends among the poor, and will learn many
lessons from their patience, and resignation, and kindness to each other ; and all who have tried to win
their confidence will testify that, though exceptions
be many, there are noble spirits and tender and true
hearts among them, rare jewels in rough setting—

> " Alas, 'tis far from russet frieze
>   To silk and satin gown,
> But I doubt if God made like degrees
>   'Twixt courtly hearts and clowns."

Who has not met with illustrious snobs in glossy hats and patent-leather boots? Who has not found brave gentlemen in corduroys, and true gentlewomen in humble serges, whose only ornament (it cannot be gotten for gold, neither shall silver be weighed for the price thereof) was a meek and quiet spirit.

Again, there is a frequent complaint that the poor are so ungrateful.

> " I've heard of hearts unkind kind deeds
>   With coldness still returning;
> For me, the gratitude of men
>   Hath oftener left me mourning;"

and I do not hesitate to say that, to my experience, where the accusation has been loudest the obligation has been least. It is not the occasional half-crown, even though it be accompanied by the dry, inappropriate, and improbable tract, but it is the constant sympathy, the Christian sympathy, coming from a brother's heart, which wins affection. It is written, " Blessed is he that *considereth* the poor and needy"—has them often in his thoughts and prayers. A poor man said to me, " I have two rich neighbours, who come to me and give me money. One visits me very seldom, and then he enters my house without knocking, and sits down, with his hat on his head and his cigar in his mouth, and after he has lectured me and preached to me, as though I were a ticket-of-leave man, he takes a shilling out of his purse, and presents it, as though it were a golden guinea. I'm very, very poor, but sometimes

I almost wish he would not come. The other gentleman enters my mean home uncovered, and thanks me when I offer him a chair, and he talks as freely and cheerily as though we were equals, and speaks words of comfort and of hope; and then he presses money into my hand with a smile, as though I were doing him a favour—and I am doing him a favour, bless his generous heart! for I cannot recompense him, but he shall be recompensed at the resurrection of the just."

Rough men have rough ways of showing their gratitude. The story is well known of the sick man, who promised the priest that his first act of thankfulness, on leaving his sick-room, would be to "poach him a little rabbit," but a far more remarkable manifestation was made to a friend of mine, when he was located in Lancashire among the miners. He was in his study on a Saturday night, when a visitor was announced, and there entered one of his subterranean parishioners, who having cautiously looked round to see that there were no listeners, addressed his clergyman with an air of grave, mysterious importance: "Mestur Whitworth, you've been very kind to my ould girl, when she wor sick so long abed, and I want to do yer a good turn, and I can do yer a good turn. There's going to be the gradliest dog-fight in this place to-morrow, and I can get yer *into th' inner ring!*"

There are many more instances, not more hearty, but of a much higher tone, of the good

will of working men towards those who really care
for them. A stable, which had been converted into
a place for worship and instruction by the clergy
of one of our University Missions (of which I hope
to speak hereafter in their connection with the
labouring class), suddenly collapsed into a wreck.
There were no funds for rebuilding, and the disappointment was very sad, until one evening a
deputation of working men called at the Clergy
House, and offered to build a new Mission-room,
by working over hours, if the material could be
supplied. Their zealous self-denial was joyfully
appreciated, the money was found, and a most con-
venient and commodious room was erected, several
of the workers contributing articles of furniture,
as well as giving their time.

In a midland county, a number of miners came
to their vicar, and announced to him that, hearing
he would lose fifty pounds of his income in consequence of the death of the gentleman who had
paid it, they had determined, at a meeting recently
held, to subscribe that sum, and he would receive
it in regular instalments.

The shoemakers at Northampton built the Church
of St. Crispin, with the aid of their friends; and I
preached not long ago in a church, within three
miles of our cathedral, in which the carved altar
and stalls were made by ship-carpenters, and a
beautiful font was presented by subscriptions from
children of the working classes.

I cannot omit another singular expression of gratitude, though it is but slightly connected with the preceding theme. An old Oxford friend, who had a living in Worcestershire, was visiting his parishioners, when one of them, an old woman, informed him that since they met "she'd gone through a sight o' trouble. Her sister was dead, and there wor a worse job than that; the pig died all of a sudden, but it pleased the Lord to tak' 'im, and they mun bow, they mun bow." Then the poor old lady brightened up and said, "But there's one thing, Mestur Allen, as I can say, and ought to say: the Lord's been pratty well on my side this winter for greens!" Some may be surprised to hear that this woman meant to be, and was, sincerely religious. She was very fond of her sister, and only referred to the temporary loss, which was to her most deplorable, and which sorely tried but could not overcome her spirit of resignation. I need scarcely add that in saying the Lord had been on her side, she was using the Psalmist's words, or that all the green things upon the earth are as much His gift, Who openeth His Hand and filleth all things living with plenteousness, as the bread which strengthens, and the wine which gladdens, man's heart.

As different as a painted plaster of Paris peach to a "Royal George" was the sham religion of another old lady in my parish, which she used rather as a cloak for her maliciousness than as a robe of righteousness. She made great professions of charity, but was always quarrelling with her neighbours. She had much of the spirit of that preaching Ranter, who declared that " he loved everybody, but if the Lord had a thunderbolt to spare he thought it would be well bestowed on brother Gubbins's head." She came to me one morning as I was going to church, and said, " Mister Rennuds, I've got another lift towards 'eaven. Willises " (who lived next door) " has been telling more lies—blessed are the persecuted ! "

Apropos of Ranters, I cannot say, after an experience of more than half a century, that they were much believed in outside their own community. The Wesleyans were always and highly esteemed, but " the Primitives " were bumptious, self-righteous, and bitter enemies of the Church. Not satisfied with their own meeting-house and open-air assemblies hard by, they selected a vacant space within a few yards of our church for their resonant repetitions, until one of our churchwardens was suddenly seized by an irrepressible desire that three of his farming men should learn the art of bell-ringing, and sent them off at once for their first lesson—and their last ; for the Ranters ranted there no more !

We had our village demagogue, who told our inhabitants that all kings and lords were thieves and knaves, that I received a thousand pounds a year (I was at that time curate, and my income was a hundred pounds), and that I was a particular friend of the Pope. He left the church and went to the chapel, left the chapel and went nowhere, except to the public-house. There he had a very small following of malcontents, who objected to manual labour, and preferred a division of property. Sometimes he suggested abuses which were injurious, and reforms which were right and wise, and so made some compensation for the harm which was done by his lies; but his main object seemed to be to vituperate squires and parsons. The latter especially could do nothing that was right. If they took an interest in social, political, sanitary, or parochial matters, he bade them mind their own business. If they complied with his request and restricted their attention to their ecclesiastical duties, "they cared nothing for the public weal." So far as he was concerned, a clergyman resembled a certain flying-fish, on which the albatross descends, if he leaves the water, and the dolphin pounces, when he returns to the sea. I was pleased to hear that one evening, when he had been exercising his hobby, and had declaimed against the peers and the priests as living in luxury upon the industry of the sons of toil, our village blacksmith remarked " that he shouldn't care to be the particular nobleman or clergyman who lived upon his (the speaker's) earnings; he wouldn't be a fat un!"

We had our village artist. He painted the sign of the Spread Eagle, which the rustics described as " the Split Crow," and the White Lion, which they called " the Prancing Cat." It was told of a brother

artist in the neighbourhood, that this white lion
was the only picture he could paint, and that a
sailor who came home and, having saved a little
money, took a public-house in his native place, went
to consult him as to a sign. The painter, after a
preliminary intimation that he was thoroughly
master of all subjects, suggested, as a friend, that
there was nothing in the whole range of his reper-
-toire which seemed to fascinate the public, to win
their admiration, and make them feel thirsty, so
quickly and completely as a white lion. The sailor
replied that he had been to several countries, but
had never met the animal in question, and did not
care to make his acquaintance. He would rather
have a ship. The artist explained that although a
ship was in every way respectable, and a most
desirable thing on the sea, it was incapable of giving
any satisfaction on the land, and would be generally
avoided. If the sailor wished to succeed, and to
have his house full instead of empty, he must not be
led away by his old fancies, but must consider the
wish of his customers; and that which they loved
the best was a white lion. Jack would not be convinced. He applied epithets to the white lion,
which were abusive, if not profane. He went so
far as to doubt the existence of this white king of
beasts, as when Mrs. Gamp remarked of Mrs.
Harris, that she " didn't believe there was no such
person." He would rather endure the dislocation
of his members, or, as he expressed it nautically,

the shivering of his timbers, than have that humbug over his front door. The unhappy artist saw that it was vain to persevere ; but he too had a will of his own, and that will was to paint the sign, and be paid for it. He proposed a compromise. "You're a very obstinate man," he said, " and you'll be sorry for it. Of course you can have a ship if nothing else will suit you, and I shall paint you a ship, but —*it will be more like a white lion.*"

The association of the sailor with the inn brings me another remembrance, which, as Pepys would say, " mightily pleased " my sense of humour. I went to preach to the members of a Friendly Society in a village on the banks of the Trent, and afterwards dined with them. The chairman went through the usual routine of toasts, but when " The Army, Navy, and Auxiliary Forces " were proposed, there seemed to be no representative of the two former professions. There was a consultation of the brethren, and it was finally determined that the landlord of the Lord Raglan Arms should return thanks for the army, and that a bargee from the river hard by should express the gratitude of her Majesty's navy.

I would note here the gradual and gratifying change, which has been wrought by a better education, by common sense, and by the temperance societies, in the conduct of these social gatherings. Drunkenness was the rule, now it is the exception. I recall the time—it was the time when the tipsy labourer, returning from feast to farm, and followed by a bull, which he did not see, " booing " behind him, and, on his arrival at the boundary of the field, pushing him with his head into the ditch, indignantly exclaimed, as he lay prostrate, " You may be a musician, but you're no gentleman "—a time when the members of these institutions seemed to think that they were bound to make beasts of themselves, and to prove their claim to the title, which in those days was commonly given to their community, of " the Sick Club." I have seen them, years ago, staggering and reeling to and fro, and sighed, " Oh that man should put an enemy into his mouth to steal away his brains ! " degrade his manhood, and defile his soul; but on the last occasions in which I was cognizant of their proceedings, I saw no drunken man.

Happier still the transformation in our harvest festivals, the cessation of that gross ingratitude which insulted the Giver by the abuse of His gifts, and the gathering together of rich and poor in their Father's house, to praise Him who is the Maker of them all, for the fulfilment of His promise that seedtime and harvest shall never cease. Nevertheless, this service, though it is very meet, right, and our bounden duty, should not deprive those who have borne the burden and heat of the day, of their annual entertainment, their roast beef and plum-pudding, their glass of good ale, their pipe, and their song and jubilation, " within the limits of becoming mirth." They have found out, most of them, that it is possible to be merry and wise. Something better still, that without this wisdom, which cometh from above, " even in laughter the heart is sorrowful ; and the end of that mirth is heaviness."

"The old giveth place to the new," and sometimes one views this exit with a sigh, as when the parish stocks were removed to my grounds to be kept as a memorial, there being no further use for them, though they had brought many a drunkard, many a rogue, to shame. The old penfold is broken down. I should hope that the belief in witchcraft has died out ; it existed but a few years ago. A man who seemed perfectly sane assured me continually that he was bewitched by a woman in the village, who persecuted him at night, and, though he bolted his door, " *used to come and yark the clothes off his bed.*" *

One ancient and wholesome custom is still in force, " the riding of the stang," commonly abbreviated into " Rang-tang." If a man is known to have ill-treated his wife, a band of performers on penny trumpets, horns, old kettles, pokers, and fire-shovels, meet under his bedroom window at night, and serenade him with derisive verses, of which I have no copy.

* In the beginning of the seventeenth century two women were burnt at Lincoln for witchcraft, confessing that they had familiar spirits, and it is not a hundred and fifty years since Ruth Osborn was drowned in a horsepond by the mob at Tring, in the belief that she was a witch.

That expressive monosyllable " yark " evokes my sad regret that many of our rural words, some of them older than the language of a more refined society, are in danger of extinction from the higher criticism, and from those locomotive facilities which tend more and more to produce uniformity in manner and in speech. They may be coarse and dissonant to ears polite, but we who have heard them from childhood would not willingly let them die. For example, we had in our village a huge conceited sluggard, who went by the name of *Brawnging Billy*, who was much given to *gawster*, and to *lorp* about, *setting folks on the hig, slaring* his neighbours, and up to *noat* (nought) but mischief. He took to himself a wife, and it was soon manifest, to the joy of all, that " Billy had married his mestur, and she'd *gloppened* him a goodish bit." Again, is there not a concentrated essence, a condensed power, of suggestive description in the five letters *shack?* The shack is a man who objects to regular employment, but can and will do almost anything, except ordinary work. He prefers field sports, covert - beating, partridge or grouse driving, running with the hounds, opening gates, holding horses, acting as " supernumerary " in the cricket field, poaching, mowing and threshing, hoeing and weeding (in small doses), sheep-washing, hop-picking, carpet-beating, etc., etc. There is the man, in the country lane, leaning on the gate, and watching the run of that hare, for which he has a snare in one pocket, and the stock and barrel of a gun in the other. He is very sly and observant, but he does not know that he is watched by an under-keeper, who will come upon him some day, when he has the gun, or the snare, or the hare in his hand, and there will be no escape. It was an under-keeper, by the way, who gave me a rich vocabulary of Nottinghamshire words, in relating how that he had shot at a snipe in some boggy ground, but had caught his foot on a tuft of grass, when he was in the act of firing; that the gun flew out of his hands, and he had a heavy fall. "It *yarked* up, and *screeted*, and I *nipped* round, and *blazed*, but I catched my toe on a bit of a tussock, and she flew—I should think she flew thirty yards, and I come down *such a belper!*"

Shacks and poachers are not restricted to villages. They abound where men most do congregate, at the corners of the streets, in the clubs, and in the parks.

"*Bofen-yed*" and "*noggin-yed*" were terms applied to persons who were stupid and obtuse. "Yed" for "head," as when the Lancashire witness, badgered by a young barrister who wore a new wig and a *nez retroussé*, and falsely accused of having contradicted his own evidence, suddenly turned on the lawyer and exclaimed, "*Why, yer powder-yedded monkey, I never said nowt o' sort. I appeal to th' company.*"

The rustic is sometimes plain of speech. He has no scruples in saying to an invalid, "You're looking fine and ill;" and an old man will bellow into the ear of his deaf contemporary, " You're breaking very fast." " Well, Booth," a visitor said to his sick neighbour, " thee'd like to get better, wouldn't thee, Booth ? But thee mun dee, this whet." Their announcements startle now and then—" If you please, sir, the corpse is waiting ; " " If you please, sir, the corpse's brother would like to speak to you."

A village has generally its Mrs. Malaprop, the uneducated female who loves long words, whether rightly applied or not. She " thought it her duty to inform me, as them Browns was a conspirating to get rid of Sally's misfortune (baby) in as genteel a form as they could, and the poor little thing looked quite emancipated."

CHAPTER XVII.

Parochial incidents—Boring for coals—The traveller by the wayside, half dead—The village murder—The carrier's dog—
Visions of the night—Coincidences.

BEFORE I leave our village, I would refer to the few
crises of excitement which have lashed our little
pond into a sea. In my father's time it was confidently announced that there was a rich substratum
of coal in the parish, and Mr. Bristowe, the owner
of the hamlet of Beesthorpe, the head of an old
Nottinghamshire family, now honourably represented
by Judge Bristowe and his brother, Sir Henry, Vice-
Chancellor of the Duchy of Lancaster, was induced
by some plausible adventurer to employ a large body
of men on part of his estate in boring for the
precious mineral. The process went on week after
week, to the satisfaction of the chief conspirators,
one of whom, the clerk of the works, was ever
hopeful of proximate and prosperous results, but
failed to tranquillize his employer, who day by day
grew more and more doubtful, not only as to the
result of the undertaking, but as to the honesty of
those who advised it. It became evident that they

must find coal or go, and as they were in comfortable circumstances, they decided to find coal. One
of the miners was to bring a few small fragments of
the article in his pocket, on his return from dinner,
and, as soon as they saw Squire Bristowe approaching on his pony from the hall, the men were to
stand round the pit with ringing cheers of joy, and
he was to be welcomed with the glorious announcement, " We've found coal! "   Now, the squire,
though on this occasion his inclination had over-
powered his discretion, was a man of brains and
keen observation, and when he had closely scruti-
nized the sample put into his hand, he returned it
to the clerk of the works, and said, " I shall be the
richest man in all England. You have not only
discovered a mine of coal, *you have found a mine of
bread and cheese!* "   The conspirator who brought
the bits of coal in his pocket had not noticed that a
few small fragments from his luncheon were blended
with them, but they were quickly detected by a
readier wit and by a more piercing eye. Two hours
after this interview, not a man was to be seen upon
the spot.

Then came in my boyhood a tragedy, with a
strange *dénouement*, which made a deep impression
upon me. Two labourers going to their work at
daybreak on a summer's morning heard the most
pitiful moans and groans from a plantation which
adjoined the road, and looking into it they saw a
poor fellow tied with ropes to a tree, his head bound

with some dark material. They released him and uncovered his face, but he fell to the ground in a state of complete exhaustion and unable to utter a word. Seeing that there was no probability of his immediate recovery, one of them returned to the village, while the other remained with the sufferer, whose horror lest his assailants should return was painful to witness. Then a cart was brought, in which he was conveyed to the inn. Stimulants were administered, and he gradually regained the power to tell that, on his way to Newark the evening before, he had been attacked by three men, who had knocked him down, robbed him of his watch and all the money he possessed, and then, dragging him through a gap in the fence, had tied him with ropes to a tree, and had also fastened some sheets of brown paper round his head, cramming it in his mouth, and meaning, as he believed, to suffocate him; that he had succeeded, by rubbing his head against the tree, in loosening the paper so as to breathe a little more freely, but that he felt as though death was coming upon him when they arrived to rescue. He remained three weeks at the inn, receiving every attention, many of the parishioners coming to see him, and sending him presents of wine, jellies, and fruit; and when he was strong enough to continue his journey, a collection was made, which, after the payment of his expenses, left a balance of seven pounds in his favour. A few weeks after his departure, the subscribers were perturbed in spirit, as they read in the newspapers that the same performance had been successfully repeated in a distant part of the country, the only variation being the earlier exit of the hero, who thought it safer to make a more rapid recovery, and left the day after his discovery with £4 10s. in his pocket, and in high spirits, for the next murderous on-slaught.

Another catastrophe, which was a tragedy in-deed, occurred also in my boyhood. The village shop was kept by a widow, who sold, with other articles, laudanum and tincture of rhubarb. Through some sad mistake, she gave the poison instead of the medicine to a neighbour, whose husband was ill, and who came to her for the tincture. The man died, and his widow openly declared that she would have revenge. She had one son, a farm-labourer of weak intellect, but quite capable of self-control and of going about his business like other men. It was always believed that his mother urged him to do what he did, and many years after—for she lived to be an old woman—I felt convinced that she had a burden on her conscience, and quite expected her confession; but she died, and made no sign. Her son came back one night from a circus at Newark, with some other villagers, and, when he left his companions, went straight to the shop, broke through the door, and strangled the poor widow in her bed. I shall never forget seeing her next morning, for my father was from home, and, though I was but fourteen, I was sent for as his representative, turned a crowd of gossips out of the house, and despatched a messenger for the police. They found the poor widow's watch and money on the person of the murderer, who was at work in the fields, and he was tried, condemned, and hanged at Nottingham. A very pious lady in the neighbourhood visited him in prison, and sent him, with questionable taste, a white camellia on the morning of his execution, which he wore upon the scaffold!

About this time, and in the adjoining county of Lincoln, there occurred a far more remarkable tragedy, and I give the details as related to me by one who was then residing close to the scene of this sad, eventful history. Two sisters, who kept a toll-bar in the neighbourhood, both dreamed in the same night that an attempt was made to break into their house. They were greatly alarmed, and as the next day wore on they confided their fear to a carrier returning from the market at Stamford. He lent them a large dog, which always accompanied his cart as a guard; but the animal got away soon after his master had left, and rejoined him on the road. The carrier had been so impressed by the nervous anxiety of the two women that he left his conveyance in the care of his passengers, returned, and, taking off his outer coat and placing it on the floor close to the window, he bade the dog watch, and said, "He'll stay with you now until I come again." In the middle of the night they heard a noise outside, and, silently leaving their beds, they escaped through the back door into a side lane, and hurried to the nearest dwelling, then occupied by a blacksmith. He was not at home, but his wife gave the poor creatures shelter, and soon after sunrise the trio went back to the toll-bar. There they saw a strange sight—the lower part of a man's figure outside the window, the upper part being evidently in a stooping position within the house. The form was motionless, and when, accompanied by some labourers who were going to their work, they entered the apartment, they found that the burglar had forced open the window, and that, as soon as he had thrust in his head and shoulders, the dog had seized him by the throat and held him until he died. The dead man was the husband of one of the three women—the blacksmith!

Are these dreams coincidences only, imaginations, sudden recollections of events which had been long forgotten? They are marvellous, be this as it may. In a crisis of very severe anxiety I required information which only one man could give me, and he was in his grave. I saw him distinctly in a vision of the night, and his answer to my question told me all I wanted to know; and when, having obtained the clearest proof that what I had heard was true, I communicated the incident and its results to my solicitor, he told me that he himself had experienced a similar manifestation. A claim was repeated after his father's death, which had been resisted in his lifetime and retracted by the claimant, but the son was unable to find the letter in which the retractation was made. He dreamed that his father appeared and told him that it was in the left-hand drawer of a certain desk. Having business in London, he went up to the offices of his father, an eminent lawyer, but could not discover the desk, until one of the clerks suggested that it might be among some old lumber placed in a room upstairs. There he found the desk and the letter!

Then, as regards coincidence, are there not events in our lives which come to us with a strange mysterious significance, a prophetic intimation, sometimes of sorrow, and sometimes of success? For example, I lived a hundred and fifty miles from Rochester. I went there, for the first time, to preach at the invitation of one who was then unknown to me, but is now a dear friend. After the sermon I was his guest in the Precincts. Dean Scott died in the night, almost at the time in which he who was to succeed him arrived at the house which adjoins the Deanery. There was no expectation of his immediate decease, and no conjecture as to a future appointment, and yet, when I heard the tolling of the cathedral bell, I had a presentiment that Dr. Scott was dead, and that I should be Dean of Rochester.

CHAPTER XVIII.

GAMBLERS.

My first experience—Fallen among thieves—Gambling at
Oxford—Suicides, abroad and at home—Racing and
betting—Results—Remedies—*Principiis obsta*—Power of
example.

I HAD a very early and startling experience in the
matter of gambling. Before my father had decided
whether he would buy me a commission in the army
or send me to Oxford, he thought it desirable that I
should make " the grand tour," as it was then called,
through France, Italy, etc. ; and as I was then but
a stripling of eighteen, without experience, I was
to be accompanied to Paris by a dear old German
gentleman, who was compelled in his adversity to
leave Fatherland, and had established himself as a
teacher of languages in the little town near my
home. He was to remain with me a month in
Paris, and then I was to go on alone. As the time
of our separation drew near, and I had discovered
that my ability to translate a few French fables and
the easier portions of Telemachus did not empower
me to converse with the natives, I began to dread

aud lament my silent loneliness in a strange land, and I advertised in *Galignani* for a companion. A bright, good-looking young English gentleman called on me on the following day to say that he proposed to follow the same route, and should be thankful to have a fellow-traveller. He had been for some time in Paris, and could speak French fluently. I went with him to his hotel in the Place Vendôme, and we were there joined by two of his friends, both bearing, like himself, honourable names, but older men and less attractive in appearance. We strolled about the Champs Élysées, and it was proposed that we should enter a shooting-gallery and have some pistol practice, at which they seemed to be adepts. In the evening we dined at the Trois Frères in the Palais Royal, and afterwards adjourned for coffee to the Place Vendôme. *Vingt-un* was suggested, and, as the stakes were to be small, and I suspected no evil, I sat down to play. Gradually the stakes rose in amount; the success of the two senior competitors rose with it (the junior kindly accompanied me in my losses); and their supernatural agility in dealing themselves aces and tens first evoked an impression, and then, as I watched, a conviction, that I had fallen among thieves. I declined to play longer, and, asking each of the winners "how much he *said* I owed him," put the sums down, amounting together to over £300, in my note-book. Then one of them, assuming an air of virtuous indignation, inquired what I meant by "said." And he was evidently astonished, and I have been ever since astonished, at my coolness in replying, "What I mean is this. I shall make inquiries to-morrow whether there is any ground for my suspicion that the money has not been honestly won, and shall act accordingly." There was a good deal of bluster about apologies and satisfaction (the pistol practice in the Champs Élysées was not without a purpose), and then the younger of the trio pressed me to leave, and offered to accompany me home. On our way to Meurice's he expressed a most affectionate sympathy, assuring me, at the same time, that I had made a deplorable mistake, which he knew I should acknowledge on reflection, his friends being members of distinguished families and men of undoubted honour. He reminded me that he had himself lost over a hundred pounds, and urged me to pay at once (he knew that I had the amount in circular notes), promising, if I would so do, to appease the righteous wrath of the receivers. Then he left me, and the latter part of the journey to my hotel was a very gloomy proceeding. I might be wrong after all, and then to ask pardon and go back to England moneyless was a vision which oppressed me with despair; and I have rarely known such a jubilant relief and reaction as when I met my German chaperon on my arrival, and he told me he had been sitting up in great anxiety, having received information, which he could not doubt, that I was in the hands of a lot of unscrupulous villains, whose rascalities were notorious to all Paris, though hitherto they had evaded the penalties of the law. We went next day to the Procureur du Roi, who received us most kindly, heard our statement with attentive sympathy, and then told us that he had listened to many similar accounts, that he knew all about these conspirators, but could not see his way to a prosecution, and that he advised me to take no further notice. I received no application from these genteel brigands. I met one of them a few days after, making his promenade, his rogue's march, through the streets, and, after a brief but brisk exchange of incivilities, we parted, and I saw him no more. On counting my loose money, I found that, as we had left off payment in coin when the stakes were raised, and had used counters, I was a richer man by a dinner and a few francs than when I left my hotel. They must have experienced that profound dejection which comes to the angler when the fish nibbles off his bait; and it must have been a long and bitter recollection that a raw lad from the country had dined at their expense!

My next experience was at Oxford. There was no cheating, but gambling did great harm. We can say, all of us, without compunction, " We have heard the chimes at midnight, Master Shallow;" but they who have wasted the after-hours on cards and dice, champagne, cigars, in anxious and sometimes angry excitement, must recall them with regret and shame. There were many instances, moreover, in which it might be said of gambling, that "it separateth very friends;" and I have seen the sad estrangement of those who had been long and affectionately attached, because one had lost to the other a sum which he could not pay.

Since those Oxford days, I have seen, as any man may see, the results of gambling, in estates heavily mortgaged, ancestral homes sold or let to strangers, or desolate and empty—

> "No human footstep stirs to go or come,
>   No face looks out from street or open casement,
> No chimney smokes, there is no sign of home
>   From parapet to basement"—

in incomes reduced one half by payments to life insurance companies, to secure sums borrowed for gambling debts; in quarrels between fathers and sons; in the exile of impoverished families to countries where they can live more cheaply; in the flight of those who have robbed their employers to foreign lands, where the runagates continue in scarceness, unless they are caught by the police; in hundreds of youths who have taken money from the till and cash-box, who have embezzled, and made false entries, and forged, because they have gambled and lost.

In suicides. Again and again we read in our newspapers, "Suicide of a Betting Man." The number who commit self-slaughter at Monte Carlo is exaggerated, but it is a long and gruesome list. The last time I was in the neighbourhood, the purser from a Russian man-of-war came ashore, and won a few napoleons; came again, and lost; came, and lost more and more; appropriated some of the " ship's " money, lost it, and shot himself dead.*

A young man was boasting, on the rail between Monte Carlo and Nice, that he had won thirty golden coins, when an old man quietly remarked, " I am glad they were not silver, or they might have suggested the price of blood."

Rather more than two years ago, the senior verger of the cathedral at Rochester was talking to my butler at the entrance to the Deanery grounds, when they heard a strange, gasping, gurgling sound, from Gundulph's Tower hard by. They looked in, and saw, with horror, a man hanging, and nigh unto death. He was cut down, and, when sufficiently restored, was taken in charge by the police. I saw him next morning in the cells of the station, and a more miserable object never stirred the soul with pity. It was long before he could answer my inquiry, what had driven him to do this desperate deed ? but at last he said, " *Gambling and drink.*"

Racing will not harm a man any more than a rubber of whist. I would subscribe to races, and go to view them, over the flat or the fences, and rejoice

* The latest, and one of the saddest, of these terrible records is that of the American heiress, who, having lost the whole of her fortune, 250,000 dollars, on Monday, September 12, 1892, returned from the Casino to her residence at Ventimiglia, and was found dead next morning, shot through the heart with a revolver, which was lying beside her.

to see working men on a Bank Holiday enjoy the
sport, if I could be assured that the best horse would
win, that knaves and harlots would be warned off
the course, and that drunken men would be taken
away and whipped.   Neither the race nor the
rubber are hurtful, until they become secondary and
subservient to that love of money which is the root
of all evil, and has nowhere a more abundant crop
of its rank, vile produce than on our English *Turf*.
A man who loves racing for its own sake may be as
much *sans peur et sans reproche,—integer vitæ scelerisque
purus*, as the best of preachers, but as soon as the
greed of gain has the mastery, and he loves the
chink of the gold and the rustle of the crisp bank-
notes more than he cares for the horses, and the
honour, and the sport, he begins to deteriorate.   I
know cases, as numerous as they are bad, of young
men, who could not do a mean action, and who disdained a lie, gradually lured by temptations, or
goaded by deceptions, to deviate from the straight
course; to say with Iago, "To be discreet and honest
is not safe," or, in the humbler language of the
vendor of apples, "If I must chate or be chated, why
raythur of the raythurest I'd raythur chate."   If
they resist and refuse, as so many honourable men
refuse, to take any unfair advantage, what security
have they that they will not be duped by others?
And if they are men of culture and refinement, must
they not be often disgusted (as Mr. Greville tells us
in his Memoirs that he was continually offended)

by their inevitable association with depraved, unscrupulous men ? And there are no men, the gaol chaplains tell us, whose conscience seems so seared, as it were with a hot iron, who are so hopelessly given over to a reprobate mind, as the habitual gambler and cheat. Some years ago, a visitor to the Sheffield Workhouse was surprised to see among the inmates an elderly woman whom he had formerly known in comfortable circumstances, and he said to the master, " That woman's son is earning at the present time about four pounds a week, and it is disgraceful that she should be here." The master went to the son, and expostulated with him as to his unfilial conduct. And this was the answer: " If you'd lost forty pounds on that cursed handicap, as I did last week, you'd be none so keen about maintaining other folks ! "

Gambling and cheating are doubtless as old as the other vices. I have seen, in the museum at Naples, the loaded dice which were brought from Pompeii, but their antiquity does not make them venerable ; and when we are told that youth must have its fling of these dice, we can only answer, as Talleyrand to the beggar, who said that he must live, that we fail to see the necessity. The fling may be finished at the end of the hangman's rope, and is always more perilous than any flight from the trapeze. It is wiser and kinder to tell youth that he will be safer and happier on terra firma, and to warn Phaeton in plain language as to the disastrous consequences of driving the sun. Let him have his four-in-hand, and his tandem, his hunters, his moor, his deer forest and salmon stream, if they come to him by inheritance, or he can afford to pay for them, and if his enjoyment of them does not interfere with the duties of his position and the work which is given him to do ; but let him be told plainly that he may lose all, if he is induced to gamble and bet. My father heard the owner of one of the best estates in the midland counties say, just before the St. Leger was run, " Now, it's lands or no lands" (I substitute this word for the name of the property), and a few minutes later it was " no lands." And yet you will hear it said, that " a man has a right to do what he will with his own," as if there could be any *right* in breaking up happy homes, bringing in the auctioneer to scatter their heirlooms and their ancient and modern treasures among the brokers, pauperizing their children, to enrich those who will exult in their ruin, and gloat over the last notes which they could pay.

I would that youth could have a few object-lessons ; that apprentices and clerks who are tempted to gamble and bet could visit those who, having lost more money than they could pay, have been detected in pilfering and false entries, and could hear their regretful admonitions ; and that young men of property could see, as they might see in every English county, the comparative results of reckless gambling and of a rational economy—the evil which is done in a neighbourhood among tenants and poor folks, the dreary, dilapidated farmsteads, the impoverished soil, the broken fences and gates, which there is no capital to renew; and the substantial buildings, the well-cultured fields, the neat cottages, of the owner who cares not only for himself but others, and who recognizes his responsibilities, as a steward who must render an account.

What else can we do to expel or restrain this evil spirit, which inflicts such degradation and distress? *Principiis obsta.* Rebuke, repress, the first signs of an inclination to covet and desire other men's goods, to be enriched at the expense of others, to receive without giving, to reap where we have not strawed. They are sparks, which, if they are not extinguished, will kindle a conflagration. You may take a wasp's nest with a squib, but a ton of dynamite will be useless when the grubs are hatched and gone. You may uproot a young thistle with a spade, but who can calculate the harm when it has flowered and run to seed? Habitual gambling becomes an infatuation. I can vouch for the following illustration, and know the names of the persons referred to. One of them had a marvellous success in all games of chance, but refrained, on principle, from playing for money. The other was possessed by the fascination of gambling. They had dined together, and the latter signified his intention of going to the tables. He had already lost a large amount of money, and his friend earnestly endeavoured, but all in vain, to dissuade him. Finally, he consented to accompany him, on the condition that if he won five hundred pounds he would return home. This he accomplished, following the directions of his "lucky" friend, and they came back together. At breakfast the next morning, he who had given, congratulated him who had followed the advice, and expressed the hope that he would keep his winnings and run no further risk. He was perplexed to see that his words were received in silence, and without a smile, but the mystery was quickly dispelled by the dolorous confession, " I'm awfully ashamed, but I must tell you that when you were in bed I could not resist the temptation to go back to the tables, and I lost not only all I had won, but another five hundred pounds also." As the prophet wrote, men are " mad upon their idols," and to-day, as when he wrote, more than two thousand years ago, men make this very madness an excuse for sin—" I was mad with drink, mad with excitement, mad with rage; " but of all insane idolatries there is not one which seems to have such hopeless, absolute, irresistible control, as that of gambling for money.

Wherefore, begin with boyhood, and despise not the day of small things. Let boys be taught that there is something contemptible, and unworthy of a gentleman, to be hankering after money which does not belong to them, which they cannot gain without inflicting loss and pain upon others, and that games which do not interest them unless their object is money, are not worth playing at all. It seems a severe restriction to forbid the smallest stakes. I once thought it unnecessary and absurd, but I have been convinced by argument and reflection that it is the wisest and kindest rule ; and, after all, the players are just as happy without them, and the thought of winning money would never have occurred to their mind, had it not been suggested to them. *L'appétit vient en mangeant,* and the desire to win pennies may develop into a craving for pounds. I should never have been involved in the misadventure which befell me at Paris, had I not played *vingt-un* for lesser sums at home. It has been said that it is silly to denounce those who play only for stamps and pence, that in the large majority of cases no harm has come, that some of the worthiest men and women we have known have enjoyed for years their sixpenny points ; but I think now that, for the sake of those in whom the first taste may produce insatiate thirst, I would have *no* playing for money. I have little faith in legal restraints, much in the power of example. The nobility copy the court, the squires and other magnates copy the nobility, the working classes their employers, children their parents.

These are wise human precautions, but, after all, the only sure safeguard is the spiritual conviction that our minds and bodies, our money, our nights and days, are given to us for a nobler purpose than the gratification of mere selfish instincts ; that the first lessons which we learned were the best—" not to covet nor desire other men's goods, but to learn and labour truly to get our own living, and to do our duty in that state of life unto which it shall please God to call us."   " Ah, my lady," the Scotch girl said, when she was pleading with the queen for her sister's life, "it's nae what we've done for self, but what we've done for others, that'll make us happy when we come to die."   " Lockhart," said he who recorded these touching words, Sir Walter Scott, just before he died, " be virtuous, be religious ; nothing else can bring you peace at the last."

CHAPTER XIX.

The love of flowers innate—Children's gardens—Flora forsaken for Pomona—The love and practical knowledge of horticulture should be encouraged and instructed—Allotments—Schools for gardeners—Window-plants.

Is it the dim innate remembrance of Paradise lost, or is it the bright inspired hope of Paradise regained, which makes our childhood so happy among the flowers of the garden and the field ? The sunny bank on which we found the first violets, white and blue; those favoured plots in the great wood which were the homes of the primrose; the pastures where we made the daisy chain and cowslip ball; the grassy lanes with their huge hedges of wild roses (stubbed up now, to make way for the model farm); the pond which, surrounded by marsh-mallows, looked like a mirror in a golden frame; the brook which flowed by the red campion and the white meadow-sweet, with the blue forget-me-not beneath— all these are present as vividly to my imagination as, more than sixty years ago, to my eye. Do any forget, who have ever known, these blissful hours in the groves and in the meadows by the stream ?   A lady, whom I know, took a fresh posy of primroses into a miserable attic in Whitechapel, and placed them on a table, by which sat a poor creature, from whom sin, and disease, and want seemed to have taken away all trace of womanhood. She looked at them for a few seconds with a stupid stare of apathy, and then suddenly they suggested some thought which seemed to thrill through her, like a galvanic shock, and she burst into tears, " tears from the depths of some divine despair, while thinking of the days that are no more." The flowers spoke to her of a time when she was joyful in her innocence, and she might have said to them as Burns to the banks and braes of Doon—

> " Ye mind me of departed joys,
>   Departed never to return."

" He that is without sin among you, let him first cast a stone at her." Who recalls those days, and scenes, and companions, without some sad regrets, without Job's prayer, " Oh that I were as in months past ! Thou writest bitter things against me "—the recollection of disobedience to those who loved us dearly as their lives, unkindness to those who were younger or weaker than ourselves ?

> " And by the brook, and in the glade,
>   Are all our wanderings o'er?
> Oh, while my brother with me stayed,
>   Would I had loved him more ! "

But the gladness of our hope expels the sadness

of the fear—the hope that once again, as little children, gazing on such beauty as eye hath not seen, and listening to such music as ear hath not heard, we shall rejoice in the eternal sunshine of our Heavenly Father's love.

Returning from the woods and the fields, we find those dear little gardens at home wherein we planted the twig, and were annoyed next morning to see no signs of foliage; sowed the melon seed, and were disappointed because, unlike Jonah's gourd, it grew not up in a night. The doll's house (the door of which occupied the entire frontage, the architect having forgotten the stairs) stood centrally at the upper end of our domain, representing the family mansion; " the gardener," a tin soldier in full uniform with fixed bayonet, spent most of his time lying on his stomach, his form being fragile and the situation windy; and the fishponds were triumphs of engineering skill. Mine was a metal pan, which had been formerly used for culinary purposes, placed in an excavation prepared for it, and containing a real fish, about the size of a white-bait, and caught by hand in the brook hard by. One of my sisters produced, I must confess, a more brilliant effect with some bits of looking-glass, but they lacked the gracefulness of nature and the charm of reality. The grotto, an oyster-barrel placed on its side, and tastefully ornamented with broken pieces of ivy and other evergreens, contained the wives of Noah, Shem, Ham, and Japhet, taken from our ark, and attended by a dog, a cat, and a parrot. They remained in a perpendicular position night and day, and had a fine effect. The former inmates of their bower, the oyster-shells, were also present on our parterres, for ornamental and, as in Lord Macaulay's history, for territorial purposes. There is nothing in his biography more delightful than the record how, when his sister had been rearranging the boundaries and readjusting the shells, he rushed into the house, exclaiming, "Cursed be Sally! cursed be he that removeth his neighbour's landmark!" The conservatory was a noble structure adjoining the family mansion, but of larger dimensions—a square hand-glass, which looked as though it had been in a phenomenal hailstorm, and had only one qualification for plant culture, a free circulation of air.

I dwell upon these adjuncts to horticulture rather than upon the produce of the soil, because in the latter department we did not attain a like success. We were not on the best of terms with our gardener—the real gardener, not the tin soldier—and he would not help us. Our ways (over the flower-beds) were not his ways, and he objected to the promiscuous use of his syringe and the premature removal of his fruit. We differed, again, on the subject of transplanting. It seemed to us an easier and more satisfactory process to transfer specimens in full beauty from his garden to our own, rather than to watch their tardy growth and tedious efflorescence. Unhappily for us, the specimens themselves did not seem to like it, and we were finally forbidden by parental authority to continue our importations.

We obeyed cheerfully, for we loved the flowers, though we had erred as to their treatment—loved them from the first snowdrop to the last Christmas rose, from the flowering trees and shrubs to the " bachelor's buttons" and "fairy" roses, which almost rested on the soil.

" The child is father to the man," and I, to whom was granted in after years the privilege of suggesting and organizing the First National Rose Show, presided in my childhood at a floral exhibition, of which my little sister was the general and executive committee. A few petals of pansies, roses, etc., were spread upon paper and covered with the largest pieces of broken glass which we could find (the idea was taken from dried flowers in an old scrap-book), and then, when the edges of the paper were turned over the glass, we called it a " Flower Show," and the servants said it was " beautiful ! "

Dear also to our happy hearts were the trees of the garden, the tree in which was the swing (who does not remember the first mingled sensations of joy and terror which accompanied him to and fro ?), and the two trees of weeping ash, which, surrounding us on all sides with their boughs drooping to the ground, made for us " here, in cool grot," a charming summer-house. Here we kept our Feast of Tabernacles, jubilant as those children of Israel who, more than three thousand years ago, dwelt in booths in the feast of the seventh month, and who, a thousand years later, in the days of Nehemiah, went forth into the mount and fetched olive branches, and pine branches, and myrtle branches, and palm branches, and branches of thick trees, and made themselves booths, every one upon the roof of his house, and in their courts, and in the courts of the house of God, and there was very great gladness.

These umbrageous retreats were transformed at the will of our childish fancy, as swiftly as the scenes of a pantomime by the touch of Harlequin's wand. Sometimes they were palaces and castles of the nobility, and the marchioness would go in state on the top of a wheelbarrow, filled with mown grass from the lawn and propelled by an under-gardener, and would be graciously received by the duchess dwelling under her palm tree like Deborah, and would be hospitably entertained with surreptitious black currants, served on a cabbage-leaf, or with clandestine toffy from the village shop. The finger-ends and mouths of the nobility after one of these interviews were remarkably rich in colour, and might have evoked the jealousy of the rosy-fingered Morn and of Phyllis with "lips crimson red." To be accurate, they only evoked the wrathful expostulations of nurse, with unpleasant allusions to the prevalence of cholera, and to the marvellous merits of castor oil.

Sometimes these arboric abodes were the dens and lairs of fierce brigands (my younger sisters as reprobate villains, with corked eyebrows and moustaches, were a sight to make your blood run cold), and the under-nurse, dragging with difficulty a garden-roller over the gravel, and supposed to be a merchant of enormous wealth, conveying bullion to the bank, was robbed, and fled for his life. Sometimes the woman who weeded was startled to hear a sweet treble voice demanding, " Your money or your life!" On one occasion she looked up, and answered, " Oh, Miss 'Lisbuth, what a Guy Faux you be!" Sometimes a lovely princess imprudently sauntered within a few yards of the robber's cave; the tenant emerged armed to the teeth with the garden-shears, and intending prompt decapitation, but fell in love with his victim, and, throwing away the shears, went down on his knees, proposed, and, with that slight bashful hesitation which befitted the brevity of their acquaintance and the disparity of their social position, was affectionately accepted.

Sometimes these sylvan homes were supposed to be the head-quarters of the English and French armies, the tents of the two commanders-in-chief. A sentinel, armed with a rake, walked backwards and forwards in front of the British encampment. At intervals his Grace the Duke of Wellington, arrayed in a cocked hat and sword belonging to an old court dress, came out with a long telescope (parasol) and anxiously surveyed the enemy's position about fifteen yards in front. Napoleon followed his example, and gazed intently from time to time, through a roll of music, on the English lines. The soldiers on guard occasionally varied their monotonous exercise by exchanging their weapons for musical instruments, the French contingent performing on a drum, and the English on a penny trumpet. These warlike preparations and sounds of defiance were quickly followed by a general engagement. The flower of the French army (sister No. 2) was slain to a girl, and the unhappy Napoleon, having been freely prodded with a pea-rod by the heroic Wellington, sought refuge among the rhododendrons.

I must acknowledge sadly, that at an early age, soon after my promotion from frock to jacket, I forsook my first love, Flora, and the Naiades and Dryads, for Pomona; and, in my boyhood and early youth, even in the groves of Academus and on the slopes of Parnassus, I ceased to woo.

But why—descending to common sense from Olympus—why is not a more anxious, practical endeavour made in our schools and colleges to encourage this love of the beautiful, and this knowledge of the useful, by teaching horticulture? I maintain that such an instruction would add largely to the comforts and enjoyments of our community. The majority of our boys and girls will some day have a garden of their own, and under our present *régime* they will take possession of it without knowing when to sow a seed, where to plant trees, shrub, or flower, or how to cook a potato. Beginning with those who have the more extensive domains, I speak that which I know, namely, that nineteen men out of twenty are absolutely at the mercy of their gardeners. They have no notion how much produce they might expect, or when it should be forthcoming. They dare not complain, lest they should expose their ignorance. They either employ more labour than they need, or the auxiliary force is inadequate. They either expect to have everything which they admire elsewhere, or they survey it with abject despair. They come home from a flower show, and express their desire and intention to have the same roses which they have seen at the Crystal Palace, Sir Trevor Lawrence's orchids, Mr. Barr's narcissus, Mr. Turner's carnations, Mr. Laing's begonias, without further notice; or they have been present at some great banquet, and, on their return, request to be supplied in the future with Jersey pears and "Cannon Hall" Muscats.

To those of smaller means and measurements, a knowledge of flowers, vegetables, and fruits, suitable soils and manures, multiplying, training, and pruning, would not only suggest peaceful, restful hours of happy employment, but also an economic and delectable improvement in the variety and quality of their daily food. Where there is adaptation and careful culture, where the best kinds are in the soil and in the situation most favourable to their growth, they attain an excellence and an abundance incredible to those who have not seen it. And so it may be said of the art of horticulture, more truly, I think, than of any other, that it not only elevates and refines—"*emollit mores, nec sinit esse feros*"—but brings substantial benefits to the body as well as to the mind.

Nor are these advantages restricted to the upper and middle classes. " Nature never did betray the heart that loved her," whether the proprietor be peasant or peer. There are no better gardeners, no men who know better what to grow and how to grow it, no men who produce more things pleasant to the eye and good for food from their gardens, than those Nottingham mechanics who have their small plots of ground and tiny greenhouses just outside the town; and in many parts of the country you may find examples of the same enthusiasm, crowned with the same success—examples which might be multiplied a hundred-fold if there were more encouragement and more accessible instruction.

By all means let the working man have his allotment of land for pasture, for corn, for orchard, and garden, but let him be taught at the same time how to make the best of it. What is the good of giving a man a flute, if you do not teach him how to play it ? Tell the poor man how to grow vegetables and fruit, and his wife how to cook and preserve them, and the rich man to help both, starting them with a few good trees and seeds, and requesting his gardener to give occasional advice, and you will deserve and win the gratitude of your fellow-men.

Youths who propose to make horticulture their vocation should of course have a special training; and a scheme which emanates from the Royal Horticultural Society, for their technical education in gardening and spade industry, deserves general sympathy and support. The promoters of this laudable enterprise invite a more general recognition of the importance of fruit culture, and the further development of gardening, together with the more careful and scientific treatment of small holdings, as a practical reply to the problem, " What is to be done with the land? " And in order to realize their design, they propose to establish " a British School of Gardening, where lads from fifteen to eighteen years of age may receive a thoroughly practical training in all the details of their crafts, together with such simple elementary scientific instruction as may be sufficient to enable them to take an intelligent interest in the manifold operations of nature, with which their after-life will be concerned. With these objects they intend to furnish a house at Chiswick, in the immediate neighbourhood of the gardens of the Royal Horticultural Society, for the reception of students; to appoint fitting persons as instructors and lecturers;

and to establish classes for the practical teaching of the Craft of Gardening and Spade Husbandry in the Society's gardens. To carry out this project, an initial sum of £1000 is required, with a further annual sum of £250 for three years, after which the school should become self-supporting."

Might not some such institutions be established at different centres, in proximity to those large cities and towns in which there would be a profitable market for their produce ; and why should not schools and colleges, which consume such a vast amount of vegetables, supply their own necessities, and over the entrance of a grand garden, in which horticulture should be exemplified in all its branches, write, " *Omne tulit punctum qui miscuit utile dulci* " ?

These arguments and intentions are, of course, appropriate to that science of agriculture which is always of supreme importance to the welfare of a nation, and seems now to be in sore need of new developments. There is a comic, a serio-comic, element in the inheritance of a large estate by a gentleman who would be perplexed to distinguish between barley and oats, turnips and mangolds, who could not tell you approximately how many sacks of wheat should be grown per acre, who likes sand better than clay because it's better for rabbits —in a word, knows nothing whatever of the management of his own affairs. Some young men nowadays, who are heirs to broad lands, very wisely locate themselves for a season in the home of a clever farmer, and there learning how to buy and sell, how to breed and feed horses and cattle, sheep, pigs, and poultry, the wages and the ways of the labourer, draining, fallowing, manuring, sowing, reaping, threshing, laying down ploughed land in grass, marketing, the rotation of crops, and all other details, they find themselves masters of the situation when they succeed to their estates, take their part with a much deeper interest in their management, and, with regard to those in their employment, can distinguish the men who are doing their duty from those who are shirking it, and can accordingly reward or rebuke them. Honest men will respect, idle men will fear them, and they will not only get more work, but it will be better done. No servants will do their best for a master who cannot appreciate exertion nor detect inertness.

Thus finding new admirations in their gardens, and constant occupation on their estate, making their homes beautiful and their lives useful, they will not crave for excitements which can never sate, nor go in search of happiness, because it is already at their feet. I would entreat those fretful vagrants who run to and fro after contentment, like men looking for spectacles which rest upon the nose, and who are further from their object every step they take, to read " A Tour round my Garden," by Alphonse Karr, and try to see, as he did, some of the marvellous revelations of an infinite Power and Love, which are written everywhere, for those who have eyes to read.

The same principle of appreciation, which does the work that is given to every man, in the workshop where he is placed, and with the tools which he finds at hand, which can be merry and joyful with the mates of his childhood and in the playgrounds near his home, should have and might have the same benign influence and the same beneficent results with the labourer as with the nobles, and squires, and other wealthy folk; and if he finds pleasure and profit in his garden, his orchard, and his "bit o' land," he will seldom be attracted by those costly fascinations of the public-house, which are always so fugitive in fruition, and sometimes so disastrous in results.

No one walking in London streets, noticing the exquisite treasures in the windows of the florists, the orchids, the bouquets, and button-holes, the baskets and bunches of less expensive specimens, the cartloads of plants in pots, offered to him by the locomotive agent, the tasteful arrangements of flowers and foliage in dining and drawing rooms, on balconies and sills; or, as he passes by more humble habitations, the window plants in the poor man's home; or, travelling by rail, glass-houses by the acre for the culture of flowers and fruit;—no one can fail to be impressed by the increase, in these latter years, of this new demand and supply.　With some it is merely a matter of fashion and *comme il faut*, another opportunity of outbidding their neighbour, constraining him by their splendour to " pale his uneffectual fire," transcending him in town by a thousand roses, as in the country by a hillock of tame pheasants; but there is with it a true and genuine love of the beautiful, and no one feels it so heartily, or enjoys it so happily, as the grower of the window plant. It is the man or the woman who strikes the cutting and sows the seed, who tends and trains and waters, protects from the frost and screens from the heat, who watches the lateral break out of the stem, the formation of the foliage and the bud, who tastes the full felicities which flowers bestow. You may buy flowers, pay others to grow them for you, and admire them when they are grown, but if this is the extent of your affection, you miss, and deserve to miss, three-fourths of the pleasure which is given to those who cultivate and care for the plant. " I am not the rose," said the perfumed earth in the Persian fable, " but cherish me, for we have dwelt together." How much more tenderly should we revere the mother of these lovely babes! What a wealth of flowers they always have, who are their most faithful ministers! They seem to find them wherever they go, or receive them as offerings from those congenial gardeners who have heard of their devotion. That which they plant seems ever to thrive, and that which they nurse to recover.

Cut flowers, which they arrange, seem to place themselves at once in the most graceful contrast and combination. There seems to be a reciprocity of mutual, mysterious love, an interchange of smiles. The only good thing I ever heard of the Mormons was their belief in a sweet sympathy between the florist and his flowers.

CHAPTER XX.

Our gardens sixty years ago—Landscape-gardening—Beautiful
trees and shrubs—Herbaceous and Alpine plants—Roses
—Famous gardeners, and writers about gardens—Realities
and shams.

CONCERNING gardens. I subpœna my memories to
give evidence, and my verdict is that sixty years
ago the gardens of England were more pleasingly,
because more naturally, arranged than now. Mr.
Marnock, the best landscape-gardener of his day,
acknowledged and acted upon this conviction. I
see him now with his arms folded over his broad
chest, and his keen gaze surveying the site on
which he is to form a garden, in reverent meditation
how he should keep the congruity between Nature
and Art by a careful obedience to the Latin rule,
" *Ars est celare artem.*" He marked out a plan for
a bed here, and a tree there; there was to be a walk,
and there to be water; and, when the plan was
finished, on that amplitude of greensward which he
ever regarded as of primary importance, you would

not find a straight line or an angle. The poet who
wrote—

> "He wins all points, who pleasingly confounds,
> Surprises, varies, and conceals the bounds,"

was a true gardener; and he is a true duffer who
thinks to give the idea of magnitude by exposing
the whole extent of the ground to the spectator,
who maintains a rigid uniformity, "balancing" bed
against bed, tree against tree, conducts the visitor
on straight walks from corner to corner, and finally
embellishes and crowns his stupidity with a hideous
arbour, or a huge construction of iron arches and
chains, on which the roses, for which it was designed,
indignantly decline to grow. As for a quiet nook,
in which to think or read, a sun-trap, or a shelter
from wind or heat, an ambuscade for "I spy"
and "hide and seek," or a spot which might embolden
a bashful lover to whisper the avowal of his love,
you might as well try to conceal yourself in the
middle of the road, or propose on the top of an
omnibus. .

There can be no stereotyped designs for a
garden, because the plan must be adapted to the
extent, formation, and surroundings of the site, but
the laws as to a natural grace and congruity, as to
outline, variety, and the planting out of boundaries,
must be observed. The question what should there
be in a garden may be answered more definitely.
There should be in every garden which has room
for them an abundance of trees and shrubs having

beautiful flowers or leaves — *arbutus, aucubas, almonds, acacias, crabs, limes, Malus floribundus, Pyrus japonica, Prunus Pisardi, laurels, laurestinus, lilacs, laburnums, Guelder roses, Forsytheas, weigelas, sweet - briars, thorns (pink, white, and scarlet), rhododendrons, kalmias, azaleas,* and *andromedas* (where the four latter will prosper), *maples (silver and gold)*, and *copper beech*, etc. There should be broad borders of herbaceous plants in front of the shrubberies, round the beds, and on either side of walks in the kitchen garden; and at the backs of these borders should be tall screens, flower-walls of climbing plants, roses and honeysuckles, clematis, jasmines, golden and silver ivies, ceanothus, holly-hocks. A space should be set apart for Alpine plants, where large stones can be arranged as they are found in their natural stratum (not set up on end as by an earthquake) and soil placed about them. This rock-garden must have all the sunshine which comes to our cloudland, and it should be one of the " surprises," which are not only so charming at first sight, but, like Phyllis, " never fail to please." Roses should have a bed to themselves—the queen " brooks no rival near her throne "—and they should be " dwarfs " budded on the briar. Standards may be planted behind the herbaceous borders—elsewhere they are unsightly. Should the soil and the climate seem specially to favour any particular flowers, such as narcissus, lilies, gladioli, or carnations, these should be extensively grown in all their beautiful varieties, and made a prominent feature in the garden. On the other hand, it is a waste of time, money, and space, to persist in the cultivation of trees or flowers which are manifestly wretched in their exile from congenial homes. You may import cartloads of peat and of clay, and for a time you may have some success, but deterioration follows —*naturam expellas furcâ, tamen usque recurret*—and there is a gradual but sure decay. Then, as a false note spoils the harmony, or a discoloured tooth the set, your failure mars your success, and, where you might have commanded admiration, you hear a titter!

It has been my great privilege to know, and to number among my friends, the most accomplished gardeners, professional and amateur, master and servant, of our time, and in the society and the studios of these artists I have spent some of the happiest hours of my life. Foremost among these horticultural heroes, I place that "grand old gardener," to whom I and all loyal subjects of the queen of flowers are so much indebted for his "Rose Amateur's Guide," Mr. Rivers of Sawbridge-worth. It was the perusal of this book, the utterance of a loving heart, so clearly and concisely spoken, which revived my reverent admiration of flowers, kindled the spark into a flame, and gradually extended my garden of roses, until I was lord of five thousand trees. He sent me the editions of his charming manual, as they were published, with some kindly inscription, and in the last he wrote, after my name, " once my pupil, now my master; " but he had forgotten more than I ever knew. I went to see him in his pleasant home. The house stood at the top of a bank, on which he had planted and trained the Ayrshire roses, so that he looked out in the summertide on a white cascade of flowers. He was hale and handsome, tall and erect as one of his own " standards," and with some of their roseate hue on his kindly, clever face. Apropos of standards, he told me that when they were first imported into this country from Belgium, the Duke of Clarence paid a thousand pounds for the same number of trees. He was among the first to reproduce on English soil this new discovery, and to import his stocks, not from the foreign nurseries, but from the hedgerows of Herts. The old foreman protested in vain against " Master Tom planting those rubbishy brambles, instead of fruit trees," but they proved to be more precious than golden pippins, and every briar was transformed into a magnum bonum. It was delightful to walk with him among his roses, and in the orchard houses which he first designed, to be inspired by his enthusiasm and edified by his instruction, to examine the developments in symmetry, colour, and size, the results of that patient devotion, the selection, inoculation, hybridizing, budding, grafting, layering, striking, pruning, and careful cultivation, which he and others had bestowed upon the rose. His portrait has a conspicuous place in the long galleries through which my memory roams, and I rejoice in its genial smile. I know that he helped to make my life brighter and better, and there are times, when I think of him or read his books, in which I pray and hope that, when I am gone, I may be remembered by those younger men, who have already gladdened my heart by thanking me for a new-born zeal, with something of the affectionate, brotherly regard which I cherish always for Thomas Rivers.

Again and again I have walked with " the king of the florists," Charles Turner, through " the Royal Nurseries " at Slough; have inspected the Crown jewels (I might say, held the *regalia,* for all gardeners must fumigate now and then); have admired the arrangement, order, and government of his extensive empire, the industry, the prosperity, and beauty of his subjects. Over the tribes and families known as the pelargoniums, azaleas, auriculas, carnations, dahlias, and pot roses, he maintained his royal supremacy. His specimens were magnificent, so large that on one occasion he was a victim to that " vaulting ambition which o'erleaps itself," one of his azaleas attaining such abnormal dimensions that, when it was wanted for conveyance to a London show, it could not be got through the door, and it was necessary to remove one of the side-posts, at much trouble and expense. He could charm the ear as well as the eye, and if he had cultivated his exquisite tenor voice with the same assiduous attention which he gave to his garden, he would have been as distinguished in the concert, as he was in the exhibition, hall.

I have been with representatives of two generations of the Veitches, among the precious enrichments to our glass-houses and gardens which they have brought from all parts of the world, treasures for which men have imperilled their lives and lost them, as Douglas, who sent us the beautiful *Pinus Douglasii*, and who fell into a trap set for wild animals, and was gored to death by one of them. It is a joy and refreshment to go from London streets, and in the King's Road Nursery, at Chelsea, to see all plants which require protection in our colder clime—from the gigantic tree-ferns in their lofty home, to the tiniest gem in its thumb-pot— lovely and luxuriant as in their native land. Messrs. Veitch not only supply us with plants, but with planters; they have not only a nursery for flowers, but a school for florists, from which many pupils have gone forth with grateful recollections of sympathy in their comfort as well as of education in their art.

I have been personally conducted by Mr. Bull through his marvellous display of odontoglossum and other orchids, and his choice collection of novelties in stove and greenhouse plants; and, to make a triumvirate of orchideous potentates, I have passed many pleasant hours with " Ben Williams," of Holloway, in judicial labour and in social converse.

I have visited Switzerland-in-miniature with Mr. Backhouse, where he has formed in the suburbs of York the most perfect of rock-gardens, a natural conjunction of mountainettes and streamlets, in which you are shut out from the world beyond, and surrounded by fascinations, countless, and vying with each other in beauty as in their distant homes, where " hills peep o'er hills, and alps on alps arise." Here we find ourselves fully qualified to answer the inquiry of Mr. Alexander Selkirk, " O Solitude, where are thy charms ? " for here " there is society, where none intrudes."

I have seen many interesting Alpine gardens, notably at Lamport in Northamptonshire, where my old Oxford friend, Sir Charles Isham, by introducing among the Liliputian trees and caverns the figures of wee men in various attitudes, has produced a most artistic, quaint, weird semblance of reality ; and I have heard of many other proofs that gardeners are beginning to appreciate this precious addition to a garden, which comprehends such manifold attractions in so small a space; but I have neither seen nor heard of any consummation so successful as that at York, where, in addition to this *chef d'œuvre*, there are broad borders of herbaceous plants, and a most interesting collection of rare ferns.

I have been with Mr. Barr among the narcissus, with Mr. Laing among the begonias, with Mr. Waterer among the rhododendrons, Mr. Pearson among his pelargoniums, with Mr. Cannell among his dahlias and primulas, with Mr. Sutton among his giant cyclamen and grand gloxinias. I have been with Mr. William Thompson, king of the vineyards, the raiser of the finest grape ever seen—I mean " the Duke of Buccleuch "—under his grapes at Clovenford, and with Mr. Bunyard, the emperor of pomologists, among his apples at Maidstone. I have been among the roses with the chief rosarians, by the side of the *Rivers*, in the midst of the *Lanes* and the *Woods*,* with the Pauls of Cheshunt and Waltham Cross (Mr. William Paul, Mr. John Lee, and myself are, I think, the only survivors of the old rosarians), Francis of Hertford, Cant of Colchester, Prince of Oxford, Cranston of Hereford, and many others, to whom I have awarded, as one of the judges, some scores of cups and of cheques. I have talked bad French to Victor Verdier, and been told by Jules Margottin how an English rosarian, expecting to gain advantage over his fellow-countrymen by obtaining his roses direct from France, having heard that M. Margottin lived at Bourg la Reine, but not being certain as to the orthography, and seeing in a catalogue the name of a rose, " Belle de Bourg la Reine," copied it and wrote at once; and the jolly old Frenchman very nearly choked himself on receiving a letter addressed to him as the belle of the district. *Risum teneatis, amici?* You, messieurs, sometimes misapprehend, as when our Bishop of Bath and

* Rivers of Sawbridgeworth; Lane of Berkhamstead; Wood of Maresfield.

Wells was entered in the book of your hotel as *L'Évêque de Bain et Puits*, and our Bishop of Sodor and Man, as *L'Évêque du Siphon et d'Homme!* I have known other famous exhibitors in their various departments of horticulture—William May, the Coles, and Mr. Baines. I have wandered with Mr. Boscawen in his wild garden in Cornwall; with Mr. Ingram on Belvoir's lovely slopes; with Mr. Fish around beautiful Hardwicke, with its valley of ferns and its vistas, through which you look down on Bury. I have known our chief horticultural writers, the editors past and present of our garden periodicals, Dr. Lindley, Dr. Masters, and gentle, genial Mr. Moore of the *Chronicle*, Donald Beaton and Dr. Hogg of the *Cottage Gardener* (now the *Journal of Horticulture*), Shirley Hibberd of the *Gardener's Magazine*; and, coming to more recent dates, I sat with my friend, William Robinson, under a tree in the Regent's Park, and suggested *The Garden* as a title for the newspaper which he proposed to publish, and which has been so powerful in its advocacy of pure horticulture of the natural, or English, school, free from rigid formalities, meretricious ornaments, gypsum, powdered bricks, cockle-shells, and bottle-ends.

I have been with the peasants of France and Italy under the vines, and among the oranges and lemons, and by the long beds of excellent vegetables, which they grow on the terraces formed from the rock; and I should like to show some of our indolent gardeners, who are ever complaining about their soil and other disadvantages, what can be done by pickaxe, trowel, and spade to utilize and beautify the barren mountain side. With all my heart I honour these men and women (for the women work as hard as the men), as, under the burden and heat of the day, they patiently obey the Divine edict, " In the sweat of thy face thou shalt eat bread ; " and to them, if to any, may be spoken, when labour is over, or the *festa* comes, these happy words, " Go thy way, eat thy bread with joy, and drink thy wine with a merry heart ; for God accepteth thy works."

And last, but not least, I have ofttimes been with the artisans of whom I have spoken, the labourers, who take a real interest in their cottage gardens, and their wives, who watch with anxious care the window plants at home ; and this is the conclusion to which I have come, from an intimacy long and close, that this appreciation of the beautiful is a divine instinct, and that it is so conducive to tenderness, and gentleness, and reverence, and love, that he who has it may be readily taught, if he has not already learned, to look from Nature up to Nature's God, from the flowers of the garden to Him whose breath perfumes them, and whose pencil paints. This conviction has been confirmed by my clerical experience, as well as by my floral friendships. The gardener ought to be always, and is, as a rule, not only a man of refined taste, but of religious principle ; and this principle is, I believe, the chief source and stay of our brotherly attachment. It is not only similarity of inclinations and habits, but a more pure and sacred sympathy, which creates and maintains our alliance.

The apron of the gardener, like the apron of the Freemason, which I have worn for half a century, not only means honest work, but brotherhood, and wherever I have been, with rare exceptions, I have found in him a brother. I do not claim for the gardener exemption from those infirmities of temper which flesh is heir to, and he may mistake his vocation as others do. There are cases in which his museum of red spiders, mealy bugs, and aphis seems to indicate that he should have been an entomologist; there are instances in which the abundance of his groundsel suggests his removal to the Canary Islands. There are examples of meanness and self-conceit. There is the selfish little " Horner, who sits in his corner " away from his fellows, eating his pie, but asking none to taste ; and " he puts in his thumb, and pulls out a plum," exulting in his display of something which you have not got, and saying, " What a good boy am I ! " whereas he wants whipping. There is the gardener who cultivates one specialty, and ignores all other plants. He can only ride his own hobby, and can only play one tune, which he gives you, *da capo*, until you are bored into disgust. If you have not seen his *Bougainvillea glabra* (anybody may fill a stove with it), he has an astonishment in store for you; if you have not worshipped his calceolarias, you are in heathen darkness.

I exclude from the category of gardeners the miser, the braggart, the ignoramus, and the impostor, and must sorrowfully attach the latter appellation to those ladies and gentlemen who profess to be "so fond of flowers," who grow them, and buy them, and wear them, and are pleased with them as ornamental adjuncts within and without their homes, but never study, in a wonder of delight, their infinite beauty of colour and of form, never think of them, never speak of them, when they are out of sight. I don't believe in those who call them "sweets," and "pets," and "darlings," and let them die for want of water. Take notice of these professors at a flower show, or a garden party, or among the "lilies of the field," and you will know the quality of their devotion. What disappointments they inflict, who are "so anxious to see your garden," and with whom you anticipate an earnest interchange of sympathies and experience, and they rush through your grounds as though they were in training for some pedestrian feat, or stop to notice the most common plant in your borders, and call it by a wrong name. Yet more objectionable, because you do not get rid of him so soon, is the man who prides himself on the extent of his collection, and, as one who buys books but never reads them, cares only for the mere fact of possession. He comes to see whether you have anything which he has not. He will hardly look at your latest acquisition, because he has " grown it for two seasons," and he speaks of some of the loveliest flowers in creation, as he would speak of his grandmother, as " poor dear old things." He feels towards them as I to himself; he tolerates, but wishes they would go.

Solace comes to you with the real enthusiast, who shares your admirations, your successes and disappointments, as though they were his own ; who is as anxious to receive, as he is willing to give, information, as grateful as he is generous. How quickly and happily the hours go as, in his garden, or in yours, or wherever your favourites grow, you suggest to each other new charms, new combinations, new methods of culture. I went to one of the most beautiful of our great English gardens, and, meeting the head gardener, asked permission to walk through the grounds, and told him my name. To my momentary surprise, he made me no answer, but turning to one of his men at work close by, bade him, " Set the fountains playing." That was his brotherly welcome, and it stirred other fountains besides those which suddenly arose and sparkled in their silvery sheen, and made my heart glad. In this delightful garden, there stands a statue of the noble owner, who reclaimed it from the waste, and underneath an inscription, " He made the desert smile ; " and so our love of flowers and florists makes " green spots on the path of time." In this land of gardens, the gardener has troops of friends, and even in places which the world calls desolate, he shall find companions to cheer him, so long as there are lichens on the mountain, ferns in the valley, or algæ on the shore. "The wilderness and the solitary place shall be glad for him, and the desert shall rejoice and blossom as the rose."

In referring to standards, by which you may measure, and scales, in which you may weigh and distinguish, the true and the pseudo florist, I have included a flower show as one of the tests, and it may interest some of my readers to have the memories of my long experience with regard to the flower show itself. I am often asked, Can these exhibitions be easily established and profitably managed? Is it desirable for gardeners to exhibit?

CHAPTER XXI.

GARDENERS— *Continued.*

Floral exhibitions, committees, and exhibitors—Town and
country shows—The Knave of Spades—Judges, righteous
and incapable.

IT is not difficult to establish a flower show. The
Marquis of Carabbas, the nearest nobleman, is invited
to be patron, and the mayor to call a meeting.
This meeting is attended by a letter from the peer,
regretting a previous engagement (a day's hunting
or fishing, which he, not being a florist, naturally
and wisely prefers) ; by those who have originated
the scheme; two or three exhibitors not quite so
disinterested ; the publisher of a local paper, who
is prepared to print the advertisements, schedules,
etc. ; a gentleman who has a field to let which would
be a most eligible site for the show ; and a rash,
good-natured young man, who, with no prevision
of the perils to ensue, overrating the importance
and underrating the work of the office, consents to
act as secretary. A committee is formed, a subscription list (the patron has kindly sent a cheque
for £5) is opened, a list of prizes is prepared, the

judges nominated, the day fixed. If that day is fine, the opening of the exhibition by her ladyship may bring success; but I have never known an instance—I am speaking of country towns—in which that success was permanent, without the addition of other attractions, balloons, black faces under white hats, banjos, roundabouts, steam organs, stalls, booths, etc. I do not denounce these galas; I like my fellow-men to enjoy themselves in their own way, so long as they are merry and wise; but I desire to warn those who think that the public will be so far interested in a show of flowers, fruits, and vegetables, as to pay its expenses, even with the aid of a considerable subscription, that they will be disappointed. The attendance will diminish, and a few thunderstorms, drenching the tents, will turn that gay young secretary into a sadder and a wiser man.

In our populous cities, and in our villages, more prosperous results may be attained. Some years ago, when the financial condition of the Manchester Botanical Society was a subject of grave anxiety, my friend, Mr. Bruce Findlay, the curator of the gardens, astonished the directors by a proposal to offer one thousand pounds in prizes, and to admit the public to see the results, on a Bank holiday, and at one shilling each. The executive bravely accepted the suggestion, and on the following Whit-Monday sixty thousand persons paid for admission. The success continued, and might be realized elsewhere by a like spirit and organization. If it were known, where men most do congregate, that the best specimens of horticulture, in all its branches, which science could produce, might be seen on a day of leisure, in pleasant grounds, and with an accompaniment of good music, for a shilling, the click of the turnstiles would sound merrily in the ears of the executive committee; and I do not see how generous employers could do a more gracious act than by distributing tickets of admission among the working-men and their wives.

In our larger villages, where cottage gardens are numerous, an exhibition, chiefly of fruits and vegetables, may be encouraging and instructive. I do not advise that this competition should take place with that of nurserymen, gardeners, and amateurs, because visitors will not care for John Smith's potatoes when they can gaze on stove plants; and Sally Brown's posy of wild flowers "looks mean and poky," as Martha Penny remarked of the Protestant religion, in the midst of Roman splendour, when placed in proximity to a bouquet of my lord's orchids. Let the attention of all present be concentrated on the skill and industry of the grower, and let those who excel monopolize the rewards and praises. Let the squire's garden be offered for a tent, or the village schoolroom, if the weather is untoward, and all unite in hearty and practical alliance. There might be a cotemporary cricket match, or other athletic sports, and I have known kind ladies and gentlemen discourse excellent music and give pathetic and humorous recitals.

There must be vigilance, as well as vigour and self-denial, in the committee. The trail of the serpent is still to be found among the flowers. The exhibitor is tempted and falls. No class is free from frailty. He wants just one more dish in his collection of fruit, and he begs or buys it. He has not "twenty-four distinct varieties," so he puts in a duplicate under another name. Sometimes, very rarely, you will meet with the thorough scamp, the knave of spades, who·has taken Luther's words for his motto—*Pecca fortiter*, win anyhow. Judging at a show, I was informed by one, who inspired me with confidence, that an exhibitor, to whom we had awarded a first prize, did not grow six plants of the flowers of which he had shown a dozen varieties, and had purchased his specimens from a famous nursery. As soon as we had made more important awards, I left the remainder to my judicial brethren, hired a dogcart, drove some four miles into the country to the garden of the suspected competitor, and was back in time to have a brief conference with the authorities, before the public were admitted, and to write, instead of " First Prize," upon his card, " Disqualified, and expelled from the society."

I remember another exhibitor, who seemed to think that you could not have too much of a good thing—*decies repetita placebit*—and who, ignoring the condition demanding " distinct varieties," showed

Charles Lefebvre under five, and Maurice Bernardin under four different appellations, with several other duplicates, which we placed in the same tube, to intimate "how good and joyful a thing it was for brethren to dwell together in unity."

On my way to another exhibition, held by working men, my cab was stopped by an elderly dame, who was of Celtic extraction, raising her arms in benediction, and accosting me with, "Bless your rivirence, there's going to be an illigant show intirely. Our boy's been sleeping a fortnight with the roses, and it's the first prize your rivirence 'll be for giving the darlints as soon as iver you set your oiyes upon 'em." But why had he slept in the little greenhouse with the roses? Alas! they would not have been safe without a custodian from rogues, who had backed other exhibitors to win, and who would have stolen and sold his blooms; but the jockey guarded the stable and won the cup in a canter.

One more warning to make a committee cautious. I was staying with a brother florist in the neighbourhood of a large town, where there was to be a show next day, and very early in the morning, being anxious about the weather, he awoke and looked out of his window. To his sorrowful surprise he saw his under-gardener, with a stranger, carefully selecting and cutting some of his best roses, and in the distance he could descry a confederate, with horse and cart, waiting to convey them away. The window opened, simultaneously with the eyes of the petty larcener and the mouth of his master. His words were few, but full of a fire and force which powerfully impressed his audience, for they complied at once with his suggestion that they should "drop those roses," and the basket fell to the ground. There was a dissolving view, which included the undergardener, "departed, never to return," and there was a lovely bouquet on the table when we went down to breakfast.

These *mauvais sujets* are not gardeners; they are the weeds which grow among the flowers, and the slugs which devour them, to be uprooted by the hand and crushed beneath the heel. The loyal florist will have nothing to do with treason, treachery, and spoils; and, with the exception of those fellows of the baser sort, whom I have named, there can be no class of men more scrupulously honest than the exhibitors at our flower shows. They are of Plato's mind, that there is something so vile and ugly in lying and stealing, that if they were sure of escape from detection they would not demean themselves. He who would desecrate "whatsoever things are lovely, whatsoever things are pure," by using them as instruments for sin, would rob a church, or cheat a child. The rule of the exhibitor is, Βούλου κρατεῖν μεν, συν θεῷ δ'ἀει κρατεῖν, "Make up your mind to win, but always honestly."

I am aware that the exhibitor may occasionally

make a fool of himself—"We are the sons of women, Master Page," and I have seen a competitor of the highest respectability tear a card in pieces on which he read, "Second Prize." There was no doubt with the unprejudiced as to the justice of the award, but his vision was distorted, and his temper followed in its track.

Sometimes an exhibitor has come to me in my judicial capacity, with a pallid countenance and quivering lip, to inquire, in the calmest tone at his disposal, whether I would be so kind as to inform him why Mr. Black was honoured with the first prize for a lot of old rubbish which had all but gone out of cultivation, whereas he, Mr. White, had shown the latest novelties from the first growers, at home and on the Continent, and at enormous outlay? And when the answer has been given, that we were to decide on the merits of the flowers, and not on the date of their introduction, on the culture and not on the cost, it was evident that we made little impression, and that, if common sense could not be confuted, he thought slightingly of common sense.

Wandering about the show, unknown, I have heard myself referred to as one of the umpires in terms opprobrious and severe : " I should say the man as judged those bouquets had just come out of a blind asylum;" "That orchid in No. 4 was worth the whole lot in the first prize," etc. Sometimes we are accused of deliberate partiality : " I know'd how it would be when I see Tom Jones shaking hands

with the judge at the station." But the ebullitions
of disappointment are not seriously intended, and
are soon forgotten. I only remember one instance,
and that was associated with fowls, and not with
flowers, in which a spirit of resentment lingered in
the breast of an unsuccessful exhibitor. At the
time of the Crimean War, a friend of mine, who had
served as an officer in the 16th Lancers, and was
then our Master of Hounds, was president of the
Bolsover Poultry Show. A farmer, who had entered his name as a candidate for a prize to be given
to the best three ducks, finding that one of his birds
was much inferior to the others, substituted in its
place a fine young goose, and was of course disqualified. On this he vowed vengeance on all connected with the show, and especially against the
president, who had nothing whatever to do with
the awards. He deliberately planned his vendetta.
Meeting the M.F.H. one morning as he drove to
covert, he stopped him with uplifted hand and inquired, " Morning, major; how long has thee been
out o' th' army?" This strange question was politely
answered, " Fourteen or fifteen years." The reply
was not in harmony with the plot of the questioner,
but he had loaded his gun and must fire it, hit or
miss. "Oh," he said, "yer know'd t' war were
coming; yer nipped out o' th' army. Yer lig nice
and snug in bed when them cannon-balls were
a-rolling and a-bowling about Sebastopple. Yer'd
raythur smell a fox than powder. Yer know'd t'

war were coming; yer nipped out o' th' army. Good morning, major."

The righteous judge must solace himself with the consciousness that he understands his business and has done his best; but it must be remembered by those who appoint him, that he cannot be righteous unless he is thoroughly conversant with the objects submitted to his arbitration. He must know from practical experience their habits and capabilities. He must be quick to detect duplicates or additions. He must concentrate all his attention upon his work, and be intensely patient in his scrutiny, until he is fully convinced. I remember a rosarian, who had a large collection and wrote cleverly about roses, entering a show with his two coadjutors (myself and a well-known nurseryman), and when I took him to our first function, the inspection of six collections, each containing seventy-two varieties, he threw up his arms (and his appointment), exclaiming, "I'm dazed at the very sight of them! As for judging, I should never dream of it." Nor could we persuade him to make the experiment. I have met with others far more incompetent, but not so scrupulous; clever in some special department, but not in that which had been assigned to them as judges. I recall one of my coadjutors who had a quaint method of concealing his ignorance. He knew the securities of silence, and never volunteered a remark, but feeling that he could not consistently remain entirely aloof, he would from time to time hold a pencil, which he carried, over some particular flower, as though he were meditating upon its merits, or wished to direct our attention to it. If it was a poor specimen, we were to infer that he desired us to notice its inferiority; if it was a fine bloom, he commended it to our admiration; if there was nothing remarkable about it, that was just his perplexity, whether to praise or condemn it. When the other judges made a remark, he boldly intimated that was exactly what the pencil meant.

My memory records examples of incapacity yet more strange than these. The Rev. E. Pochin, one of our most accomplished and successful rosarians, having won the chief honours at the Crystal Palace Exhibition, took collections quite as good as those which he had shown in London to a provincial show, and, there being no question as to the superiority of his flowers, was surprised to find them unnoticed. Venturing to communicate his astonishment to the judges, he was politely but positively informed that " his roses were not the right sort for exhibition "!

Having denounced the incapacities of others, I am conscientiously bound to acknowledge an infirmity to which, in common with my learned and thirsty brothers, I have yielded more than once, namely, in devoting more time than was absolutely necessary to fruits, which were " to be tested by flavour." After two or three hours in a hot tent on a July day, the difficulty of arriving at a unanimous verdict as to the relative merits of the strawberries and the melons has been unduly magnified, and a superfluous number of witnesses have been examined by the judicial committee.

Should gardeners exhibit? Some of their employers are apprehensive that objects of special cultivation may divert attention from others, which seem of less importance to the gardener, but are quite as interesting to the owner. My experience is this, that if a man achieves signal excellence in any particular department of horticulture, he deserves the encouragement which he obtains at a show, and that he who has this excellence will not restrict it to one ambition. It is, moreover, advantageous for a gardener to see the best specimens of his art in all their varieties, to gain and give information. Exhibitors will not tell you all they know, but they will tell you much, if they find you zealous and ready to communicate your own experience. Letting my memory range among the many gardens which I know the best, it brings home the conviction that, as a rule, the gardener who has some special superiority rises above mediocrity in his other productions, and that he who has no remarkable success is satisfied with a decent debility, a conventional standard, which just satisfies, and evokes neither praise nor blame. The same flowers (of the same size), the same fruits and vegetables (of the same flavour), appear, at the same time, in the same places, and might be under some act of uniformity, which, like the law of the Medes and Persians, altereth not.

*　　*　　*　　*　　*

Flowers never seem to me so happily placed, as when offered upon His altars, who gives them to us, and who bids us, " Consider the lilies." Most beautiful of all these lilies, for this sacred purpose, the eucharis, the arum, *L. auratum, longiflorum, Harrisi, candidum.* The Christmas rose, protected by glazed frames, is a precious addition at a time when the Japanese anemone and other outdoor white flowers have bloomed ; and some of the snowy chrysanthemums are fair emblems of purity and innocence. The white camellia has ever a stiff, artificial look, but this may be modified by inter-mixture with ferns and other flowers. I would choose all that were fairest and sweetest, not formally arranging them by ecclesiastical rule or pattern, but with a natural grace—sometimes using only one variety, sometimes many. As a flower by itself, the arum is of all most effective, and its easy cultivation, size, and endurance combine to make it, in my opinion, the most valuable of all for church decoration. At the consecration of the first Bishop of Truro, there were two vases upon the altar, each containing five flowers of arum, and every white, ivory chalice was visible throughout St. Paul's. The larger orchids, such as *Lælia purpurata ;* stove plants, such as the lovely dipladenia; roses of one colour, or mixed, or in combination

with lilies—La France is, perhaps, the most charming; the diverse shades of the pæony, pale yellow
and bright rose; with countless other flowers, and
many varieties of foliage, are available and effective.

A silly and inaccurate objection is sometimes
made to placing flowers upon the altar, because it
is a practice of the Roman Catholic Church. The
question is whether the use is right, and not whether
it is Roman; and Roman it is not, so far as my
experience goes, seeing that it would be a misnomer
and an insult to designate as flowers the artificial
rubbish which is so often placed upon Roman
altars.

I am sorry, but not surprised, to see from time
to time in our obituaries, "*No flowers.*" A cross and
a crown upon the coffin, expressing the humble hope
that work is over, and that the worker rests from his
labours; that the souls of the faithful, after they are
delivered from the burden of the flesh, are in joy and
felicity, may bring welcome solace to the Christian
mourner's heart, and it may be right that sincere
affection and respect should lay their wreath upon
the grave; but when hundreds of pounds are thus
spent on a single funeral, reason and religion must
protest against the waste. Then especially, when
these floreated coffins are made a public show.
There is a natural desire to take a last fond look of
those nearest and dearest, but to make a display
of the dead with scenic surroundings, such as have
been recently described in the London papers, must

be suggestive to many minds of profanation rather than of piety. It is recorded in the *Standard* of February 11, 1892, that "four memorial services were held at the Metropolitan Tabernacle on the day preceding, each attended by 5500 persons. At each service, *all eyes were centred upon the grouping of coffin and bending palms, of white lilies, ferns, and myrtles, with hanging drapery, bearing texts or words spoken by the deceased, and the white bust in the centre, a striking likeness of the late pastor.*" The same paper, on February 12, had an admirable article on the subject, in which the writer says, "The public pulse is getting into the habit of being at fever heat; and unless the popular humour soon changes, men really great and eminent will shrink from the humiliation of public honours, whether in life or posthumously. The exaggerated demonstrations, held at the obsequies of those who have had their little day, will compel the surviving kindred of really great citizens to ask to be left alone with their sorrow, and to insist on a quiet interment in some country churchyard." It is a matter of thankfulness to know that in our Church these spectacles would be impossible, and that any such display at the funerals of our great ecclesiastics, such as Dean Church and Canon Liddon, would be universally condemned.

> "Our mother the Church hath never a son
> To honour before the rest,
> But she singeth the same for mighty kings,
> And the veriest babe at her breast;

> And the bishop goes down to his narrow home
> As the ploughman's child is laid,
> And alike she blesses the dark-browed serf,
> And the chief in his robe arrayed."

Of flowers for festivals, I love the primrose, so fresh and sweet, for Easter, in bunches *and in water;* the holly and aucuba for Christmas; and the bright dahlias, among the oats, for harvest.

I conclude my reminiscences of florists and flowers with some verses, which appropriately combine ecclesiastical and floral themes, and which I have permission from the author, the Rev. John Spittal, to publish. The lines are addressed to Lord Penzance, a most scientific student of the rose, and were written on reading an account of his most interesting and successful experiments in hybridizing his favourite flower, and which, read in the same spirit in which they were written, have been pronounced by his lordship to be " very amusing."

> "I own it was with much surprise I
>   Saw Penzance named in your report,
> By me connected with ' rule nisi,'
>   Or ' judgment for contempt of court.'
> For High Church ways, and *making crosses,*
>   His lordship sentenced Mr. Dale.
> Poor Fairthorn Green had grievous losses,
>   And spent about three years in jail.
> And while my lord prepares for taking
>   An early hold on Mr. Cox,
> To find the judge himself *cross-making,*
>   I must confess it rather shocks.
> Yet there is hope the truth may reach him,
>   As he essays to hybridize,

And wedding rose with rose may teach him
  With marriage bonds to sympathize.
Surely a man of such resources
  May find sufficient work at least,
Without insisting on divorces
  Of congregations from their priest.
But all our trouble may be settled,
  When some new rose, of splendid fame,
Brilliant in hue, distinct, large petalled,
  Bears through the world Penzance's name!"

CHAPTER XXII.

HUNTERS.

Antiquity of " the sport of kings "—Erroneous ideas about
hunting.

MR. JORROCKS, though not a student, was historically
accurate in his observation that " hunting was the
sport of kings." He who " began to be a mighty one
in the earth " was Nimrod, the hunter. In the
East, we read, hunting was always regarded as a
manly exercise, requiring courage and dexterity,
invigorating the body, and instilling into the mind
a taste for active pursuits. It was held in such
respect that the founders of empires were represented in the characters of renowned hunters, and
the Babylonians were so fond of the chase that the
walls of their rooms presented a repetition of subjects
connected with it, and they even ornamented their
dresses and the furniture of their houses with the
animals which they had hunted. The Medes and
Persians were equally noted for their love of field
sports, and, like the Egyptians, had spacious preserves,
in which the game was inclosed.

The animal to be hunted and the methods of

hunting have varied, of course, with the climate and scene of the chase. The artist who represented the Prodigal Son in scarlet, breeches, and boots, was a man of limited information; and Sir Tatton Sykes was indulging his quaint humour, when, his attention being invited to some beautiful views, by Roberts, of the mountainous districts of Palestine, he remarked, "Queer country to get across, that, sir,—queer country!"

But, *mutatis mutandis*, the same spirit has pervaded and pervades the ages. It has glowed in the hearts of kings, as we know here in England, from our royal chases, forests, and preserves, Grand Falconers, and Masters of the Buckhounds; it is the sport *par excellence* of the nobles, gentry, professional men, farmers—of all who have a horse to ride; and with those who have none, the latent love of it wakes instantly at the sound of the horn, and men, women, and children rush with eager faces from their homes, whenever the hunt goes by.

There are some who hold that hunting is a mere barbarian instinct, innate in all, but conspicuously developed in the Englishman, whose first impulse, according to Charles Lamb, is to say, "Here is a fine day, let us kill something." They affirm that it is a frivolous, dangerous, and expensive amusement; and, so far as these objections have come under my notice, I am convinced that in the case of those who make them, the vanity, the peril, and the extravagance would all be realized if they went forth to hunt the fox. They are persons who would be uncomfortable, both in body and mind, if they were placed astride a spirited horse, in proximity with a pack of hounds. They would be annoyed by his impetuosity, and would be perplexed, like Mr. Winkle, as to " what makes him go sideways ? " They would tumble off. They might require a doctor. They would rightly denounce the exercise as a waste of time, of peaceful contentment and personal security, of pounds, shillings, and pence. But their physical incompetence, it will be justly urged, does not invalidate their argument; that must be met as a principle, without personalities. Well, then, I reply, you must allow that men need relaxation, as wheels need oil, and I ask you, Where will you find it so conducive to manliness, healthfulness, and social intercourse, as in the hunting field ? I have not a word to say in defence of the man who makes hunting his business, and does nothing else. An idle man, wherever he be, who does nothing to justify his existence, who makes an idol of his lower self, and ignores the noble work and duty for which he was created, is a drone in the hive, a barren tree in the orchard, a deaf note in the instrument, a dead fish in the net. He monopolizes that which he was meant to share; " Ephraim is joined to his idols, let him alone ; " but for the man who is true to his manhood and its responsibilities, and who can afford the time and the money, I can think of no recreation so invigorating as a few weeks' holiday in the shires, or two days a

week from his home. And he will have far more
enjoyment than the man to whom, in this as in all
other excess, satiety brings indigestion.

Some, who have no practical experience, have
most erroneous ideas about hunting. They are under
the impression that every man who rides, and has
a good horse, goes out and follows the hounds. Their
conjecture is so far correct that a large majority,
when they leave their homes, entertain that hope and
intention ; but not one in ten fulfils it. At the first
stiff fence, when hounds are running, there is a
pause. An observant eye sees a distant gate, and
galloping to it, is followed by half the field. While
others are hesitating, an underbred four-year-old
smashes a gap in the hedge, and the dubious lose
their fears. Brief while ! A strong piece of timber,
too strong even for the cart-horsy quadruped, who
is down on the other side (*procumbit humi bos*),
scatters them in all directions, and they are seen no
more. Now, two or three equestrians with large
hearts and little heads seem to take leave of the
latter, and, forgetting that foxes do not always run
in a straight line, rush forward recklessly, and do
not discover until too late that the hounds are not
to be seen. The huntsman has watched their
demented disappearance with a thankful mind, for
these are the men who override his hounds—the
men of whom Will Derry said, " That's Parson Wills,
sir, Parson Wills. He will be atop o' th' 'ounds.
Whips blow'd him up, and he tuk no notice ; and I

blow'd him up, and he tuk no notice; and master blow'd him up, and he tuk no notice; *so we tuk the 'ounds 'ome.*"

A goodly number still remain· with the pack, but as the pace grows faster, and the line of chase leads over some heavy " plough," a deep drain, and a " beastly double," others begin to veer and skirt, the roads and lanes and gates allure the unstable mind, and, after thirty-five minutes, only six men, all of whom might have been named before the fox was found, have kept their place with the hounds.

The explanation is, that it requires something more than a man and a horse, though the man be courageous and the horse can gallop and jump; it requires a man " with brains, sir! " to ride to hounds. It is possible for a person of weak intellect and strong limbs to win a steeplechase on a superior horse; he can only go in one direction, and go he must, between the flags; but to keep with hounds in a long and difficult run is altogether a different thing, and the exceptions are very few to the rule that he who rides always with cool, courageous judgment, has other accomplishments, other superiorities above his fellow-men. One of these leaders, who could not only ride in a run, but describe it afterwards, as no other man—Whyte Melville—writes in " Market Harborough," after describing the Honourable Crasher as reading the " Idylls of the King," " There is something of poetry in every man who rides across country." He who " dares do all that may become a man" delights to read in the old romance of gallant, knightly deeds; and if sometimes he lays it down, and sighs—

> "So then I see the good old times are gone,
> When every day brought forth a noble chance,
> And every chance brought forth a noble knight,"

then let him remember that stile in the corner, at which he disposed of a bumptious rival, or let him anticipate next Thursday's meet, when in all probability they will have *the* brook. Days of chivalry are still in store *au cheval* and his rider.

I shall ever remember with a grateful respect the groom who taught me to ride. As soon as my father, a keen sportsman, could persuade my mother that I was much too old (*æt. meâ* iv.) for a rocking-horse, I was transferred to a pony, ancient and of blameless character, and to the tuition of our master of the horse. My memories are dim as to the initial process, but most distinct and joyful of a day when, having taught me what he called " quite an 'unting seat," and having inspired me with confidence to canter, sitting behind me, and with his hands in readiness to help in case of need, he slipped off unnoticed, except by my parents, who had just come to see, and who watched me with amused anxiety, as I approached to realize the triumphant dignity of my new-born independence. Once assured that I could swim without the corks, I plunged boldly into deep water. My teacher came with a proud smile on his face, and my father put a sovereign into his

hand. It was well earned, and quite appropriate to
the golden opportunity, for which he had waited
with so much careful preparation. When he left me
without his supporting arm, he knew that I no longer
required it, and he saw that if I missed him and
mourned his loss, there was the best of help at hand.
Many a child has been frightened into a dislike and
dread of riding by want of thoughtful sympathy, just
as many a young horse has been spoiled by violent,
instead of gentle treatment. Horse-breaking and
heart-breaking may be synonymous terms.

If a child is afraid when he is first mounted on
a rocking-horse, or on a pony, take him off, and
wait until he has lost his fear by watching others
that are fearless. Then that love of imitation, which
some would have us believe (but we don't) that we
inherit from ancestral apes, and that instinct of
jealousy, which we know too well, from the history
of his sons, that we inherit from Adam, will soon
make him wish to be replaced. Do not thwart, but
guide, his inclinations. Let him always think that
he is master of the situation. Exalt him gradually
from the dull to the lively, from the pony to the
jumping cob, from the jumping cob to the hunter,
and it will not be your fault when the ordeal comes,
when he gets his first fall, or is run away with—
such " fate is the common lot of all "—it will be his
fault, not yours, if he is not a horseman. There
must come a selection of the fittest—a crisis, when
the timid goes home, and the brave goes to the next

fence, with an utterance of indignation, and other stimulants, which cause his steed to bound like a buck. The faint-hearted disappears—

> "At puer Ascanius mediis in vallibus acri
> Gaudet equo, jamque hos cursu jam præterit illos."

It gladdens my heart and kindles my hope to see our boys ride. They get a little intermixed with our horses' forelegs in the woods and lanes, but they are out of the way when business begins, and when it is slack they are worth watching. They are off at full gallop as soon as they see a fence, and either clear three times the necessary space, or, if their steed abruptly determines, on reaching the obstacle, to give them notice to quit, they bound over it like a flying-fish, are up in five seconds with a merry laugh, and evidently regard their aerial flight as part of the day's fun. This is the raw material, from which we make our cavalry officers, explorers, and pioneers. I had two young brothers-in-law, who were the joy of John Leech's heart. He represented one of them in *Punch*, riding at a deer-fence about nine feet high; and he declared that the other was only prevented from charging a canal by a barge in full sail. They turned out excellent horsemen. Harry bought and trained a young horse at Oxford, rode him, and won "the Aylesbury," and the other was thrice M.F.H., and said to be one of the best judges of hounds in England.

Returning home after the first day on which I

was permitted to remain with the hounds until the hunting was over, my father told me that a tall gentleman in a brown coat, who had been talking to me long and kindly, was the Marquis of Tichfield (afterwards Duke of Portland), and that he was considered to be the best horseman of his day. I do not remember to have seen him again, but I often met his brother, Lord Henry Bentinck, who was also, though he was shortsighted and wore glasses, an admirable rider, a popular Master of Hounds, and a man whose quick and pungent humour glittered and pierced like a sword. It was he who said, though the splendid rebuke has been ascribed to others, when he was canvassing North Nottinghamshire, and a furious opponent informed him, "Lord Henry, I'd sooner vote for the divil than for you!"—it was he who replied, with the most polite demeanour and blandest suavity of tone, "Perhaps, sir, in the event of your friend not coming forward, I might hope for your support." It was he who inquired from a rash cavalier, who was overriding his hounds, "May I ask, sir, do you smell the fox?" and who said to a large landed proprietor, suspected of vulpecidal acts, on his remarking that he regarded a particular wood as "quite a seminary for foxes," "I think, general, you mean *cemetery*." "I've an unpleasant duty to perform this morning," he said to a friend on the hunting-field; "I told my two whips the other day that they were the two biggest fools in

England, and I've been out with Lord Yarborough's hounds, and seen two bigger, and must, of course, withdraw the observation." A fox crossed the Trent near a ferry, and Lord Henry had just got his hounds, horses, and men into the boat, and was leaving the banks, when a member of his hunt, called "The Bird" (he being of the first flight), arrived, and foolishly endeavoured to leap into the boat. The distance was too far, and the gallant horse, though he made a noble effort, fell with his rider into the Trent. Lord Henry calmly surveyed the misadventure, and all that he said was, "The Dun Diver!" The poor "Bird" returned to dry his plumage ashore. Spending Christmas with a friend, he was asked at luncheon by the rector, after service in a church at which, profusely adorned with evergreens, the congregation had been small, "what he thought of the decorations?" "I thought," he replied, "that there was *plenty of cover, but very little game.*"

In those days a meet of "the Rufford" was indeed a sight to see. "The Dukeries" alone made a gallant show. Worksop Manor, then the property of the Duke of Norfolk, now of the Duke of Newcastle, was uninhabited; Clumber, although the reigning duke did not hunt, was represented by the heir, the grandfather of the present duke, and an influential member of the Government at the time of the Crimean War; Welbeck, as I have noted, by the marquis and his brother, Lord Henry; and Thoresby by Earl

Manvers, the most considerate of landlords, the most generous of benefactors to the poor and sick, the kindest and truest of friends. I have never since seen such a charming "turn-out," an equipage so *comme il faut,* as that in which he came to the meet—an open carriage with four grand sixteen-hand horses, ridden by postilions in cherry-coloured jackets, buckskins, and black-velvet caps, with two outriders. He could say a severe thing when a knave or a fool required it; but he was a delightful companion in his normal state, full of quaint and genial humour. Though he was always a munificent supporter of the hunt, he was not a prominent hunter; in fact, he preferred the *fallentis semita vitæ,* and followed in the wake of the hounds, "far from the madding crowd." If he met with obstacles which seemed to him unduly obtrusive, Robert, a favourite groom, got off his horse and removed them. One day a timid stranger, admiring this method of hunting made easy, attached himself as equerry, and followed through the gaps, until the earl, turning towards him with a solemn courtesy, said, as he raised his hat, "I am quite sure, sir, that you are not aware that for many years I have enjoyed in this hunt *the exclusive privilege of being last;* and I know that I have only to inform you of this fact to secure your respect for my claim."

On another occasion, when a new pack had been brought into the country, hastily got together, and comprising the drafts of many kennels, only unanimous on one subject, that it was their duty to hunt whatever they could see or smell, an officer came from the barracks at Nottingham to one of our meets, who was evidently an expert. The hounds had been but a short time in covert, when a hare came forth, in front of the horsemen outside, pursued by half a dozen puppies, full cry. The officer immediately followed, and, with considerable shouting and cracking of his whip, turned them back into the wood. Whereupon Lord Manvers rode up to him, and addressed him, with a courteous bow, " Pardon me, sir, for the intrusion, but, seeing that you are a sportsman, I think it only right to warn you that in undertaking to correct the delinquencies of this incorrigible pack of rebels, you are entering upon a task which is superhuman. ' All the king's horses and all the king's men ' could not stop them from running hare."

Robert aforesaid, though blameless as a groom, was *sans peur*, but not *sans reproche*, as a rider, and, on being requested by his master to try a mare recently purchased at a fence, he lost his seat, and, as he alighted, scored her with the spur. " Robert," the earl quietly remarked, " if the spur is required in taking a horse over a fence, the application is usually made before, rather than after, the leap."

Lord Scarborough, irreverently designated " Black Jack," came also with four horses from Rufford, and " Dick Lumley," heir to the title, and a striking contrast to the solemn peer, bright with health, high spirits, and good looks. Lord Galway came from Serlby, himself a Master of Hounds, and no better sportsman rode horse or carried horn. The Foljambes from Osberton; George the squire, also M.F.H., and Frank, his brother, one of the most popular men of his day, and always to the fore. They were sorely afflicted, these two brothers, the elder with blindness, and the younger with a fatal cancer; but the fame of the Foljambes in the hunting (and cricket) field is safe with those who bear the name. The Bridgeman-Simpsons from Babworth; the squire, who was the husband of the accomplished lady to whom I have previously referred as an artist, and his brother, the rector. The Denisons from Ossington, the home of the elder brother, Evelyn, afterwards Speaker of the House of Commons, and Viscount Ossington. They were all of them what we gardeners call "specimen plants," men of genius and culture. Four, I think, were first-class men at Oxford, including Edward, Bishop of Salisbury, and George, Archdeacon of Taunton. Lord Manvers spoke of the latter as "St. George without the dragon," and right worthy is he to be ranked among the champions of Christendom, for no man has fought more bravely than he against the enemies of his Church and creed.

Mr. Denison was always a very generous supporter of the hunt, and took an anxious and practical interest in its management, not only because he liked the amusement, but because, as he said to me more than

once, it seemed to him a matter of importance to the
common weal, that all sorts and conditions of men
should have opportunities of meeting together for
pleasant recreation, interchange of thought, and
enlargement of sympathy. At the time when he was
made Speaker, he was specially hopeful, on the election
of a new M.F.H., and the auspicious commence-
ment of his new *régime;* and Davis, the huntsman,
with whom I was discussing our future prospects,
said to me, " As for the Speaker, sir, I never saw
him so pleased, and I'm only afraid of his calling
out, 'Forrard, Fallacy!'" (one of his favourite hounds)
" in the 'Ouse, instead of 'Order, gentlemen!'" No
need, I thought, to encourage Fallacy in a place
where it never ceases to assert itself; and as for
" Order, gentlemen," in those days all members of
Parliament were gentlemen and knew how to keep
order for themselves.

There were many other good men and true : Sir
William Miles, M.P. for Bristol, but then residing
at Beesthorpe Hall, Notts., a most powerful horseman,
who excelled all in piloting a " screw;" Sherbrooke
of Oxton (formerly Lowe, the brother of Robert,
Chancellor of the Exchequer and afterwards Lord
Sherbrooke), the model of a country squire; Manners-
Sutton of Kelham; Pegge-Burnell of Winkburn;
" Will Need" of Fountain Dale, of whom more
anon; the Handleys of Muskham; Francklin of
Gonalston; Trebeck, Beecher, and Warrand, of
Southwell; Milward of Hexgreave. And now?

The last time I saw the hunt go by, I counted but six scarlet coats, and those of other tints were few; but it was solace to hear that some of the great houses still maintained their ancient zeal, pre-eminently those of Welbeck and Thoresby, supporting the chase in person and in purse, and that "the Rufford" never had a more successful and popular Master than now in Launcelot Rolleston.

CHAPTER XXIII.

HUNTERS—*Continued.*

My first horses—A sad catastrophe—Squire Musters—The
Belvoir Hunt—Will Goodall—The Quorn—The Pytch-
ley—Rufford incidents—Captain Percy Williams—Jack
Davis—Colonel Welfitt—Hunting parsons.

REVERTING to early youth, the first hunter which
was mine exclusively was a cob of fifteen hands.
His name was David, and I loved him like another
Jonathan. He was a demure, and yet an eccentric
horse. He galloped demurely, he jumped demurely,
he never reared, or kicked, or shied, and yet on one
occasion he suddenly and irresistibly darted from
the riding of a wood into the thicket, and rushing
under the bough of a tree, where there was not
room for both of us to pass, he left me, like Absalom,
among the branches; and again, on a sunny afternoon,
when we had been waiting for some time in a
grass field outside the covert, in which hounds
were drawing, he with his usual deliberation sank
gradually down. Before he had time to roll, or I to
dismount, my father, who was happily close by,
gave him such a cut with his whip as roused him to

an abnormal liveliness, and kept him wide awake
throughout the day. History repeats itself, and,
after a lapse of some thirty years, I had a similar
experience. I was returning from a distant meet
on a warm day towards the end of March, and was
riding very slowly on the grassy side of a lane,
when "Paddy," a very old Irish horse, went down
abruptly, and I had only just time to free myself
from the saddle, before he was lying on his side.
I thought that his end was come, and, having loosed
his girths, I stood by in a most doleful mood, for
a better horse never rose at a fence; and I was
doubting whether I should bleed him in the mouth,
the only form of depletion which I should dare to
practise, when, to my astonishment, lazily and
leisurely, but with evident satisfaction, the old
horse began to graze! Aware that only condemned
criminals partake of a hearty breakfast on the eve,
or rather the morn, of annihilation, I joyfully
tightened Paddy's girths, raised him on his legs
with a chuck of the bridle, mounted, and trotted
him home. I believe that the horse was fast asleep
when he fell.

This incident, comic in itself, evokes, nevertheless,
one of the most tragic memories of my life. I was
riding a very promising four-year-old over some
small fences, as we went from covert to covert
(hounds not running), and came to one which had
a dyke of some four feet on the other side, and a
drop of about a foot from the level of the ground

from which he sprang. He seemed to clear the leap easily and completely, but I suppose that one of his hind legs must have alighted below the bank. We had not gone far into the field before I felt a tremulous vibration under me, and when I had dismounted, and led him a few paces onward, he fell, never to rise again. I have always had one thankful consolation: I am sure that he felt no pain. When ten minutes afterwards he heard the distant horn, he raised his head, and his bright eyes glowed, as he longed to join the chase. I could have thrown myself on the ground and wept, and I never hear that most pathetic song of Whyte Melville's, "The Place where the Old Horse died," but a flood of thoughts comes gushing, and fills mine eyes with tears.

David was soon too slow for my ambition, and a generosity which never failed supplied me with a much more rapid conveyance, in the form of a bright well-bred bay with black points, a beautiful head, clean shoulders, and strong propelling powers, though anything but a screw. My singing sister insisted that he should be called Lochinvar, but it was I who should have had the appellation, convinced as I was, after a brief acquaintance, that "in all the wide borders my steed was the best." Accustomed to the dignified demeanour of David, I was somewhat perplexed for a brief season by the incessant gaiety of his successor, but I quickly discovered that it was only an indication of his desire for those more active employments which I was fully prepared to supply, and that he loved galloping and jumping as much as I did. We had only one quarrel, which resulted in a brief separation. We were approaching a fence, when he saw, and I ought to have seen, the hounds on the other side make a sudden turn. He turned with them, and as he resisted my endeavour to keep him in his former line, I struck him sharply with my whip. In three seconds I was on my back by his side. I really don't know how he did it, but if a box of dynamite had exploded under me, I could not have been more summarily dislodged. Then the horse never attempted to move. I believe that if he could have spoken he would have said, " I'm very sorry ; please get up ; but you mustn't do it again." I never felt more humiliated. I arose a sadder, a wiser, and a dirtier man. Lochinvar offered no resistance when I put him again at the fence. He never swerved an inch from my guidance, though I turned him, of course, on the opposite side to rejoin the hounds. He went, if possible, better than ever, and made no mistake. When I reached home my father, who had not been out that day, met me in the stable-yard and said, " I don't know, Reynolds, whether you have brought the brush, but I never saw any one in greater need of it." I told him what had happened, and he laughed, until I thought he would be ill. I claim some appreciative sense of humour, but I never could fully grasp the comedy of that situation.

I rode Lochinvar for two Christmas holidays, and then I was promoted from the cob to the hunter, raised from the lower to the upper horse. At that time the famous "Jack Musters" was still hunting hounds in Nottinghamshire, and his clear musical voice rang through our big woods in "The Clays." The husband of Byron's "Mary," a great athlete in his earlier days, was a powerful horseman, and had a method of pressing his horse through a fence, whenever it was possible, rather than of leaping over it, which was not graceful, though in the case of such a heavy rider it required less exertion from his steed. In the first days of my promotion, I was riding a very tall animal, appropriately named Leopard (one of those horses which, too good for harness, and not quite good enough for hunting, form the fag end of a stud, and are rarely ridden by the owner), and in the course of a very slow run, for the scent was bad, we came to a flight of strong rails. As there was no hurry, Mr. Musters ordered one of his whips to get off and remove a bar. Alas! the pride which goeth before a fall came upon me, and I rode at the rail; but Leopard had no pride about him, and instead of rising to the occasion, he smashed two bars. While I was communicating to him my views as to his behaviour, I heard the cheery voice of Musters, "Thank you, sir, thank you. Get on, Jack." The vote of thanks, seconded by the whip, was carried unanimously, but it failed to impart to me the gratification with which it was proposed.

I went now and then into " the Belvoir " country. First, when the Duke of Wellington, a guest of the Duke of Rutland, came to the meet at " Scrimshaw's Mill," and it seemed as though every man who could ride or drive, in the four counties of Leicester, Rutland, Lincoln, and Nottinghamshire, was there to welcome our great hero. From the high ground on which the hill stands, the surrounding country appeared like—no, I shall not say an ant-hill; everybody would say an ant-hill—seemed to be as full of moving life as London of twinkling lights, when you look down upon it in the night. " The Belvoir country " —words musical and full of meaning in the ears of hunting men ! " Beautiful to see," whether on the broad uplands of Lincoln Heath, or (to him who has a stout heart and strong horse) in the heavier soil and larger fences of the Vale. " Beautiful to see," the best-looking, the best-bred, the most even pack of hounds in the world ; and he who can follow them, when they meet, and there is a scent, at Stubton (the only appointment which was well within my reach), will bear witness that they are as good as they look. " Beautiful to see," with Will Goodall, rightly named, like the place from which he came, for he was good all round, in looks, in temper, knowledge, horsemanship, riding before them to covert, or close behind them in the chase—close behind, so long as his steed would carry him. I remember an occasion when he was not so well mounted as usual, and the mare which he rode, hardly rising at a fence, fell into a deep ditch on the other side, and depositing Will on the bank, seemed quite content to remain where she was. At that moment the hounds lost the scent, but Goodall's keen eye had seen the tired fox in front, and running forward, cap in hand, he put them on the line. Then returning to the mare, pulling at her head, and touching her with his whip, he said, " Now, old lady, get up, and let us have another try ! "

" Beautiful to see," as I have seen, such gallant cavaliers as Lords Forester, Gardner, Wilton, Sirs Frederick Johnston, Thomas Wychcote, Mr. Gilmour, " Harry Howson," Rector of Brant Broughton (and memory presents him, making for his favourite place over the Brant aforesaid, on whose banks so many will be " left lamenting "), Colonel Dundas, the Gordons, John Marriott, and many more.

I have only one memory of the illustrious "Quorn," the recollection of a happy day which I spent in " high Leicestershire," at the invitation of my friend, W. Clowes, then Master, in the neighbourhood of Cream Gorse and Ashby Pastures. I went, as a heavy weight, only to look on, but I saw much more than I expected. There was an immense " field," but, like all other fields, it grew small by degrees and beautifully less. Not so the fences—they were several sizes larger than I liked; but I had a powerful horse, and to rise from the elastic sward, instead of from the tenacious clay, was like leaping from a spring-board to an athlete.

"The Pytchley" I never saw, though I have been often in their country, and had the pleasure of knowing some of their foremost men, Whyte Melville, H. Nethercote, R. Bevan, and others. It must be a grand country to ride over—a little too grand now and then; indeed, I have heard Percy Williams say that there was a certain district, not far from Market Harborough, which no horse could negotiate. His name recalls my excursive thoughts to the Rufford, of which he was for many years the successful Master. He was a thorough sportsman, lived at the kennels, like the old tradesmen over their shops, turned out his men, hounds, and horses in excellent order, and was always punctual. Sometimes too punctual, as when, in the days of cub-hunting, he appeared very early on a September morning in a distant part of the hunt, and, not finding a fox in the first wood which he tried, said to a boy waiting outside, "Well, my lad, and where are all these foxes, of which I have heard so much?" "Oh, if you please, sir," replied the guileless youth, "fayther hasn't brought him yet." The keeper had a bagman in reserve, to deceive his master, whose orders to preserve foxes he had disobeyed, and his delay in producing him lost him his situation—his employer gave him the sack.

And this incident again reminds me of Jack Davis, who was long chief equerry to Captain Percy Williams, and of a conversation which I overheard, to my intense delight, between him and another keeper, who loved the pheasant more than the fox, and who joined us at the centre of a large wood, which the hounds were patiently drawing without any audible results. " Good morning, Mr. Davis," said the keeper. " Morning," growled Mr. Davis. " Has your dogs had pretty good sport, Mr. Davis ? " " We don't call 'em dogs," said Jack, " we call 'em hounds." " Oh, don't yer ? " said the keeper. " I thote yer did." " Oh, you thote so, did you ? " replied Davis. " You're like Thompson's dog ; he thote they were a-bringing him his breakfast, and he came up, a-jumping and wagging his tail, and—*they took him out and hanged him !*" And if he had been wearing the black cap of a judge, and not of a fox-hunter, I believe he would have pronounced then and there upon that keeper the extreme sentence of the law.

Jack's contempt for game and gamekeepers amounted to monomania. We were returning one afternoon by a famous preserve, and from the grassy lane on which we rode the pheasants rose before our horses in such numbers, that I could not restrain the exclamation, " What a lot of pheasants ! " On which Mr. Davis replied, drawing himself up into an attitude of dignity, and gazing into the firmament with a sudden interest, as though he had just been made Astronomer Royal, " *We don't take no notice of them things !* "

The Master of the Rufford whom I knew best and cared for most (with the exception, of course, of my brother-in-law, Francklin, who showed good sport for a couple of seasons, and greatly improved the quality of the pack, chiefly by introducing the Belvoir blood) was Colonel Welfitt, to whom I have previously referred as "Will Need," and who was the president of the Ornithological Show at Bolsover, falsely accused by a disappointed exhibitor of "nipping out o' th' army" to avoid the Crimean War. He was past mid age when he accepted the office, and when he informed old John, the kennel-man, that he was going to be Master, the reply was not encouraging: "Are yer? Yer twenty years too old for the job." There never was a more matter-of-fact or plain-spoken man than John, and when he was called upon at the hunt supper to propose a sentiment, he rose and said, with a solemnity befitting the occasion, "Gentlemen, the sentiment as I've got to propose is this—I wish as I wor twenty year younger!"

Welfitt was "a fellow of infinite jest," one of those bright spirits who make the sunshine of society, dispelling its dreary gloom, and thawing its rigid and chill constraints. Dignity forgot its self-importance at the sound of his joyful laugh, and in him were fulfilled the wise man's words, "A merry heart doeth good like a medicine." His experience, military (he was a captain in the 16th Lancers, and afterwards commanded our yeomen regiment of "Sherwood Rangers"), magisterial, and sporting, supplied him with a fund of anecdotes, always well told and worth hearing. Moreover, he knew the "time to laugh," and that "it is good to be merry and wise," but below the sparkling surface there was a stream of "living water," deep and clear.

Dulce est desipere in loco—occasionally, opportunely, harmlessly. Welfitt delighted in a practical joke. He had promised to give a Dorking cock to a neighbour, and presuming upon his credulity, although not, as the result showed, overrating it, he put an egg into the hamper which contained the bird. By an early post he received a thankful acknowledgment of its safe arrival, with the information that, to the intense surprise of the writer, the cock, during his journey, had laid an egg! The donor immediately wrote back to say that the fowl had undoubtedly "beaten the record," that he was the only cock who had ever done it, and that his friend would find, to the increase of his astonishment, that "the egg was laid hard boiled!"

He who attacked Welfitt rode for a fall. He lost a valuable hunter, which was accidentally "staked" and died. At the same time, a member of the hunt, who had more money than manners, had bought a black horse for two hundred guineas, which, to his sore disappointment, had fallen lame. He was under the impression that his misfortune was only known to his grooms; but Welfitt, whose ears were always open, had heard of it, and therefore when he was rudely addressed, "And so, I hear,

you've killed your grey horse," he was quite prepared with a reply—"Yes, he's dead and buried.
It is a sad loss to me, but I have been much com-
forted in my sorrow by a most kind and considerate
letter, written by your black horse, and *expressing
his deep regret that he was too lame to attend the
funeral.*"

Silence would have been more prudent in
another of our *nouveaux riches*, who would quote
Latin and other languages which he had never
learned, and who, when asked why he suddenly
disappeared in the middle of a capital run, frankly
owned that he came to a fence which was larger
than he liked, and that, seeing an open space in the
distance, he had made for it, only to find a still more
formidable dyke. "And so," he said, "I went from
Skilly to Carrybedees, and never saw the hounds
again."

*   *   *   *   *

Is it right for a clergyman to hunt? Again I
say, as of cricket previously, if I were a bishop, and
that question were put to me by a priest, I should
answer, "If you can assure me that you can spare
the time and the money, that you can take a day's
holiday in the week without neglecting any of your
duties, reducing your charities, or getting into debt,
you have my permission to hunt on one immutable
condition—*that you ride straight to hounds;* and if I
hear of you craning and shirking I shall withdraw
it at once."

In these happier days of clerical energy very few have the time, and in these sadder days of clerical penury very few have the means, to hunt; but I should be sorry to hear that the ecclesiastical element was banished from the chase. The presence of the parson contradicts an impression which, silly as it is, has been accepted and repeated by those who are disaffected towards us, that we lose our virility on taking Holy Orders; and the black coat and the white tie may sometimes be a wholesome restraint. I am sure that my influence with my parishioners was not diminished when I hunted once in the week, and I know from the clergy with whom I stayed when I went from home as a preacher, that on several occasions there were men in the congregation, whom I had met in the field, who " had not been seen before in church on a week-day." I recall another incident which illustrates my argument. On a certain day, when two foxes were before the hounds in a large covert, one of them came out with more than half the pack in front of the huntsman and myself, who were the only horsemen on that side of the wood. He blew his horn for the rest to follow, and away we rode with a burning scent. We had gone about a mile, and were in a high state of delight, when the Master, who had remained with the rest of the hounds in pursuit of fox No. 2, sounded a recall, and obedience was inevitable. As he rode forward to turn the hounds a malediction, brief but vehement, came from his lips, "D—— that horn!" Before I went home he came to me, and, touching his cap, he said, "I'm very sorry, sir, that I lost my temper and spoke those words this morning."

Other memories of the chase will suggest themselves, when I revert to old Oxford days; meanwhile I would introduce a few reminiscences of another form of hunting, the pursuit of game with a gun.

CHAPTER XXIV.

SHOOTERS.

Johnny Jebb and his gun—My first partridge—Joyful memories
—The past and the present—The old keeper's lamentation
—A clever auctioneer.

SOME sixty years ago there lived in our village a
poor hunchback, named Johnny Jebb. He had
not only the pity but the regard of us all, for,
though he was deformed in body, he had a ready
wit, a genial temper, and gentle ways, and could
make himself useful in many little matters. He
was the public scribe of those who could not write,
acting as their amanuensis, and even making wills
and drawing up agreements in a neat, legible hand.
He cut the hair and shaved the cheeks and chins of
the rustics, the shoeing-shed of the blacksmith being
his barber's shop, when not otherwise engaged.
He sold oranges and nuts. I knew him first as a
painter, and though I have since seen the galleries
of the Vatican, Florence, and other famous collections, no pictures have ever made such an impression upon me as those of Johnny Jebb. He begged
old copy-books, which in those days had some object

delineated on the cover, with a brief description or moral (Charles Dickens tells us that one of these represented a virtuous lion, constrained by his conscience to devour a young man who had contracted a habit of swearing), and these engravings were minutely, elaborately coloured, and converted into pictures which absorbed all my admiration. Two of these, a parrot, and Westminster Abbey, were purchased, on my urgent solicitations, by my mother at an outlay of one shilling. Afterwards I saw in the Zoological Gardens and elsewhere a large number of parrots, and I also saw the real Westminster Abbey, St. Peter's at Rome, and other famous churches, but neither in ornithology nor in architecture anything at all resembling Johnny's brilliant variety of tint. Every feather in the bird, and every stone in the building, had its own distinctive hue.

He was very poor, and every one was anxious to give him a preference when there were "odd jobs" to be done. "Bird-tenting," the watching and scaring away of crows, wood-pigeons, sparrows, etc., from the corn, freshly sown or ripening in the ear, was one of these employments, and was performed by blowing a horn, shaking a wooden rattle, or by the firing of a gun. Wandering about the fields one August afternoon in my early boyhood, "all among the barley I heard this frequent gun," and, guided by the sound, I soon discovered that the gunner was Johnny Jebb. After much persuasion and solemn vows of secrecy, I induced him to let me handle the weapon, and in a state of high nervous excitement I had my first shot; and after numerous failures, the results of blinking, and twitching and wobbling of the implement, I triumphantly brought down—at a distance of not less than twelve yards, and after aiming for not more than two minutes—a "spink"! John said it was a spink, but there was not much left to indicate its species.

What a contrast that gun would make with the latest improvements in the hammerless, smokeless, self-loading, self-ejecting breech-loader! It had the longest barrel and the shortest stock I ever saw in conjunction. The former gradually dwindled from a full-sized breech to a bore about the size of a fourpenny-bit. The small, stunted stock was bound with brass, and, being more convex than concave, seemed to be always slipping from the shoulder. The cock, or hammer, held a large flint, which, when the trigger was pulled, struck the steel opposite, uncovering the small pan, and igniting with its sparks the powder which was placed therein, and which passed through a touch-hole into the barrel. Johnny kept his powder in a tin tobacco-box, in one pocket of his trousers, and his shot loose in the other. These he measured out in the head of an old clay pipe, placing over the powder and over the shot a liberal supply of newspaper, which he produced from another portion of his raiment; and which required the vigorous use of his ramrod to be kept in position.

It was, I think, on the occasion of my third visit to the barley, and when I was anxiously stalking a yellow-hammer by the hedge side of the field, that I was startled by a sound of rushing wings, and a covey of partridges, the first I had ever seen, rose from the corn, and flew towards me. I heard Johnny call, "Don't shoot! don't shoot!" but, whether I lost my presence of mind, or was impelled by sporting instincts, or by memories of bread sauce, or whatever may have been my motive, I heeded not his warning voice; I closed my eyes, raised my gun, and fired. The hen-bird piloted her young ones safely over the fence while I was elevating the long tube and inducing a tardy obedience to the laws of combustion, but the old cock, the father and faithful guardian of his family, fell, dead as a stone, in the grass field beyond. I should say that Johnny's lineaments, when he saw him fall, very much resembled those of the gentleman who

> "Drew Priam's curtain in the dead of night,
> And told him half his Troy was burned."

The most accomplished tragedian could not have assumed his look of horror. "The keeper would kill him, and the squire would put him in jail;" which seemed a superfluous appendix. For myself, though I felt, at first, something of that compassion which, we read in the "American Æsop," distressed the tender-hearted elephant, when she accidentally set her foot on the hen-partridge, and, seeing the young birds in the nest below, sighed, "Alas, what have I done! I have been a mother myself," and sat down on the callow brood—I must confess that, on the whole, my emotions were more jubilant than grievous. Ignoring the fluke, I proudly remembered that I had brought down my first game. My only regret was that I could not go home and make a full confession, for fear of bringing Johnny into trouble. Gradually he recovered his confidence, as he lost his fear of discovery, and he put the bird in his pocket, to be buried at nightfall, as he informed me, in some secret place. No long time after, when my old companion was gone, I told my father the incident, and he said "it would be one of the best suppers poor Johnny ever had!"

At an early age I was presented with a gun, about the time when the old "flint and steel" was superseded by the "copper cap," and was instructed how to use it. My father gave me some simple rules: "Never carry your gun 'on full cock,' except when you see, or expect to see, game; and take care to have the muzzle always pointed downward or upward, so that if the charge accidentally explodes, no harm can happen. If you ever present to me a view down the barrel of your gun, I shall send you home." He was a man of his word, and had the courage of his opinions. I went home once, but it was ἅπαξ, once for all. I never repeated the offence.

Then (and for fifty consecutive years) I took out a certificate, and was duly " licensed to kill game ; " and of all my holidays with the gun, the first have the fondest memories. I have held my own with my companions in the stubbles and the turnips, in the woods, and on the moor ; I have wiped Green's eye and walked Brown off his legs ; I have shot in some of our best preserves, but I can remember no days so delectable as those of boyhood and youth. It is not so in other sports. In hunting, for example, in cricket, and in fishing, experience adds to enjoyment, and *the man* has more power and skill with his horse, his bat, and his rod ; but in shooting there is no joy to compare with the first partridge, pheasant, woodcock, black-cock, grouse, mallard, snipe, or running game. Who does not rejoice to recall those mornings at Christmastide when, with a supreme effort, he rose at the dawn of day, and went by the brookside, silently over the untrodden snow, with his gun and his retriever ; and there was a rustle among the reeds, and a flapping of wings, and, with a single note of indignation or of fear, the wild drake rose, and sped upon his flight, until a louder utterance resounded far and near, and he lay on the ground, a far more attractive sight to the eyes of the young sportsman and to the recollection of the old than a hundred yards of pheasants—reared in coops, and shot in corners—placed side by side in the riding of a wood, as the *spolia opima* of a grand battue? As a result, I prefer to this wholesale (and retail) carnage the foreign baron, returning proudly from *la chasse*, with his retainers shouting in their joy, and a brass band playing triumphant music, while four foresters bear before their lord (on horseback) a diminutive rabbit on a pole!

Or what shall we compare with the eager, intense felicity of boyhood, wandering about the woodlands on a summer's eve, creeping, gun in hand, to the corner of the covert, whence the rabbits come forth to graze, and intercepting one of them ere he can reach his refuge? Or, when crouched in ambush, half in the fence and half in the dyke, we wondered whether that leveret nibbling the clover on our right was within range of our artillery, or whether we should shoot the rabbit some three yards nearer on our left? Or, who forgets the supreme fruition of hedgerow shooting in the winter months, when the adjoining wood has recently been shot (not surrounded by nets as now), and with a friend on the other side, a couple of beaters, and a lively terrier, we saw the nimble rabbit dart from his lair, amid the rattling of sticks, the shouts of the men, and the barking of the dog; back again sometimes, ere we could raise the gun; sometimes, wisely, running out of sight down the dyke, not showing himself until, out of reach of our artillery, he neared the wood, and then wagging his little white scut, as though in derision, before he disappeared in the thicket; sometimes, unwisely, making for the open and turning a fatal somersault, with the terrier not far from his heels.

I am not surprised that the young men of our present day do not enjoy partridge-shooting as it was enjoyed in the days of my youth. I am not surprised that they go forth some two or three hours later, and return some two or three hours earlier; that they dawdle over their elaborate luncheons, pipes, and cigarettes, and may be found in the billiard-room, or the morning-room, or the easy-chair in the drawing-room, when they might have been, as we were, still in the fields. I am not surprised, because, though they have some advantages, though they no longer need the paraphernalia with which we were encumbered—the powder-flask, the shot-belt, the ramrod, the wads, and the caps—though they have more birds to shoot at, artificially reared, and driven in the earlier hours of the morning into the turnips, the sport itself is comparatively uninteresting, dull, formal, monotonous. When the sickle was superseded by the scythe and the mowing-machine, and the face of the earth was clean-shaved, when the high hedges were cut down and the broad dykes filled in, when fields were added to fields, or only separated by the light iron fence, when the old order changed and gave place to the new, there were manifest gains in facilities of cultivation and in the increase of produce; but to the artist and to the sportsman, to those who loved the picturesque, and to those who followed the partridge, the transformation was indeed deplorable. I remember an old gamekeeper sorrowfully surveying a model farm, as though it had been some fair city overthrown by an earthquake, some shore strewn with wrecks, or some plantation of goodly trees laid low by the hurricane, and saying, " I've known the time when that farm was as pretty a spot for game as could be found in the county, and now—why, there ain't a place where a partridge can make a nest, or a hare or a rabbit can hide! You see the grass field yonder. Well, you'll scarcely believe it, but it wor once the beautifullest bog for a jack snipe as ever you'd wish to see. I've killed three couple of a morning among the tussocks and rushes afore they spoilt it with them drains!" And when I nobly suggested (for my sympathies were with the snipes) that he must not forget that there was more wheat, more food, than before, he wished to be informed " what was the good of wheat, which it did not pay to grow at thirty shillings a quarter, when them foreigners were sending more than we wanted, and *folks never left no stubble !* "

The jack snipe is a fascinating bird (whether on the wing or on the toast), but he is not an adjunct of true agriculture, and the keeper's denunciation of modern improvements must be regarded as " not proven." It recalls to me another plea for bad farming, as quaint, but far more ingenious, which I heard many years ago from a Notts auctioneer, the cleverest of his craft in the midland counties. He was offering for sale a farm in our neighbourhood, which had been long neglected by idle and impoverished tenants, when one of his audience proclaimed in a loud voice, " that he wouldn't have the place as a gift; that it was more like a *dock*yard than a farm, and he didn't think it would produce a new corn from an old one."   The auctioneer heard him patiently, and, when he had concluded his disparagements, he replied to the effect " that he should make no attempt to conceal the fact that the farm was not in a satisfactory condition; but the land itself was excellent, and he was sure that any occupier possessed of the intelligence of the gentleman who had just favoured them with his candid and gratuitous remarks " (hereupon all eyes were fixed on the commentator, to his evident discomfort), " any tenant with his quick discovery of defects, his knowledge of *draining* " (the sale took place on the afternoon of a market day, and the countenance of the critic, who had just come from "the ordinary," was still aglow with alcoholic fire), " would speedily restore order, fertility, and abundance.   And I think," he continued, " that this gentleman has not duly considered the present advantages, as well as the future profits, to be derived from a farm such as this which I have now the honour of offering to your notice.   I would ask you to reflect for a moment upon the temptations which beset a young man who has entered upon a farm on which everything has been done which capital and culture could do. He goes out to find that no repairs are required, no improvements can be designed, no alteration can be made in the regular routine of work. So he returns to his home, has a glass of brandy and water, and smokes a cigar. Takes another walk after his dinner; same results, more brandy and water, more cigars — contracts a habit of drinking, loses his money, loses his health, dies in the workhouse! Whereas, a young man who takes the tenancy of the farm which is now on sale is compelled to be industrious, and has not a moment of spare time upon his hands; his active habits make him healthful, a beautiful wife and lovely children make his home happy, frugality makes him rich, and he dies at an advanced age, respected by all, and bequeathing a thousand pounds to the Nottingham Infirmary." After this introduction the speaker, having put all his hearers but one in good humour, proceeded to business.

CHAPTER XXV.

SHOOTERS—*Continued.*

Partridge-shooting in the olden time—The sickle and the scythe —Tame birds—Temptations and inclinations to poach— The poacher.

LET me describe a day's partridge-shooting in the olden time, that the young sportsman may, if he please, compare the present with the past. We breakfasted early, and left the house about 9 a.m. The keeper waited with the guns; a brace of pointers whining in irrepressible excitement, and receiving us with joyful embraces, which, as Mrs. Nickleby said, when one of her admirers persisted in carving her initials on the pew-door during divine service, were "gratifying, but embarrassing;" and a miscellaneous youth, who was everything by turns, and nothing long, sometimes in the stable, sometimes in the garden, a messenger, a cleaner of boots, whose service everybody claimed, especially "the maids," but who was in September definitely annexed to the shooters. A short walk brings us to a field of wheat-stubble—some fifteen inches of straw has been left by the Irish reapers, who came over in those days by thousands with their sickles—and as

soon as the gate is open, our plan of "beating"
the ground having been previously decided, and
the miscellany sent off to "mark," the pointers
rush right and left in front of us, the limit of
their range being intimated to them by the whistle
of the keeper, and, crossing each other at intervals,
pursue their quest of the game. See! Sancho suddenly changes his gallop to a walk, and the walk,
after a few slow, cautious steps, into a halt. Then
he stands, and moves not, unless it be to crouch upon
the ground, as he finds himself close to the birds, or
to follow as they run before him. Juno sees him,
fifty yards away, stops and "backs." Distance does
not lend enchantment to the view, and her curiosity
(said to be a feminine infirmity, but I have noticed
it quite as largely developed in Sancho and other
males) impels her to make a stealthy advance towards
her mate, until the upraised hand of the keeper, and
his "Steady, Juno!" enforces a reluctant obedience.
The guns draw nearer to "the point," and this is a
crisis in which you may frequently distinguish the
superior from the second-rate sportsman, the silver
from the electro-plate—I might almost say, the gentleman from the snob. The former, when he is nearest
to the game, waits patiently for his companion, and
seems more anxious to give than to take advantage;
the latter either hurries forward with a selfishness
which disdains disguise, or moves onward step by
step when he thinks that he is unobserved, and in
either case puts up the birds. Prematurely or not,

sooner or later, they must rise from their covert, some to fall and the rest to be accelerated in their flight—as though they were not sufficiently scared by the report of the guns and their family bereavements—by loud holloas of " Mark! mark!" to the lad in the lane, who has an engagement with some blackberries in another direction, but is expected to see every bird alight, wherever he may happen to be. Then, as the well-trained pointers obey the word of command, " Down, charge!" the guns are reloaded, the birds are bagged, and the sportsmen either follow the covey which they have sprung, or go in search of other game.

All around us the deep stubbles offered board and lodging for the birds, but, when disturbed, they would seek other refuge; and following them in the clover and the grass, the turnips and potatoes, the hedgerows and the late crops of beans, we had a continual and charming diversity in the scene and manner of our sport. Sometimes they would alight on the fallows, and then, when the sun was up, and the great clods of clay were baking into bricks, you required a good courage and a good pair of boots. Both the beans and the ploughed land suggested Leech's delightful sketch of the lazy gunner, giving directions to his friend to do the walking, " and I'll stay here and mark." But there was no shirking, no loitering, in those days; the exercise and its results were too enjoyable, and *"dum perspiro, spero"* was on the sportsman's crest.

Sometimes the farmer would join us on his lands —for the tenant had not been then informed that it was his duty to hate his landlord—and would walk with us, and show us where to find the game, and have a pleasant, friendly talk about the harvest and the markets, until he left us, with a hare in one hand and a brace of birds in the other.

And then, just when our energies were beginning to flag and the pointers beginning to tire, when our collars were limp and our ties were loose, when the birds, as always in the middle of the day, were more difficult to find, and we were becoming more and more severe with the lad in the lane for not marking those birds which he could not possibly have seen—then Tim, the stableman, not remarkable on ordinary occasions for his personal charms, but now beautiful in our eyes as the Apollo Belvidere or the Flying Mercury, approaches with pony and cart, bringing luncheon to restore our vigour, and Don and Jewel to replace our weary dogs. Then the white cloth is spread under the umbrageous oak, or on the bank which is shaded by the tall hedge, and the cold game-pie, or the hot Irish stew, the puff, the cheesecake, and the peach, with the beer, which in that primitive period was made from malt and hops, with the brown bottles of "pop," and a *soupçon* of sherry—there might sometimes be what Mrs. Brown calls "just the least as is" of cognac to blend with the aerated water—are spread out for our refection, together with the rugs and the wraps, on

x

which we seat ourselves around. Sometimes the ladies joined us, and then, if Jupiter had seen our cup-bearers, he would have given poor Hebe warning; but our *séances*, though delightful, were brief, and as soon as the small cigar or pipe was smoked (the combination of paper and sawdust, called cigarette, was not then discovered) we resumed our sport, Sancho and Juno, refreshed by their rest, struggling with Tim, who had them in couples, and almost pulling him off his legs in their efforts to follow the guns.

In the afternoon the birds were again in the stubbles, and we continued our pursuit until "the sun was westering to its close." In those days, when we had no breech-loaders, and when we followed and found the game, instead of its being driven to us, we considered twenty brace a satisfactory "bag" for two guns, and it required good walking and good shooting to accomplish such a result. Under the present system of driving the coveys into turnips before the shooters go out, and then walking them up with a long line of beaters, much larger quantities are easily secured; but this process cannot be compared for a moment with the diversity of enjoyment which we had in the olden time, and hardly deserves to be described as sport. The rearing of tame birds by the hundred in itself invalidates any claim to the title, and my memory suggests an illustration in support of my argument. There was a numerous assemblage of shooters, keepers, loaders, and beaters, on the estate of a great breeder and preserver of game in my neighbourhood, and a multitude of partridges were congregated in two vast fields of turnips. There was a piece of grass land between these two fields, and on it stood the house and premises, kennels, and coops of the head keeper. As the company passed from one piece of turnips to the other, some scores of young birds, late hatched and little more than half-grown, gathered themselves around the keeper, and affectionately insisted, to his intense disgust, in following him across the field! I would rather see the Italian and French chasseur stalking the linnet, and bringing him down in triumph, because he has little else to stalk; I would rather see "'Arry from London" shooting at the seagulls, as they flap their great wings overhead, because, as a rule, he misses, than look upon that procession again.

Similar exhibitions may be witnessed in the coverts as well as in the field—young pheasants following the man who has reared them as he passes the place where they have been fed; and I protest against these poultry shows, this excessive and artificial multiplication of game, not only as detracting from the manliness of the sport, and converting healthful, vigorous, sustained exertion into the brief battue, half luncheon and half lounge; as creating a spirit of jealous competition which induces the competitors to appraise the merits of a day's shooting rather from the quantity which has been shot than from their enjoyment of the diversion; as interfering in many cases with another recreation which, being offered to all who can avail themselves of it, gives a much more extensive pleasure—I mean hunting, sometimes forbidden, and sometimes only permitted, because there is nothing to hunt;— but, in addition to these objections, I denounce this extravagant display as an additional temptation, which allures men to disobey the law of trespass, to disregard the rights of property, and to defy those who defend them.

I hold no brief, I make no apologies or excuses for those who heed not the Divine commandments, " Thou shalt not steal," " Thou shalt do no murder," but I maintain that it is every man's bounden duty to oppose rather than to encourage all tendencies to evil, to minimize rather than to increase the suggestions and opportunities of vice, to make it more easy to do that which is right, and more hard to do that which is wrong. If I find a burglar in my house I detain him, if I can, until he is trans- ferred to the police, but I do all that is in my power to keep him out of it; and I do not have any silver spoons on the lawn to show how rich I am in plate. I grow my apples in an orchard, and not upon way- side trees, and do not wear my handkerchief pro- truding from my pocket when I am in London streets.

Proclivities to poach are among those baleful weeds which are indigenous in " the ground of the heart," and which, if they are not checked, corrupt and cover the soil. Boys will go where they have been warned not to go, and to be pursued by some irascible owner, sudden and quick in quarrel, but slow in action, is a supreme delight. I have heard that after a holiday pies have come from the baker to the school containing rabbits not purchased in the market. Nay, I have heard grown men say that to see coveys of birds, bred on their own ground, flying over the boundary fence, and settling in a manner which seemed to them designedly and offensively ostentatious in their neighbour's fields, was a most severe ordeal. Indeed, one of them candidly confessed that a certain beanfield, to which a magnificent covey always resorted as soon as he entered the adjoining stubble, had finally led him astray. "I brought back two brace," he said; "but when, a few days afterwards, I succumbed to the same temptation, and was nearing the spot where the birds had dropped, in a state of profuse perspiration and some little nervous anxiety, I was horrified to hear a loud and angry voice exclaiming, 'What, yer in them be-ans agin! Young Lovegrove seed yer in 'em last Wednesday; but it's not now, and it's not then—it's for iver!'"

Speaking generally, these nomad and acquisitive instincts are satisfied by legitimate sports and games; but to those who have no means, and no lawful opportunities for such a gratification, they present themselves as seductive allurements to crime. A

friend of mine, a squire in the midlands, an enthusiastic sportsman, with a large experience both at
home and abroad, and an irrepressible desire to
narrate his adventures, was staying in the same
house with the Right Hon. John Bright, and one
night in the smoking-room he had for some time
entertained the company, as chief speaker, with
records of his prowess, when the famous orator,
having finished his pipe, rose up to go. My friend
pressed him to refill and remain. "I thank you,
sir, for your invitation," Mr. Bright replied, "but
having listened with much interest to your conversation, and having formed my conclusion, I think
that I will go to bed." "And may I ask," said the
sportsman, "what that conclusion may be?" "Certainly you may," it was answered. "My conclusion
is this: *that if you had been a poor man you would
have spent most of your time on the treadmill,* and I
wish you good night."

The poacher is not an educated man, and does
not read, like the Honourable Crasher, "The Idylls of
the King," but he is a very clever artist in his craft.
He knows the habits and the haunts of all the
animals, furred or feathered, which he desires to
annex, what they eat, and where they find it. He
knows their lair and roost. He can speak their
language and imitate their utterance so accurately
as to draw them almost within his reach. He
removes the top from a tailor's thimble, and covers
the vacant space with parchment, through which

he passes a piece of fine "gut," and, by drawing it backwards and forwards, produces the partridge "call." His snares, and traps, and "gins" are most cunningly devised, neatly made, and skilfully set. His manipulation of trout is delicate as it is fatal. He attaches a running noose of whipcord to the end of a stout rod or pole, and, passing it adroitly over the head of a pike basking on the surface of still clear water, he will tighten it with a sudden jerk as the fish opens his gills, and lift him at once to land. He knows where to set his night-lines in the pools of the brook, or by daylight to dislodge the eels beneath its banks, and spear them in midstream.

He watches not only the game but the keeper, and rejoices to elude and deceive him. Guns are fired by one or two of his company far away from the covert, in which the rest are engaged with their nets. Nor does he confine his devices to the keeper. A dealer in game at Nottingham came to the police-office to state that a man had driven to his house early that morning, bringing two large sacks containing hares in his cart. Each sack, he said, held twenty-five hares, and he opened one, and took out three or four specimens, to show that they were fresh and good. The bags were old and worn, and the legs protruded and the skins were visible here and there, where a rent had been made. The seller was in a very great hurry, as he "thought the bobbies were after him," and the dealer agreed to take the sacks as they were, and to give three pounds for the lot. On emptying them, he found himself the proprietor of the four sound hares which had been shown to him as a sample, seven hares' feet, several pieces of fur which had been deftly sewn on the sacks, and a various collection of old rags, grass, papers, and other rubbish!

The poacher will sometimes indulge in a quaint, sarcastic humour, as when he delineates in chalk upon the wall of the keeper's wayside home a rude representation of two men, carrying between them a long pole laden with game, and scrawls underneath his mural fresco, " Good night, Billy; 'ow you does snoar!" or when he wrote to a dignified and reserved peer of the realm, one of whose Christian names was Robert, the following epistle : *—" DEAR BOB,—You will be delighted to hear that we had first-rate sport last night in the big wood, and much regretted your absence. One of your keepers ran against a wire, placed in his way by some malicious person, and when he fell among the brambles, and his gun went off, his language almost made us blush. It seems a pity that his mother took him from the Sunday School afore they had finished his education, and he ought to know better than to carry his gun on full cock, when he's a-scrambling among the briars in the dark."

* I have seen the letter, but cannot remember the spelling and grammar *verbatim et literatim,* but otherwise it is accurately repeated.

Many years ago, I had an interview with a poacher, which, though it was very brief, and not a word was spoken, produced a great excitement, a memorable alternation of despair and victory. Walking with my gun by the side of a brook which ran through my property, in search of the wild duck, which sometimes came in the winter from the frozen lakes in the neighbourhood, and from the Trent, to our running stream, I had reached a point where it was crossed by a bridge and a public road. On this road, to my right, and but a few yards from the bridge, stood a man, who also carried a gun, and who, my keeper informed me, was a notorious poacher. The words had only just passed his lips when a fine mallard rose in front of us, and flew towards the bridge. I suppose that I was nervous in such an august presence, but, whatever was the cause, I fired and missed! The mallard was now an easy shot for the poacher, when, as he deliberately raised his gun, I pulled the trigger of my second barrel, and the bird fell dead at his feet. I shall never forget the dissolving view on the keeper's countenance, from the scowl of disgust to the grin of delight, when he went to fetch the drake!

CHAPTER XXVI.

OXONIANS.

Preparatory schools—Newark-upon-Trent—Young Mr. Gladstone—Memories of the elections—Arrival at Oxford—
Magdalen Bridge—The anxious freshman—College friends.

I went to Oxford to finish the education which
began with the archer and the frog. Soon after I
had mastered the alphabet, my parents seemed to
lose their yearning to " keep their only son, myself, at home." I had been systematically spoiled,
and trained to be a nuisance, and I was sent to a
preparatory school for very small boys, which was
kept by an excellent old lady, Mrs. Gilby, in the
town of Newark-upon-Trent. I am ashamed to state
that I made a most unfavourable impression upon
my schoolfellows, soon after my arrival, more
particularly upon the head of Master Charles Gilby,
at which I threw the king of the ninepins, when he
forbade me to join in the game.

Worse than that, to make full confession, when
Mrs. Gilby commenced the preliminary process of
breaking in the colt, by placing the bridle in his
mouth, and I, the motto of our House being " *Fræna,
vel aurea, nolo* " (" I'll have no bit, though it were

gold "), began to rear and kick; when, to drop metaphor, I was shut up in the cellar—then (ah, reader, remember, I pray you, my loneliness and darkness, and the longing for liberty which glows in British hearts)—then I did a desperate deed; I turned the tap of the beer barrel, and, with a loud voice, announced the fact through the keyhole. Listening, they heard the splash upon the floor. The door opened—I was free. A brief emancipation. The toe of retribution was on the heel of crime, and there was quickly a second overflow, Mrs. Gilby manipulating the taps.

Some sixty years afterwards, and one hundred and fifty miles from Newark, I, the dean, was conversing with the bishop, Dr. Thorold, of Rochester, and mentioned that I had seen Mr. Gladstone, canvassing, before he was a member of Parliament. "That is strange," said the bishop. "I saw him chaired after election." And when I inquired how he came to be there, he replied that his home in Lincolnshire was no great distance from Newark, and that he was sent there to a school which was kept by Mrs. Gilby. As the older boy, I had left her tutelage when Master Thorold came, but I had only moved up the street to the Grammar School, some hundred yards away, and it was a curious coincidence that we should again meet in such close (and to me most happy) association, after a severance of so many years, and so far away from the homes of our childhood.

Both schools had a holiday to celebrate the election of " young Mr. Gladstone," as the Conservative member for Newark. He came to us with a great reputation, having just taken his " Double First " * at Oxford, and I have a most vivid remembrance of the spot on which I first saw him, of his gentle manners, and of his kind, thoughtful, intellectual face. From that day, and for more than half a century, he was of all public men the one whom I most admired and revered. I read, believed, and still believe, a book which he wrote, in the maturity of his manhood, and the fulness of his faith, to defend that connection between the Church and the State, which was threatened, he said, by the infidel, the Romanist, the professor of political economy, and the democrat. He maintained " that the State in rejecting the Church would actively violate its most solemn duty, would entail upon itself a curse, would be guilty of an obstinate refusal of light and truth, which is the heaviest sin of all; and that such a separation would be a practical atheism, that is a human agency, knowingly, deliberately, and permanently divested of regard to God."

Gradually in the half-century which has passed since this book was written, more rapidly in the later years, the Churchman (as it seems to me) has

---

* His Mathematical First did him special honour, because in his boyhood he had a great aversion to arithmetic, but, when he was told that a statesman must be conversant with figures and statistics, he overcame his objection; and, as Chancellor of the Exchequer, was the first financier of his day.

been merged in the statesman, the statesman in the politician, and the politician into the lover of popularity and power; but the old arguments, unchangeable as truth, against the disestablishment of a national religion, the dismemberment of the empire, and the sacrifice of principle to expediency, may still be used in all charity, and though the hero of my long and loyal worship is little more to me now than a broken idol, I protest against the opprobrious reproaches, scurrilous slanders, and false accusations which are recklessly uttered against the most famous statesman and the most impressive orator of his age, against an accomplished scholar and linguist, a consummate financier, a Christian gentleman, perfectly sincere in his convictions, and prepared to defend them.*

It is currently and credibly reported that Mr. Gladstone in his early life desired to take Holy Orders, and were it not for the belief that " whatever is is best " in the end, many would be disposed to think that he would have been more successful as Primate than as Premier of all England. He would have been the greatest theologian and preacher in Christendom, and, once established at Lambeth, with his excellent wife, no temptation in the form of

* An absurd instance of this antipathy occurred recently. A volunteer regiment set up a pioneer, who marched with his axe in front. Whereupon, a gentleman in the neighbourhood withdrew his subscription, under the impression that the man with the hatchet was a complimentary representation of Mr. Gladstone!

a cardinal's hat or a papal tiara could have suggested itself to his ambition.

The Radicals were much perturbed by the defeat of their candidate, Sergeant Wilde, afterwards Lord Truro and Lord Chancellor, and gave us schoolboys a very striking proof of their indignation. We were enthusiastic Tories, and we knew the reason why. It was not remotely associated with politics—we were sublimely ignorant and indifferent as to party opinions—but we had discovered that the gentlemen who, from their social or official position, had the most influence in obtaining half-holidays, were Conservatives, and we never doubted for a moment that such men were in the right. Accordingly, when, after Mr. Gladstone's victory, " the Blues," Sergeant Wilde's adherents, paraded the town at night with music and torches and barrels of flaming tar, we threw open the windows of our dormitory as the procession passed, and shouted " Red for ever." In two minutes we saw through our error, for there was hardly an unbroken pane, and these sermons in stones were followed next morning by other homilies of a practical character, with illustrations by " the Doctor " and his cane.

Rough ways and rude speeches had freer scope in those days, when the rival candidates stood on the same hustings, with great crowds of their supporters before them. Woe to the man who had done some mean or foolish act, or said some silly words. They were proclaimed in a tone which all must hear;

and with a simplicity of language which none could fail to understand. Nor were these animosities satisfied with the breaking of windows or the strife of tongues. Instigated by demagogues, exasperated by taunts, inflamed by alcohol, the rivals attacked each other when they met with their bands in the streets. It was the custom to convey the successful candidates, mounted on triumphal cars, through the town, and I remember an occasion when two elegant chairs, draped with lace and pink satin, were brought from the head-quarters of the victorious army into the market-place, and before they could be placed upon the conveyance prepared for them, and the conquering heroes seated, an assault was made by their opponents. I watched the lovely sedilia swaying to and fro over the heads of the contending crowd, saw them totter and fall, to become mere rags and matches. They were lively days, those days of election, when I was at Newark School. Not only was there fighting in our streets, the walls covered with addresses and appeals, " Vote for Gladstone," " Plump for Wilde " (I thought of these placards as I walked through Pompeii, and saw traces of the *graffiti*, " Vote for Marcellinus," " Verus for ædile "), parodies, lampoons (rightly named as " squibs," fire and brimstone, ending in smoke, with a villainous smell of saltpetre); but every secret inducement, promise, persuasion, intimidation, and deception was used on both sides to influence voters. Men were stupefied with drink on the eve of the poll, and driven to distant parts of the country. Bribes were freely offered and received. One of the electors made no secret of his plan of campaign : " I takes the brass from both on 'em, and then I votes as I loikes." Another boasted that he had got a five-pound Bank of England note for his suffrage. A subtle acquaintance met him on his way to vote and whispered in his ear, " They've given you a ' flash ' note—it ain't worth tuppence." Whereupon the possessor took it from his pocket, tore it to pieces, and voted against the candidate whom he had promised to support.

*   *   *   *   *

I have lingered too long over my memories of school-days and their surroundings; the coach waits to take me for my matriculation to Oxford. There were at that time but a few miles of rail laid down, of those *viæ per Angliam ferro stratæ*, which was afterwards the subject of a prize poem, and the first sight of the University from the hill of Headington was far more admirable and impressive than that which is presented to us now as we approach on the level. There was a flood in the foreground, and to the poetic mind Gray's lines on Eton College came at once and of course—

> " Ye distant spires, ye antique towers,
>   That crown the watery glade,
>   Where grateful Science still adores
>   Her *Alfred's* holy shade,"

even as, from the non-poetic mind, came, in later

days, the exclamation of "Spiers and Pond!" Sentimental, or facetious, or both, for there is a time to weep and a time to laugh, the old Oxonian never forgets that first sight of Oxford, beautiful Oxford, which he saw from that rising ground. We claim no superiority, mental or muscular, over our brothers on the banks of the Cam; we have no chapel so exceeding magnifical as King's; we have no quadrangle to compare in expanse and dignity with that of Trinity; but when you come to a close and complete comparison of the city with the town (which ought to be a city), of street with street, college with college, of our parks and gardens, our river and its banks, with "the backs" and miserable stream at Cambridge (all honour to the men who from such vile material achieve such grand results!), why then no eyes in good working order can fail to see that, though Granta is quite as clever and quite as amiable as her sister Rhedicyna, she is not so pretty to look at.

What city has so fair an entrance as Oxford, over Magdalen Bridge, by the stately tower and the famous college which King James commended as "the most *absolute*, that is, the most complete building in Oxford," and which the old historic Antony à Wood declared to be " the most noble and rich structure in the learned world;" with its Founder's Chapel, once profaned by the malignant Puritan, who broke down the carved work thereof with axes and hammers, but now "set in its state,"

Y

and hallowed by a reverent worship, thanksgiving and the voice of melody; with its pinnacles and turrets, its cloisters, library, and hall, with its deer park, and streams, and trees? Where is there a street like " the High," with its churches, colleges, and schools? These edifices, it must be confessed, are not of uniform merit—*sunt bona, sunt mala, sunt mediocria:* did not Dr. Ashhurst Gilbert, afterwards Bishop of Chichester, declare, in preaching in St. Mary's, and in deprecation of an incongruous similitude, that " as well, my brethren, might you compare the solid masonry of University with the meritricious architecture of Queen's?"—but the combination, the *tout ensemble*, has no counterpart.

There are many incidents in boyhood and youth which are as evergreens in the garden of memory, never losing their glossy leaves—the first prize we won, the first pony we rode, the first watch we wore, love's young dream (of a tragic actress coeval with our mother); but there is no event which, as it seems to me, impresses itself so distinctly and permanently upon our remembrance as our introduction to college life. There is a delightful fascination in our new experience of comparative independence, possession, and authority. We exult in the exclusive tenancy of our small but snug habitation (the bedroom a mere slice of masonry, just holding the inmate and his appurtenances, but of all dormitories the most delightful, and no king " laid in bed majestical can sleep so soundly as the "—undergraduate); we are impressed by a supreme sense of our dignity as masters of an establishment—item, one joint-stock servant—and as proprietors of six dessert and six tea spoons, real silver, hall marked, and engraved with family crest, three dozen of port and ditto sherry, an armchair which might have been made for Falstaff,* and a series of richly coloured prints in which the achievements and catastrophes of the chase, over or into the wall, the timber, and the brook, were cleverly portrayed from " The Find " to " The Finish," from " Gone Away " to " Who-op! " " Then ' the oak ' is such a blessing! " as Shelley said to his Oxford friend and biographer. In a moment, by closing that outer door, you ensure stillness and peace; you can rest, you can read, you are secure from touts and bores, you can enjoy uninterrupted the genial parlance of some kindred spirit, some friend to whom you can open your heart on subjects which would be incongruous " where men most do congregate." Some of my dearest, happiest memories come to me from these hours, when " oft in the stilly night, ere slumber's chain had bound us," our secret thoughts and holy aspirations, so seldom uttered, rose high above our studies and our sports, and we spoke, with mutual trust, and brotherly affection, and

* Suggesting the observation, made by the professor from Padua, "that Oxford had a right to be called ' the seat of learning,' because it was a seat in which Learning sat very comfortably, well thrown back, as in an easy-chair, and slept so soundly that nobody could wake her."

humble reverence, of our faith and duty, of our hopes and fears.

Then came the anxious, nervous curiosity concerning our companions, as we met them for the first time in chapel, lecture-room, or hall. Would they like us; would they be kind, and call on us; or would they regard us as too puerile, too awkward, too "rugged and unkempt," for their patronage? Was our tie correct? Was the cut of our coat *comme il faut?* Should we go to the wrong pew and be contemptuously repulsed? Should we demean ourselves creditably at meals? Certainly, we should not commit ourselves as the notorious freshman, who put his knife to his lips, and was sternly rebuked by his neighbour, "Sir, you can't juggle here." That first awful lecture! Should we be "put on"? Should we utter a false quantity, omit an aspirate?

What were the results of these solicitudes? Few disappointments, because *animal implume* is gregarious as birds of a feather, and men of like minds and habits soon fraternize and keep together. There is an instinctive sympathy. I remember that when I first dined in hall I made a selection of several faces, having a faith in physiognomy which has rarely misled me, of those whom I most wished to know, and all of them eventually were numbered among my friends. There were exceptions to my rule, preaching *"fronti nulla fides," "nimium ne crede colori;"* and if these memories have a reader going to the University, I would impress upon him the wise instruction which Polonius gave to his son—

> " Do not dull thy palm with entertainment
> Of each new-hatch'd, unfledged comrade."

Beware of the effervescent spirits, who are prone to call you Jack, or Billy, or Bob, as soon as they know your surname, and who, if you accept their first familiarities, may annoy and depress you always. Mate with your equals, with men of your own grade and means. Otherwise, you may be led, or you may lead others, into habits of extravagance, into vain conceits and expectations. These sudden ascents and condescensions are spasmodic, as a rule, and rarely establish a lasting friendship. The exceptions are, when men are united by spiritual sympathies in the service of One who is no respecter of persons, and then in all ranks we may find "the friend that loveth at all times, and the brother born for adversity."

CHAPTER XXVII.

OXONIANS—*Continued.*

Dons and undergraduates—Reading, hunting, and boating men —Humiliation of pride—Want of religious sympathy and instruction—How supplied in later and happier days— The Universities and Public Schools Missions.

THE collegians of my day might be divided, like the universe, into four quarters—dons, reading, hunting, and boating men. There were some undergraduates, including the manliest and wisest, who were not only eager students, but brave horsemen, stalwart oars, agile cricketers (lawn-tennis was unknown, football was not in vogue, and golf had not come over the border); men who, when they were invited to self-indulgence, seemed almost to apologize for their splendid courage, " because they did not think it right to give, or could not afford to give, more time or money to amusements, in which none had greater enjoyment "—they might have added, " or in which none had greater success." I remember a signal illustration. At a large wine-party one of these heroes, who had just come up as a freshman, was invited by his neighbour to go out next day with the hounds, and when he replied that he must stick to his books, one of our foremost riders (the only one who was bumptious) remarked in a tone which pretended to be a whisper, but was audible to all, that he should not think the young gentleman had ever heard of any horse but Pegasus and the wooden quadruped which they took into Troy. I saw a frown and a flush on the young gentleman's face, and a quivering of the lips, and an upward movement, as though he would rise from his seat; but he was learning the noblest of all lessons, and was silent. Not many days after, we had a fast run in the Bicester country, and a dozen of us, well up with the pack, were stopped for a time by an impossible bullfinch. There was a partial aperture in the centre of the fence, but this contained a huge, grim, dreadful stile, with a step crossing the lower bar, and surmounted by a beam of strong oak, polished by friction with wayfaring men, and clamped with an iron band. The sarcastic critic, to whom I have just referred, was the first to inspect it, and he pronounced it " not negotiable." Cheerfully accepting his verdict, we were turning to seek some practicable exit, when to our astonishment a young horseman, quietly attired in black, and mounted on a steed which some of us recognized as an unruly but well-bred four-year-old, recently imported from Ireland by one of our Oxford dealers, rode calmly but resolutely at the stile. It was evident that both the horse and his rider meant business, and that the former required restraint rather than encouragement. But he was well in hand (only lunatics gallop at timber), and just steadying himself for a second, to concentrate his power and measure his distance, he rose and cleared that formidable obstruction. Then he who had done the deed turned with a pleasant smile to him who said that it could not be done, and, uttering but one word, rode on. The word was "*Pegasus!*" Then he, to whom it was spoken, made a show as though he would follow the speaker; but we knew, and he knew, and his horse knew, that there was no real intention. No effort was made, no second attempt after the first ignominious "refuse;" and the freshman had pounded the field!

Unhappily this composite order of undergraduate, of men who are as zealous in their work as in their play, and who, whatsoever their hand findeth to do, do it with their might, has few examples; and I therefore repeat that, speaking generally, we may classify the members of the University as: (1) men who rule; (2) men who read; (3) men who ride; and (4) men who row.

Wherefore, first of the dons, or domini, who exercise dominion over us. Remembering that not a few of them were of humble origin,* had come to

* The Christ Church swell may be reminded that Wolsey was a butcher's son, and I remember that in my day the son of a butler took a First Class soon after the son of his master was ignominiously "plucked for his Smalls"!

Oxford from secluded homes in the country, or from streets in manufacturing towns, with no surroundings to elevate and refine, and therefore had little in common, outside the lecture-room, with those who, living among the beauties of nature, the elegancies of art, the accomplishments of culture, the luxuries of wealth, the

κηπία καὶ ἐγκαλλωπίσματα πλούτου

measured all men by their own standard, and enlisted none who did not reach it, who refused the title of "gentleman" to those who had a provincial accent, dishevelled hair, unseemly raiment, creaking shoes, prehistoric hats; when it is recollected that, in those days, heads of houses were regarded as ornamental rather than useful, figure-heads rather than pilots, as sitting in serene expectation of bishoprics and deaneries, and tutors were looked upon by parents as teachers and economists to help their sons in obtaining classes and degrees, and in keeping them out of debt—by the sons themselves, as hindrances to their enjoyment, to be interviewed only on restraint;—it seems to me that our rulers fully and faithfully discharged the duties which they undertook, as they understood them, as they were understood by those whom they succeeded, and as they satisfied the public expectation. They were learned, and, as a rule, apt experts in imparting knowledge; they were just; they were patient and kind. In addition to their regular instructions, they were always ready privately to help the ignorant to pass his examination, as well as the more intellectual and erudite to win honours in the schools. They were men of high moral integrity, with discreet appreciations of their good old common-room port.

As for the realization and promotion of the sacred purposes for which the University was designed, for which the founders built and the benefactors endowed its colleges and halls, it would be a false compliment to speak of failure, because failure implies effort, and no effort, worthy of the name, was made by our rulers in my day. Ever since the days of St. Frideswide; ever since King Alfred, according to the old black-letter verse—

> " In the yeare VIII. hundred LXXX. and tweyne
> Did found and make a study then againe,
> And an Universitee for Clerkes in to rede,
> The which he made at Oxenford indeed,
> To that intent that Clerkes by sapience
> Again Hereticks should make resistance ; "

in the days of Ethelred, Guimond, Canute, William of Durham, Walter de Merton, John de Balliol, Walter de Stapledon, Adam de Brom, William of Wykeham, William Waynflete, Bishops Fleming and Smith and Fox, Knights Sutton and Pope and White, the founders or restorers of University, Merton, Balliol, Exeter, Oriel, New, Lincoln, Magdalen, Brasenose, Corpus, Trinity, and St. John's, the multitude of generous men who endowed them with money and estates, were all of one mind that while Oxford was to be a place of general instruction, having Schools of Arithmetic, Astronomy, Geometry, Grammar, Logic, Music, Moral and Natural Philosophy, Metaphysics, and Rhetoric, these studies were absolutely subservient to the queen of all science, Theology, mere tributaries to the river which maketh glad " the city of our God," helps to the Christian faith. The design of Oxford was not only the development but the consecration of the intellect. "There are those," St. Bernard writes, " who desire to know only in order that they may know, and this bears the taint of curiosity; to know that they may be known, and this is but vanity; to sell their knowledge, and this is a shameful trade; but some that they may be built up in the love and fear of God, and that is wisdom." "Knowledge puffeth up, but charity edifieth."

This wisdom was not taught. No appeals were made by our tutors, privately, personally, to our spiritual instincts of love and fear. At a time when the influence of good and that of evil are alike most powerful, when holy ambitions and noble thoughts are contending with worldly motives and with carnal lusts, when earnest words of encouragement and warning fall as the gentle dew from heaven on the hard ground beneath, no advice was offered, no sympathy was shown. No attempt was made to understand our special qualities, inclinations, temper, temptations; no study of character with a view to its improvement, no gentle pleading face to face, as the Master bade, "If thy brother trespass, go and tell him his fault between him and thee alone; if he shall hear thee, thou hast gained thy brother." Golden opportunities lost for ever; many a crisis, in which a kindly hand on the shoulder and a tender voice in the ear might have saved from sin and shame.

It may be said you had constant services, sermons, and divinity lectures. The services certainly were frequent; but they were also compulsory, and therefore attended grudgingly and as of necessity. They were said in a dreary edifice, and, as a rule, in a cold, monotonous, perfunctory tone, which did not invite devotion. I never heard a note of music in our college chapel; the University sermons (I do not remember that any were preached in college) failed to impress the undergraduate mind, except when Newman, or Pusey, or Claughton preached. No advantage was taken of lectures on the Greek Testament for exhortation, or reproof, or instruction in righteousness; but they were occupied by the consideration of textual arrangements, diverse interpretations, parallel passages, commentaries, descriptions of scenery, dates, and statistics. It was a time in which ugliness and dirt were regarded as bulwarks of the Protestant faith, and beauty and order were "marks of the beast." Doctrine was bigotry, reverence was idolatry, and zeal was superstition.

I remember two sad examples of disinclination

and incapacity on the part of our teachers, spiritual pastors, and masters (all tutors of colleges were then in Holy Orders), to commune with their pupils concerning the one thing needful, to strengthen and to guide. An undergraduate, who was very earnest and anxious about his religion, went to his tutor for explanation and instruction on certain perplexities which had harassed and oppressed him. His appeal was received with a manifest surprise, and when he pressed it with some fervour, it became more and more apparent that he was supposed by his senior to be suffering from nervous or mental disorder. Finally, he was recommended to see a doctor! Another, who was in great trouble from a remorseful conscience, went to his superior, as invited by the Church, to open his grief, to receive comfort and counsel and the benefit of absolution, and was curtly informed "that if he meant confession and that sort of thing, he had better go to some popish priest," which advice, I grieve to say, he ultimately followed.

These are extreme cases, but they promoted distrust, and restrained others from the risk of similar repulse. The intercourse should have been initiated and encouraged, instead of being suppressed, by the elders, and then, as we know from the happier experience of later years, there might have been "showers of blessings." It is indeed a matter of deep thankfulness to be assured that this spiritual sympathy is now more largely and lovingly offered, and that where indifference and unbelief had risen in its place, like weeds where there is no culture, it is earnestly contending with doubtful disputations, oppositions of science (falsely so called), rationalism, materialism, false doctrine, heresy, and schism, for " the faith once delivered to the saints." Its power may be estimated by the wonderful work which one man, Ἄναξ ἀνδρῶν (true to his name), having the desire, received the power to do among the undergraduates for Christianity and the Church at Oxford; and its results may be seen throughout the land in devoted priests and generous laymen, nowhere more admirably wrought than by our University missions among the London poor. Nowhere, in these later days, has been shown more convincingly the marvellous influence of Christian love in uniting all sorts and conditions of men, nowhere has the Church given a more beautiful proof of her heart's desire that the poor should have the gospel preached to them, than in those parts of the metropolis where the Oxford, Cambridge, and Public School Missions (the latter having been organized by Oxford and Cambridge men) are doing their noble work.

At the opening of the new Oxford House the Archbishop of Canterbury said, " I should wish to emphasize that what before was predicted and believed in—the idea which brought Oxford men down to Bethnal Green—has been realized beyond their most sanguine expectations. It has been found by absolute experience that among all the differences, which evil powers or false principles use to divide men from one another, there is really nothing more untrue and nothing more fatal than the distinction which so many people quite unconsciously draw between class and class. Here in this Oxford House it has been found that people of all the so-called classes mingle harmoniously together. They desire the same things, they have the same aspirations, the same amusements, the same morals, and they find that both one class and the other, as we so mistakingly and commonly speak, are really one. This Oxford House is one of the ways in which a combination of all kinds of people, of men of all sorts of positions and various employments, has been effected in the happiest and most harmonious manner. It is founded on true definite religious principles, the principles of the Church of England; and these, it is found, so far from separating man from man, are the truest and best cement, the most binding power which can be applied."

CHAPTER XXVIII.

OXONIANS—*Continued.*

The first lecture—Timidity and impudence—A brave beginning
—The fascinations of the chase—Mr. Drakes' Hounds, and
the Heythrop—Jim Hills—Buying and selling horses—
Perils and penalties—" The Grind "—The river—The race
with seven oars.

DESCENDING from the heights of Olympus, from the
potent, grave, and reverend seniors, to the *nondum
ad Parnassum graduati* at its base, I joined the
latter, with resolute ambition to reach the mountain-
top. I went to Oxford, as thousands before me, to
take a First Class. An insuperable objection on
the part of my Pegasus to cross the Ass's Bridge
had destroyed my hope of mathematical honours;
but I had made good progress in the *literæ huma-
niores*, had a real admiration for Æschylus and
Thucydides, Theocritus, Horace, and Virgil, and had
transformed many stanzas of " Childe Harold " into
Greek iambics, which would have amazed the
author of " The Isles of Greece." I began to read
with a brave industry, got up my books, and was
commended for translations which would have lashed
Sophocles into fury and choked Aristophanes with

laughter. Half a century has passed since my first "lecture," but the scene is presented to imagination by memory with a reality which no artist could paint—the anxious freshman in his new gown and cap, feebly imitating the nonchalance of his elder brother as they enter together the tutor's room, furnished with the most beautiful of old furniture, well-bound books by standard authors, and surrounded by chairs for the students, wherein they await the word of command—"Line 505—Mr. Aspen-Leaf, will you be so good as to begin?"

There are exceptions to this timidity. I recall an occasion on which there was some doubt as to the locality of a city mentioned in the text, and the lecturer addressed a youth, who had just come from Shrewsbury School, "Now, Mr. Bentley, you are a pupil of our great geographer, Dr. Butler, the Atlas of our age, who carries the world, not on his shoulders, but in his head" (enthusiastic applause, as always when a don condescended to a jest), "and you can probably enlighten us as to the position of this ancient town." "I believe, sir," it was promptly replied, "that modern travellers are of opinion that the city ought to be placed about ten miles to the south-east of the spot which it now occupies on our maps." Alas! I am constrained to add that, after receiving respectful thanks for his information, the informer told us, when we left the lecture-room, that he had never heard of the venerable city before, but that, "for the honour of

Shrewsbury and the reputation of the doctor, he felt himself bound to say something." Retribution swiftly followed; and on his second experiment in transplanting cities, the fiction was detected, from the delight of the audience, too audibly and visibly expressed, and the disconcerted topographer was brought to rebuke and shame.

For two or three terms I sailed smoothly over Learning's solemn seas; then the sirens began to sing. The men who read were not, as a rule, such cheery companions as the men who rode and drove, and played cricket, and wore gay clothing, and smoked fragrant regalias, and were always jubilant. There were some, as I have intimated, who combined diligent study with moderate relaxations and joyous demeanour, such as Buckley, who rowed in the College Eight, took a First, became Fellow and Tutor, Professor of Anglo-Saxon at Oxford, and of Classical Literature of Haileybury, and who, from his large sympathies and pleasant genial ways, always won the undergraduates' love; and Forbes, afterwards Bishop of Brechin (who apologized to his father when writing for money, but " ventured, at the same time, to remind his parent that a son was an expensive luxury "), a delightful companion, a most earnest Christian, and one of the most learned theologians of his day; and there was handsome William Lea, one of Dr. Arnold's favourite pupils, who was also in the Brasenose boat, rode occasionally with hounds, took a Second, and was

Archdeacon of Worcester. I think that if I had known these men sooner, or if some kindly tutor had shown me, with words of brotherly affection and common sense, my privilege and responsibility, and had proved to me from such examples as those which I have quoted that it is possible to be both merry and wise, I think that I should have listened to the lyre of Orpheus, and turned my back on the sirens.

I read resolutely for two terms and a Long Vacation, but when once more "the horn of the hunter was heard on the hill," and I met a siren in a black-velvet cap and scarlet coat, a blue bird's-eye tie, buff kerseymere waistcoat, buckskin breeches, and pale brown tops, coming adown our staircase on his way to the chase, I could resist no longer, and was lured to the rocks. He dazzled my eyes, he bewildered my brain, he caught my affections, so light and so vain; I wrote home for my pink, I bought a horse, and joined the equestrian order. I ceased to court the Muse, and wooed the " Goddess Diana, who calls aloud for the chase."

The freshman who is fond of hunting may find his photograph, and see his semblance, as from a mirror, in the epistle which Horace wrote to the Pisos—

> " Imberbus Juvenis, tandem custode remoto,
> Gaudet equis canibusque, et aprici gramine campi,
> Cereus in vitium flecti, monitoribus asper,
> Utilium tardus provisor, prodigus æris,
> Sublimis, cupidusque, et amata relinquere pernix ;"

which may be translated freely, " The youth who does not grow a beard, released at last from his mother's apron-string, and far from his father's frown, rejoices in horses and hounds, in galloping over the grass of the Bicester country, or in leaping the stone walls of the Heythrop. He is easily led into mischief; kicks if touched by the whip; improvident about common things; ignorant of the value of money; flighty, flirty, quick to leave old loves."

Irresistible to him the fascinations of the chase at Oxford, the merry companions, the cantering hacks, the high, commodious dog-cart, oft requiring, when the meet was distant or the hills were steep, the prefix of a second steed (again suggesting the quotation, " *tandem custode remoto*," a " leader," where no proctor is seen), and then the grand excitements of the hunt, and those " moving accidents by flood and field," which immersed the rider in the deep Evenlode, or brought the brush to his saddle-bow. Going forth, or returning home, cloud or sunshine, our spirits never flagged. " Why do you call that grey hack of yours Δίκαιος ? " I asked a friend one morning as we rode " to covert." " Because," he said, " a fellow in my form at school once translated δίκαιος ' white horse; ' and when asked the reason why, he replied that he had looked the word out in the lexicon, and it said, *candidus, æquus*, ' white horse.' " On another occasion I inquired from the same comrade, just when the hounds were beginning to draw, why he did not exchange the grey aforesaid for his hunter; and he answered with all gravity that he had just received intelligence of the death of his uncle, and was consequently in mourning. It was a remarkable demonstration of grief, seeing that the afflicted nephew was in full hunting costume, and that, being one of the best riders in the University, and the grey hack having some galloping and jumping powers, he was for a time foremost in the run.

Never weary, nor dejected, a perpetual proof of Addison's statement that "man is the merriest species of creature; all above and below him are sad," the undergraduate of my day of all the cheeriest was the man who rode to hounds, sometimes it may be transgressing " the limits of becoming mirth," and too practical in his jokes, but ever ready to retract and recompense. I remember that, as we were drawing near to Oxford, and the light began to fail, on a December day, we had just ridden through the toll-bar famous in history,* when we saw

* Famous as the scene of the interview in which the head of a college, having informed the gate-keeper that he had forgotten his purse, and expecting profound obeisance and prompt permission to pass, on adding the announcement, " I am the Master of Balliol," was astonished to see a hand on his bridle, and to hear a gruff voice reply, " If you ben't master o' tuppence, you don't go through this gate to-day."

There was a rookery at that time in the grounds of Balliol College, visible from the Master's lodge. " I am grieved to observe," he (the Master) remarked one day to a friend, "a very serious epidemic among the crows. The symptoms are before us the tall form of Dr. Hawkins, Provost of Oriel, and my comrade, Charley Allen, who had marvellous mimetic powers, turned to me and said, "I'll make him believe I'm Mainwaring." Now, our friend Mainwaring was reading for his degree, and had made a solemn promise to his chief that he would abstain from hunting until the examination was over; and therefore it was very naughty and mischievous on the part of Master Charles to pass Dr. Hawkins at a hand-gallop, holding up the collar of his scarlet coat and hiding his countenance, as one who feared recognition; and his conduct was the more deplorable, because a similarity of form and the surrounding gloom were auxiliary to his purpose, and made his deception a success. I met the innocent victim on the following day, and he informed me that he had just had an extraordinary interview with the provost, who had sent for him, and received him about as cordially as though he had been a burglar, and commenced the conversation with, "Mr. Mainwaring, I always thought you were a gentleman," and when Mr. Mainwaring responded that "he hoped such was the case," the provost had exclaimed with loud indignation, "No,

in all instances the same: a sudden quiver of the wings, followed by vigorous, but futile, attempts to cling with their claws to the branches, and then they fall dead. The carrion is immediately removed, and interred by the college servants." I need hardly inform the sagacious reader that the rooks were picked off by the air-gun of an undergraduate, and "interred by the college servants" in a pie!

sir; you gave me your word of honour that you would not hunt this term, and you have not only broken it, but, conscious of your deceitful conduct, have vainly endeavoured to conceal it. I recognized you at once, when you rode past me yesterday." The result was that the accused proved an *alibi*, and the provost was convinced of his mistake; but when I explained the mystery to my friend, he was for some time unable, though he had a very keen appreciation of humour and a great regard for Charley Allen, to enjoy in all its fulness the success of that little scheme.*

The sport was excellent with Mr. Drake's hounds

---

* The practical joke was, and will always be, a favourite occupation of the undergraduate. The results, as in the instance quoted, are sometimes serious. "Oxford mesmerism" was introduced in my time. The operator, having asserted his power to mesmerize, and having selected a subject from those who disputed it, produced two plates, and placed upon each of them a tumbler containing water. After a few preliminary manual evolutions, he took one of the plates in his hand, and requested his *vis-à-vis*, on whom the experiment was to be made, to take the other (which had previously been held over a candle and made quite black by the smoke), and then to watch his movements and copy them minutely. Dipping his forefinger in the water, and then rubbing it with slow solemnity on the under side of the plate, he passed it from the top of his forehead over the nose to the chin, and then made a transverse line just above the eyebrows. The result, with a few supplementary spots, was fascinating, but in one case much to be deplored. The victim left the room and the college, quite unconscious of his facial enrichments, and seeing a church lighted and open for evening service, went in with the best of motives, and, to his intense surprise and indignation, was angrily ejected by the beadle and two churchwardens.

in a fine hunting country, although the rash under-graduate sorely tried the patience of John Wingfield, huntsman, and his "Now, do 'e, gentlemen, keep back," could hardly restrain him from spoiling his own amusement. He preferred the cheery voice and frequent horn of Jim Hills, and his "Tally-ho, for'ard!" whether there was a fox or not. Most of us, I fear, "in our sallet days, when we were green in judgment," cared more for the riding than the hunting—too often when there was a scent we pressed the hounds off it, or blamed them for not running when there was none. Experience brought a truer enjoyment as we began to note the clever-ness and perseverance of the pack, until in our elderhood we were flushed with righteous anger to see mere boys riding on before us, charging prepos-terous fences with indecent haste when hounds were close in front of them, and there was an open gate not a hundred yards to the right.

The right way, doubtless, is to let them alone, and I remember bearing a caustic message from one M.F.H. to his neighbour, "Tell him that if he will put his hounds into such a covert, and then ride home, he will probably hear in the course of the day that they have killed a fox."

Horsedealers are not universally regarded as men who would prefer pecuniary loss to the use of exaggeration or guile, but I have found them, in my purchases at Oxford and elsewhere, as honest as their fellow-creatures. Buyers should know something of the article which they require, and should have a warranty. I recall a letter, written by a veterinary surgeon to a young collegian, who had instructed him to inspect a horse which he proposed to purchase: " Sir, I have examined the horse. The interesting family of quadrupeds to which he belongs is liable to a great number of diseases and injuries, hereditary, climatic, accidental, and I have no hesitation in stating that he has got most of them. He would be a very precious acquisition, as an object lesson, in our veterinary college, but I do not feel justified in commending him to you, with a view to use or recreation."

Inseparably from this letter, as a Siamese twin from his brother, is associated another example of the wisdom of making exhaustive inquiry before you invest in horses. A graduate, who had left the University, and who was a most accomplished performer both in the saddle and on the box, increased his slender income by purchasing, breaking, and educating horses. At a large public auction he secured at a low figure, without a warranty, a very handsome and well-bred steed, which turned out the most obstinate, vicious, hopeless, and worthless of his kind. His owner could do nothing with him, and sent him back to the repository from which he came, to be sold for what he would fetch. Another customer was attracted by his showy appearance, and when he had bought and paid for him he came to his recent proprietor, and said, " Now, sir, seeing that the horse is mine, and you can incur no further liability, I should feel much obliged if you would candidly tell me what sort of animal he is." And the answer was promptly given, "Well, sir, *if you don't want him to ride or drive, you'll find him a very nice horse.*"

I may not leave the subject of hunting at Oxford without making my confession that the pleasures of memory are accompanied by a regret—*surgit amari aliquid*—that too much time and money were spent in the delectable pursuit of the fox, and I rejoice to hear that the restrictions upon this pastime are not so elastic as they were in my day. *Post equitem sedet atra cura*, and many a young Nimrod and reckless Jehu has brought sorrow to his home, and encumbered himself with debt for years, by his extravagant outlay in riding and driving, and in expenses incidental thereto. One day a week should suffice for those who are in *statu pupillari*, and that only when their tutors know that they can afford it, and have their parents' or their guardians' consent. "It is not right," Archbishop Laud wrote from Lambeth two hundred and fifty years ago—"it is not right to put such a charge upon parents without their particular leave and directions," and if that permission is withheld, it is a tutor's duty to enforce obedience. Not many young men have the magnanimous self-control of an undergraduate, to whom, knowing him to be one of the best riders in his county, I offered a mount. "You are very kind," he said, "because you know how I love the sport; but you don't know that the best friend I have in the world, my father, is making sacrifices to keep me here, and I have promised him not to hunt." The cynic, who "rejoiced to be told that virtue was its own reward, because, as it seemed to him, there was no other remuneration," would be disappointed to know that not many years elapsed before my friend had a couple of first-rate hunters, the results of continuous and careful work.

At Brasenose we invented "The Grind," though I am unable to explain the origin or meaning of the word. It was applied to a small company of under-graduates, meeting, after lectures and luncheon, at a rendezvous outside of Oxford, mounted on the ordinary hack, selecting some building or plantation two or three miles away, and racing towards it as our winning post. The excitements of the contest were heightened by the incapacity of the steeds, and by the appearance on the scene of the furious farmer encouraging his men to pursue and capture. With an impracticable fence before, and a man with a fork behind him, the trespasser was sometimes in the sad predicament of a certain flying-fish, of which we read that the albatross attacks him when he leaves the water, while the dolphin waits for him below.

*　　*　　*　　*　　*

Although we were divided at Brasenose College into the men who rode on the land, and the men who rowed on the water, and I was a bigoted dry Bob, I had many dear friends in the boats, and especially among those who maintained our supremacy. Gilbert Sandbach had left the college, before I entered it, with the reputation of having found our crew in a low place on the Isis, and, after "bumping" a boat every night of the races, having rowed finally at the head of the river. He was succeeded by three admirable strokes—Bishton Garnett, Somers-Cocks, and Francis Tuke. Somers-Cocks had been taught by Aleck Reed, when at Westminster, the noble art of self-defence, and when he was insulted and attacked by a blustering bully, who went by the name of "the Henley Pet," he punished that hero so effectually, that no entreaties could induce him to resume the perpendicular attitude, from which he had been dislodged.

How they loved the river, and the boat, those grand, genial, brave-hearted, strong-armed men! Again I see those eager faces, striving in vain to hide their anxious zeal, as they listen for the signal, "*Incumbite remis!*" and the eight oars dip and rise as one, and "Bravo, Brasenose!" tells our joyful hope. Will you not pardon the captain who, in his sad despair, silently approached the coxswain, who had lost the race, raised him by the collar of his coat, and dropped him into the Isis? Will you not almost believe that an enthusiastic "No. 5" was last seen walking down Bond Street with an oar on his shoulder?

In the summer of 1843, there was a large exodus

from Oxford in vehicles of all denominations to see the Henley Regatta, especially the great race between the crews which represented the two Universities, the Oxford University Boat Club and the Cambridge Subscription Rooms. Our men were giants, adroit as they were strong, and we were sanguine of success. The oarsmen had just taken their places for the start, when one of the brothers Menzies, in the Oxford boat, fainted and fell. He was taken from the boat, placed on a large sofa, and carried on the shoulders of his comrades to the Lion Hotel. He lay at full length, pale and motionless as though in the last sleep, and no sound was heard as this strange procession went, like a funeral, slowly along the street.

Leaving their invalid to the speedy restorations of the doctor, the crew returned to the river with a substitute, whom, though he was not in training, they proposed *faut de mieux* to put in Menzies' place. Unhappily the Cambridge captain objected to this arrangement, and refused to allow an additional oar. While the Oxonians, and, as it was reported, some of the Cambridge men, were protesting against his decision, and the former were discussing whether they should row or not, the steward, Lord Camoys, informed them that the signal for the start would be given at the appointed time. Both the boats went down—the Cambridge with eight and the Oxford with seven oars. I never saw an assemblage of faces on which disappointment and disgust were so plainly and universally expressed, or heard so many exclamations, not loud but deep, of "mean," "cowardly," "sneaking," "snobbish," etc.   We mounted the drag which had conveyed us from Oxford, and was now placed on the bridge, and there we waited to denounce and deride the imminent and inglorious victory.   I shall never forget the roar of "*Bravo, Oxford!*" which reached us as the boats came in view, nor the amazement, which could not believe what it saw—the boats close together, and our own gradually drawing ahead, until the race was over, and, by half a boat's length, *Oxford beat Cambridge with seven oars!*   Had they been the Seven before Thebes, or the Seven Champions of Christendom, or the Seven Bishops,* who stepped out of their boat at the Tower, they could not have been cheered more heartily.   It was a strange result, so strange that some regarded it as supernatural, a penal visitation on injustice.   None were more surprised than the victors.   "The boat," one of them said, "seemed to trim and go as though no change had been made."

The Cambridge captain undoubtedly made a mistake, but *nemo mortalium*, etc., and all men know, who have seen the Isis and the Cam, that Cambridge has quite as brilliant a record as Oxford in the annals of aquatic fame.

* I may notice here that four oarsmen who have rowed in their University Eights, Selwyn and Wordsworth, Pelham and Hamilton, have been made bishops.

CHAPTER XXIX.

PREACHERS.

My experience—No help at Oxford—The "Evangelicals" the
best preachers fifty years ago—Ordeal and result—Dr.
Dollinger and Newman—Objections to preaching without
manuscript—The matter and manner of preaching—The
Great Example—Read and think—Savonarola—Utterance
—Length—Preachers.

I LITTLE thought when I first heard the ancient
Oxford story of the vice-chancellor on his way to
St. Mary's exclaiming, in a tone of dignified rebuke,
to the undergraduate who was going in a contrary
direction, "Is this the way to the University Sermon,
sir?" and receiving the affable answer, "First turn
to the right, sir—anybody will show you;" still
less, when, like young Harry, with my beaver up
and buckskins on my thigh, gallantly armed, I leapt
on my steed like winged Mercury, at the corner of
Brasenose Lane,—that I should ever walk through
that sombre avenue preceded by the University
bedel. I little thought when I first heard Newman
preach, in such a pathetic and impressive tone that
the words with which he began his sermon have
never been forgotten, "Sheep are defenceless
creatures, wolves are strong and fierce," that I should

ever stand where he stood. Nor should I refer to the subject, were I not more severely conscious than any one else can be that the contrast is as between Handel playing the organ and a schoolboy learning the flute, and yet believe that my experience as a preacher may be helpful to other ordinary mortals, whose duty it is to preach.

There are hundreds of clergymen who have never really tried to preach. There are hundreds of clergymen who can write far better sermons than mine, who fail to impress their hearers, because they don't know how to preach. These men I would entreat, with all brotherly love and humility, to ponder my history. It has been useful, I am thankful to know, to some of those who have heard it.

In the years which I spent at Oxford, I did not receive one word of advice or instruction as to the composition or the utterance of a sermon. The preachers, as a rule, with few exceptions, such as Newman, Pusey, Claughton, of Trinity (afterwards Bishop of Rochester and St. Albans), failed to interest their hearers. There was a public orator, but I do not remember any lectures on oratory. He appeared annually at Commemoration, not to silence and engross the undergraduates with his splendid eloquence, but rather to evoke than suppress their jocose admonitions, "Don't be shy, sir," "Mind your h's," "Cut it short."

There was then no theological college, no school of preparation for Holy Orders ; and, therefore, for many years after my ordination I composed and copied feeble discourses, which I read in monotonous and soporific tones.* The clergy known as "Evangelical" were almost the only preachers, and they were either regarded as having a special gift and genius, which was innate, and could not be acquired, or as mere Methodists and Ranters, whose enthusiasm was glaringly inconsistent with the dignity and gentility of the Church of England. The rest were either high (far over the heads of their hearers—I remember preaching, as a deacon, to the farm labourers concerning "the Anglo-Catholic Church and the Œcumenical Councils," and at the same time a quotation which appeared in the *Times* from a sermon by one of our greatest theologians to the rustics at Ambleside, in which he reminded them that they were surrounded by "an apodeikneusis of theopratic omnipotence"), or they were dry as the desert, or both.

Then came a momentous epoch. An evening service was so long delayed that I was unable, on entering the pulpit, to read a word of my sermon. In my brief, but awful perplexity, the thought came to me, "Surely you have some words for your Master," and I prayed that I might speak them, remembering

* Well might Sydney Smith inquire, " Is it a rule of oratory to balance the style against the subject, and to handle the most sublime truths in the dullest language, and in the driest manner ? Is sin to be taken out of man, as Eve was from Adam, by casting him into a deep sleep ?" After one of these dreary discourses in a Lincolnshire church, a member of the congregation said that the text should have come *after* the sermon. It was, " Awake, thou that sleepest ! "

the promise, " It shall be given unto you what ye shall say." I repeated the text, without chapter or verse, forgotten, began to utter the thoughts which came into my mind, preached for the first time in my life (to read is not to preach) some twenty minutes, and then thankfully concluded. Nor should I ever have repeated the experiment, had not my churchwarden informed me in conversation afterwards, that the congregation were much more impressed by my extempore address than by the ordinary sermon. " You see, sir," he said, " the enemies of the Church are always jeering our folks, and telling them that the parsons buy their sermons at so much a yard, and that any Cheap Jack from Newark Market is a better speaker. They say that no one would employ a barrister who read his brief, or go to see an actor who repeated his part from a book ; and that preachers who would win souls must speak from the fulness of their own hearts, and not from other men's brains." The incident, and these commentaries upon it, constrained me to obey the wishes of those who had the first claim upon my sympathy and service. I had always entertained the ambition, but never until now the hope, of preaching without a manuscript. Had I been requested, when I entered the church on the occasion to which I have referred, to speak without reading to my people, I should have replied, as thousands of the clergy would reply to-day, that it was simply impossible.

I had been much impressed by Dr. Dollinger's words to Mr. Gladstone: "*Depend upon it, if the Church of England is to make way, and to be a thoroughly national Church, the clergy must give up the practice of preaching from written sermons.*" I remembered Newman's statement: "*For myself I think it no extravagance to say that a very inferior sermon delivered without book answers the purpose for which all sermons are delivered, more perfectly than one of great merit, if it be written and read.*" And I recalled an occasion when Mr. Simeon, who was then the great preacher of his day, being kept at home by illness, sent a sermon, which he considered the best he had ever written, but which made very little impression, though it was well read by his friend.

Now it seemed that the time was come to give some practical expression to my belief in this suggestive instruction, and I began at once to comply with my convictions, and to realize my resolutions to preach from memory my own thoughts. I had fallen into easy ways of transfer and adaptation, which required little time or reflection; and I soon discovered that my new ambition demanded and deserved all my energies in anxious and persevering work. I never had faith in "extempore" preaching, except in cases. of unforeseen necessity. It is profanity to offer unto God that which costs us nothing, and it is folly to contemplate success except on His immutable condition, "In the sweat of thy face thou shalt eat bread." But when there is earnest, arduous preparation, it will be accepted and blessed, as were the firstlings of Abel, because we bring our best. That preparation means prayer, a definite purpose, meditation, plan, study, illustration, simplicity. It means laying foundations, that is, thinking and reading (above all *the* Book); then the scaffolding, the scheme and outline; then the building, the sermon itself, solid in structure, and yet attractive in form, enriched, like a cathedral, with reverent ornamentation. Then the architect must contemplate his completed work until it is reproduced like a photograph on his brain—he must learn his sermon by heart, not word by word, but with such a comprehensive remembrance of the sentences and arguments as will ensure a continuity, though it may not be an identity, of words.

"I wish I could do it," it has been said to me again and again by my younger brethren, "but it is not in my power. I know that I should forget and break down." And my reply is: How do you know? How can you know, having never tried? You cannot be more fearful of failure than I was, and as to forgetting, did you never hear what the Scotch elder said to the minister? The minister made a very free use of notes in the pulpit, and his congregation did not approve. They decided to expostulate, and sent a deputation. He heard their remonstrance, and he informed his visitors, somewhat rudely, that his memory required assistance, and that he intended to use it. " Weel, then, minister," said the chief of the legation, " if ye sae soon forget your own sarmons, ye'll nae blame us if we follow your lead."

" Have there been no failures ? " I have only heard of one authentic case, that of Bishop Sanderson, but of course there may be collapses from want of faith. Twice in twenty years I have come to a brief silence—once for want, not of faith, but of food, having travelled nearly four hundred miles and foolishly postponed my meal until the service was over. I had not preached two minutes before it seemed as though the upper part of my head was petrified. I had just enough consciousness to tell my hearers that my memory failed, but that I was sure that God would come to my help, and then the stupor left me in a moment, and I preached without further interruption. Once again, and more recently, I was thoroughly exhausted by a long series of engagements in different parts of the country, including the Church Congress at Rhyl, and while speaking at a great meeting of working men at Leeds I was seized with blank oblivion.

> " Keen was the shaft, but keener far to feel,
>   I nursed the pinion which impelled the steel."

I had ceased to take with me the few written words which suggest the chief topic of sermons or of speech, which would have released me from my dilemma, and which I shall not forget in the future. though I hope that I may never want them.

Usually, in case of embarrassment, the repetition of a sentence, in substance not verbatim, will enable the speaker to remember and to follow his line of thought, to pick up the thread which had fallen. He must expect the disappointment of forgetting now and then some argument or example, which he regarded as of special importance ; and though some new ideas and enforcements may suggest themselves when he is speaking, he should always have more material prepared than he is likely to want in delivering. Happily for me, there was a programme of musical interludes, and Dr. Talbot, with prompt and merciful consideration, gave a signal to the organist, and while he discoursed most excellent music I remembered, though imperfectly, the remainder of my speech.

Wherefore I maintain that sermons should be spoken from memory, and not read from a book. I believe that hundreds of the clergy, who write excellent discourses, would make a more general and a deeper impression upon their hearers, if they addressed them without a manuscript, face to face. They would rejoice to find that difficulties, which appeared to be so huge at a distance, dwindled and disappeared as they approached them in the courage of their faith, and that they possessed a new freedom and a new power in running the race that was set before them ; and they who have not the same cleverness in composition would, I feel sure, have more influence if, after the best attention of thought and study has been bestowed upon their subject, they would speak instead of reading the results. St. Paul tells us that his speech and preaching was not with enticing words of man's wisdom, but in demonstration of the Spirit, and where that Spirit is, there is an earnestness which speaks from soul to soul. It is not from incapacity, but from a mistaken diffidence, or from want of zeal, from indolence, that so few sermons are preached.

Let me ask, in proof, would any unprejudiced observer say that the clergy of our Church were inferior in abilities and education to the Romanist or to the Nonconformist? I assert, on the contrary, that, having the same intellectual power, the Churchman has advantages, many and great, over the Dissenter, in his more complete education, in his orders, sacraments, creeds, and liturgies, and the English has this precedence over the Roman Catholic, in that he preaches a purer doctrine, and knows more of the men to whom he preaches. They use no manuscript, and if he dares not disuse it—

> " He either fears his fate too much,
> Or his deserts are small."

*   *   *   *   *

As to the matter and the manner of preaching, it must be "very meet, right, and our bounden duty" to follow in all meekness and lowliness of heart the example of One who would have all men know that He is the Christ, because "the poor had the gospel preached to them," and of whom it is recorded that the masses (ὁ πολὺς ὄχλος) "heard Him gladly." We should copy "the simplicity of Christ," and, like the Apostle, "use great plainness of speech." We should be bold in rebuking sin, as He who drove the money-grubbers from the house of God, and denounced the Pharisees as hypocrites and children of the devil; yet tender and pitiful and compassionate as He who wept over Jerusalem, and said to the woman taken in adultery, "Neither do I condemn thee: go, and sin no more."

We should illustrate our sermons, as He did, by parables, by connecting them with the events and surroundings of our common daily life, speaking to our hearers of those matters which interest us all most deeply—our nation, our occupations and homes, our common anxieties, our temptations, our troubles, and our joys.* There are too many preachers who seem to forget that God teaches us by the dispensations of His providence, as well as by the revelations of His Word, and that it is for them to demonstrate the fulfilments of prophecy, the teachings of history,

* And so George Herbert writes of the parson in his " A Priest to the Temple:" " When he preacheth, he procures attention by all possible art, both by earnestness of speech, it being natural for men to think that where is much earnestness there is somewhat worth hearing. Sometimes he tells them stories, and sayings of others, according as the text invites him; for them also men heed, and remember better than exhortations; which though earnest yet often die with the sermon, especially with country people; which are thick and heavy, and hard to raise to a point of zeal and fervency, and need a mountain of fire to kindle them; but stories and sayings they will well remember."

the adaptation of the gospel to all the conditions and necessities of human life, to lighten the darkness of our sorrows and our sins, and " to guide our feet into the way of peace."

In words which all could understand, our Lord, who afterwards sent " unlearned and ignorant men to go into all the world and preach the gospel," has connected the Divine truth which He taught with the objects most familiar to us. His people would not hear His voice, even as now they will not hear or read His Word, but He has made all creation to preach of Him. He has associated those things which are ever before us with the blessings and the lessons of the Incarnation, and has signed them with the sign of the Cross. "From morn to noon, from noon to dewy eve," we are compassed about with so great a cloud of witnesses—" the bright and morning star," the light that " lighteth every man that cometh into the world," " the sun of righteousness," sleep and resurrection, the water that cleanseth, the bread which strengthens, the very door through which we come and go, the stones and the streets, the banks, the market-place, the courts of justice, the prisons, the hospitals, the little children, the men standing idle ; or, out in the country, the sheep and the oxen, the trees barren or bearing forth good fruit, the grass and the corn, the fowls of the air and the lilies of the field, the burning of the weeds, the ploughing, sowing, and reaping ; or, beyond city and country also, the sea, and the ships, and the fishermen.

And not to the Apostles only, but to us the command is given, " What ye have heard, that preach ye." " The message which we have heard of Him declare we unto you." We must "preach *the Word*." A young clergyman came to an older priest, who was greatly respected for his goodness and learning, and for his impressive preaching, and asked him what sermons he would recommend for his study and imitation. And the reply was promptly given, " The sermons of Jesus Christ. Read them, with prayer before and after, again and again, mark, learn, and inwardly digest them, until it is with you as with the two who journeyed to Emmaus on the first Easter Day, ' and they said one to another, Did not our heart burn within us, while He talked with us, and opened to us the Scriptures ? ' "

Asked to name books which, though not inspired, were most helpful, he said, " To me, the works of St. Augustine and St. Bernard ; the commentaries of Cornelius à Lapide and Bishop Christopher Wordsworth ; the writings of Bishops Andrewes and Jeremy Taylor, Isaac Barrow and Isaac Williams ; the sermons of Dr. Pusey, and the poems of Herbert and Keble. Read, and reflect on what you read ; but books will not make you a preacher. You must study your own heart as a surgeon studies anatomy, that from self-knowledge you may know your hearers. It is specially true of preachers, that ' the proper study of mankind is man.' Keep your ears and your eyes open, and then say what you have to say, plainly, bravely, to others."

Not many months ago, I was in the Duomo at Florence. No church in the world has witnessed more marvellous manifestations of the preacher's power. Rude mountaineers from the Apennines and crowds of peasants from all sides of the city came in at daybreak, and waited for hours in all weathers until the cathedral was opened, to hear Savonarola preach; and such was the effect of his sermons that ladies burnt their ball-dresses and finery, as being the hateful proofs of worldliness and pride, and sold their ornaments and jewels, that they might give more alms to the poor.

Five hundred years after Savonarola's martyrdom, a similar sensation and scene was witnessed in the same church, and thus described: " Day after day through the greater part of Lent (1887), and down to Easter Tuesday, the Duomo at Florence has presented a striking spectacle. The great veil of dark green silk spread over the nave, a few feet higher than the sounding-board of the pulpit, has thrown the church into mysterious gloom. From seven o'clock in the morning till eleven, men and women have sat on chairs and benches to keep a place. Long before eleven, the whole dark area has been crowded thick with human beings, and the crowd has swelled and spread till it has filled the aisles and all the westward parts of the vast building. At eleven o'clock, men carrying a sedan-chair have made their way to the pulpit steps; their living freight has passed with an effort into the pulpit, to pour forth for a whole hour a torrent of impassioned words, addressed to the working classes by a preacher who has stirred them as no one has since Fra Girolamo—Padre Agostino de Montefeltro. It is computed that an audience of seven thousand, chiefly of the working classes, has steadily attended his course of thirty-two sermons." *

How did those preachers attain this irresistible influence? They prayed for it, that utterance might be given them, that they might speak boldly as they ought to speak, and then they were not ashamed of the gospel of Christ. They who had preceded Savonarola had preached the dry dogmas of abstruse theology, the subtleties of Aristotle, Aquinas, and the Schoolmen, even as they who preceded Montefeltro had declaimed on Papal Infallibility, Mariolatry, and other "fond things, vainly invented;" but these men, as the eagle mounts from the cold barren rock, and soaring upward

> " Bathes in the bickerings of the noontide blaze,"

raised the thoughts of their hearers above sophistry and superstition, legend and myth, to Him who came to bear witness of the Truth, exhorting them to repentance and " newness of life," because the Saviour will soon be the Judge, because " the wages

---

* A selection from these sermons has been admirably translated by Miss C. M. Phillimore, and is published by the Church Printing Co.

of sin is death," and because "in Jesus Christ neither circumcision availeth anything, nor uncircumcision ; but faith which worketh by love."

*   *   *   *   *

As to utterance, the voice should always be distinct, and audible by all ; not monotonous, but varying with the subject-matter, not failing .at the end of a sentence.   If there are no inflections, no modulations of speech, attention will succumb to drowsiness, and drowsiness to slumber.   If there is no indication of intense feeling in the heart of the preacher, he will excite no emotion from his hearers—

> "Si vis me flere, dolendum est
> Primum ipsi tibi."

The manner should be spontaneous, natural, and the parson should follow Hamlet's advice to the players, "Let your own discretion be your tutor; suit the action to the word, the word to the action."

As to duration, happy is the priest, and beloved by his people, who can say with Apelles, "I know when to leave off." *   There is no more cruel tyrant than "one whom the music of his own sweet voice

---

* Lord Chancellor Halsbury, speaking on this subject, " remembered when the head of his college was asked by a distinguished preacher at St. Mary's what he thought of his sermon, the former gravely replied that he had heard in it what he hoped never to hear again.   'What was that?' asked the alarmed preacher.   'I heard the clock strike twice,' was the reply.   A sheriff's chaplain had once asked a judge what was the proper length of a sermon.   'Well, twenty minutes,' was the answer, ' *with a leaning to the side of mercy.*' "

doth ravish like enchanting harmony," while it wearies all beside. I have known a popular preacher join three sermons into one (it was easy to distinguish the connecting links); the first was heard with eager admiration, the second with calm approval, the third with a weary impatience. To such a discourse a lady, it is said, who adored the preacher, took Bishop Magee, and when she exclaimed, as they were going home, "Oh, what a saint in the pulpit!" his lordship added, " And oh, what a martyr in the pew!"

I may not speak of our great living preachers. Of those who are gone, " where beyond these voices there is peace," they who impressed and instructed me the most were Bishops Wilberforce, Magee, and Lightfoot, Doctors Pusey and Liddon. One of the best preachers I have heard, unknown to fame, a quiet gentle spirit, but endued with a wonderful power to make men think and try, was the Rev. R. H. Parr, the Vicar of St. Martin's, Scarborough.

CHAPTER XXX.

As a child extracts the candied peel from his cake, or the epicure reserves the plumpest oyster on his plate for his last *bonne-bouche*, or as, when leaving a mixed company, we keep, if we can, our final farewell for him or for her whom we love the best, so, *parva componere magnis*, I come in my concluding chapter to the happiest of all my memories—recollections of hours (I would they had been multiplied a thousand-fold!) which I have spent with working men, in public worship and in private prayer, in fields and factories, on land and sea, on road and rail; in their sorrow and pain, in sick-rooms and hospitals, in homes darkened by the shadow of death; in their hours of relaxation, in their gardens and their games. My heart is with the working man who deserves that noble name, who "goeth forth to his work and to his labour until the evening," not believing in those malcontents who imagine mischief, and go astray, and speak lies, and stir up strife all the day long, denouncing all rulers as tyrants, all rich men as knaves, and all parsons as hypocrites.

No long time ago, my son heard one of these demagogues orating in the Park. "My brothers," he said, "the trumpet of war is sounding through the land. Even the village 'Ampton is hup in harms, and the worm which has been writhing for centuries under the 'eel of the landlord is shouting for the battle. Listen, my friends, and I'll tell you what poor 'Odge is adoing to deliver himself from the oppressor. One Sunday he ventured to take a walk in my lord's park, a-thinking that as it contained twenty thousand acres it might, perhaps, be big enough for both, and hup comes the noble-hearted peer, a-blustering and a-blowing, and he bellows out at poor 'Odge, 'Now, feller, what are you adoing, a-trespassing on my land?' And 'Odge answers, 'Who guv you this land?' And my lord, he says, 'My faythur guv me the land.' And 'Odge, he says, 'And who guv your faythur the land?' And my lord, he says, 'My grandfaythur guv my faythur the land!' 'And who guv it your grandfaythur?' says 'Odge. 'You himpudent snob,' says the 'orty peer, 'it has been ours ever since the Conquest. We fought for it, and the king guv it us.' 'Ho,' says 'Odge, 'you fought for it, did you?—and we mean to fight for it, and we mean to have it;' and then he walks up to his lordship, and snaps his fingers close to his noble nose, and finishes the discourse with, ' We don't care *that* for kings! ' And this is what we must do, my brothers. We must fight for the land," etc., etc.

But the working man, having quite as large an amount of brains as any other section of the community, is aware that if 'Odge, in defiance of law and equity, in the absence of the police, the army, and the auxiliary forces, were to take possession of the land, Dodge and Podge, with a few hundred thousand " brothers," would lose no time in asserting a similar indifference to the rights of property and of title deeds, and would claim their equal share ; that this portion would be too minute to maintain the few who knew what to do with it ; and that if every man had three acres (which he could not cultivate) and a cow (which he could not milk), the industrious, temperate, and acute, would in a very short time annex the possessions of the idle, the drunken, and the dunce.

Wherefore, if only as a matter of common sense, the working man declines to be humbugged by these " murmurers and complainers," who not only covet and desire other men's goods, but openly avow their intention to let him take who hath the power, and let him keep who can. It is a policy which dates from a remote antiquity, and was once the dominant principle of our own British Constitution ; but it has proved to be incompatible with national progress and domestic happiness, and the character of those who desire its revival does not inspire confidence. They are roughs, and they are distrusted and despised by working men, not only because they are incapable, but because they are immoral. I have lived a long life among all sorts and conditions of my brethren, and I am convinced that no section of the community has a more appreciative respect for honesty, justice, and truth than the genuine working man.

Splendid evidence has been given to the public. I remember the case, referred to by the present Archbishop of Canterbury, of the printer employed in the Oxford University Press, who refused an offer of five hundred pounds for a surreptitious copy before publication of the Revised Version of the Holy Scriptures, and that of the working carpenter, who was not to be outdone in generosity even by such a man as Frederick Denison Maurice. Maurice accepted an offer for the lease of his house, forgetting that he had let a stable and coach-house at the end of the garden to the carpenter. His solicitor proposed to make the best bargain he could; "but," said Maurice, "you must tell him exactly how the case stands, and let him know his advantage. "Well, now," said the working man, on receiving the message, "that's what I call a real gentleman, and I'll give up the stables any day, and take nothing for going out." *

* *Economic Review,* vol. i. No. 2.

When he is assured of a sincere, practical interest in his welfare, the working man is grateful and sympathetic;* but until he is convinced, he is coy and suspicious. He is losing faith in " the true Friend of the working man," in placards which only profit the printer. He is ceasing to care for promissory notes, which are renewable, but never cashed. Like the pupil at Dr. Birch's school, on receipt of a hamper from home, he is surrounded by admiring friends, desirous to lend him their knives; but, when they have got at the cake, he feels " like one that treads alone some banquet-hall deserted." He is distrustful alike of words which are softer than butter, and of words which are very swords. He does not believe that he is superior (or inferior) to his fellow-men, that he is an hereditary bondsman or an hereditary monarch.

Nevertheless, though the working man has many would-be leaders, who disappoint him—inflated windbags, who collapse when they are pricked with the pin of common sense: *rem acu tetigisti*—he has " troops of friends " whom he can trust, who regard him as a brother and not as a machine, of whom it may be said that—

> " In making their thousands, they do not forget
> The thousands who help them to make."

I mean the men who give parks, and gardens, and playgrounds (if you don't now and then take the kettle from the fire, and let it sing on the hob,

* See p. 185.

you will burn a hole in it), who build hospitals, and restaurants, and swimming baths. I mean such men as Francis Crossley, who, when he gave large and beautiful recreation grounds for the people of Halifax, told them on the opening day that he attributed his prosperity in business very largely to the fact that, when he first commenced it, his mother had said, "If the Lord prosper us in this place, the poor shall taste of it." I mean those who, having ascertained that working men have minds as well as muscles, provide libraries, and galleries, and museums, and interesting entertainments.

Including music. It was my privilege to meet, not many weeks ago, a gentleman who told me that, having been successful in his business, he had made it a subject of anxious consideration how he might best lay out a portion of his wealth for the happiness of his fellow-men. "I have always," he said, "had a strong faith in the influence of music to refine, to solace, and to cheer, and I am therefore taking part in building premises for the professors and pupils of the Royal College of Music, with a view to the promotion of good music among all classes, by sending accomplished performers and teachers through the length and breadth of the land." This Royal College of Music will cost him £40,000.

They are his friends who help him to reduce his expenses by co-operative stores, and to obtain fair remuneration for his work. It must surely be right for the tradesman and the working man to make the best market of his labour, so long as there is no violence (there is a tyranny of numbers as well as of individuals), and justice is done to all.

He is a friend of the working man who helps him in his brave self-denial to provide for the time of sickness, who subscribes to those societies which obey the wise man's counsel, "If a man live many years, and rejoice in them all; yet let him remember the days of darkness; for they shall be many." And here, appropriately, I would refer to the advantage of inducing working men to join an ambulance corps, those especially who are engaged where accidents are frequent, so that they may know what to do in a perilous emergency. A traveller not long ago rescued two children from a canal, in which they had fallen. They appeared to be dead, and, had he not known the process of restoration, life would soon have been extinct.

They help the working man, and he knows it, who establish and maintain technical schools, in which the young may learn from skilled masters the best methods of using the best tools in the craft which they propose to practise. And with these technical schools for boys I would connect schools of cookery and thrift for girls, that they, who will be hereafter the wives of the working men, may be useful as well as ornamental, and know how to make the most and the best of their resources. *If*

*there were more wives who were good cooks, there would
be more good husbands at home for supper.*

The working man has no truer friends than
those who are doing what they can, whether as
owners or from any other influence, to improve his
home. No place deserves that beautiful name, in
which men and women, husbands and wives, brothers
and sisters, cannot maintain both their moral and
physical integrity, in which they lose the shame
which is a glory and grace, in which they cannot
breathe the pure air, and enjoy the pure light, which
God designed for us all.

I shall be disappointed in my estimate and expectations as to the sagacity of the working man, if,
being now master of the situation, he does not direct
his attention, and the attention of his representatives
in Parliament, to the abolition of the smoke nuisance.
It has been proved, by Mr. Fletcher of Bolton and
others, that the process is easy and inexpensive, and
it is for those who suffer from it most to insist on
its removal, with other pollutions and noxious exhala-
tions, injurious to human life. Such a purification
would be followed by infinite blessings to the bodies
and souls of men ; the restoration of sunshine to
darkened homes, of smiling health to wan, sallow
cheeks, of green leaves and singing birds to blackened
and stunted trees, and of fish to poisoned streams.

And, brightest of all, the splendid and sure results
would be such a grand help to temperance, by the
removal of temptations to drunkenness, as no other

human scheme, within my conjecture, could ever hope to win. Not only medical men, but all of us who know the crowded homes of the poor in our large cities and towns, can testify that a foul atmosphere induces a craving for stimulants. " You come. and live in our court," a drunkard said to a philanthropist, " and you'll soon take to the gin." It has been asserted, and not disputed, much less disproved, that, wherever men are engaged in a healthy outdoor employment, and where their homes are also situated in healthy localities, these men, as a rule, are sober, and that drunkenness may be attributed more to atmospheric impurity than to facilities for drinking in the number of public-houses ; and that men who are employed in mines or works, where they breathe for hours a highly noxious atmo- sphere, with their homes in proximity, are more or less intemperate.*

The best lecture I ever heard on intemperance was from a working man. He was sitting on a bench by the Midland Railway, looking somewhat weary, when a drunken fellow staggered alongside, and began to mumble nonsense. " I don't want you," said the working man to the sot. " Go away ; you're drunk." " Now just you listen to me," it was answered. " Do you suppose as a mighty Power would make the barley to grow in the fields,

---

* A very interesting letter on this subject will be found in the *Times* of September 6, 1892, written by the author of " The Topography of Intemperance," Mr. Thomas Glyde, of Cardiff.

and the hops to grow in the hopyards, and then put it into the mind of another party to make 'em foment, and me not to drink 'em? Why, you know nowt." "Well," said the other, "I believe in a glass of good ale, and I should like one now, for I'm fine and dry, but I'm quite sure as a mighty Power never made the barley and the hops to grow and foment for you to take them and turn yourself into a beast."

*   *   *   *   *

What are the special helps which we clergy can offer to the working man? First of all, we must win his confidence and affection. It is not difficult, when he is assured that we do not want his vote, or anything he has, but himself. He seems to know by intuition when, for the sake of the Lord our God, we seek to do him good, when we have too much respect for him and for ourselves to flatter him with "mere verbiage, the tinsel clink of compliment," and when we go to him with some of Christ's love in our hearts.

Moreover, he must be assured that we too are working men, for bees love the hum of the hive, and they who labour rightly condemn those

> "Who by their everlasting yawn confess
> The pains and penalties of idleness."

"Do you know why I came to your church?" an artisan said to a clergyman. "Because I saw you going about your business early and late, and I don't believe in blinds down at nine o'clock in the morning, churches locked up all day, and six Bank holidays a week."

And when once he believes, he will return your affection. "Thou hast gained thy brother." He will listen, when you speak to him of the truth as it is in Jesus, the love of the Saviour, and the justice of the Judge—that "the gift of God is eternal life, but the wages of sin is death." You will help him and he will help you, as ye "bear one another's burdens," to fulfil the duties and attain the promises set before us in the Gospel.

You will welcome him to his Father's house, and he shall know that—

> "Our mother the Church hath never a son
> To honour before the rest."

You will try to make his life happier, his home brighter. You will be the friend that "loveth at all times, and the brother born for adversity," until "the night cometh in which no man can work"— the night and also the day—until—

> "Where the dews glisten and the song-birds warble,
> His dust to dust is laid,
> In Nature's keeping, with no pomp of marble
> To shame his modest shade.
>
> "The forges glow, the anvils all are ringing—
> Beneath its smoky veil,
> The city, where he dwelt, is ever swinging
> Its clamorous iron flail.
>
> "But by his grave is peace and perfect beauty,
> With the sweet heaven above,
> Fit emblems of a life of Work and Duty
> Transfigured into Love."